STAR OF THE
RISING SUN

Further Titles by Evelyn Hart

THE GREEN FIELDS BEYOND *

MOUNTAINS OF THE SUN

SPRING IMPERIAL

THE STARS STILL SHINE

THE ORDER OF THE STAR *

available from Severn House

STAR OF THE RISING SUN

Evelyn Hart

SEVERN HOUSE

This first world edition published in Great Britain 1998 by
SEVERN HOUSE PUBLISHERS LTD of
9–15 High Street, Sutton, Surrey SM1 1DF.
First published in the USA 1998 by
SEVERN HOUSE PUBLISHERS INC., of
595 Madison Avenue, New York, NY 10022.

British Library Cataloguing in Publication Data

Hart, Evelyn
       Star of the rising sun
       1.   World war, 1939-1945 - Hong Kong - Fiction
       1. Title
       823.9'14 [F]

       ISBN 0-7278-5323-6

Typeset by Palimpsest Book Production Ltd,
Polmont, Stirlingshire, Scotland.
Printed and bound in Great Britain by
MPG Books Ltd, Bodmin, Cornwall.

*To my darling daughter Fiona Evelyn
who so loved Hong Kong*

The Story So Far

LOUISE WINN journeyed to the Far East from America as a pioneer at the end of the last century. Marrying the dynamic British entrepreneur James Winter, she watched the Japanese Treaty Port of Yokohama grow into an international city, and her husband honoured by the Imperial Japanese Emperor Meiji. The highest award for a non-Japanese citizen, the *Order of the Star of the Rising Sun*, became the symbol of James Winter's achievements, and Louise's most prized possession after his death in 1909.

The devastating Yokohama earthquake of 1923 robbed Louise and her three-year-old granddaughter of the beautiful Camille. Summoned to England, Izolda was sent away to an unscrupulous establishment by her father and suffered years of abuse and neglect. Meeting her granddaughter years later, Louise rescued Izolda and took her to live in exile on the French Riviera. But as the threat of another war overshadowed their sunshine existence, Louise and Izolda were forced to leave their home again.

Booked on a steamer bound for Hong Kong to escape escalating tension in Europe, Louise feels she is at last coming home. Izolda, at eighteen, believes her life is just beginning . . .

Part One

'Fragrant Water'

1939

Chapter One

IN a misty haze, early on the morning of 29th March 1939, SS *Chitral* headed at half-speed past green Lantau Island.

Louise stood alone, still and quiet, at the starboard rail. Her silk dress fluttered in the breeze under her open navy-blue coat. She wore a hat firmly pinned on to keep her hair tidy. Her little high-arched feet were placed neatly together, and her gloved hands held tightly onto the rail to steady herself as the liner glided on and began to veer round. The powerful engines were throttled back until they were virtually soundless.

She had not been up and dressed at such an hour for many a year, but she was not going to miss one minute of this day of days; a day which for a long time now she had anticipated with joy and gratitude. It was the last of her worldwide travels. She had come into harbour at the end of her journey through life; she had come home – home to the East. Under the brim of her hat her brown eyes shone with youthful enthusiasm, for to her thrill she felt she had never been away from the familiar sights she saw through the mists. And the odours!

They came with the wind wafting down through the narrow Lye-mun channel to the east, past North Point and Causeway Bay. The wind brought with it all the scents compounded in the back streets of Wanchai and in the tin shacks climbing the hills behind Happy Valley. There was the sweet acrid tang of cooking oil, sour pig meat, putrid rotting vegetables all mingled together with smoke from charcoal fires. These were basic, pungent, earthy odours of the East – the have-not smells of human poverty.

With a rush Izolda came to join her grandmother at the rail. "The Chinese call this harbour 'Heung Kong' which means 'Fragrant Water'," Louise turned to her with a smile, "so named in the old days when ships called here to take on fresh water from a spring."

"What have I missed?" Izolda asked rubbing her eyes. She had overslept after a late night of dancing with Chippy, a childhood friend now an officer in the Royal Navy. She woke to find that her grandmother's bed was empty. She had thrown on some clothes and come up without even brushing her hair. Chippy had kissed her goodnight on deck again. His lips were soft and rather sweet and he had said that he loved her.

"You haven't missed much. It's been quite misty; beginning to clear now."

"Oh, isn't it stunning!" Izolda looked ahead at Victoria Island with its city of solid business buildings built close together on the rugged, rocky coastline that, on the western side, descended steeply to the sea. Mr Lauder had told her that the Island was only thirty square miles in size on which ninety-eight percent of the populace of one million were Chinese. He had said what a lucky girl she was to be coming here to live, a safe and healthy place with malaria – once rampant – now controlled. She gazed at the shifting vapours over the mountain peak where she would be living in her uncle's house, sudden peeps of vivid green appearing through the clouds.

"Phew! 'Fragrant Water' my foot." Izolda wrinkled her

nose as a long barge passed the ship, and a noisome stench was blown over.

"Known as a *fu-fu* boat. It carries night soil to the mainland where it is destined for vegetable patches in the New Territories. Makes excellent manure," Louise informed while pointing northwards to the undulating land beyond Stonecutter's Island. "Those blue hills over there are in China proper."

Now, barely moving, the liner began her slow turn preparatory to several tugs nosing her into a berth at the ocean terminal on the mainland of the Kowloon Peninsular opposite Victoria Island. The sun, as if from behind a white chiffon curtain, turned the Peak to soft emerald. As the haze thinned the mountain appeared to be necklaced in half-veiled white strings. Below, the bulky shape of HMS *Tamar*, immaculate in her black and white paint, lay anchored offshore, gun ports open.

"Chippy's headquarters, isn't it?" questioned Izolda. But Louise didn't answer. She was far away.

The sight of the old battleship filled her with a feeling of affiliation. They had much in common. By the grace of God both of them were seemingly indestructible with all the disasters and wars they had encountered and managed to survive. And they were by no means defeated yet, neither sunk by the vagaries of fortune, nor even down in the water, not awhile, not they. They were still floating, the old hulk and she, at rest and now firmly anchored in a safe harbour.

Nothing less than a most monumental disaster would finish them off!

"Mother! At last," Jimmy boomed. He bounded up to embrace Louise in burly arms, at the same time knocking her hat askew.

7

"How did the journey go?" Antonia asked, kissing her mother-in-law on both cheeks.

"Mighty pleasant, Toni dear," Louise said, setting her hat straight, "a long sea voyage is so health giving." Izolda was embraced by uncle and aunt in her turn.

"Sea journey healthy? Bunkum, Mother! I'm in need of a rest cure after one, and if you're a bad sailor you might as well be put in a shroud, weighted down, and slipped on a plank overboard," Jimmy raised his thunderous eyebrows comically.

"I bet you enjoyed yourself?" Toni looked with interest at Izolda whom she had not seen since a toddler: her beloved friend Camille's daughter. The resemblance was there – colouring different, though there were Titian glints in the girl's golden hair.

"I guess she's exhausted; up half the night dancing with a naval officer."

"Oh Grandma, really . . ."

"You know perfectly well, Jimmy, I've been a good sailor ever since I crossed the Pacific in a sailing ship," Louise ignored the interruption.

"You're wonderful, Mother," Toni took her arm. "We have a too-big house now the children are grown; it's going to be good having you living with us to help fill it up. You should both have come years ago."

"Her father wouldn't hear of it, not until war was nearly upon us."

At this, husband and wife exchanged a quick glance. Louise did not notice, but Izolda did, and a frisson of disquiet passed through her. Perhaps the East was not so safe after all. Captain Roger Stamford on board ship had spent ages questioning her grandmother on the Japanese. What was he getting at? Ah Roger, would she ever see him again? Would he have written, a letter perhaps here waiting for her? In the meantime there was Chippy. She'd make the best of Chippy, her first real boyfriend.

As well as being allowed on the ship before others, it seemed that Jimmy Winter could also usher them off first. He bypassed such encumbrances as immigration and passport officials, and there was barely time to introduce Chippy, and for the Lauders to come up and meet them, before temporary farewells were said and they were off. Izolda found her grandmother and herself suddenly elevated from the position of poor white nonentities in France, to mother and niece of a tycoon in a new world of cosmopolitan commerce and wealth. She forgot all about talk of wars and basked in the luxury.

Within a short time Jimmy had their cabin luggage packed into the Chartered Bank's private launch bobbing up and down beside the huge liner, and his family down the gangway and helped aboard to cross Victoria harbour to the Island. The harbour was a magnificent one: a sheltered, azure, deep water roadstead that had first caught the imagination of Captain Elliot in 1841, who annexed it and made it possible for European traders to descend in their thousands.

To Louise the trip across the harbour was full of gladness for the present and nostalgia for the far past. To Izolda it was all new and exciting; from the Chinese crewmen in the launch to the crowds of ships on all sides. There were junks with huge slatted sails like ribbed fans, their bows low, their sterns high, anchors dangling in mid air, to *walla walla* taxi-launches holding up to twelve passengers, and the many small sampans bursting with families. There were spick and span anchored warships flying the White Ensign and painted in the pale grey of the China Fleet, and old rust-peeling freighters low in the water, pregnant with heavy cargo. Larger craft tooted, hooted and blasted as they blundered their way through the traffic. Lesser boats shrilled and rang warning bells, their crews emitting Cantonese curses at anyone who crossed too near in a whole bustling, noisy chaos of what seemed to Izolda to be a series of near misses.

"Remarkably few collisions," Toni answered Izolda's unspoken query. "Here, have a jumper," she threw one over from a locker, "it's been cold for a week. I'm still wearing my winter clothes," she tweaked at her smart lightweight woollen suit which reflected the grey eyes that some twenty-five years ago had captivated Jimmy. Her peroxided hair remained lacquer-fixed and unruffled in the wind. A double-decker green Star Ferry with its stubby funnel passed near, the top filled with first class passengers, the lower deck packed with second class humanity.

"There are two ferries," elucidated Jimmy, "one named the *Day Star*, the other *Morning Star*. They constantly ply the seven-minute crossing from the terminal near the Kowloon-Canton railway station – that long red brick building with a clock tower over there – to Victoria Island. The Chinese craft come as near as they dare to foreign ships, and dash disconcertingly across one's bows at the last second to 'cut off the evil eye'. You'll find the Chinese are a very superstitious nation, in fact riddled by superstitions from the cradle to the grave."

The launch came to rest by some slimy steps covered in weed up which Jimmy helped his mother. By the wharf waited a large six-seater black Cadillac. An ageing Chinese chauffeur dressed in beige uniform stood by the limousine. He beamed at Louise.

10

"Remember Ping-Li?" Jimmy asked. "He was my rick-shaw coolie when we were in Wei-chu. Both of us have come up in the world since then."

Louise nodded at the man. She recalled the name but not the face. After all they had left Wei-chu a good time ago – before the Great War.

Ping-Li ushered the family into the back of the car. He took particular care of the remembered old lady. The older generations were revered by his people, and Ping-Li found it quite right and proper that Master's mother had come to live in the household. The vehicle he drove was more like a plush room inside than a car. Jimmy sat roundly, legs apart, on the back seat between his wife and mother, while Izolda took one of the jump seats opposite. Jimmy lit up, neatly cupping his small, square-fingered hands over the match. He drew deeply on a cigarette and tapped on the window division for Ping-Li to start. He was in a hurry, but would see his mother home first . . . had an important engagement with that thirty-three-year-old half-caste right-hand man who was personally attached to the Generalissimo by being a member of the large Chiang Kai-shek family. Brigadier-General Sha-Kwo, a boyfriend of Ying-Su's and known as 'Bungy' – modern lot! Bungy had been rapidly promoted and was especially useful, in the present crisis, for his European education. With his own knowledge of the language, he himself was up to his neck in it; dragged in. No wonder he smoked heavily. He was absolutely delighted to have his mother with him; worth a guinea a minute, she was! Now that he was at the top he would enjoy being ticked off by her in the manner he had so resented as a youth when number three in the bank. How much did she remember of Hong Kong? He was not too sure . . .

"That's the post office on our right." He indicated a

11

mammoth arcaded four-storied building on Des Voeux Road, "The waterfront used to come right up here in the old days."

"You don't have to tell *me* about the old days," Louise put her middle-aged bigwig son firmly in his place, "I first visited Hong Kong with Papa on a trip to Europe before any of you were born. 1887. I remember it very well as it was then. They called these parts a *praya* where each merchant owned a waterfront and jetty by his warehouse *hong*. I've been to Hong Kong many times since. For a while I actually lived here, with Camille on Macdonnell Road . . ."

"Oh, I'd like to see that," Izolda said, as she always did if it was anything to do with her mother. The street was crowded with what appeared to be extremes of wealth and poverty; Rolls Royces and limousines such as theirs had to vie for space with lesser cars, taxis and rickshaws and many trams.

"I'll ask Ping-Li to go via Macdonnell Road so that you can have a look," Toni suggested. She took up the speaking tube to address the chauffeur.

"Did they call this part 'Central' in those days, Mother?" Jimmy teased while giving his wife a huge wink. "There's the Hong Kong and Shanghai Bank," he continued undeterred while waving his hand at a fortress-like building, his cigarette glowing, ash dropping onto the thick piled carpet. "See the bronze lions at the front, Izolda? Over the portals is written 'Abandon hope all ye that enter here'. Maybe that's what put Winn off. It is the tallest building on the Island. That squarer one next door is my Chartered Bank. I'll take you to see the boardroom one day." Jimmy looked at Edouard's watch he kept in his waistcoat pocket . . . His brother, a brilliant athlete, had died from meningitis as a young man, and Camille, who had been in England at the time, had brought the watch out to Wei-chu to give him . . . Humm, he was just all right for time. He'd be meeting Bungy in a private room at the back of the bank building. The room was regularly tested for those new-fangled listening devices the Japs were planting. The wretched little buggers were infiltrating everywhere.

"On the left is the supreme court, see Izolda?" Toni took up the commentary, "old colonial style, as is the Army headquarters further along, and Government House you'll see up the hill."

"Remember the H-K Club, Mother? Famous place, exclusive, all European though that won't last much longer the way things are going and a damned good thing too when families like the Ho Tung's aren't allowed in. Secluded green cricket club beyond . . ." Jimmy choked on a cough while puffing out a cloud of smoke.

"You shouldn't smoke so much," chided Louise, "I don't like the sound of that cough."

"There's nothing wrong with my chest. It's a good loose cough. I'll challenge Izolda to a game of tennis this evening just to show. I gather she's a bit of an expert, eh?" He gave Izolda his bellowing laugh.

Smoothly Ping-Li steered the car to climb up the Lower Heights. They drove past St John's Cathedral where Izolda's mother had once given a recital, passed the Peak tramway station in Garden Road with the Helena May Hostel for women above, and went on to the Mid-Levels or 'Half Peak' as the Chinese called it, after which, in the Upper-Levels, only the wealthy and their servants resided.

"There it is – No 12, Macdonnell Road, that's where Camille and I had a flat, on the second floor, in 1912," Louise said craning her neck excitedly to see better, "Fancy that now, it looks quite the same except that it's gotten a new lick of paint. My, how it takes me back. We were on our way to her singing training in Paris, and she was heartbroken."

"Over what, Grandma?"

"I guess having to leave behind one of her beaux, the chief magistrate in Wei-chu."

"Your mother had to choose between marrying him and living in China or singing. She chose her career," added Toni.

Twisting and turning and rounding the southern side of the Peak, the car purred on and up. Now there were few cars to be seen on the road. The rickshaws they passed, the coolies straining between the shafts, others pushing from behind, four to a rickshaw, were quickly left behind to continue the struggle up the hill.

Swerving into Peak Road, the Cadillac took a sharp hairpin bend and directly after turned to the right and passed under a red and green pagoda-arched gateway off the main road. Tyres crunched down the loosely gravelled drive of 'The Falls', so named for the waterfall that splashed down through the large property. On a terrace directly up behind the drive lay a hard tennis court, below were close-cut sloping lawns surrounded by well tended beds of marguerites and yellow flowering lantana, with azalea bushes backed by mimosa trees just coming into flower.

The car came to rest before a gleaming three-storied mansion built at the turn of the century on a platform carved out of the slope of the mountain. The turquoise tiled roof glistened in the sun, the corners curving upwards in true Chinese fashion. Red gargoyles and carved dragons with open mouths leered out from under the eaves, and on the deep verandahs Chinese scenes were painted in relief.

Well away from the north face of the Island from whence they had come, there was not a sound to be heard above the splashing of the stream and the twittering of birds. The house, the setting, the faraway views, lay basking in the sun in the quiet of deep country, way above the busy city and the empty China Sea.

"I know what it puts me in mind of," Louise exclaimed as she stood on the drive gazing up at the house.

"Where's that?" asked Toni.

"Temple court in Yokohama," elucidated Izolda. The story of the red mansion where her grandfather had proposed to her grandmother at a ball in 1887 was an old favourite.

"Not unlike," Jimmy, who also knew the story, laughed, "that American tycoon who made his fortune in armaments for the Japanese, built it for his peachy wife. This house is just as fine, four-square and sturdy enough to withstand the invasion of my mother and niece!"

"Whatever the house reminds you of, Mother, I hope you will be very comfortable in it," welcomed Toni. "It is solidly built which makes it warm in winter with the mountain behind protecting us from the northeasterly wind – freezing in January – and yet airy enough in summer to be at least six degrees cooler than down in the city." She led the way into a large marbled hall where a group of servants had assembled.

"This is Cookie," Toni did the honours, "and here is Fung Wan, our Number One Boy. Ah Hoong is the washee-washee maid, and Ah Fan will be your personal amah."

This last little woman, with finely lined face and grey hair shiny with pomade ointment, wore the usual high buttoned jacket, trousers and soft cotton slippers. Louise was glad to see that her feet had not been bound and crippled into the 'golden lilies' shape as small as a toddler's, as her previous amah in China had suffered.

15

Jimmy took his leave to go back to the office, and with Ah Fan following her new 'old Missie' Toni led the way up a wide flight of shallow marble stairs to a substantial landing on which reposed an antique opium couch as big as a small double bed. Over it hung a huge portrait of a wispy bearded Mandarin in full length brocaded robes. Off the landing Toni ushered the the newcomers into a sumptuous drawing room full of heavy blackwood furniture. It was a darkish room, shaded as it was by the arched verandahs surrounding the house on the southern and western sides. Fans like propellers rested overhead; heavy crimson curtains hung at the french windows, and two exquisite gold and blue patterned Tientsin carpets lay on the polished floor.

The room was full of treasures that Jimmy and Toni had collected in China and particularly, in recent years, in the markets of Peking. A fabulous red scroll-panelled draught screen stood between granite fireplace and landing doorway; a valuable pair of matching 'famille-verte' jardinieres reposed on either side of the mantelpiece. Two illuminated glass cabinets on the inside wall contained a collection of pale jade ornaments, stone manganese figures and much delicate white procelain. But the most important piece in the room was the priceless bowl embossed with writhing yellow dragons. It stood on its own carved wooden base to hold it safe. The dragons had the distinctive five clawed feet which showed any connoisseur that it had once belonged to an Emperor.

Off this room was a Wedgewood-blue bedroom, almost as big as the drawing room again, which Toni had allocated for Louise. Through it lay an elaborate blue tiled bathroom where steps led up to an old fashioned tub with a whole panel of taps. "You must let Ah Fan help you in and out, Mother; it is rather deep and you might slip," Toni warned. "Ring for Ah Fan or Fung Wan for anything you want. Jimmy's study, the main dining room and the kitchen quarters are on the ground floor, otherwise we are self-contained up here and you will only need to use the stairs when you want to go into the garden or out in the car with Ping-Li. You can get plenty of fresh air and exercise round the verandahs. I do hope everything's to your liking?"

"To my liking? You've thought of *more* than everything for sure," Louise praised. "All is quite perfect, Toni, bless you."

Izolda had said nothing through all this. She felt superfluous and slightly overwhelmed by the house and its servants. But now her aunt took her up another flight of stairs to what used to be the nursery floor. "Yours is next to Winn's old room beyond Ying Ying's. Her pet name stands for 'brightness'; she's as bright as a tack is our Ying Ying! They still use this floor when they stay. Winn's up-country at the moment. He works in a shipping broker and insurance firm attached to 'Butterfield and Swire'. Spends the weekends with the Hong Kong Volunteer Defence Force banging guns off in the New Territories. Is mad about it – all the Volunteers are. He has his own pad in the city. Ying-Su comes and goes all the time; mostly goes! Well, my dear, I must leave you now to unpack. It's my afternoon stint at the Queen Mary Hospital." With a smile Toni left the room with her quick, sprightly nurse's tread. Izolda had gathered that not only did her aunt nurse for several shifts a week and was on the municipal hospital board in charge of nurses training, but she also ran a crêche for abandoned children, was active in Red Cross, and had raised enough money through bazaars and mah-jong mornings to build an extension to the Sailor's Rest Home. Altogether her aunt was a live wire, and she, Izolda, would have to get her skids on in the bustling noisy town down below where everyone seemed to work, both rich and poor; she would have to compete with the throngs of pretty office girls wearing their colourful *cheongsams* slit to the knee.

On her floor below, Louise's thoughts were in much the same vein on how her daughter-in-law was an exceedingly busy and efficient woman who had kept her looks, though she herself did not altogether care for that bleached honey-coloured hair. Peroxide was said to ruin the scalp as lacquer did. Funny how the modern generation had taken to shellac which the Japanese and Chinese had put on their hair for centuries. The Japanese always said it helped to keep the grey away.

With Ah Fan hovering about, Louise unpacked her suitcase for immediate needs. Then she looked around for somewhere to put her precious *Order of the Star of the Rising Sun* which in the old days had rested on the grand piano in Yokohama, and more recently on the mantelpiece in the Villa Micheline. No mantelpiece over a fire grate in this room but instead stoves, very necessary for the rainy season in the summers when the walls dripped endlessly and leather shoes and boots turned green overnight. She decided on the dressing table and propped the Order up against the mirror where she could see it when lying in bed. It was destined for Jimmy when she passed on. Until that day arrived she would not part with it.

Izolda came down to join her grandmother. They were served tea with wafer-thin black and white sesame cakes by Fang Wan who stood by with a grin on his face and a cloth over his forearm in case 'old missus' needed mopping up as he used to mop up the two children of the household.

Afterwards Louise and Izolda wandered out onto the

18

verandah. They looked down on the garden where violet-blue magpies with long wavy tails chattered in the branches, and kites with hooked bills built their nests in the pine trees. The land fell steeply away to the south-west through soft green hills wooded with stunted firs. No other house was visible. The view was of a peaceful wilderness of semi-tropical verdancy undulating down to the blue water of the Pokfulam Reservoir in the distance, and further still to the sparkling waters of Telegraph Bay. Far beyond again, dozens of small islands lay as if floating on the calm azure sea.

"We've gotten ourselves here!" Louise expressed triumphantly. "I guess I couldn't ask for a better place to end my days. Nothing, but *nothin'* will induce me to move again, not earthquakes, nor landslides – of which they get many when it rains. Wild jackasses, world holocausts are not going to prize *me* out. No, I shall be carried out from here feet first willy-nilly, and don't you say 'Oh Grandma I wish you wouldn't go on', for it will be a happy time as the Japanese say about joining their ancestors; one in the very order of things."

Chapter Two

"HOW do I ring Kowloon?" Izolda asked her aunt on the day after their arrival.

"Just lift the receiver, dear. The operator will put you through. Use the telephone on the landing by the opium couch. All calls in Hong Kong are free."

"Free? How extraordinary."

"Yes," said Louise, "they've been free in China ever since the days of the first eastern cables. Your mother used to spend hours phoning her beaux."

"Hello, hallo . . . Maisie? It's me, Zol. How's Hugh? . . . I'm looking forward to meeting him . . . Oh, out in the New Territories with the Sappers . . . Yes, I knew that, you told me a dozen times on board. What? The bridesmaid's dress . . . say again? . . . Thai silk; sounds lovely . . . a fitting? Where? OK I get it, we meet at 'Mickey's Kitchen' up Ice House Lane at three tomorrow. What fun! No, I won't be late. Bye for now."

The following day Toni drove Izolda down in her Austen to the large departmental stores where she left her with instructions to walk on westwards deeper into Victoria town where she could shop in the many narrow stone 'ladder streets', each a flight of steep steps up the encroaching mountain, and told her to bargain for any purchase.

"Don't accept less than ten per cent; sometimes you can

get up to twenty if you spend long enough at it – they expect you to. Retrace your steps to Ice House Lane near where we parked the car. It's the favourite venue of the Holdens and Winters; they keep a table permanently for us there. You can't get lost in Hong Kong. To get home catch a No. 15 bus to the Old Peak Road. Why don't you wait for Ying-Ying at the Peak tram terminus and come back with her?"

Fascinated by the lane-like streets of gaudy calligraphic signs and posters hanging over the open shop fronts, Izolda successfully bargained for some silk stockings, which she had run out of on board, and then made her way back to Ice House Lane where Maisie soon joined her for tea.

"We're having the wedding at the Union Church – I think I told you," Maisie gabbled away.

"You did – where you and Hugh went to Sunday School as kids," Izolda remembered. She proffered an envelope from her handbag, "A pre-wedding party invitation from my aunt. The Holden parents and Chippy have already accepted."

"Oh, what a dear your aunt is to give a party for us. Hugh is dying to meet you, the tear-stained girl he used to know in that ghastly English parsonage! His parents are lovely and will fill the gap when Ma and Pa go."

"How long are they here for?"

"About a month, then back to Boston. Ma fusses over the grandparents who are pretty ancient now. We've found a sweet little bungalow on the golf course at Fanling until we're entitled to married quarters," Maisie informed excitedly. "You *must* come and stay. Hugh will be going off to his Fortress Company every day and leaving poor little me pining all alone!"

"What does the Fortress Company do?"

"Guards the frontier, I suppose."

"Guarding it from what – the Chinese?"

"The Japs, you dim-wit. Don't you read the newspapers?"

"*Le Figaro* didn't report much on the far east – in any case I'm not interested in reading about war politics."

"Well you'd better catch up on the situation since we've landed in the middle of it. The Japanese have occupied French Indo-China. They took Canton no distance from here, ignored Hong Kong for the time being, and last month landed on Hainan Island with an enormous fleet."

"Where's that?" Izolda said sulkily. She loathed all this talk of war. They'd come here to get *away* from war. She wished Maisie would shut up.

"In Tong-king Bay, hundreds of miles to the south, but Hugh says it's ominous."

"As they left Hong Kong alone I don't know what all the fuss is about," Izolda aired. She was determined to believe her father's 'safer clime' theme, and would stick her head in the sand like an ostrich if need be.

"Pa Holden says that since the Rape of Nanking two years ago with its grisly mass orgy when they ran amok – like our Lascar on board ship – and murdered over two hundred thousand civilians with twenty thousand women raped, the Chinese can't loathe the Japs enough. But unless the nationalists and communists bury the hatchet and unite properly against the common enemy they haven't a hope of defeating them. Every now and then they forget the Japanese and are at each other's throats again. Hopeless."

"Oh, do stop it, Maisie. I want to see what you've chosen for the bridesmaid's dresses . . ." They got down to some samples and sketches. Maisie, in a flurry of wedding preparations, soon left, and Izolda made her way past the cathedral up to the Peak tramway station to meet Ying-Su. On the way she thought how convenient it was to have Chippy as a friend in Hong Kong, but she didn't want him, not really. There had been no letter from Roger waiting for her at her uncle's . . .

She was early for Ying-Su. It was not yet the rush hour, and waiting for her to come across from her office, Izolda examined a poster of the tramcar: a boxy funicular railway reputed never to have been out of order in all its fifty-one years. It worked on two separate steel cables; one car ascended while the other descended with a passing place about halfway up the mountain. The ascent looked alarmingly steep. She studied the Chinese crowd. They all looked alike to her. Would she be able to pick out Ying-Su? She had a problem with her; the first problem she'd encountered in Hong Kong.

Izolda took a seat on a bench and pondered on Ying Su whom she had met on her first evening at The Falls. An unexpected feeling of umbrage had hit her at first sight, a feeling she could not account for. Ying-Su was a small, sophisticated, fashionably and expensively dressed Chinese girl. That she was an integral part of her own blood relations, hit Izolda as incongruous if not thoroughly false. In a nonchalant middle-class accent, alien to her oriental heritage, Ying-Su had given her a kiss, said how nice to have a cousin turn up, embraced her 'parents' on her return from a trip to China and called them 'Dad' and 'Mum'. This, Izolda told herself, was only natural since she had been adopted as an abandoned child whose exact age no-one knew.

Ying-Su was greatly loved by the family, and she was undoubtedly attractive with her slanting black eyes in a piquante face with a provocative bow of pouting red lips. But what affected Izolda most was the way Ying-Su and her own grandmother took to one another in what Izolda could only describe as a sort of love affair. Louise expounded straight

23

away on her times in China to Ying-Su's fascination, egging her on to tell her more which the old lady was delighted to do, always happy to have an audience hanging onto her words. For years now, Izolda had found herself embarrassed by her grandmother's oft repeated reminiscences and had cut the words off rather than encouraged them.

Soon a mass of humanity began to pour out from the Government offices across the way. "Hallo," exclaimed Ying-Su, dancing up to her. All the resentment Izolda felt on their first meeting returned in a rush. "Waiting for me? How nice. Let's take a walk round the Peak when we get there. I need some fresh air after being incarcerated all day."

"What's your job?"

"Secretarial. Translating mostly." Ying-Su waved an immaculately manicured hand in the direction of the Government offices. She led the way to the cable car. The funicular started off smoothly at its acute angle which forced the passengers' backs against the slatted seats. They stopped at Macdonnell Road – Izolda related to Ying-Su how her mother and grandmother had once lived there – after which the car came to a halt in the middle of nowhere. There was a dead silence and then a lot of loud talking.

"Oh hell," Izolda expressed nervously, "it *would* choose to break down for the first time in its life when I'm on board."

"You *are* funny," tinkled Ying-Su in her so-English voice. "Danger's the spice of life, don't you think?" She struggled upright and poked her glossy head out of the door. A rapid exchange in colloquial Cantonese ensued. "Minor landslide, that's all – we're always having them. The coolies will soon clear it up." Ying-Su sat down again and tucked her feet under her. "I think our grandmother's superb, don't you?" she said conversationally.

"I wouldn't have said superb exactly . . . she does go on rather, and lately she's begun to drop her food," Izolda commented cautiously. *Our* grandmother. Really.

"They say you never can see the best in your own kith and kin; adoption has its advantages."

"Does your . . . er . . . having been adopted worry you sometimes?"

"Heavens no! I am eternally grateful to Mum and Dad for taking me out of the gutter and giving me a first class education and a brother to boot."

"What is Winn like?" He was going to be like a brother to *her*, a blood relation.

"Well, he's as dark haired as his father with Mum's light eyes. Devastating combination."

Izolda did not answer this remark. 'Devastating' used for a brother? Most peculiar. Could it be? It could . . . they were not related.

With a jerk the tram started off again on its thousand foot climb. The higher they progressed the more spectacular the view became with the city below, the sea and Kowloon etched out before them like a colourful map to make an almost giddy spectacle.

Disgorging with the others at the Peak terminus the girls started out on the flat Lugard Road which followed the indented hillsides, the road soon narrowing, cars banned as they left behind the old colonnaded houses of bankers, business men and government officials. The path progressed through trees and bushes of opalescent greenery upon which rested tortoiseshell and tiger butterflies the size of small birds sunning themselves with spread wings of white spots and yellow and black daubs. Steep tracks could be seen

25

descending in a wilderness of shrubby, slippery and inaccessible slopes where dripping rivulets ran by clumps of thick bamboo.

"Those tracks are made by the Hash Harriers," Ying-Su informed.

"What on earth are they?"

"A sort of club; quite mad, I think. You won't catch me joining it," Ying-Su turned up her dainty nose. "They rush out at weekends to race one another up and down. It used to be men only but now a women's Hash Harrier club has been formed. They get lost in bad weather, invariably break bones and turn ankles, and the police and fire brigade have to go out in foul weather to search for them when they have far more important things to attend to, such as the influx of so-called Japanese businessmen."

"Do you think the Japs might be getting ready to attack Hong Kong?" Izolda asked bluntly. Ying-Su in her government job must know whether the rumours had any foundation.

"It is just as well to be prepared for any eventuality," Ying-Su replied evenly, her fathomless eyes on the view from Look-Out Post. "There's Government House squeezed between Upper and Lower Albert Roads with St John's cathedral below. See? Standing out clearly with its black slate roof and square tower. That's Victoria barracks further away on the hillside and you can see the China Fleet Club to the west of North Point near where the noontide gun is fired at twelve o'clock to tell Hong Kong they can knock off for lunch. That's Causeway Bay," she continued, "and the typhoon shelter where all those junks are jostled together; an ammunition dump on that small island offshore. Across the harbour you can see the Kai Tak aerodrome with its dirt runway and the seaplane station. Hair-raising approach by air. There was a crash into the mountain only the other day – everyone on board was killed."

"Have you flown?" asked Izolda.

"When I go to China – sometimes," Ying-Su said vaguely. "Those pimples in the New Territories are called the Nine Dragons."

"Well, I think the whole setting is quite fantastic, so beautiful with all those pretty islands."

"There are countless of them all waterless and uninhabited. They're the ones to watch . . . I'm glad you appreciate my country," Ying-Su switched. "It *is* Chinese of course, pure Chinese. Should never have been separated from the Motherland. *We* believe it worth fighting for."

Ying-Su's emphasis started Izolda thinking. What exactly did the Chinese girl mean by 'we'? We British, the country of her adoption, or we Chinese, her country of origin? Ying-Su had been to college in China. The Chinese communists talked of liberating Hong Kong; so, was Ying-Su's 'we' a patriotic Chinese one? *'The Motherland – pure Chinese'*, she had said.

The more Izolda listened to Ying-Su talking about Mao Tse-tung and how they'd fought the nationalist party in a 'peasant revolt', the more she suspected that Ying-Su had become a communist in her student days. If her suspicions proved correct the girl was in a strong position to double-cross her adopted family and the Hong Kong government for which she worked; as if the communists were anti the Hong Kong government it went without saying they must be pro Japanese. Therefore she would watch the Chinese girl like a hawk, and if treachery were proven in her own mind, warn her uncle or Winn or someone about it before more damage could be done.

* * *

27

"I found it in a back street in Peking," Jimmy lit up a cigar after the family had had dinner at The Falls. He was answering his mother's query about the ornately carved couch on the landing which had caught her fancy. In ebony, it was intricately inlaid at the back with mother-of-pearl, the arms carved into curving scaly dragons. Toni had scattered gold braided cushions over the hard, shiny surface.

"We were told it once belonged to a wealthy mandarin," Toni took up, "so Jimmy thought it appropriate to hang the portrait of the pigtailed gentleman in his robes above it."

"The mandarin was a friend of mine," Jimmy belched out smoke through his nostrils, "he lived in opulence in a palace in Peking with his family of wives, concubines and dozens of children. I'll let you into a secret, Mother. The couch has a hidden panel."

"How romantic! Where?" Izolda exclaimed.

"I'll show you sometime. Used to keep the opium in; it still has that curious and unmistakable tang about it. In those days, after a meal, instead of having a Havana like this," Jimmy waved cigar ash over himself, "guests were offered a small pipe. They called it 'chasing the dragon'. No ill effects unless used to excess when it becomes compulsive, but rather—"

"Compulsive like your smoking?" interrupted Louise.

"Not at all, Mother. I could stop tomorrow if I wanted to."

"Tomorrow perhaps, dear, but not today," Toni put in smoothly.

"What twaddle, Dad. You know you couldn't give up smoking if you tried."

"You against me too, Ying-Ying? *All* of you agin me?" Jimmy mocked mournfully. "What I *was* going to say to Izolda when I was so rudely interrupted is that in moderation the pipe soothes yet stimulates the mind as the old Dowager Empress Tzu Hsi knew very well. Despite

28

what a lot of people thought, she was no addict. The smoker wakes refreshed and ready for anything after his afternoon's restoring nap under its influence."

"Well, for crying out loud," burred Louise on the top of her form, "you sure sound, Jimmy, as if you've tried it out. I declare you know ALL about it!"

"We are talking of opium, Mother, heroin is another story, smoked by the old crones and sunken-eyed men one sees in Wanchai and over West Point way, gaunt skeletons who are picked up in their hundreds by the police and passed through the magistrate's courts. Both opium and heroin is smuggled in waterproof packs brought in ships from Siam and Burma and dropped into the harbour at certain points where they are retrieved by junks."

"Do they get caught?" Izolda asked.

"Not often; those who traffic in it have plenty of funds with which to pay off the officials in the right places. Impossible to completely eliminate police corruption in such a teeming place as this."

"That couch could sure tell a story of the people who have lain on it and gone off into a pain-free world of hallucinatory bliss, an end I wouldn't be averse to myself," Louise stated firmly. "I'll have you know *I* could be an addict."

"WHAT?" the company exclaimed aghast, all except Izolda who interpreted her grandmother's mischievous look which usually appeared when she was about to say something intended to shock.

"Could be true. I'll have you know that I've taken chlorodyne on and off all those years since I contracted sprue in Wei-chu. Guess what? It has opium in it!"

"Valuable medicinal drug; calms and warms the stomach," Toni added in the silence the old lady's unexpected statement produced.

29

"You are a card, Grandma; you really had us taken in for a moment there," Ying-Su's bell-like laugh rang out. She went over to sit on the arm of Louise's chair and put her hand affectionately over her shoulder. It seemed the last straw to Izolda. Resentment flooded over her. She couldn't stomach the 'Grandma' from the cuckoo in the nest much longer. Why did Ying-Su have to pinch *her* pet name? Why not 'Grandmother', or even 'Granny'? OK, she had to get used to sharing her grandmother with the family she had wanted to join so much, but she hadn't bargained on a rival, one who wasn't a granddaughter proper, and a Chinese one at that! She knew she was being childish; she was used to having her grandmother's full attention focused on her and her alone. Spoilt, that's what she was, abominably spoilt. She hadn't wanted to be tied any longer, or have the sole responsibility of looking after an increasingly decrepit old lady. Now her chance had come to stop fuming and take her freedom with both hands and go and live at the Helena May hostel with other bachelor girls, find a job, go out with Chippy, make lots of friends, forget about Roger . . .

"Come into my room will you, Jimmy?" Izolda heard her grandmother saying, "I want to show you Papa's Order. It will be yours when I'm gone. As well I want to talk about a new Will – not that there's anything much to leave . . ." Louise took her son's arm and walked out of the room.

Now what is she up to? Izolda said to herself, well, whatever it is, *they* can jolly well deal with it!

Chapter Three

IT was the evening of the Winters' party for the engaged couple Hugh Holden and Maisie Lauder. Out in the drive Ping-Li waited to show the chauffeur-driven cars where to park. A succession of white coated servants walked up the marble steps carrying trays of delectable eats from the kitchen below. Fung Wan was busy in the small dining room upstairs decanting various bottles, seeing that there was plenty of ice available, and giving the sparkling glasses a further polish.

Toni was also in the room checking that all was as it should be. She sampled the cocktail Fung Wan had mixed. "Excellent," she praised, and put the glass down in a corner where she could find it again. "Nice and dry."

Louise ensconced herself in the drawing room in a winged chair with high back before the painted screen, a position from which she reckoned she could best view the scene and would not have to move. Because her feet barely touched the floor, one of the servants brought her a footstool. Though she had no connection with the event the assembly was celebrating, she was looking forward to playing the part of the host's mother to all and sundry. She was going to stay put and let them come up to her. Neither did she need to search her memory for names. She knew the Lauders and Chippy Paine-Talbot from on board

31

ship, and she had since met Mr and Mrs Holden and their son Hugh who was to marry Maisie.

It was going to be intriguing to sit there and watch the wealthy business husbands of expansive waistlines and their overdressed wives. There was only one other woman coming who was as old as she and that was Lady Ho Tung, Sir Robert Ho's wife. Toni had had them to tea to meet her. Charming couple. They had talked about the Manchus and the China she had known during the revolution of 1911, and they had struck up a friendship. The old couple were coming up for their sixtieth wedding anniversary party. She had been invited to attend which had pleased her no end.

Entering the drawing room and seeing his mother sitting there, Jimmy chuckled to himself. She looked the dead replica, down to the eyebrows and pallid colouring, of Tzu Hsi, that 'Old Buddha' who had held court on her throne in the Winter Palace outside Peking. Even her hat skewered on with its shining jet hatpins looked not unlike the Dowager Empress's elaborate headdress of many jewelled pins.

Automatically Jimmy searched for his cigarette case in his pocket, took one out, and tapped it prior to lighting up. No. Curse it all. He'd show 'em he could cut down on the nicotine. Good moment to start when about to shake hands with the stream of guests Toni had invited. He could not for the life of him remember who was coming, notwithstanding that Toni had previously read the list out to him. Fiery little wife she could be. Kept him on his toes! He beckoned to her and they moved over to the landing by the opium couch to start receiving the company.

"Real good you can come to the wedding ceremony," drawled Mrs Lauder, the first guest to come up to Louise, four strands of milky pearls gleaming on her cocktail dress. "We've reserved a seat in church for you near the front."

"Most thoughtful," Louise eyed the head of newly set tight waves. "I believe it is the only Union Church left in the East. The trend started way back in Yokohama with my uncle. All denominations came. Such a good idea."

Mr Lauder joined his wife, cocktail in hand. "A pity they didn't keep on more of those broad-minded ministers to lessen the schisms among us non-conformists in Scotland," he caught on the gist of the conversation.

"Do try one of our fried-in-batter canapes," Toni made way for Fung Wan in the group round Louise, "they're fish roe, Mother, from Macao."

"Scrumptious," Mrs Holden agreed after Louise had helped herself. "Though I shouldn't . . ." She took a second one.

"Your health might benefit by losing a little," Louise frankly scanned Joan Holden's stout figure, at the same time taking in the blue-rinsed hair and mouthful of prominent teeth.

"Oh dear, oh dear, is it so apparent? Compared to my hubby I'm slim."

"Bulk's a good thing," Bill Holden declared. He came up with Jimmy to join the ladies, dark double whiskies in their hands. Bill, a florid man with heavy jowls, was head of the Colony's waterworks department.

"Absolutely," Jimmy agreed, patting his rotund stomach, "gives one a reserve to fall back upon in hard times. Ah, Winn my boy, good to see you back. Sorry about this hullabaloo. How's business in China?"

"International affairs running on much the same, Dad, certainly in the insurance line. Plenty of Japs about," Winn added, his grey eyes looking meaningfully into his father's brown ones.

"Suppose so. Same as here – huh? Come into my study later and tell me about it, that is if you young-uns don't go gallivanting off to some nightclub."

"This young-un for one won't. I've some sleep to catch up on."

Izolda had come into the room and stood by her grandmother's chair looking around her. "Some cousin," Winn remarked to his father, "she's gorgeous!" He had met her for the first time earlier that day and found her radiant.

Winn was not the only one who noticed the glow about Izolda that evening. Her grandmother had as well as her uncle and aunt who'd observed to one another how quickly Izolda had blossomed in Hong Kong, and that in no time she'd have a collection of young men round her just as her mother had had before her. None of them knew that Izolda's radiance was due to having received her first missive from Roger. She was thrilled that he had penned her a note however brief, thrilled that he liked her enough to write at all. W.J. Turner's poem, *Romance*, learnt at school, jumped into her mind as she read the note: '*I stood where shining Popacatepetl in the sunlight gleams . . .*'

"Zol!" called out Ying-Su from the door, "a pal of yours has arrived."

As Izolda darted across the room she noticed Ying-Su talking to the Chinese General Sha-Kwo, friend of her uncle's he called 'Bungy'. She brushed past them suspiciously and went over to find Chippy. "Oh well done," she said enthusiastically, "you found your way up here."

"Sorry I'm late. The Commodore kept me; can't do without me," Chippy grinned.

"You're not really late," Izolda said, pink-cheeked and

34

glowing with her secret happiness. She had decided not to tell anybody about the letter, not even her grandmother. They might make pertinent remarks, especially Maisie who had said that Chippy was 'mad' about her, and was bound to pass it on to Hugh who knew Roger. "Come along and meet my family and the Holdens," she ushered him into the crowd.

"Nice to see you on terra firma, my boy," Mr Lauder extended a large hand.

"My, isn't it jus' the nicest thing all us *Chitral* friends meetin' up again?" Mrs Lauder enthused.

"Hallo Chippy," Maisie edged into the circle. "Where's Hugh got to? You must meet him. He's gone and done his famous disappearing trick I bet. Doesn't like cocktail parties – says he can't hear his own voice!"

Maisie, Izolda and Chippy went in search of Hugh and found him seated on the landing couch in earnest conversation with Winn and Ying-Su. "Oh, there you are, darling," Maisie rushed up, "here's Chippy, friend of Izolda's, met on board ship."

"I've heard a good deal concerning the trip out." Hugh unfolded his long legs from the couch and rose to shake hands, "In fact I gather a riotous time was had. I'm surprised Maisie remained faithful to me. I suppose you did?" he turned to her with a quirk.

"I can vouch for it," put in Chippy, "she did nothing but talk about you, especially to Roger Stamford."

"Great guy," remarked Hugh. "I had a card from him on the North-West Frontier wishing us all the best for the wedding."

It was on Izolda's lips to blurt out that she'd had a card from Roger too, but she stopped in time. Best to keep that to herself. Instead she stood in the group examining the three men and thinking of Yvette and how envious she would be if she could see her now. Hugh nearly matched Roger in height, but there the resemblance ended. Hugh was reddish haired with a loose-knit slighter figure, his looks aquiline and arch-nosed, unlike Roger's ruggedness. Winn, standing next to her, was different again, really striking with dark hair, grey eyes and a moustache, unusual for a civilian. She'd liked him on sight and agreed with Ying Su that he was 'devastingly' good looking – film-starish, she'd have put it.

"You've certainly gathered a family round you, Zol," Chippy remarked, "I remember how as a kid you went on about having none. You can't do that anymore. I can see the likeness between the cousins."

"The Winter strain is a dominant one," Winn smiled indulgently at the naval officer who, a lieutenant he gathered, looked as if he were hardly out of the egg. As for his cousin – she was lovely, luminous somehow. What a treat. He was one for the girls and this coz was a bonus. He put an arm affectionately over her shoulder.

Winn Sutherland Winter had not been sent to boarding school in the UK. Jimmy and Toni had kept this precious only child in the far east to whatever posting. He had gone to excellent local schools and had recently got his honours degree at the Hong Kong University. He was a true colonial and due to his sophisticated cosmopolitan upbringing he seemed older than his twenty-three years.

"I'm exhausted, I must sit down," Maisie settled herself on the opium couch.

"Same here," yawned Ying-Su taking a perch on a cushion at the back of the divan.

"Neither of you look in the slightest bit tired," Chippy declared chivalrously. He offered cigarettes all round from his flat silver case. Izolda noticed his middle finger was more nicotine stained than ever. One day she'd suggest he scrub it with pumice stone and lemon juice. Knowing Chippy, he would take the hint amiably.

"Don't believe a word she says, Chippy," Winn settled down beside his sister. He tweaked her short black hair teasingly. "She's as strong as an ox. Far stronger than I."

"I'm not," Ying-Su pouted, her doe eyes on Chippy. She liked to play on her piquante littleness to rouse the protective spirit of the British male.

How subtle she was, Izolda thought, catching the look. She'd be after Chippy next no doubt. There they were, Izolda mused, six young people sitting close together on the opium couch away from the crush in the drawing room, and all because Hugh Holden did not care for cocktail parties! Ying-Su was curled up, like a self-satisfied cat, to the rear against the ivory pattern where the hidden panel was. Hugh was sitting in front of Ying-Su with Maisie leaning against him for a back. She, Winn and Chippy sat at the foot of the couch. They were all touching and everyone's scents mingled. From Ying-Su emanated a heavy exotic scent; Maisie had Chanel No. 5 and she herself had used some of her grandmother's eau-de-cologne. Hugh smelt of tweedy Englishman; Winn of rather pleasant aftershave lotion, and Chippy of the oil which failed to keep his unruly lock of hair in place.

"It's a bit like being on a raft at sea, I mean all of us sitting here," she said dreamily.

"Winn and I spent hours playing on it as kids."

"We used to nab some of Dad's cigarettes and pretend we were smoking 'snow'," said Winn.

"I like it here. It's a peaceful raft away from that racket in there."

37

"*Hugh!*" protested Maisie, "that's extremely rude of you when Mr and Mrs Winter are giving this party for us . . ."

"Yes, I know, and I humbly apologise. My excuse for appalling manners is pre-marital nerves. I feel quite neurotic about it. I wish to God the whole bloody tribal exercise were over."

"So do I. If it weren't for our four parents taking charge, we'd have gone off and got married on our own."

"You know you wouldn't, Maisie. You'll enjoy every moment of the great day," Izolda scoffed.

"I agree with Hugh. I'd rather stay a bachelor than go through all the palaver," said Winn.

"Well I think a white wedding is romantic," Izolda expressed her feelings. "What about you Chippy?"

"I could take it, Zol. I'm really rather a sociable creature," he laughed. "I gather you're a Sunday soldier, Winn? In which case we'll be on manoeuvres together this coming summer – combined ops with all three services plus police and every available volunteer roped in. We've been working on it on *Tamar*. Should be good fun."

"Right. I'm a dead keen Gunner; Sergeants' Mess to you, sir! Proud motto of the Hong Kong Defence Force is '*nulli secundus*' and second to none are our gun sites. I'll show you one up behind The Falls if you're interested?"

"Like to see it very much. From the news today the guns in Europe will be blasting off in earnest at any moment."

"But not here," evaded Izolda.

"That's wishful thinking, Zol," said Ying-Su. "Don't be too sure."

"Canton is crawling with Japs. I happened to notice in passing," Winn declared cheerfully.

"Grandma doesn't think the Japanese will attack the

British, and she should know," Izolda said, stoutly sticking to her theory.

"Then why," snorted Hugh, the regular soldier, "are there sentries posted all along the twenty-two mile border in the New Territories if not against the Japs?"

"Oh darling, do shut up," remonstrated Maisie, "Zol can't bear talking war, and it is not the moment to anyway." But nothing would silence the men on the subject.

"Have the brave Volunteer Gunners noticed that all their guns point inwards? What if the enemy takes you by surprise and comes by sea?" jeered Chippy. Izolda had already learnt in the short time since her arrival that regulars tended to look on the 'Sunday' soldiers as playing at the war game.

"It's no secret the government has plans for women and children to be evacuated," Ying-Su remarked.

"Where would they evacuate us to?" Maisie enquired.

"The UK or Australia, and I believe there's some suggestion of the Philippines."

"At least that's nearer. I shan't go."

"You'll have to, darling," Hugh said kissing the top of her head, "I'll make you."

"Neither will my grandmother go." Izolda thought of Louise's words on their arrival about neither landslides nor earthquakes budging her. "Don't let's think war. Here we are safe on our little opium raft . . ."

". . . and what becomes of *me* when the typhoon blows?" Ying Su's voice tinkled out.

"I'll give you my lifebelt," Chippy responded exactly on cue. Izolda said nothing.

"You and I, Zol, don't need lifebelts," Winn breathed into her ear. "We'll swim together to one of the deserted islands, and live there happy ever after. What think you?"

Did he mean it? Was he teasing? The grey eyes looked steadily into hers, his body close and attractive. For a moment there was silence on the opium couch, and then Maisie jumped up and pulled Hugh to his feet. "Enough," she exclaimed, "we simply must stop being unsociable and circulate with the guests. There are plenty of folk we haven't thanked personally for their presents. Come on, Hugh, into the drawing room with me and do your stuff."

"Bullied already," Hugh replied with a grin.

In her bedroom that night, Izolda took the letter out from a drawer and looked lovingly at the Indian stamp overmarked with 'Rawalpindi'. The envelope was addressed to Miss ICV Richardson – so he had taken in all her names as she had his! Inside was not a letter as such but a regimental card with message written in neat handwriting. The card was crested with: '*Ubique – Quo fas et gloria ducunt*'. Izolda had asked Hugh what '*Ubique*' stood for, and he replied that it was the same as the Sappers, only they translated it differently: *Ubique* for them meant '*Everywhere*' while for the Gunners it meant '*All over the place*'. The card had a picture of action in mountainous country in 1917 during the Great War. There were men's bodies lying by guns surrounded by barbed wire, craters and explosions. On it Roger had written: '*Hope you arrived safely. Do write and tell me about it. I'm up to my eyes in work. Please forgive blood and thunder. I know it is not your choice; neither is it mine.*' And then the beautiful words: '*Sayonara, Izolda, till we meet again. Yours ever, Roger.*'

At first Izolda, never having had a letter from a man before, thought that 'yours ever' was a strange way to end a note. Then, when she pondered on it – which was a good deal of the time; she slept with it under her pillow and was always taking it out to read again – she thought how 'yours ever' could equally mean 'yours *for* ever'. Izolda pretended that 'forever' was what Roger did mean, and she treasured the card all the more for that fantasy.

Part Two

'A million lights shall glow'

1940–1941

Chapter Four

THE Holden-Lauder wedding passed off splendidly. Maisie and Hugh were seen off on their honeymoon to the Philippines, and the Lauders left for the States.

When the news came over the air on 3rd September 1939, following the German invasion of Poland, that war had broken out in Europe, and that in Great Britain the Territorials had been called up and everyone was in uniform including DD (as Izolda's father was known in the Royal Navy), it seemed a good moment for Izolda to claim her independence. She moved down to the Helena May hostel and took a nearby job as a typist. One of the reasons for the move was her increasingly hectic night life and the difficulty of getting back to The Falls. Only on rare special occasions did the late Peak tram depart for the 12.45 a.m. run.

Louise put no opposition in the way of Izolda's leaving. She felt it right for her to branch out on her own. She had instilled in her since childhood the moral values of her own generation and did not think her granddaughter would deviate from them any more than Camille had. As for herself she was content to be where she was, proud of her grandson Winn – so like the previous generation of Winter men – and pleased with the close association formed with Ying-Su whose intelligence and perspicacity attracted her.

*   *   *

45

Despite her resolution, it was Izolda who most missed the singular attachment that had existed for over ten years with her grandmother when they had been solely dependent upon each other. Ironically, through gaining a family, Izolda now felt she had lost this unique relationship she had once believed could only be severed through death.

But unrecognised by Izolda at the time, though the special bonding between them may have been loosened to include others, it was neither lost nor severed, and often they met in the dark lattice-windowed rooms in the intimate atmosphere of Mickey's Kitchen where she and Maisie had met soon after their arrival. Here Louise, when she felt like it, was driven by Ping-Li; Jimmy went there from the Chartered Bank, Toni from her hospital, Winn from his office block on Des Voeux Road, and Ying-Su from the government offices. Hugh and Maisie popped in from time to time when they were over in Victoria from their Fanling bungalow, and Chippy frequently hopped on a tram from the naval base to join the family in the lunch hour.

It was on one of these gatherings on a hot May day in 1940 when Izolda had been in Hong Kong for over a year, that, unexpectedly, Roger's name came up. Izolda had replied to his card via his base address in the Rawalpindi HQ Mess. She had written about the wedding and her doings in Hong Kong – perhaps, in retrospect, over-emphasising the full life she was leading. When no answer came, she wondered if this had put him off. Too late she remembered how he'd said he was not a great party man. After months of fruitless watching for the post, she resolved to wait until Christmas as an excuse to try again. With the seasonal card sent when December came, she added a note enquiring if he'd received her letter. There was no reply to this, not even a Christmas card. All the elation she'd felt on receiving his first – and it seemed only – missive had by now long left her, so that it was quite a shock to hear Roger's name.

"I read about Roger Stamford in a military news letter," Hugh mentioned over the meal.

"Oh? What about him?" Izolda asked, keeping her voice even with difficulty. After all this time the mention of his name could still affect her and bring back the pang of the memory of him. Despite overhead fans whirring to stir the sluggish air, Izolda felt herself breaking out in a sweat.

"Hugh showed the citation to me," Maisie, red-faced and bursting at the seams in the last month of pregnancy, said. "Roger has been awarded the MC on the North-West Frontier. They had a scrap with the Pathan tribesmen last cold weather."

"The citation read, 'For outstanding courage'," Hugh informed.

"Well done, whoever he is," exclaimed Winn.

"Bravo Roger!" Chippy added, "he's the sort of chap who deserves a gong. Bags of pluck."

"Any more details?" Izolda enquired faintly. Roger lived in another world from hers.

"Apparently a cavalry patrol was attacked by a party of tribesmen," Hugh, who had himself served at one time on the North-West Frontier of India, explained, "they attacked from the heights on one side of the well-known Darwaza Pass, causing casualties. The Mohmands of that district then had the temerity to come down and fire into the camps of the various regiments wounding more including two officers from one of the 'Piffers', as the Punjab regiments are known. Can't allow that sort of thing," he laughed.

"Go on," urged Izolda.

"Well, when an incident like that occurs, the Frontier Force Brigade forms up with its infantry, artillery and all the rest and especially the indispensable Mountain Gunners, a battery of which Roger commands. With their 'screw-guns'—"

"Explain to us girls," Maisie demanded.

"'Screw-guns' are light Pack Howitzer guns," Hugh elaborate for the women. "The barrels, in two parts, are carried on the backs of mules; when needed the guns can be put together in a couple of minutes. Mules can climb with their burdens at considerable speed up precipitous mountains where heavier guns can't go. Roger would have crept his way with his men and mules up a mountain in the dark to a certain high point to open fire on the enemy at first light and prepare the way for the infantry crawling up the ridges. Once the opposing sides clash, and the guns cannot be aimed into the mêlée, Roger was probably ordered to leave his guns and fight as infantry with his men. The citation says he went to the aid of some Piffers who were being decimated. He encouraged and rallied his men to keep at it, succoured the wounded and fought on through a long day of being hard pressed against hordes of tribesmen until the latter at last had had enough and retreated to their fortress mountain villages."

Izolda pushed her plate away from her. War. Roger in the thick of it. Ugh. Blood and thunder like the picture on his card. Yet he had written '*not my choice*'. It was a long time since she'd sent her Christmas card. He had never answered. By now she knew he would not get in touch with her again – certainly not when he was engrossed with bloody struggles like that . . .

"To bring us back from mountainous frontiers to sweltering Hong Kong," Chippy said cheerfully, "who can come to a bathing party next weekend on Commodore Collinson's

48

yacht *Taipan*, flags flying? Ask Ying Su too when she's back. Room for us all."

Winn nodded. "Count me in," he said.

"Me too," added Izolda determined to put Roger out of her head.

"Not for us; sorry," Hugh helped his wife to her feet, "wouldn't do for the baby to arrive on the Commodore's yacht! Thanks all the same."

"She wants a son," Izolda said wistfully to Winn as she watched Chippy following the pair out.

"Must you go out quite so much with him?"

"With Chippy? Why not? Don't you like him?"

"Of course I like him. I don't think anyone could not, he's so . . . innocuous somehow. Perhaps it is that I'm envious of all the attention you give him."

"We're good friends," she replied.

For some time now Izolda had felt at a loss to know how to deal with Winn, whose kisses were anything but brotherly. After a party he would sometimes stay on for the night at The Falls. He would come into her room when she was in bed to chat, and on several occasions he had actually got into bed with her! In his pyjamas, he had taken her into his arms and held her to him, and she had felt the excitement and daring of being in bed with a man, a rather darling man who wasn't a bit like a brother. He had kissed her and cuddled her and run his hands over her nightie and said how sweet she was and wouldn't it be nice if one day they decided to marry and had lovely children and so strengthen the Winter clan. It had made her all mixed up with emotion. Intimacies with a cousin sounded like incest to her, though Great Aunt Maude had married her first cousin – but then they couldn't have children. And whoever she married she *must* have children to make her own family. She felt thoroughly bemused about

the whole thing. Winn was another reason why she had left
The Falls.

Now in Mickey's Kitchen when the others had left, she
asked Winn about Ying-Su. "I don't understand her," she
said. "I mean . . . does she *think* British?"

"I don't know what you mean."

"I mean, well, her job is highly secret, isn't it?"

"So I believe."

"But being basically Chinese . . ."

"What *are* you getting at Zol? Speaking like as native
has its uses. Dad's been roped in—"

"To do what?"

"How should *I* know? I haven't been roped into anything,
thank God. I'm a straightforward weekend soldier, and I've
got more than enough to do looking after my guns than
poking my nose into dangerous stuff. Stay out of it, Zol
darling."

"You and Ying-Su don't behave like brother and sister,"
Izolda was determined to keep ferreting.

"No we don't. We're not brother and sister. We were
brought up together and we found out about life together on
the top floor when we were pretty young. Nothing wrong
with that except that Mum and Dad would have a fit if they
knew, so don't tell them."

"No, of course not."

"I took myself off to the Bowen Road flat before they
could suspect anything."

"Do you still . . . ?"

"No," Winn laughed at Izolda's expression. The darling
girl really was a treasure. Just what he wanted for a faithful
wife – so refreshing. Transparently genuine after the hard-
boiled girls of Hong Kong. He had often been tempted to
go the whole hog with her . . . but no, their relationship

was too delicate for that and she too precious to him to risk destroying it by being over hasty. He wanted to protect her from designing males, marry her himself in the end when it was time for him to settle down. But he was worried about this Chippy business. To Winn he was a thoroughly weak specimen. Ribby, no chest to him; a bit of a sop – a good natured milksop, a prissy. Whatever, the thought of those thick pink lips kissing the golden girl sitting beside him – ugh, it revolted him. He could give her everything – money too; he'd been promoted in the firm and was canny over his investments. He'd teach her about passion . . . they would make a most handsome couple! And he'd be faithful to her – like Mum and Dad.

Winn looked at Izolda and saw the query still in her eyes. "The truth is, dearest Zol, that Ying-Su went on to various men friends. Her present one is that Chinese general you met at The Falls – most suitable. I've had my paramours too, but then my most beautiful and utterly delectable cousin comes into my life. I fall flat. What do you expect?"

"Before we stop talking about Ying-Su . . . I think she's gone communist from all those trips to China."

"Aha, my beauty, so that's it is it? That she has picked up revolutionary leanings? Yes, she could have. Well, if you find anything suspicious my advice is tell Dad. Let him sort it out," Winn advised, looking at Izolda straight from his dark-lashed grey eyes.

The intense heat of summer was fully upon them with the temperature in the nineties and humidity at an oppressive ninety-three per cent, on the day of the Commodore's picnic. The dry leaves on the trees drooped tiredly and fell. The vivid greens of the Peak had faded to fallow, and the harbour scene of ships and craft lazed in a shimmering heat haze as the noontide cannon on Jardine's Wharf boomed the hour.

Izolda, Winn and Chippy were ferried out to the *Taipan* in a sampan by a barefooted water-woman who sculled them along with a flat oar at the rear of the craft. Ying-Su was not with them. She'd sent apologies to Chippy and gone off somewhere on the spur of the moment.

"She's always doing it," remarked Winn, "she'll get married one day on the spur of the moment without telling anybody."

Once on board the *Taipan*, the guests found themselves jumping to obey the barked orders of the Commodore to hoist sail, and in a very light air they glided off round North Point. On their slow progress they watched a civilian plane approach, and turn sharply to land at Kai Tak airport. Overhead an RAF Walrus Amphibian roared low and landed as gracefully as a large falcon by the sea base. It came to a halt beside a great deep duck-shaped Clipper flying boat. Glassy water slapped against the yacht's keel, and *Taipan* glided on to sail through the Lye-mun Narrows between the Devil's Peak of the mainland and the Island. Then she headed on to anchor in Junk Bay.

While Chippy with the others stowed sails, Winn and Izolda dived overboard to swim to the barren shore. Winn, having lived in the tropics all his life, was a strong swimmer and from her Menton days Izolda was like a fish in the water. Having a date that evening with Chippy, she wore a white bathing cap to keep her hair dry. She and Winn crawled side by side, pacing one another smoothly, shoulders gleaming half in, half out of the warm water. They watched one another's progress in enjoyment as heads held sideways rose and mouths opened to take in quick gulps of air. On shore they shook themselves like animals do, and Izolda turned up the rubber from her ears to hear better what Winn was saying. Her striped bathing suit with brief skirt

and narrow belt clung to her slim figure showing her hip
bones and emphasising the smallness of her waist.

"She's lovely. I love her," Winn thought as they wandered
alone on the bare ochre-dun beach in the blistering sun, the
water on his body running in rivulets through the dark hairs
on his tanned legs.

He put his arm about Izolda's shoulder, and she responded
by tucking her hand into his waistband above his trunks. His
flesh was cool to the touch though the sun was rapidly drying
their wet skins, and soon they must return to the yacht for
lunch under its awnings.

Izolda's feelings for Winn were as usual, mixed. She was
half in love with him, but cousins? Children? The same old
story. She wanted to be married, and she wanted to have
children. She wanted to be a young mum as Maisie was
about to be, and even though Roger's name had recently
come up again he no longer came into her calculations. She
still thought of him, remembered the marvellousness of his
strong tall figure, often dreamed of what it would be like
to be kissed by *him*. But the remembrance of his face was
fading fast, and she had no photo or snap to remind her of
the details though she could remember how his hair curled
above his ears, and the ruggedness . . .

Her meeting with Roger on the *Chitral* had been a once
in a lifetime encounter with a glimpse of exquisite marvels.
Roger with his charisma, his forcefulness, his courtesy to her
grandmother, his devotion to the army, his courage which
had won him an MC on the frontier, was not here in her
life; nor was it conceivable that their paths would ever
cross again with the thousands of miles and the fathomless
seas that separated them – and, worst of all, the lack of
correspondence which had killed hope dead. Even if in the
future they did by some fluke meet, he would take no more

notice of her than he had on the *Chitral*. Just a short period on the same liner; just a card with 'yours ever'; just a *sayonara* which was not a 'till we meet again' but a goodbye.

There was absolutely no point in denying herself marriage and children for the rest of her life for an unobtainable dream.

The crowded bus with Chippy and Izolda on the top deck, ground its way through the narrow streets of Wanchai. Here at night the flashing lights of the girlie-bar parlours enticed the sailors to enter. By day the streets were full of stalls of fruit and fresh vegetables, of large yellow Chinese cabbages, polished red tomatoes, bulky elongated green lettuces, round juicy outsize oranges, boxes of brown lychees, and huge tangerine-coloured mangoes.

From their viewing point Chippy and Izolda caught glimpses inside the open fronted shops of seated figures making swift calculations on their abacuses, of craftsmen at metalwork, ivory carvings or woodwork and every other conceivable artifice in the making in that hammering, humorous, noisy area with its ever moving population.

Leaving Wanchai behind, the bus began to climb, swaying round hairpin bends. Below them they could see the Happy Valley racecourse, distinct with its oval track round a circle of green. Laughing, Chippy and Izolda held onto the seat bar before them for dear life. They passed the old roman catholic cemetery followed by the parsi and the protestant ones with their terrace upon terrace of white graves and ornate marbled monuments. They laughed at the drunken angle of the old stones.

The road wound on up to the Wong-Nei-Chong Gap, and began to descend through undulating hills towards an expanse of blue sea. At Repulse Bay they disgorged with the crowd and ran down to the long white sandy beach. On the shore sat a Chinaman in a concrete look-out ready to ring a bell should he spot a shark. Chippy and Izolda plunged into the clean water. For a good hour they swam and splashed and ducked one another, then they dried themselves and climbed up the steps to the Repulse Bay Hotel for refreshments, and they talked. For the first time Chippy spoke of his family, the admired parents and household Izolda had known when they had hired the Villa Claude next to theirs in Menton for a few short months years ago.

The truth was, Chippy told her, very far from the perfect family. Even then in Menton his mother was having an affair with the batman-cum-chauffeur. On the family's return to India, the baby girl, through the negligence of their ayah, had toddled off on her own in the garden of the bungalow and within minutes drowned in the swimming pool. Chippy's older brother had enlisted with the British Battalion in the XVth International Brigade to fight with the republican side against Franco in the Spanish Civil War, and had been killed at the Battle of Harama in 1937 with two hundred other British volunteers. In her grief at the double calamity, Chippy's mother had taken her life.

"My father retired from the Indian Army, married again, and is settled in Canada. I hardly ever see him. So you see, Zol, I am as bereft of a family as you have been," Chippy ended the sad saga. Izolda's heart went out to him. Poor Chippy, he was so nice, such fun to be with, they got on so well . . . She loved him too – in a different way from Winn – but she loved him.

That night they dined *à deux* at the China Fleet Yacht Club. With a bar in one corner, small tables were arranged round the dance floor in a room approached from an enclosed flight of stairs lined with portraits of former commodores.

The room where they sat was shaped like a glassed-in bridge of a ship, three-quarters of its length giving uninterrupted views of the harbour. The myriads of twinkling lights of Kowloon glowed from across the water. Lights were everywhere one looked. Illuminations were draped over the boats at sea; lights to one side of the club flickered through the typhoon barrier which sheltered a thousand small craft; a thousand 'flying flames' of lanterns swung.

"'Across the water when 'tis dark a million lights shall glow . . .'" Izolda quoted.

"Where did you get that from?" Chippy asked.

"I found it in a book in Uncle Jimmy's library; a prophecy written in the Sung dynasty, and it has come true," Izolda gazed out through the windows at the brilliant skyline.

"Let's get married," suggested Chippy.

"What's that got to do with the Sung dynasty?" countered Izolda.

"Nothing. It's just that I love the way you come out with quotes like that. What about it?"

"Yes," smiled Izolda. A proposal! The one which from childhood she was going to accept if he was 'nice', and if anyone was nice, Chippy was.

"We're engaged then?" Chippy looked almost as astonished as Izolda felt at this sudden turn of events.

"I suppose so," Izolda laughed.

"Boy!" Chippy clicked finger and thumb, "Wanchee bring champagne."

"Yes Master; quicklee Master," the boy beamed.

"To us," they toasted one another.

"When shall we get married?" asked Izolda.

"The sooner the better as far as I'm concerned. No reason to hang around."

"I agree. Don't let's have a long engagement like Hugh and Maisie did. They said it nearly killed them."

"Especially if there's going to be war, Zol."

"*Especially* if there's going to be war, Chippy."

"I like him very much," Louise said when Izolda burst into her bedroom with the news, "a bit immature perhaps, but you can grow up together. He is sincere and has a nice honest face. Sure, honey, he'll make a devoted husband."

"Won't Daddy be thrilled that my fiancé is a naval officer? Mummy would have been pleased too, wouldn't she, Grandma? The wedding's to be in the cathedral where she gave the recital. Isn't it all perfect?" Izolda enthused, bubbling over with excitement.

Everyone was delighted – everyone that was except Winn. "For God's sake, Zol, pull yourself together," he had said furiously on hearing about the engagement. "Break it off right away."

"Why should I?"

"You know perfectly well why, damn you," Winn exploded. 'You're playing a dangerous game. For some reason you've taken it into your head to marry this chap. You'll find yourself landed . . ."

"I'll be landed with Chippy; that's what I want."

"No you don't."

"How do you know? I wish you'd stop interfering."

"Look here, Zol," Winn attempted to cool the situation. "Wait a while. If all else fails you can always marry me!"

"Don't be flippant. For that matter why didn't you marry Ying-Su?"

"Ying-Su doesn't come into it," Winn ground his teeth.
"Don't dodge my question."

"I'm not dodging anything."

"You are. You're avoiding the fact that you are *not* in
love with him."

"I *am* in love with him," Izolda replied, eyes bright. She
twisted her engagement ring round her finger. It was a
lovely diamond ring. She liked seeing it there. She liked
being engaged.

"You're marrying him for the sake of getting married."

"I'm not. I *do* love him, Winn, really I do."

What more could he say, especially when his was a
lone voice?

They cabled DD with the glad news, and he cabled back
his delight and that he was going to put an announcement in
the *Times*. His cable ended with: '*Glad you are not here. We
are under siege with our backs to the wall. Every best wish
for your future happiness. Your loving, Daddy.*'

By now the 'phoney' war in Europe was well and truly
over. The British Expeditionary Force had been pushed back
by the strength of the Reich onto the beaches of Dunkirk,
and DD was one of the many who went out with the small
boats to rescue a whole army to fight again.

On the September afternoon on the day that Japan ominously
signed the Tripartite Pact with Germany and Italy to help one
another if attacked, Louise was sitting in her room wearing
an old mauve satin kimono Toni had fetched from some
tin-lined box in the basement. The kimono was embroidered
with chrysanthemums in white silk. The whole smelt of
mothballs. Louise liked the smell and would not let Toni
have it cleaned. The scent reminded her of her furs in Japan
when they were taken out of their boxes after the summer.

She liked to wear it when playing her 'Thirteen Demon', or as some called it, 'One Man' patience.

She had always enjoyed the feel of a shiny stiff deck of cards in her hands, the small hands which Jimmy had inherited. Her nails were shiny from polishing them on a rouged shammy buff – her green-fingered hands no longer sore-cracked now that she gardened no more. Detached, she watched them expertly shuffling the cards, spinning back with a flip the bending pack to interlock in exact measured neatness. Those hands could still play the piano! Known only to herself and the servants, sometimes when she was alone in the house – and often she was alone with the busy working family out much of the time – she went upstairs to the nursery floor and tickled the keys in the games room, mostly hymns from memory. And she sang. Actually she could still sing rather well. In her day she had had a powerful contralto and because the voice was so deep it had not cracked with age.

Sometimes she played her patience on a board while sitting up in bed at night when she couldn't sleep. She kept a tin of Bath Oliver biscuits by her bedside to nibble, and also a flask of brandy for when she felt ill – she never took more than a teaspoon; neither did she cheat at patience. A teaspoon of neat brandy was enough to stimulate the heart, and cheating oneself at cards would be just plain stupid! A card would hold everything up, and when it was impossible to make a move she would change one card round, once only: therefore '*One Man*'. If that didn't work she would shuffle the cards thoroughly, and start a new deal. When starting again, there was always the anticipation, and the satisfaction when a game *did* come out – a rarity – all thirteen reserve cards used up, four tidy stacks in front of her. Then she would look across to the dressing table at the Order propped against the mirror, and settle down to sleep to dream of that red-letter day when she and James were driven in their brougham to the station for Tokyo and the Imperial Palace where the Grand Chamberlain, in full court dress, met them for the investiture by His Imperial Highness the Emperor Meiji . . .

Next day Izolda arrived at The Falls to see her grandmother and discuss wedding arrangements. Toni came in. "I've just been listening to the news on the wireless," she said. "Full of battles in the sky over England."

"Preparatory to an invasion, I guess," Louise aired, "I for one am disgusted at Japan for signing that Tripartite Pact. They ought to know better."

"As a result of the Pact the border has been closed with China, and about time too," Toni enlarged. "Jimmy tells me a barrier has been put up on the road and rail bridge over the river at Lo-Wu."

"I suppose Hugh and his Sappers will be blowing up the roads and bridges next?" said Izolda gloomily.

"It hasn't come to that yet, dear, but we've got to face that it well soon may."

"Does the border closure mean that Winn can't go on his business trips into China any more, Aunt Toni?" Izolda wanted to know. She had not seen Winn since their clash of words. He was obviously avoiding her.

"I shouldn't think Winn will have time to go anywhere now. He spends every weekend out on the Fanling golf course kneeling with his battery behind his field piece and making a fearful noise. He's as happy as a sand boy!"

"Men love a fight. If there were only women in the world there wouldn't be wars," Louise commented sourly.

"At the Helena May hostel there's a notice pinned on the board to the effect that women who are not nurses or

working in key office jobs will be evacuated. That includes
service wives. I wonder what Maisie and the baby will do;
she won't want to leave Hugh."

"As yours isn't a key job, you're in the category to leave,
Izolda. Have you thought of that? You could become a
VAD."

"No thanks, Aunt Toni. I hate the sight of blood, not that
I've seen any . . ." Izolda's voice trailed away. She was sure
she'd faint at the sight of it. And she envied Ying Su who
was in a key job and wouldn't have to leave. But . . . ?

"Let me think," Toni said pensively. "The auxiliary
medical corps is considered 'key'. You could try as a
typist or telephonist there."

"Nothing will move *me*," declared Louise for the ump-
teenth time, though no one had asked her.

"Jimmy's having the old fortified pillbox below the house
cleaned and new locks put on."

"What for?"

"An emergency foodstore, dear. Nice and cool inside. It's
so well hidden in the overgrown bushes that it is almost
impossible for anyone not knowing its position to locate
it. Jimmy is also thinking of digging a slit trench on the
terrace as a precautionary measure for us to jump into. I
told him what I thought of the manic idea."

"When the samurai get the war lust there's no stopping
them," Louise declared. "Jimmy's right."

"Grandma! You told everyone on board ship there wouldn't
be a war here because the Japanese were our allies. The Pact
is for their defence – not *offensive*."

"That was before war broke out in Europe."

"What's that got to do with it?"

"Only that it looks as if the Germans are winning – the
way they pushed the Allies into the Channel and are now

bombing England – and the Japanese like to be on the winning side."

"Mother dear, really, samurai warriors in 1940! By all accounts their army is a well equipped modern one."

"Maybe, but they sure are samurai warriors underneath all that new paraphernalia."

"Now, about the wedding reception . . ."

Later that day, Toni asked Izolda if she knew the facts of life. "Well . . . sort of," stammered Izolda. Toni took her into her bedroom and told her in clinical terms exactly what happened.

"Any questions?" Toni asked. Izolda shook her head. "What about a contraceptive?"

"No, we want babies."

"You have to face it, there may be war. You're young. Plenty of time. I think you'd be wise not to start one straight away."

"If there's to be war, more necessary than ever to replace those men lost," Izolda declared blithely, on the brink of her cure-all fun marriage to Chippy, and the start of her own family.

It was in that autumn that Chippy, smart in his naval uniform, and Izolda, virginal in white, were married by the Dean. Beautiful, crystal clear, sunny day after warm autumn day, the best season of the year in Hong Kong, the time of the Chinese moon festival when little cakes were sold in the streets. In St John's cathedral the sun shone through the open black shutters and picked out the blue designs on the high wooden trusses in the rafters.

After the service, a naval guard made a fine arcade of flashing swords for bride and groom to pass under while

cameras clicked. Ping-Li drove them in the beribboned
Cadillac the short distance to the blue and white arched
colonial Hong Kong Club. Chippy and Izolda led the way up
the grand stairs and into the large reception room where the
portrait of a one-armed officer of the East India Company,
wounded in the Sikh War of the last century, looked down
on them with a sardonic smile as if he knew . . .

The only person who suspected was Winn, and he was not
there, having unequivocally refused to come to the wedding,
though Ying-Su was present, attentive as usual towards Louise.
Laced with champagne, Izolda never gave Winn, nor even
faraway Roger, a thought. She enjoyed the party so much
that she had to be dragged away by Maisie – slim again
having given birth to a son three months previously – to go
and change in readiness to cross the harbour in the Bank's
launch decorated in more white ribbons and showered with
confetti.

Izolda and Chippy were taken to the palatial Peninsular
Hotel where they were conducted to an enormous bridal
suite. Next day they caught the boat for the four hours'
journey to Macao, the oldest colony on Chinese soil. It was
a good place for a honeymoon couple, well away from anyone
they knew. There was plenty to occupy their time, with casino
gambling late into the nights, and the island full of historical
and architectural relics to explore by day.

Chapter Five

"ISN'T it just the nicest thing to wake up in the night, to stretch out your hand and find your husband there beside you." Izolda caressed the double bed fleetingly while placing Louise's coat upon it.

It was Louise's first trip to her married granddaughter's new home. The fact that the flat on Macdonnell Road was in the same block as the one she and Camille had lived in in 1912, pleased her no end. "What a cute way to express married love," she smiled, peering into Izolda's mirror. She dabbed her nose with *poudre blanche* from a gold compact Jimmy had given her on her birthday, adjusted her hat to the slight angle she liked, and stuck the hatpins in more securely.

"Maisie's asked me to be Tommy's godmother. Isn't that super? They're having to bring the date of the christening forward to comply with the deadline for evacuees leaving."

Izolda settled down beside her grandmother in the small drawing room. She waited for the squint-eyed boy to bring tea. He always made her wait. She'd never liked him and recently had become nervous of him now she often found herself alone in the flat. The apartment was a rented one; money was short, and she had to economise. She had not expected that. On their return from honeymoon Chippy had

64

been put in command of a motor torpedo boat which meant he was away at sea a great deal. Izolda had not been prepared for that either.

"Where is Maisie going?" Louise asked.

"To Manila. She has some American friends living there who are putting her up."

"And you are nicely settled into your auxiliary medical . . . whatever it is?"

"Yes. The military hospital switchboard is pretty dull, my lowly jobs usually are, but I like doing the daily trip to Kowloon and back. The crossing fairly blows the cobwebs away!"

"You've made this apartment nice and homey," Louise looked about appreciatively at the comfy chairs, pictures and photographs.

"Second-hand furniture hired from Cat Street, due to your generosity, Grandma."

"I gave your mother a marriage *dot*, and I was determined to give you one, however small."

Louise had done the unheard-of. She had sold out at a loss her small capital rescued from the earthquake and had given it to her granddaughter, all except for a few hundred pounds which she reckoned would see her out. Now she had no money left to worry about. It was as much a relief to her not to have to write business letters, as it was not to have to make out any more cheques.

"To help fill in the weekends when Chippy's away, I've joined the Hash Harriers," Izolda informed, "Ying Su told me about them."

"Who are they, for heaven's sake?"

"We run along set courses up the Peak, and return grimed with mud. It is the greatest fun, I can tell you! Easy to get lost though, especially on these winter days when the mist comes

65

down to Mid-Levels." Izolda looked out of the window at the swirling clouds.

"Doesn't sound much fun to me," Louise grumped. She wondered what induced her granddaughter to take such violent exercise and endure the discomforts of getting soaked by the rain and wet undergrowth – but she would keep her counsel. Young marrieds were best left to their own devices to work it out. "What does Chippy do when he is away?" she asked instead.

"Anti-pirate patrols up near the border – Tolo Harbour and Plover Cove way. He also has to check the Japanese aren't infiltrating into the uninhabited islands. There are such conflicting opinions floating around, one doesn't know what to believe."

"I met Sir Van . . . what's-his-name; you know, head of the Hong Kong Bank. Your uncle and aunt had him to dinner. *I* didn't stay up for it, but I had a nice chat beforehand. He was emphatic that war would *not* come to us here, and he said he had sources from his branch in Japan to prove it."

"Sir Vandeleur Grayburn, Grandma. Everyone seems to have their theory. Chippy says we ought to be watching for the Fifth Columnists who are bent on snooping out our defences."

"Fifth Columnists? For crying out loud what are they?"

"From the French . . . *cinquième*. Remember in the Spanish Civil War when the four columns marched on Madrid and the fifth were already in it?"

"Sure. I had forgotten the term."

"Well, here the equivalent are Chinese traitors who want to get Hong Kong back from the British." Izolda believed that Ying-Su was one of them though she would not dream of saying so to her grandmother.

"Humph. It seems to me a mighty stupid moment to be sending our naval vessels right now to Singapore. Remember how when we arrived the harbour was stuffed with ships flying the white ensign?"

"I do, Grandma. Now, according to Chippy, all that's left is one last war destroyer and a pea shooter! That's why the little MTBs are so hectic. Hugh told me that General Grassett is getting some of his Canadian battalions sent over to strengthen the army. Oh, blast, why does the wretched subject of war always come up? Let's talk of something else, Grandma."

Carrying a bulky shoulder bag, Ying-Su slipped through the crowds down to the ferry terminal. No one particularly noticed the young Chinese girl wearing the universal *cheongsam* in a discreet shade. In her traditional dress she jostled for a place on the lower deck of the boat. Without makeup, her hair tied severely back, she looked plebian: just one more of the millions of ordinary Chinese faces.

On Kowloon-side she made for the Castle Peak bus which started off crammed with humanity through the narrow street of Tsim-Sha-Tsui. It progressed along the winding coastal road that ran north-westwards, and wove its way in and out of the rugged contours, stopping frequently to set down and take up passengers.

At Tseun Wan Wai, in the bay opposite the island of Tsing Yi, Ying-Su left the bus and proceeded off the main road down an alleyway. She disappeared into a scruffy chop house. Not even her parents would have given her a second glance when she reappeared dressed like a farming Hakka woman in a large straw hat shaded round the edge with a black cotton frill, straw sandals on her brown feet.

With the tripping steps such as these women took, she

made her way out through the town towards the mountains to the north. Her route took her across the defensive Gindrinker's Line beyond where, zig-zagging up Yellow Hill, she left the mountain road and turned down a track to the left. It twisted between strips of cultivation, and came to a stop in a small cluster of trees where a farmhouse lay hidden. Ying-Su knocked on the door. Suspiciously, the inhabitant surveyed her through a slit.

"What dost thou want at this time of the evening?" a high pitched voice from the interior cackled. "If thou art one out to make a living loitering on the roads at night, thou wilt find white soldiers from Scotland further on who wear skirts with no under-garments – no occasion to remove trousers! Tee-hee!" the voice shrieked in derisive laughter.

"Nay, mother . . ." Ying-Su began in the Hakka dialect.

"Get thee away – I take in no wanton harlots here! Off with thee!"

"Old mother, I seek thy welfare and a night's lodging."

"I have little to eat and less comfort, not even a pig for pork," the woman whined. She opened the door a crack.

"Thou speakest truly, for the sow has not yet farrowed and there are no piglets."

"Come in, thou," hissed the voice cautiously from within, "that is if thou hast brought the silver with thee?"

"Aye, mother, I have the dollars . . ." And Ying-Su sidled into the dark interior.

In the half light before dawn Ying-Su was on her way again. All day she walked. Skirting the Shing Mun Redoubt by Jubilee reservoir that the troops called the 'Battle Box', she ran into some Jocks on guard. They did not bother to challenge her. She saw trails of mules with their pack guns on backs; she saw Rajput and Sikh soldiers digging in. She carried on through them and down into the plain where the villages lay concentrated. At dusk she sought out another isolated house on the outskirts of a hamlet. A man's quavering voice answered her knock.

"What dost thou want, daughter of the night?"

"I seek thy welfare and a night's lodging, old father."

"We have not much by us, not even a pig."

"That is understood, for the sow has not yet farrowed and there are no piglets."

"Enter . . ."

Ying-Su's slow journey went on, with the information passed on and the silver changing hands, until she reached the border at the Sham Chun river. Two miles east of the closed road and rail bridge at Lo-Wu, like a small dark wraith, she slipped into Japanese-occupied Kwang-tun Province.

Two weeks later Ying-Su crossed back into the New Territories, thinner, travel-stained and deeply bronzed by exposure to the elements. She made straight for the railway station where she bought a ticket which took her through Fanling and Tai Po to Shatin. There she made her way through marketing crowds to the floating fishing village of hundreds of sampans tied to each other on the water. Some time was spent in isolating one with a certain blue smock drying on the bow. Then she hired a garrulous woman to ferry her out.

She was making her way back to Shatin station through the market, when she heard the click of a camera close to. For a fraction of a second her eyes looked up from under the frill of her Hakka hat; then she stuck out her tongue and averted her head in the peasant's instinctive countering of the camera's evil eye.

Izolda had seen only a Hakka woman by the colourful

stall she was photographing, and it was not until the snaps were developed that she looked a second time at this one. She looked closer, and gasped at the likeness.

It was Ying-Su!

So she *had* been right. The snap proved to her mind that her suspicions were true. Winn had said that if she discovered anything, to go to his father. Izolda promptly rang up Miss Maureen at the Chartered Bank and made an appointment to see her uncle officially.

Miss Maureen, long-standing personal secretary to Jimmy from his Peking days, had become part of the Winter set-up. A manishly dressed Irish woman devoted to the Winter family, she was often in The Falls closetted with Jimmy in his study in the continuation of the confidential work she did at the Bank. For relaxation she liked nothing better than a game of tennis. She would come up to play after office hours, work late with Jimmy, spend the night at The Falls, and be driven down to the bank next morning in the Cadillac. Now, bespectacled and looking rather like a middle-aged schoolgirl with her flat, buttoned shoes, cropped hair and tie worn over white blouse, she ushered Izolda into the innermost sanctuary of her tycoon boss.

"My dear," Jimmy rose good naturedly. "Private business, eh? What can your old uncle do for you?"

"Look at this, Uncle Jimmy," Izolda did not beat about the bush. She handed him the photo across his desk.

"Yes?"

"I was on my own in Shatin taking snapshots of the scene on my afternoon off. Chippy is away on patrol. I could swear . . . a bit blurred I know, but it is Ying-Su, isn't it?"

Jimmy scrutinised the photo. "Did she see you?"

"I'm pretty certain she did. She looked up."

"What occurred?"

"She stuck out her tongue like they do and melted into the crowd. It was uncanny. I was just taking this snap of the stall when she appeared in the lens."

"Thanks for bringing it in, my dear," Jimmy said thoughtfully, "thanks very much; very observant of you, and quite right to come straight to me. I'll keep the photo and the negative please – can't be too careful. Now don't say anything to anybody and most certainly not to Ying-Su, nor even to your husband or your grandmother. Can I trust you? Everything, absolutely everything in the family goes on as normal. Normal relationships. Your part in the affair is over. I want you to forget about it. Can you do that?"

Miss Maureen came into the room. "Mr Winter, General Sha-Kwo has arrived," she announced. She put a file on his desk and swept up another to take away with her.

"Good. Show him in." Jimmy dismissed Izolda with a nod. He looked preoccupied.

The one-starred Nationalist Brigadier-General, the pockmarked, moustached and light-skinned half-Chinese man, smartly dressed in pinstriped mufti suit, saw Izolda as she came out of the inner office ahead of Miss Maureen.

"Jimmy's niece," he nodded and stopped to shake hands with her briefly.

"Yes, and you are General Sha-Kwo," Izolda replied. She remembered him from Maisie and Hugh's engagement party at The Falls. According to Winn he was Bungy, Ying-Su's latest boyfriend. These Chinese . . . were they all in it together? Whatever, she was going to take her uncle's advice and not bother her head about it . . .

Inside his office Jimmy extended a warm hand clasp and clap on the back. "Cigarette? I know you like these."

"Thanks," Bungy took a Balkan Sobranie from the silver box Jimmy proferred and subsided into a deep swivel chair.

71

He lit up, inhaled and blew out smoke. Jimmy lit a cigar. "How is the Generalissimo?" he enquired.

"Well. He sends greetings from central China, and Madame sends love to Toni."

"Thank you. Is she in Wuhan?"

"Rather. She'll not leave his side in a crisis," General Sha-Kwo said, his voice exuding bonhomie. Educated at Wellington College and Sandhurst, he sounded more British than the British.

"You'll be seeing Toni and Winn tonight. Dinner at our place at eight o'clock. Working lunch with His Excellency at Government House tomorrow . . . busy time, eh? Much talk can do about the alliance. Humph."

"Unholy alliance," Bungy laughed. With gold-signet-ringed little finger he flicked ash into a tray.

"Difficult to see you two joining in earnest against the Japs," Jimmy growled.

"We will – in pockets. The talks must go on dominated though the Reds are by the Russians."

"Pockets? Not good enough."

"You'll have to lump it," Bungy said conversationally. A conservative confucian himself, he was prepared to die for the cause. "The Generalissimo is the only hope for China against the peasant hordes gathering in the mountains. Nothing must, nor will, deviate us from that policy. You know as well as I do, Jimmy, who are the real enemy – the danger from within. If they become established they will be the death of China. It is imperative that we stop the spread and not impale ourselves on Japanese swords. Those pissing little pygmies will run out of steam, and our great China will swallow them up like a python a rat."

"In the meantime you let them bleed you all down the occupied Eastern coast."

"Sooner or later Japanese expansionism will clash head-long with the Americans in the Pacific. Let *them* destroy the dwarfs."

"Hum. What about us caught in the middle? As the Generalissimo's British liaison officer I shall be first out. God, I hope it doesn't come to that," Jimmy's usual jocular face wore a worried frown, "I never thought I'd be put in a position of having to leave my family behind to their fate, and now I have my aged mother living with us as well."

"Evacuate them with the women and children."

"Toni leave? Don't be ridiculous! As for my mother, she won't budge. In any case a move of such magnitude would kill her."

"I understand your feelings, Jimmy. You're a great family man. I can but assure you, you will be most welcome at HQ," Bungy expressed sympathetically.

"And will your lot move? Goddam it, Bungy, will you?"

"The enemy will not attack here. They have their sights set on Burma."

"They mass at Canton."

"The usual show of force," Bungy shrugged.

"In any case would your bloody corrupt warlord generals move to order? You know better than I that the buggers are only interested in self gain."

"Calm down, Jimmy. The Generalissimo wishes me to inform the Governor that *should* the British be attacked by the common enemy he will order his generals to move . . ."

In the new year of 1941, Izolda had the only communication she ever received from her stepmother, who wrote of her father's death in action. His ship had been blown up by a mine but not before he had been awarded another bar to add to his DSC, DSO and bar from the Great War.

73

Chippy found Izolda with the cable in her hand. She cried on her naval husband's shoulder for the lost years when as a child she had been separated from her father; she cried because he had loved her and missed her; she cried because she had barely known him, and she cried most of all because underneath her put-on act she was bewildered, confused and unhappy.

The novelty of being Mrs Christopher Paine-Talbot had begun to evaporate when her friends, married at about the same time as she, became pregnant. Her frustration and longings increased to such an extent that no amount of late nights, or rushing off with the Hash Harriers allayed them. She came to know every inch of the tracks and paths she climbed, map in hand: up the peak; round to High West Point; down past the reservoir to deserted Telegraph Bay that could clearly be seen from The Falls; over to Mount Kellet overlooking the fishing town of Aberdeen with its packed floating community; up to Mount Gough; down to Magazine Gap, and along Mounts Cameron and Nicholson to the narrow strategic Wong-Nei-Chong Gap where the defence guns lay thickest.

During that first winter of her marriage, dressed in white shirt, shorts and plimsoles, Izolda squelched up and down the mountains in the mud. She slipped and skidded on the steep narrow tracks, glissaded down them on her backside, sweated, fell, got up and ran on, her panting breath adding its steam to the swirling vapours. She sprained her ankle, strained cartilage in her knee, bruised herself in falls, and returned to the flat filthy, plastered in mud and tired out, to bathe and fall into bed in exhausted sleep.

Hong Kong celebrated its one hundredth year under British sovereignty with a ceremony in Statue square at which the Middlesex regiment turned out smartly. There was a church parade at the cathedral, and a huge garden party at Government House. The *South China Morning Post* and *Hong Kong Telegraph* splashed their headlines with: '*A hundred years since Captain Elliot annexed Hong Kong in 1841*'; '*Hong Kong the Bastion of Civilisation one hundred years on*'; '*The Colony is immune from attack*'; '*Let them come from the sea and face our guns*'; and '*We are an Impregnable Fortress!*'.

On that same day Ping-Li drove Louise down to the apartment. Louise was worried about Izolda's hectic life spent much on her own and decided it was time she came to the point.

"I thought you were going to have a baby straight away," she drank her tea before the wood fire in the drawing room.

"Not everyone can have babies to order," Izolda threw back airily.

"Then I reckon there is something wrong; nothing much in all probability, but you should see a doctor."

"I have," Izolda blushed.

"And what did he say?"

"That's between Chippy and myself."

"You know I have never been one for prying, but I know you well enough to know there's something wrong. You're too thin. All that rushing up and down mountains ain't healthy. No wonder you haven't gotten pregnant."

"Oh, Grandma, why must you try—"

"People have problems, though I must say your grandfather and I never had any. He knew a thing or two . . ."

"From Sumuko?"

"I guess so. You can't shock me. I haven't lived for nearly eighty-four years for nought. There's nothing you can tell me

I don't know. That great act of yours hasn't hoodwinked *me*! You'd better out with it, honey."

"I can't, Grandma."

"Then tell your aunt. There's nothing you can't tell her either. Don't just sit there suffering and ruining your health."

Izolda knew her grandmother was trying to be helpful, but how could she tell her, of all ancient Victorian people, that, feeling shy of one another in the opulent bridal suite at the palatial Peninsular Hotel, she and Chippy had changed and gone down to dinner. How they had danced and drunk a great deal of champagne and had returned unsteadily to open the long window and stand on their balcony with their arms around each other. How they had viewed the festival processions with their moon-lanterns bobbing up and down in the street, the peddlars calling out their wares for sale with sing-song chants.

How could she tell her grandmother that the towel she had placed under her in the outsize bed as her aunt had instructed, had remained pristine and unstained? How they had giggled and blamed the champagne, but how in Macao Chippy's inability had continued to dog him? And most of all how could she tell her grandmother that she had believed – and still half believed – that it was as much her fault as her husband's. She *could* not confess to that failure on her part.

So she did not tell.

Chapter Six

"I REFUSE point blank to see our MO," Chippy had said in Macao. He lit another cigarette from the butt of the last, "it'd get out in naval circles that I'd visited him on my return from honeymoon – bound to make me a laughing stock! I could never face the lower deck again let alone my officers. Remember I'm in command of the boat now. Useless sod that I am I'd rather bloody well blow my brains out than face their hidden smirks. I mean it, Zol."

"Don't, Chippy. It's not as bad as that. It's probably all my fault. I know what. There's a consultant who comes to the military hospital. He's a missionary doctor – awfully nice. You could visit him incommunicado so to speak. No one would connect . . ."

It took courage to go.

"Did you know you've had tuberculosis?" Dr Lawrence, several visits later, screwed up his eyes to look closer at the x-rays he was holding up to the light. He was a small man with a kindly lined face, and quick hand movements. He spoke in a croaky voice that ended each sentence on a high note.

"I have a bit of a cough."

"A definite scar there, though healed. Could be the trouble. Get some cod liver oil and drink plenty of milk," the doctor squeaked. He gave him some powders to take, and told him to come back in a month's time and bring his wife.

The missionary Dr Lawrence was the only one in all that congested Colony to know. He became their friend and only confidant; moreover he had considerable knowledge of such cases which were not uncommon amongst his Chinese patients, though for the opposite reason to Chippy's: they indulged too much.

"Is there anything in the aphrodisiacs one sees sold in the back streets, doctor?"

"I've heard of instant cures for cancer and TB. There's usually some medicinal value in the quack doctors' prescriptions. No harm in trying." It was a terrible shame, he thought. Such a decent young couple. They deserved better.

Through the cramped, massed, thronging back alleyways of Kowloon, where cooking smells sickened, and rat-infested open gutters stank, Izolda and Chippy pushed and shoved their way to consult a herbal 'magician'. They experienced no embarrassment among the dozens of other customers jostling for the old man's wares, though they found his leering looks and yellowy-grey wispy beard repellent.

The shelves behind him in his tiny shop were filled with stacked rows of large jars full of ancient potions and remedies for every ailment that existed. Under them, in row upon row of small drawers, lay packets containing ground deer's antlers, rhino horns, bones and much else of unknown origin.

"Something-for-Englishmans-who-vitality-is-waning?" the herbalist's face peered into Chippy's, his sly knowing smile showing black gaps between stumps of teeth. "Ginseng good for you sir; ginseng fork white root have magic power, you see sir; you-make-lovelee-lady ve'y happee!" he bowed up and down, head nodding, hands tucked into the sleeves of his long robe. For a large sum he sold them a small packet. They shouldered their way back through the crowds to the *Day Star* ferry.

"Damn it all," said Chippy sitting down beside Izolda on one of the slatted top deck seats, "what a great big bloody bore I am."

"No you're not. I'm going to take some too and we'll die together if necessary! I bet it's just as much me."

"Don't be daft, Zol."

Doses of ginseng made no difference. Weeks passed and from one of his fellow officers, who was always boasting of his conquests, Chippy, in desperation, elicited an address.

By this time he was so demoralised by the depths he had sunk to in the effort to do his duty by his wife, that he went to several bars before he summoned enough courage to wander unsteadily into the red light area of Wanchai's narrowest streets. He ignored the signs to the topless bars, the black cat clubs, the joss houses and the opium dives. He brushed off the prostitutes in their skin-tight seductive *cheongsams* which exposed legs to high thigh and who grabbed him by the arm and tried to steer him into doorways. Throwing them off he checked the address he was making for and doggedly went on his befuddled way to a massage parlour run by the recommended 'Mamma' who catered for all tastes.

She turned out to be as fat and friendly as reputed, and drunk as he was, and near to tears with self-pity, Chippy unburdened himself to her. After extracting a goodly due she cheerfully promised him the works with two of her most experienced girls. Pliant and pretty Kiki and Lulu took him off to a dimly lit private room. They stripped him down and laid him on a couch.

He lay there feeling foolish, his self-pity turning to merriment at the drollness of it when they set to, one at his head, the other at his toes – scantily clad, well endowed, Kiki and Lulu with their lovely long black straight hair.

"I'm ticklish," he tittered feebly.

"We make laugh?" they giggled themselves. "We do the massage more harder!"

With highly scented oil and flexible touch they set to again with their prying, prodding, probing, postering work.

"Thasht's better," Chippy sighed eyes shut, an inane grin on his face.

After about fifteen minutes, they temporarily drew breath. They were used to men of all sorts, but, boy, this was a tough case! They turned his limp body over and called on the ultimate of their skills. The minutes ticked by as they tried every searching, groping trick they knew on the flaccid corpse. When a slight snore emanated from their subject, the girls had had enough. They went through his pockets, shook him awake, helped him to dress and with Mamma inviting him to come back for more sessions, pushed him out into the street. He stood there for a moment, dazed, dishevelled and smelling highly of the oil, but no wiser.

More weeks slipped by and then months, with Chippy increasingly occupied in exacting patrols and continuous stepped-up manoeuvres. His one caveat in his private life was that there should be no annulment. "You only have to say the word for a divorce," he told Izolda one night when they were talking in bed, "but we've had fun together, my sweet, haven't we? We've had lots of fun?"

"There shall be no annulment, Chippy, I don't want a divorce any more than you do. You know that, and yes, we *do* have fun; we get on so well together. I only wish . . . well . . . children . . ."

"What about us adopting one like your uncle and aunt did?"

"It wouldn't be the same. I want to carry it the whole nine months – I want it to be mine."

"I know what," Chippy said. He sat up in bed. "Go ahead and *have* one. It would bear my name. My God think of that! No one need ever know. It's a brilliant idea."

"How could I?" Izolda was aghast at such a proposition. "It would feel so sordid . . . and, and wouldn't you mind?"

"Not if we were still living together and we meant to go on that way. I think I'd make a good father having had quite a bit of practice on my little sister."

It was the last thing that Izolda, as a loyal wife, wished to do, but the idea once got used to had some merit to it. She could have her family and still have Chippy. It also made her see for the first time that only less than a man, an 'innocuous' man as Winn had once called him, could give his wife *carte blanche* to go and do such a thing. Chippy, amiable, kind, fun Chippy, was lacking in jealousy and perhaps hate? What would he be like when facing the enemy? Shake hands?

Half-heartedly Izolda began to look at other men, seeing them only as breeders. It did not work. They were either too thin or too fat, too sweaty or too hairy, too brainy – she could not keep up with their erudite conversation – or plain stupid, and one nice young man who might have fitted had carroty colouring; she did not fancy having a son with red hair, sandy eyelashes and freckles!

Besides, in her case it was not all that easy to manoeuvre a man of her set into bed with her. Although it was a well known fact that seduction scenes were plentiful in hotels and apartments in Hong Kong, all Izolda had ever achieved with the men she consorted with was a kiss between dances in the corners of Repulse Bay Hotel's terraced garden;

a tight, usually rather drunken, embrace from someone
when cooling down after the Gay Gordons in the Hong
Kong Hotel, or a faintly erotic petting session after the
Caledonian Ball at Government House where the popular
Sir Mark Young entertained.

Adding to the difficulty in finding someone suitable,
was that the Winters were well known in the Colony and
universally liked and respected as a family; and Chippy was
popular. All believed the pair were happily married, which
was true to a great extent. As it was, no man of Izolda's
acquaintance was going to have an affair with Jimmy
Winter's niece and Chippy Paine-Talbot's wife unless he
could not help himself – that was unless he were deeply
in love with her, and that, with Izolda's restraint and her
non-flirtatious nature, had not happened except perhaps
to Winn.

Winn was the only other person besides Chippy who had
been in love with Izolda in Hong Kong, and after their row
and her marriage he had distanced himself from her. But
by now all that had been forgotten. They often met at The
Falls and at parties and were once more good friends. Izolda
felt his physical attraction, had known the excitement of
cuddling in bed with him, and knew that at the slightest
encouragement on her part he would be there again and
this time there would be no restraint. Neither would it
worry cosmopolitan ultramodern Winn to cuckold another
man's wife. He had done it before with other wives and
he would so again if invited. The only thing Winn would
draw the line at – and draw it most definitely – was rape.
With Winn the partner had to be more than willing. He had
never had occasion to chase a girl, (they had always done the
chasing), and Izolda was the only one he had wanted – and
wanted badly – who, so to speak, had got away. Yes, Winn,

dark haired, brawny and handsome as he was, was a most attractive proposition. Yet it remained that he was Izolda's *cousin* and that had always, and still did, make her uneasy. Although he had once said they would have doubly healthy children, she would have liked to have a second opinion on that from a doctor before deliberately setting out to have his baby. To have an affair with Winn and then to produce an unhealthy child who was perhaps damaged or disabled in some way . . . NO. That was not the idea at all; must on no account be risked. Winn was out; right OUT.

In her dilemma, and for a brief period, Izolda toyed with the possibility of Hugh Holden fitting the role. The idea was a tempting one. He was a grass widower (Maisie and the baby were safely away in Manila). She liked him enormously with his lean moustached face and eyes that changed colour like a chamelion. She had adored him as a child at the Parsonage when he had been kind to her and let her be his ball boy. Since meeting him again in Hong Kong they had often talked of those unhappy times and the iniquitous Reverend Forster. Izolda debated Hugh for twenty-four hours right through a day and a sleepless night. Then she discarded him too. Of *course* she could not possibly betray Maisie to whom she had been a bridesmaid and to whose son she was godmother. If it came to that, neither would *he* betray Maisie, and at that she'd feel a right fool and spoil their friendship into the bargain.

After her sleepless night, Izolda gave up Chippy's suggestion as a crackbrained idea. She was working long hours at the switchboard in the office at the military hospital; she had to commute across the harbour daily in the crush and hurly-burly of traffic on road and water; she spent hectic weekends exercising with the Hash Harriers; she played tennis at The Falls; she swam and went to dances and sailing picnics whether Chippy was there or not. To sum up: Izolda was tired, disillusioned and worried about the potential military threat to Hong Kong.

She had neither time nor heart for chasing around after men.

Whatever Izolda's personal traumas were, life in Hong Kong went on its same hard-working, busy, social way as that fateful year of 1941 lengthened. The populace by this time was lulled into believing that the Japanese, who surrounded them on the landward side and had not attacked, would not do so, at least not from the direction of China. Even those 'in the know', like Jimmy at Intelligence Headquarters, expected that if they did come it would be from the sea where the garrison's big guns could keep them at bay.

When Japanese forces occupied the Vichy French naval and air bases in Indo-China, most Hong Kong officials heartily supported the British and United States agreement to freeze all locally held Japanese gold and other assets. The Japanese Government, through the mouth of Mr Matsuoka, their Foreign Minister, reacted strongly to this move, and rejected the British and American warning against their action in Siam as 'entirely unwarranted'. For a week tension in Hong Kong ran high, and war fever was stepped up.

Yet once again, nothing happened. The tension died away, and not only did the life of the colony return to normal, it became positively complacent. The 'spies' in the New Territories who until now had been shadowed, were ignored. They actively continued to gather details of defences on mainland and Island. A glaring case was that of Mr Yamashita, a barber in the Hong Kong Hotel; he was known to be an intelligence officer, but was not apprehended. Instead, his clients talked openly between themselves during his ministrations.

"The Japanese are always very thorough in their intelligence before an attack," Louise aired up at The Falls. No one took any notice of her remark.

'*We stay a deep water and free Port for ever*', the editor of the *Hong Kong Standard* wrote in an optimistic leader. Most of the populace thought they would.

Towards the end of the summer, some two years since war was declared in Europe, and nearly a year since Izolda and Chippy had been married, many of the evacuated wives and some of their children trickled back into the relaxed atmosphere of Hong Kong. They came on ships from Australia and further afield. Not all were welcome; everyone knew of a married officer or rating who resented the intrusion which stopped his routine of going down to Wanchai to enjoy the charms of the sing-song down-homers.

But Hugh was overjoyed when he heard that his and his father's request for Maisie and his small son to join him from Manila for a month over Christmas had been granted by the authorities. Hugh had kept on the Fanling bungalow in the hopes of just such a reunion. He, together with the Holden grandparents and the majority of other residents were delighted at the turn of events. They too, after so much time, had been lulled into believing nothing would happen.

"By the way, I've heard that Roger Stamford is being posted to Hong Kong with reinforcements from India. Some Canadians are coming as well from the other direction."

Hugh's words, thrown out casually on the tennis court of The Falls, hit Izolda like a tidal wave. The buffeting drained colour from her face as she rocked on her feet, and then the undertow took hold to suck her from the shore of her known life into the deep of the unknown. She was partnering Winn, and promptly served a double fault.

"Oh bad luck!" Miss Maureen exclaimed in her Irish lilt at the net. "Game to us, Captain Holden, four-five against I'm thinking. Change over sides; my serve."

"A giant of a man with an iron handclasp," Chippy remembered from the *Chitral*. He was sitting on the sidelines with Ying Su waiting their turn to play.

"Good shot, Winn! Posted to what?" asked Ying Su when Miss Maureen had won the first point and on the return of her second serve Winn had sent a sizzler back.

"As a Major in command of a mountain battery in the New Territories. Remember he's the chap who won the MC on the Frontier?" Hugh informed from the net after volleying out of court. "Sorry, Miss Maureen."

"Fifteen-thirty, sure there's too much talking going on," Jimmy's PA observed disgustedly. She served again to Winn.

"Sounds a good strengthening for the Gunners. We need some giants against the little men," Winn went on chatting despite Miss Maureen's caustic remark. His return hit the net cord and bounced neatly over. "Sorry about that, you two!" he conceded with a grin.

"Blather!" expressed Miss Maureen. "Partner, 'tis sure you're not attending properly. Come on now! Fifteen-forty."

By then Izolda had recovered sufficiently to manage a good return which bypassed Hugh on his backhand, and the game and set was hers and Winn's. They handed over to Chippy and Ying Su.

Without saying a word to anyone, Izolda walked down the steps, across the drive, into the house, and up to her grandmother's blue bathroom to take a shower from the extended rose among the plethora of taps. It was still very hot for late summer, humidity at its highest, and she was dripping with sweat. She let the cool water rinse over her while her thoughts raced.

The man she had fallen head over heels in love with was coming to Hong Kong!

He was the man she had first seen towering over her on the gangway of the *Chitral*; the man whose arms about her when dancing had overwhelmed her with such feelings that she had stumbled; the man who had on several occasions joined her and her grandmother for tea; the man who had sent her a card soon after she had arrived in Hong Kong but had never replied to her letter nor even to her Christmas good wishes nine months later.

With Roger living and working out in the New Territories their paths would be unlikely to cross – *unless she sought him out.* What for? On the face of it he was the perfect specimen to father a son who would be a Paine-Talbot, yet he was the last person she could lure into an affair. If she knew anything about his character she knew that he was no flirt – he had never kissed her, not even when saying goodbye. Neither was he ever likely to submit to living with her. And patently, as the *wife* of Chippy whom he had known on board ship, she would be, to a man of his type, taboo! No, if they did meet again, he would be polite and friendly to husband and wife and want to chat to her grandmother about the latest developments in the East, and that was *absolutely all.* Rather than have the turmoil of unrequited emotions that had beset her on board ship boiling up within her to fill her with despair, it would be better not to see him again.

Izolda, drying herself after her shower, her graceful young girl's body reflected in the long mirror, debated this course.

And yet, and yet, he had liked her enough to say he wanted to keep in touch, to ask for her address and to send her the card that from its very wording seemed to invite an answer. So why none? Had a correspondence developed she would never have married Chippy, nor anyone else. Why no answering letter? Why not even a Christmas card? Why the terrible destructive silence after the joy of receiving the first letter? Where was that golden land now? The awful silence had gradually, oh so slowly, stifled her happiness, throttled her and finally killed her hopes. *Why* had he not written again?

Perhaps he had met a girl in India and was married himself? That would explain everything, and it would explain his silence. She knew nothing of his army life. All she knew was that he had won the Military Cross in a skirmish on the North-West Frontier.

What *had* happened in India to so change Roger?

Chapter Seven

AFTER Hugh told Izolda that Roger had landed, she found herself going about the streets in a state of agitation lest she bump into him, and she jumped every time she saw an exceptionally tall man approaching. Once in Kowloon she was certain that she recognised his back disappearing into a bank. Stealthily she followed him in only to find that it was not Roger at all.

In the same way she deliberately avoided Mickey's Kitchen for lunch in case Hugh brought Roger over. Sooner or later she knew she would have to come face to face with him, and the day arrived when Toni rang the flat to ask her and Chippy to join them for tennis on the following Saturday. Hugh was bringing over the friend she and Chippy had met on board ship. Wasn't that nice?

Izolda's second introduction to Roger Stamford was altogether different from the traumatic experience of her first. She felt quite composed when they shook hands formally on the tennis court at The Falls, though she vividly recalled the warm handclasp. She summed him up dispassionately: yes, he was a magnificent specimen of a man. Yes, no wonder she had fallen flat for him at the tender age of eighteen years. She watched him greet Chippy and listened to his deep voice congratulating them on their marriage.

"What with Maisie on her way to wedded bliss that was quite a trip out, wasn't it?" he said, hazel eyes wrinkling up at the corners in the smile she remembered.

"Have you joined the married throng?" Chippy asked cheerily. They all knew that even if he were married he would not be permitted to bring his wife out. Hong Kong was now a 'non-accompanied' station, and the families who had trickled back were only allowed to stay temporarily.

"Not a chance, old chap," Roger's face creased, "no damsels to chose from up on the North-West Frontier!"

"I'm another of your Gunner bachelors," Winn said, bounding up the steps from the drive to shake hands. Toni then introduced Ying-Su and Miss Maureen. "We'll toss for partners," Winn took command. "Mum, are you playing?"

"Not today, darling, but Dad would like a game. Come in to tea in relays so that everyone can have a turn."

"We could do with a second court," Jimmy said on arrival. He began whacking some practice serves in. They tossed; Roger drew with Ying-Su against Jimmy and Izolda. "Come on, niece, we'll give 'em hell," Jimmy growled. He prepared to serve.

They did too: six-one.

"Let's challenge them to a return after the others have played," suggested Roger, addressing Ying-Su.

"Yes, do let's," Ying-Su's tinkle pealed out. "Zol's rather good. She learnt to play from an early age in France."

"How is your grandmother?" Roger asked Izolda when they were walking up the marble stairs to tea later, leaving Chippy and the rest to play.

"Better than ever. She's put on quite a bit of weight. It's great for her to be back in the East. Thank goodness we escaped the war in Europe. We'd have been in unoccupied

90

France, but . . . I suppose, anything might happen here . . ." her voice trailed away.

"Mother, do you remember Captain Stamford whom you met on board ship? He's a major now," Toni imparted in the drawing room.

"Aahha," said Louise in her meaningful way, her sharp eyes taking in the new lines in Roger's suntanned face, "she went and got married since then."

"Yes, indeed, Mrs Winter," Roger looked down at the old lady from his height before taking a seat, "how pleased you must be, and also proud of the way you rescued her and brought her up."

"How did you know Grandma rescued me?" Izolda demanded, startled. She sat down on the sofa beside him. She did not talk about those childhood days any more.

"You told me yourself," Roger turned to her. "Have you kept your mother's engagement ring?" he asked, looking down at her hand and seeing only a plain gold band and a diamond ring.

"Certainly. I wear it on special occasions . . . What a lot of details you remember."

"I have a good memory for – some things. When I was in hospital I meant to—"

"In hospital?" Izolda looked at him in some concern. "Were you ill?"

"Small matter of a war wound. The dear little dum-dum bullet went in one side and out the other," he laughed, and then expressed more seriously, "Actually it wasn't funny. I was in high fever by the time they'd evacuated me to Peshawar. I was going to say that when I was in hospital I wrote you a Christmas card to thank you for your letter which had reached me before I left for the Frontier. Unfortunately the card never got posted. You see I didn't

91

take any letters on campaign and I couldn't remember your address."

"*I* sent you a Christmas card in 1939," Izolda said wide-eyed. "It had my address on it."

"You did? What a shame I never received it. I could have done with a note of commiseration to cheer me up just then. Where did you address it to?"

"The depot in Rawalpindi. Wouldn't they have forwarded it?"

"Yes, but there was such a shemozzle in the campaign, letters did go astray. I never received my anxious parents' Christmas parcel that year."

"It doesn't seem fair . . ." Izolda began slowly. It was desperately unfair. Why hadn't he addressed his care of the Chartered Bank? No, he probably didn't know that her uncle was the head. Hurriedly she stopped herself from speculating and instead said the first thing that came into her head, "Where did the bullet . . . ?"

"Really, Izolda!" Louise rebuked, "one doesn't ask personal questions about such intimate matters."

"Don't worry, Mrs Winter. I am quite capable of guarding my secrets," Roger remarked amused at the *naïveté* of the question, and then, seeing Izolda's blush, which he found surprising in a sophisticated married woman, he added thoughtfully, "'*Sayonara*' wasn't it? Well, how nice that we *have* met again!"

They finished their tea and resumed their tennis, taking it in turns to sit out on deck-chairs in the shade of a tree by the tennis court. It was very hot, a damp moist heat, and they drank copious glasses of the fresh lemonade served by Fung Wan in tall tumblers jingling with ice cubes. Then Hugh and Roger went back to the New Territories and their units, and Chippy and Izolda went down to 12 Macdonnell Road. And that was all, except that for a long time Izolda felt as if she had been run over by a steam roller. She felt flat and tired and liable to indulge in little weeps when she was alone.

What Roger did not mention to Izolda was that though he had every intention of answering her letter eventually, he had rather let it hang fire for the time being. He had been disappointed in her. To his way of thinking the letter in answer to his card gushed. Admittedly it told of Maisie Lauder's marriage to Hugh Holden, but it then went on to tell of the good time she was having with innumerable cocktail parties, dinners and dances. It seemed to be a letter to impress, and it looked to him as if the opulent life with her wealthy uncle and aunt had gone to her head. There was hardly any mention in it of her grandmother, and it was the bond between these two which had at first attracted him. If she had turned into a sophisticate they had little in common. But then when lying in Peshawar hospital badly wounded and feverish his thoughts had turned to her again. What would she feel if she read of his death? She would be sorry, he believed, but it would not greatly affect her.

Naturally Roger, when he met up with Izolda again at the tennis party, did not go into the details of how his wound – which had hit him in the side like a kick from a horse and momentarily stunned him until he found he seemed to be in one piece though his shirt was covered in blood – had not been helped by his remaining on his feet and actively directing the fight for several hours more despite his orderly, Hassan Khan, begging him to go to the dressing station. Eventually, by then feeling excessively cold and faint from loss of blood, Roger had left his young second-in-command, Mike Mitchell, in charge, and allowed himself to be led away by Hassan Khan to the regimental aid post where he collapsed and ignominiously had to be carried the rest of the way down by stretcher.

After being discharged from hospital, Roger had taken long recuperative leave in Kashmir fishing up the beautiful little side valleys, and returned fit and in fine fettle, a hero to his Mountain Gunners. It was then that in the late summer of 1940 in the Mess in Rawalpindi that he read in a *Times* out from England, the announcement of Izolda Richardson's engagement to Lieutenant Christopher Paine-Talbot, RN, the young naval officer on board the *Chitral*.

The news of Izolda's imminent marriage had not greatly surprised him, in fact, after her letter he had expected something of the sort. Yet the announcement left him with the uneasy impression that he had missed out somewhere.

Captain Roger Stamford, MC, shook off his deflation, shrugged his broad shoulders and was soon submerged in arranging a troop train to take his Gunners down to Bangalore to join a division training to go into Burma. Had he gone in with the rest he would in all probability have been put in the bag with thousands of others and that would have been the end of his war. Instead, in 1941, he was promoted to Major and sent orders to proceed immediately with his Mountain Gunners to Calcutta to embark for Hong Kong.

When the mists of summer were finally dispersed from the Peak and the view was clear enough to see the little islands in the far distance, and when Louise heard on the news that the Japanese forward troops were in Burma, some intuition told her to ask her daughter-in-law to do some shopping for her.

"Toni dear, buy me some reserve bottles of Dr J Collis Browne's Chlorodyne drops when you are in Central – several, please. And when you are down there you might as well get a stock of Bath Oliver biscuits – I like the round tins best – and some half-flasks of my medicinal brandy for when needed."

"The Japanese Army is nowhere near here. They are busy annexing Siam," Toni protested.

"Well, that's as maybe, but I strongly advise you two to hurry up and increase your stockpiling of the pillbox all the same. For sure you'll need every store you can muster to last a siege . . ."

"You make it sound like the walled siege of the Legation Quarters in the Boxer Rebellion!"

"I remember that. Although I wasn't in it, thank the Lord, I had friends who *were*. By the way don't forget to hide some greenback dollar bills down there," Louise ran on undeterred. "Silver money is useful too; everythin' will be in short supply, you mark my words. Commodities vanish from the shops overnight as I well know from when Camille and I were caught in Paris at the beginning of the last war. We had to queue for everythin'. Food became very short."

"What makes you think war is imminent here, Mother?" Toni frowned.

"Several reasons, I guess. I've told you already about their intelligence thoroughness – all those Japanese on the streets and in the shops. What are they doing but spying? Another reason is that success goes to the samurai's head. Like nobody else they get the 'victory disease' – that's what we called it in the Sino-Japanese and Russo–Japanese wars. I bet they're on the bandwagon now with their success in Indo-China. And another thing: if I know anything about the Japanese mentality it's that they'll want to be on the winning side, and it looks mightily to me as if the Germans and Italians are winning in Europe."

Jimmy came out onto the verandah. He subsided into one

of the rattan chairs and called to Fung Wan to bring him a drink.

"Tired, Jimmy? Mother has been telling me to step up the stockpiling," Toni said, watching her husband light up.

"I kept my American passport on when I married, out of pure sentimentality," Louise rumbled on. "Your father could never understand why. He was a great patriot though an ex-one. The Yankees sure are keepin' well out of the conflict."

"Pshaw. You forget lease-lend, Mother, a life-saver to the British."

". . . The first thing that happens," Louise took no notice of her son's remark, "is that the banks shut and you can't get any bills, and the next minute there's panic buying and the shops close down because there's nothing coming in. Be prepared is all I'm saying, and if you children disregard my advice at least *I* shall be well stocked up with my drops, my biscuits and medicinal tipple. I guess I can live on those at my age for a *long* time."

"No you couldn't. You'd get scurvy. I'd better include some vitamins on my shopping list," Toni laughed.

"Ho-ho," Jimmy puffed out smoke, "Mother dear, I do believe you and your opium-orientated drops'll survive anything!"

"You'd be the first to come begging if you got dysentery and there were no doctors or drugs handy," Louise retorted tartly. "I venture to inform you further at the risk of more ribaldry that the next thing that happens is the electricity gets cut off. Buy some oil for heaters and get plenty of candles and matches; and then I guess the mains water will get bust, so . . ." Louise went on with her warnings. The 'children' gave up listening.

"She's right, old girl," Jimmy said to his wife the next

day on the doorstep as he was leaving for the office. Ping-Li had parked Toni's Austen in the drive ready for her to go to the hospital. Jimmy looked at his wife, neat in her nurse's uniform, her blonde waves tidy and stiff under the becoming sister's cap. They'd had a good tumble last night. By Jupiter his Toni was a luscious armful still. He loved her dearly and here they were on the treadmill to destruction. "The cunning old thing," he resumed, "instinctively knows it's coming. There's bound to be a run on commodities and I shan't be here to scrounge for you. Get in all the stores you can and the sooner the better. We'll stack them in the pillbox in the evening when the outside servants have left. The fewer who know about the depot the better. I'll get the money supply. Remember, Toni, I want you to keep the family together up here in our fortress. You'll be safest here."

"All right, Jimmy. I'll do some mammoth shopping on my way home." Toni kissed her husband goodbye with a sinking feeling in her stomach. She knew only too well that he would be the first to leave if and when things came to a head; that Winn would be the first to go up to the lines; that Ying-Su – well it was no good relying on where *she'd* be. She, Antonia Winter, would be left to look after her aged mother-in-law and the large household as well as continue her exacting hospital duties. With her nursing experience she knew she would be vitally needed there.

Chippy was away on patrol. "Don't you have to come back to refuel?" Izolda had said.

"No," he'd answered, "we have a base in China waters, only don't tell anyone I told you so."

Work was hectic at the military hospital in Kowloon. Often the switchboard was jammed with calls; at other times Izolda was asked to do extra typing and didn't get

back to the flat until after eleven. Peggy, a friend she'd
made in the typing pool and who had a pad not far from
the hospital on Kowloon-side, invited her to stay the night
whenever she worked late.

The pad was tiny – it consisted of one small living room
with a put-u-up sofa and one equally small bedroom –
but it was delightfully characterful. Situated in crowded
Tsim-Sha-Tsui off the straight, mile-long Nathan Road in a
brightly lit noisy area of non-stop traffic and trading shops, it
sat right at the top of an ugly tenement building block. Open
concreted stairs with iron balustrades ran up its four floors,
and its chief attraction – apart from the spectacular view –
lay in the roof garden. Here Peggy had installed a mass of
flowering plants. She had also installed a telephone.

Izolda took to staying there when Chippy was away. It
saved time on the journey from Island to mainland, and kept
her from the squint-eyed boy of whom she had become more
nervous than ever. That he was devious in his dealings, and
treated her with scant respect was not in doubt, and she could
never tell with those eyes, which way he was looking.

"Why don't you give him the sack?" Peggy asked.

"Chippy engaged him and he can't see that there's anything wrong with him. I have to have someone in the flat
. . . Oh it's all too difficult." So the boy stayed.

When Peggy told her she was leaving shortly to get
married to a man in the 1st Middlesex regiment, Izolda
took on the tiny flat. She went back to Macdonnell Road
once a week to check on everything, pay the boy, have
her grandmother to tea, and she was always there on the
infrequent times that Chippy stayed in port for a few days.

If it had not been for the interest in setting herself up in the
'pad', Izolda felt she might have lost her mind after meeting
Roger again. The dream of what might have been if things

had gone differently, was too agonising to contemplate. Meeting him again had brought home to her in no uncertain manner that she had gone into marriage with Chippy, as Winn had so rightly said, for all the wrong reasons. The part that was nearly driving her round the bend was that *if* only he had received her Christmas card with address reminder, and therefore sent her the one he had penned, she would have answered it straight away to express her distress at his wounding. A regular correspondence would have resulted, and she most certainly would *not* have married Chippy or anyone, and when he turned up in Hong Kong, the door would have been wide open. If, if, if only . . . it had all hung on that vital little word 'if'.

As it was she saw her life stretching before her in its barren way . . . because how could she hurt Chippy whom she had married? If she was not tough enough to sack the beastly boy, she would never be tough enough to have her marriage annulled and let the whole world know it. Hers was a hopeless case.

But once Izolda had settled into her new accommodation she began to feel better, in fact she began to enjoy herself. She had had her twenty-first birthday that last summer. She was earning good money. She was living the life of a bachelor girl without the restrictions of the hostel where she had lived before her marriage and which had its strict rules, and now she benefited too from the status of a married woman. One day she would find out about the missing part of her life and in the meantime she was free to come and go when she liked, ask in whom she liked, feed when she liked, cook or not cook. Living in Kowloon was quite different from living in a staid flat in Macdonnell Road. It was lively and a little daring, rather like she imagined it must be for the artists who lived in the *quartier latin* in Paris that her grandmother had told her about.

She was never accosted in the crowded streets, and she felt neither lonely nor afraid up in her nest. Sitting out on the roof garden bright with Peggy's potted plants, which she watered and tended assiduously, was sheer delight. In the perfect autumn weather the view across the shimmering harbour to the white buildings of Victoria was as clearly etched as if on a master's palette; light and shade stood out in bold relief. Her eyes could trace the Peak painted emerald green by the summer rains. She knew the names of all the ridges from her Hash Harrier runs; she knew them so well she could visualise those out of sight, even to the exact position of the Falls on a high west point facing south.

To her west she could see Stonecutter's Island, and eastwards the Lye-mun Narrows. Over the city she could watch the occasional plane coming in to land on Kai Tak's one runway. The roar of traffic from below came up to her muffled, while on every side there was the chatter from her Chinese neighbours hanging out their bed linen and washing on their balconies in a higgledy-piggledy of jutting habitations of which she was an infinitesimal part.

Chippy rang, and after work she caught the ferry to Victoria. She found him already in the flat. He was looking tired.

"How much time have you ashore?"

"A few days."

"What after that?"

"A long spell away – several weeks."

"You've probably forgotten, but we'd accepted to go to the Government House Ball in a party Peggy and her husband have got up. I'd better write and decline."

"Don't be silly, Zol – just because I can't go. Go yourself

and have a good time. You know how in short supply women are since the ban. Is Hugh going?"

"Yes."

"Is Maisie back?"

"Not yet."

"Well there you are. You can be Hugh's partner, and I bet there'll be other extra men hanging round."

"All right, since you say so." One of the extra men 'hanging around' would be Roger. Hugh had told her he was coming to the Ball. She had seen him once more since the meeting at tennis. He'd been lunching with Hugh at Mickey's Kitchen. She would like to dance with him again. Why not? Chippy wouldn't mind – quite the opposite.

On the Saturday of the Ball, Izolda prepared herself with extra care. It was going to be like on board ship again. A whole evening spent with Roger. With the advent of the autumn sun, Izolda's light tan had returned; her complexion was glowing, and she knew she was looking her best.

She returned to the Macdonnell Road flat and dismissed the squint-eyed boy for the night. With him out of the way she took a bath scented with bath salts, and put on a new ballgown of heavy cream satin delicately embroidered round the low neckline with sparkling beads in a lover's knot motif. The evening dress had thin beaded straps which gleamed over her shoulders, and the skirt flared out below the knee into small panels of sun ray pleating. Each panel was decorated at the top in the same charming bead motif. She wore her high heeled silver sandals that made her look her tallest and which helped to give her the poise and confidence she still lacked. Round her neck she wore her grandmother's long carved jade beads which she borrowed for the occasion, and instead of wearing her diamond engagement ring she

101

wore her mother's which matched the necklace and went well with her evening purse.

To complete the picture, she put on a modicum of makeup with a dash of cherry lipstick, a tinge of green eyeshadow, a touch of mascara and finished the toilette with a dab of scent behind ears and on wrists. She looked into the mirror critically and decided she would pass Government House standards. She checked the flat was tidy and the coffee making equipment was in place in the kitchen in case some of the party came back for a nightcap.

Izolda called a cab over the telephone, locked the door behind her, put the key in her bag and set forth on the short distance to Government House.

Chapter Eight

"ISN'T Christopher here tonight?" Roger enquired on the dance floor. He had looked over Izolda's head at the crowded room and failed to spot him.

It was a brilliant scene in the white and gold-embossed ballroom of Government House with its brocaded curtains and glittering chandeliers. Most of the men were soberly dressed in black tails and white ties, but there was a liberal dash of red mess-jackets, red tabs, naval uniforms and a sprinkling of the light blue of the RAF. There were decorations and medals galore, not to mention the gold-braided shoulder aiguillettes of the aides-de-camp. In the midst of all this finery, the ladies' gowns, both western and Chinese, made a riot of colour as bright and varied as a herbaceous border in full flower, the whole decked out with sparkling jewellery.

Broad-shouldered Roger looked particularly stunning in mess kit of dark blue monkey-jacket with red facings. He wore a stiff white collar and black bow tie. Three miniature medals dangled on his chest. The first was the Military Cross with white and magenta ribbon, the second and third were the India General Service medals. On the red lapels of his uniform shone gold-braided grenades. The outfit was completed by red banded overalls worn tight over elegant long-boned legs. And Izolda noticed how his hair still curled endearingly above his ears.

"Chippy's away on patrol; for ages this time," she answered his question. "He's been terribly overworked since they reduced the Navy out here. All that's left is one old destroyer, a gunboat and the MTBs. Can you beat it? No wonder he's exhausted."

"The policy seems to be that ships are needed more urgently in the Indian Ocean. We Army are better off. They're sending us reinforcements rather than taking them away."

"I hear General Maltby is going to be the new GOC."

"Yes, taking over next month from General Grasset. A splendid man, so I'm told. Not bringing his wife though; aims to set a good example. Too many women have been allowed back already. It must be lonely for you with your husband away so much."

"I've got used to it. I'm busy enough what with my job, the family and my grandmother to see, not to mention the Hash Harriers at weekends!" She'd told him about the latter when she met him at lunch and he had said it sounded rather like a women's army on manoeuvres.

"You must be superbly fit," now he laughed admiringly. She was as slim as a willow wand.

"I am! I've become a sort of female long distance runner." She looked at him with her wide smile.

To Roger the enchanting girl he was dancing with – he still could not think of her as a married woman – was outstanding due to her very lack of ostentation in the mostly over-bejewelled company. The cream satin she was wearing was by contrast bridal, virginal, and instead of diamonds or pearls round her throat, she wore a long old-fashioned dangling necklace of jade beads which he remembered seeing her grandmother wear on board ship. And she was wearing her mother's ring. Was that for him because he had asked about it? He found her very beautiful – even more so in the flesh than in those feverish dreams when he had been in pain in hospital and she had come back to haunt him. Since meeting her again at The Falls, he had burned with a suppressed fury that he had lost her through his own incompetence. She had been too young for him on board ship, and now she was not too young. But she had fallen for her Chippy, a decent enough fellow.

The smartly uniformed band of the Middlesex regiment playing a thumping jazz tune on a raised dais, made conversation difficult and they soon stopped trying. He held her closer and she gave herself up to the joy of dancing with him. Izolda felt none of the nervousness she had first experienced on board ship when she'd been overwhelmed by his presence. Now she only felt a marvellous happiness at being in his arms, her hand in his. She danced lightly, accustomed by now to wearing high heeled shoes, and there was no question anymore of her turning an ankle or he of stepping on her toes. He danced quietly, unstrenuously, smoothly compared to the bouncy exuberance of Chippy's dancing. But she could feel the strength lurking in his controlled body, hear within the hidden mastery of him and the seen assurance and purpose in all his movements.

Roger and Izolda danced almost exclusively together that evening in between sitting out and chatting to Peggy and her husband, to Hugh and the other members of the party. They had supper together, and afterwards, when the decibels in the ballroom had become very high, and the dancing very energetic, they went out into the coolness of the Government House gardens which were lit with lanterns of flickering globes strung between the trees. Lights streamed out from the french windows of the old house, and a sweet scent of frangipani wafted strongly over to them on the balmy night air. The perfume came from heavily petalled waxy blooms that grew thickly on the temple-shaped Pagoda trees dotted through the gardens.

They stood on the front terrace from where they could see twinkling lights shining across the harbour to the Nine Dragon hills of Kowloon. To begin with they did not speak. Izolda, for one, had no wish for talk to interrupt the magic she felt. She was so fulfilled, so happy, so content to bask in Roger's presence. This feeling of overriding gladness was something new to her, and it made her realise just how unhappy she had been since her non-marriage with Chippy. To be good friends was all very well, but now that she had met Roger again she saw the true depths of the farce she had been living.

Roger too was content to stand beside Izolda for a while without speaking. She stood to one side of him and a little in front, fine and straight in the rich satin dress, the embroidered beads gleaming out from the folds in the dim light of the hanging lanterns. She was all light, he thought. The dainty thin straps glistened on her gracefully sloping shoulders; her hair shone, burnished like cloth of gold, and her eyes shone too that night. She had wonderful eyes, shaded by those long dark eyelashes that he had first glimpsed on the gangway of the *Chitral* when she had abruptly turned away from him, eyes that were transparently true, that could be vulnerable, that were often shy, sometimes startled, sometimes happy as now; eyes that held no guile, no flirtatious coquettish glances. She was beautiful with a beauty that was quiet and ran deep, and it was a great pity . . . Strange they had no children . . . perhaps they had?

"Any offspring?" Roger spoke his thoughts aloud, and then when she shook her head and bit her lip, saw how tactless he had been in asking her. They could have lost a child, or be longing to have one. "I'm sorry," he said. "That was impertinent of me. I should not have asked," and then when still she did not speak, "I'm glad you're wearing your mother's ring tonight, and I love the jade necklace. Antique, isn't it?"

"Yes. Chinese. Each bead is different, each carved with an insect or flower. Look," she said, turning to face him and holding up the chain so that he could see for himself. He fingered the beads, close to her, drinking in the scent of her while she looked into his face, tracing in her mind his every mark or line to keep for memory.

"My grandfather gave it to my grandmother when my mother was born," she explained. "Grandma was wearing it when the earthquake struck. That was all she had left – the beads and her rings, and of course my grandfather's Order which she found in the ashes of her home next day."

". . . And your mother's ring?"

"She took it off her body."

"You know," he said severely, "you oughtn't to be staying in Hong Kong. You ought to take your grandmother away. I wonder Christopher hasn't seen to it."

"Nothing will budge Grandma. I switched jobs to Kowloon so that I could stay on. I have a small pad over there. You must come and see it one day. It's lovely. All to myself. I call it my eyrie! Anyway Maisie is bringing Tommy over for Christmas," she ended defiantly.

"I know, and I've told Hugh what I think of his ill-conceived, crackpot idea of not only allowing it, but *suggesting* it. Now I've alarmed you . . ."

"Yes," she said in her straightforward way. "You sound

107

as if war is bound to happen when most of us are still hoping it won't, all except my grandmother who has started to stockpile. But then she's always been an old Jeremiah! I'm not as brave as she is in facing things."

"You faced the kidnapping . . ."

"Gracious, you remember that too?"

They went on talking while wandering through the gardens suffused with the fragrance of frangipani. Izolda told Roger about her father's death and how it had affected her though she had hardly known him. But she did not tell him about Chippy, the one subject that was uppermost in her mind. Roger in his turn told her a little about the campaign in which he had been wounded, though he did not tell her how she had come back to haunt him in his delirium or the upset he felt when he read of her marriage. He talked a lot about his men, his 'marvellous *jawans*'.

They strolled so long in the gardens that when they returned to the ballroom they found their party had broken up. Izolda, wide awake, and not wanting the enchanted evening to end, invited Roger back to Macdonnell Road for a nightcap. He accepted with alacrity. They walked over.

"Pour yourself a brandy," she said, showing him the cocktail cabinet in a corner of the drawing room. "You'll find some ice in the icebox."

"Can I get you something?"

"No thank you; I'll make some coffee." She left him and went into the kitchen to grind the grains. She did not like brandy – leave that to Grandma with her sips! What was going to happen now? Would he . . . ? Alone in the flat with Roger; the double bed waiting to be baptised . . . All that undressing down and doing . . . well . . . the act Toni had so clinically described. And in *hers and Chippy's* bed?

Suddenly all the romance Izolda had experienced that

evening left her. She felt cold and filled with nausea at the thought of betrayal.

In the drawing room, when she returned with the coffee tray, Roger noticed that she had lost her colour. She looked as if she were the one who needed a brandy. They drank their coffee silently. She felt awful. Ashamed of herself and her thoughts.

After a while Roger broke the silence and told her he had some leave coming to him, and he was going to hire a sailing boat. "Do you know anything about sailing?" he asked.

"A bit. I've sailed with Chippy."

"What about helping me with the ropes on Sunday?" He noticed her colour was returning. What had upset her?

"I'd love to." She cheered up at the thought of a day with Roger. "I'll bring a packed lunch for two."

"Super." He finished his glass and stood up. He was going! Izolda leapt to her feet to face him.

"It's been a lovely evening," she said tremulously. Emotion overtaking her at its ending, she put up her face as if half expecting to be kissed, closing her eyes as she did so.

Smiling, Roger, accepting the invitation and with his arms at his side, bent to kiss her on the cheek. At that moment Izolda, holding her breath at the closeness of him, slightly turned her head, and their lips accidentally met. It was a kiss of lips barely brushing, yet it was electric.

Then, "I must get back to the Mess," Roger said stepping back. Firmly he walked out of the room and collected his cap from the hallway. "Thanks for the drink. See you Sunday," he said, and let himself out of the flat.

For a long while Izolda sat on the sofa trying to think it out, her hands held to her hot face, her dress in folds of gleaming cream about her. She had invited Roger back to the flat when her husband was away. She did not know exactly what she'd expected, but she had expected *something* to happen. All that had happened was that she had got cold feet and thank goodness she *had*. It would have been too awful . . . and then the kiss – the bungling kiss of lips meeting. She blushed to think of it – putting her face up like that indeed. What a perfectly idiotic and embarrassing thing to do. No wonder he had abruptly left. How was she going to pluck up courage to face him on Sunday after that?

The truth was she was not attractive enough for him to want to have an affair with her. She was as impotent as Chippy. It was hopeless and she was hopeless, and she would have to go on being a wife in name only for the rest of her life and live on what comfort she could get from an occasional encounter with Roger Stamford such as she had had in tantalising measure that evening.

Roger undressed in his billet, put on his pyjamas and undid the sheet and blanket Hassan Khan had tucked in with neat hospital corners. He stuffed his second pillow over the iron frame at the bottom, and cursing too-short beds in general, got in between the sheets.

He lay on his back with his feet sticking out over the pillow. One day he would get an outsize six-foot-seven bed, and in the meantime why the hell couldn't the quartermaster do something about finding him a decent length on which to kip? He had suffered from too-short beds ever since he'd been at Wellington College, and as for bunks – they were torture. On board ship he had often had recourse to leave his berth and stretch out on the floor. For his sailing holiday he betted the bloody bunk would be fit only for a goddamned John Chinaman!

For some time Roger did not shut his eyes. He lay on,

watching the dawn creeping up to illuminate his window. He puzzled over the enigma Izolda presented, the girl he had not been able to entirely forget. In Hong Kong he found her, as he had first found her when she was little more than a kid, unusual, sensitive, genuine and charming in her relationship with her grandmother. Tonight, in that dress, she had been outstanding, and if he were honest with himself he had to admit that he was sexually attracted by her. And she? She seemed fond of him. The enigma was that she looked to him all wrong as a married woman. She appeared vulnerable and virginal. Since his wounding he had not had an affair, nor wanted one again. The wounding had properly sobered him up. What he had come to want, to positively hunger for, was a true partner in life. Yet this was no time to contemplate partnership with anyone. The situation in Hong Kong was far too explosive, and if it exploded they all knew what they were in for: out and out total war with their backs to the sea wall all the way. Compared to what might come here, the North-West Frontier campaign would seen like a benign picnic!

Roger's thoughts turned again to Izolda and how she had come in holding the coffee and looking as pale as her dress, veiled fear showing in her flecked eyes. Had she feared that he was the sort of man who would pounce? In which case why had she invited him back? And that kiss of tremulous trusting lips – no demands there, no passion, rather an enquiry . . . He *simply could not understand her*.

Roger turned on his side and swept the top sheet untidily over his shoulder. His untucked bed was by now in a complete shambles. Never mind. Whatever the answer to the riddle of Izolda, he would ask questions and find out more about her on Sunday.

*   *   *

111

They sailed round to Junk Bay and anchored near the beach where the Commodore had had his picnic party more than two years before. Now Izolda had Roger as companion, incomparable Roger about whom she was in turmoil. Her moments of bursting happiness alternated with despair at what she had thrown away by marrying Chippy. She was in love, in love, *in love* – with Roger.

In bathing suits they ate the sandwiches Izolda had made, drank Roger's beer and talked about the war in Europe and how he, after his wounding, had asked for a posting back to England to get into that conflict only to be sent in the opposite direction further East.

"I'm glad you came east," she said.

"It's fate," he answered.

They talked of holidays they had had as children and how he had learnt to sail as a boy round the Isle of Wight; and Roger said the only time he'd been in France was on a school trip to Brittany, "I seem to remember the highlight there was a French maid seducing some of us more senior boys – a most enlightening time," he said with a grin.

"I wouldn't know anything about that," Izolda replied and promptly dived into the sea.

Puzzled, Roger went in after her. Why did she like to play the innocent with such dropped remarks?

They spent the rest of the day bathing from the boat or walking along the beach collecting shells as she had once walked with Winn. She wanted to put her arm round Roger's waist and feel *his* flesh, but refrained: no more advances after that last bungled kiss!

So they walked apart, each thinking his own thoughts. Later, on the yacht again, they sat by the tiller in their damp suits, cool skins glistening with water, and watched the lowering sun turn the clouds in the sky to balls of fiery orange and red in the glory of an Eastern sunset.

"When you asked me back to the flat after the Ball," Roger said quietly, "did you expect . . . ?"

"Yes-no," she answered quickly, and then more slowly. "I wanted you to kiss me, though, because we had had such a lovely evening together, and because I fell in love with you on the *Chitral*."

He did not touch her. He sat on in silence as if a thunderbolt had hit him. "I didn't know," he said after a while, "I didn't know that – and yet I knew there was something . . . I wanted to keep in touch with you. That is why I wrote, and then you fell in love with another bloke." He spoke the words as facts. "I suppose it happens."

"It wasn't as simple as that. You didn't answer my letter, and when there was nothing at Christmas I never expected to hear from you or see you again. And I wanted so badly to be married and have a family—"

"But you didn't have children," he interrupted her. "What went wrong?"

"My relationship with my husband is not up for discussion," she said stingingly, head up.

"*Entendu*," he said with a little nod. "And now," he went on, very still beside her, "now that you have met me again, how do you feel about me?"

"I find," she said simply, her eyes downcast on her hands in her lap, "I find that I am still in love with you."

He did not touch her or put his arm around her to kiss her as she longed to be kissed, and though she could feel his eyes upon her, she could not look at him for fear of what she would see in them. Those brown eyes might be full of contempt or even disgust at the implied betrayal of her husband.

After a little, after his long silence, and non-reaction to

the confession torn out of her heart, which now felt like a sledge-hammer banging uncomfortably within her, she began to shiver. She rose and went down to the tiny cabin to change out of her damp bathing suit. She stripped off, stepped out of it, biting back tears of mortification and hurt, took up a towel and began to wipe her cold midriff in desultory fashion.

A shadow cast itself across the strip of worn carpet at her feet, and she looked up to see Roger standing at the entrance, his bulk half blotting out the exotic sunset with its kaleidoscope of rapidly changing brilliant colours. And the darkening cabin filled with slanting dancing stars of mauves and blues and purples shot through with threads of gold-dust.

Chapter Nine

ROGER stood in the doorway watching Izolda towelling her back. To him she looked like a Grecian statue, one hand over her head, and all her youthful gleaming figure exposed. His eyes descended from her small firm breasts to her little waist, her flat stomach, curving hips, shapely thighs and long slim-ankled golden brown legs. He stooped his great height and stepped down into the cabin.

Izolda stopped towelling when she saw before her a new Roger, not the one she knew with eyes that wrinkled up at the corners, but one with black mirrored pools, deep, dark, demanding, and brooding on her body. He was unsmiling, his mouth set, straight – even grim. She felt herself trembling as she held the towel to one side where it drooped on the floor. He was an unknown quantity, a stranger with a beautiful set of head, strong torso and slim hips and he exuded power and passion – a silent man who did not speak. Everything, all there was to say, lay in the look.

And under his gaze Izolda felt like a bud unfolding towards the sun. She dropped the towel and with longing held out her hands to the warmth.

He stripped and came to her and the last of the sunlight flooded into the cabin behind him. In a stride he caught her in his arms, and kissed the fluttering pulse in her neck and up to her face and all over it until his lips came to rest on hers and stayed there long and deeply and passionately.

At first she was astonished, her loins suddenly heavy and she full of amazement and throbbing excitement. She put her arms around him to make sure she wasn't dreaming, her fingers running through his springy thick hair, down his back and over a puckered piece of flesh at which she felt him flinch – dear God, his wound . . . Soft and yielding to his embrace, she abandoned herself to the learning of new feelings and undreamed-of sensations.

He laid her on the bunk and she followed him trusting and submissive in the unfolding of what she had to do. It hurt a little and it was not the slightest bit like what her aunt had told her would happen in her oh-so-clinical way, but was warm and luscious and sweet as a stolen peach ripe from a sun-blessed wall in a secret garden. With open eyes she watched the deepening sunset ever paling and changing and darkening to cast magic patterns on the low dingy roof of the boat as Roger moved over her. She gave a little laugh when with a thump she heard his feet kick against the panel of the board and a responding muffled curse came from him. She lay, holding him to her without moving. In blissful content she folded herself against the muscles of his stomach, against his strength. And all around her she could swear there lingered the scent of the frangipani Pagoda tree.

"I hurt you?" he half asked, not sure.

"Oh no," she said, lying at his side in the narrow bunk and burying her face in his shoulder, "Oh *no*! Now I've found out what Maisie used to go on and on about after she married Hugh . . . and all in a rocking, tiny boat, quite inadequate for your size – all on the South China seas!"

"What do you mean you've *found out*? NO!" he exclaimed, leaning up on one elbow to look at her in the near dark; and she was glad the shadows hid her face.

"Yes," she said. "I can't say it, not even now." And she turned her face further away.

"Christopher incapable? My God, the poor bastard . . . then I *did* hurt you?"

"No, no," she said again, "I'd had . . . the doctor suggested it . . . it was nothing, but the operation didn't help." She took his face between her hands and with joy kissed its roughness. "How could it hurt me when I love you; when you've loved me?"

"He must have known," Roger said severely. He took one of her hands away from his face and kissed her open palm.

"He didn't. Truly he hadn't an inkling. We were both of us utter innocents. He's so decent, he wouldn't have married me had he known. Of course he wouldn't. You see, he's thoroughly *nice*, that's why it's been so difficult. We consulted a doctor. He suggested various things . . . Oh, don't let's talk about it. I don't want to talk about it."

"Why didn't you have an annulment?" he asked, as she knew he would.

"*Please*, Roger. Put yourself in Chippy's position." (At this Roger gave a great guffaw which made Izolda smile.) "Everyone would have guessed *why*. He said he'd rather blow his brains out than have it known in the Navy."

"Divorce then?"

"I suppose we will in the end. But straight away there didn't seem to be any great urgency. Oh, do we *have* to go on talking about it? It's got nothing to do with us."

"Nor has it, thank God," Roger's face crinkled. "It's just as well I didn't know . . . I'd have been too scared."

117

"You scared?" she scathed. "Rot!"

"I've only known married women."

Roger got up and tied a towel round his waist to make a skirt so that he looked like a light-skinned giant from the south of India. He picked up her towel from the floor and drew it over her. He left her and went to put on the boat's bow light to add to the other myriad of lights sparkling into life in the short tropical twilight.

"Can you get away for my leave and come sailing round the islands with me?" He looked up as she came out to him dressed.

"I will, Roger, somehow I will," she said, her heart in her eyes.

"And get yourself fixed up?" But she knew she would not.

"Then I'll damn well have to find a boat that has a longer bunk."

"All the same," she laughed with pure gladness, "all the same I think you managed pretty well in this one!"

She helped him to hoist sail, and they returned to Kowloon. In the dark they walked to her pad where he left her at the entrance. All the way back they talked about what stores she was to collect, and how he would bring the champagne. They were going to do it in style, this honeymoon she had never had, floating round the islands, floating on the blue, blue sea – floating on air . . .

"Did you get bitten?" Roger rang Izolda the next evening after work.

"Yes, did you?" she laughed, her face rosy.

"In the most intimate places, the impertinent little brutes. I'll have to see to it that our junk gets fumigated first. What did the military hospital say about some leave?"

"They looked surprised at the short notice, but they said OK. I'd have taken it anyway."

Izolda rang up The Falls and told them she was going on a sailing jaunt with friends from Kowloon. She would be back in ten days' time well before Chippy returned. Louise wondered at the unexpected holiday, but said nothing.

It was the most idyllic interlude, a golden time in the sparkling South China seas, a time of peace, of sun and calm weather, of autumn breezes, ruffled surface waves and slight swell; of hot sand and an ocean of clean clear water for swimming in.

Roger and Izolda soon mastered the hired junk with its patched sails which made it look like a muted orange moth. Small enough for them to handle with ease, yet it had a roomy cabin with two decent-sized bunks below. And as the leisurely days passed and they got to know one another better and ever more intimately, their relationship grew into something deeper than mere physical attraction. To them it was as if two destined souls had met in the firmament and fused, as if all their lives they had wanted each other.

For the present that was enough for both of them. Let the future take care of itself! The present was perfect and with it there was no future nor even any past. Roger would look up from the beach or the other end of the junk and hold out his hand to Izolda, and she would go to him and in the few steps that separated them take in again his face and his thick dark hair and his bronzed body, and in those moments would once more fall in love all over again. He said she was beautiful and he made her feel beautiful, but he was beautiful too – a beautiful man's body with courtesy, consideration, understanding and gentleness. The intelligence was there in the keen eye, the toughness was there when called upon, and the integrity was there holding

119

the whole together. With Roger, Izolda felt herself come alive. She found they were in harmony in everything they did together, and her entire mind and body was permeated with happiness.

From Castle Peak in the New Territories, where they had picked up the junk, they found anchorages for the night in places with quaint names such as 'Dragon Head' and 'Pearl Beach'. They sailed over to Lantau Island, twice the size of Victoria Island, and walked up the twin-peaked mountain to stay one night in the Buddhist Lin Po Monastery with its enormous figure of Buddha. There they ate a vegetarian meal with the shaven-headed monks and nuns, and slept in dormitories where the sexes were segregated – the first night they had been parted since the beginning. The next morning they were awakened at four a.m. by the reverberating clash of gongs and the boom of the great bronze bell, and they met again at the long refectory breakfast table, their hands brushing in greeting. They smiled at one another, and asked, smiling, how their night had been, and saw themselves giddy with love; and that next night was all the sweeter for the abstinence.

Sailing on eastwards, they passed Stonecutter's Island, waterless and somehow forbidding. For a moment a cloud of reality penetrated Izolda's heady ecstasy when Roger mentioned that there was a section of sixty-pounders on the island. The next moment she was laughing with him at the antics of a woman in a tub madly trying to round up a water crate of paddling, squawking ducks. With the breeze failing Izolda took over the steering, while Roger started up the junk's engine which sparked obediently into motive power, and she navigated them through Victoria harbour's scurrying cross-traffic as if she had done it all her life.

They passed through the familiar narrows of Lye-mun

that Izolda knew so well, and sailed on round Junk Bay to spend an enchanting day watching fishermen at work by a sleepy village in Clear Water Bay where the old stone walls were garlanded with sweet-smelling honeysuckle. Near there they visited some of the many temples on the mainland peninsular – each with its gods and cloying scent of incense – before turning southwards to round Hong Kong Island past Big-wave Bay to Shek-O, the prettiest cove of all with its sheltered beach and small island offshore.

In the evenings, after a champagne supper on board under the stars, Roger and Izolda would go down to the cabin and there spend the night together, entwined, engrossed in one another – two people alone in the whole universe. And by day wherever they went there were all those two-hundred and thirty-five islands waiting for them to explore. Anchoring off some of these, they swam together from the junk to the deserted beach of their choice. Here, in complete privacy they savoured the caressing freedom of bathing as nature clothed them, water lapping on skin. Here they made love in the shade of sun-blistered rocks, or on a grassy bank by a rill now dry. Afterwards they lay still and watched the swallows diving to sip the water in the few pools left. Sometimes the love sessions were lengthy langorous half-asleep ones; at other times they were short and urgent when they snatched at, and for a sublime moment held, a shooting star.

"I don't care what happens next," Izolda said in Roger's arms, "life can do what it likes to me after this."

"I care, dearest," he said, "I want us to live together until we fade away with age."

"By that time you will be a blimpish old General."

"In that case you will be the senior wife on the station."

121

"I should be hopeless at it; all that entertaining and—"

"You are steadfast and brave and I love you very much and you will be marvellous at it."

"Yes," she said tracing his face with a finger, "I will be marvellous at it with you. For with you I have no faults and love can do no wrong."

Slowly, they made their way on round the rocky Stanley Peninsular without a care in the world, without premonition in their minds of what the Fort standing out prominently on the headland was to mean. They saw it for what it was: an ugly block with the massive old jail, grim-stoned standing sentinel behind and next door to the Anglican St Stephen's Boys College.

"I'm badly in need of a bath," said Roger that day. "I'm itchy all over and I need to wash my hair in fresh water. What d'you say to a night ashore?"

In the fishing village of Stanley, nestling in the neck of the peninsular, they tied up, left an old boatman in charge, and repaired overland to the Repulse Bay Hotel of low long lines a short way up from the expanse of sandy white beach.

By this time Izolda cared nothing for anyone who saw them together in the hotel where in the past she had danced with Chippy; she was so rapturously in love after the starved years. Neither did Roger care much who saw him with this virgin girl who had changed his life so unexpectedly, a girl in a million; lovely, laughing, truthful.

In the event they met no one they knew. They indulged, after their scratch boat meals, in a three-course dinner at one of the many tables lit by red-shaded lamps dotted along the open terrace, while punkahs turned overhead ruffling their hair. The menu bristled with Lucullan dishes in the hotel renowned for its good food, and their choice finally rested on a starter of French-dressed insides of palm branches, suckling pig to follow, and the hotel's famous chocolate soufflé to end – and they drank champagne.

"I've never had so much champagne in all my life as I've had this last week," Izolda waved her glass in the air, "I'm bubbling over with champagne!"

"Watch it," Roger laughed. "I don't know that I'm steady enough myself to carry you to the bedroom!"

In that electric atmosphere, Roger only had to touch Izolda's arm with the tip of a finger, only to look into her eyes, to set the scarcely dying embers of her new-found passion alight. She was light and buoyant with love, heavy and longing with love.

"Extraordinary that for so long I didn't know," she said, lying with Roger and looking out of the bedroom window at the stars in the fathomless sky above the sea, her head on his shoulder, her feet entwined in his long legs, "I truly thought I was a hopeless case and that it was all my fault."

"Hopeless, my foot," Roger's voice was in her ear. "Sometime, dearest, we have to talk about the future . . ."

"But not just yet, darling, not just yet." She turned and lay on him. "You're like the Dorset man."

"What Dorset man?" he asked smiling, his eyes half shut.

"You know, the one on the Cerne Abbas hillside picked out in white gravel. I drove past him once when I was staying with my father."

"Oh him. Well . . . here's another." And he took her to him.

They walked round the scenic Deep Water Bay with its small golf course inland, and over the hill past Aplei-chu Island and the naval base. They went to Aberdeen with its jam-packed harbour, and high-hulled gaudily painted houseboat restaurants where Izolda got irrepressible giggles at Roger's maladroitness with chopsticks.

They sailed across to Picnic Bay in green Lamma Island where they swam once more, diving into the transparent water from the junk with exuberant shouts, ducking each other, racing each other, bodies like sleek porpoises crawling side by side. They heaved themselves on board and lay panting on the deck, skins bronzed, sopping hair dripping. They were young, beautiful, healthy, strong – in love.

"You are the dearest thing that has ever happened to me. I want you to belong to me."

"I want to belong to you."

"Will you marry me, Izarling?"

"I will marry you, darling Roger."

"What will your grandmother say?"

"She'll keep her counsel, or she'll have it out good and proper. But she will understand – she always understands."

"Wonderful, wonderful Grandma!"

With time running out, indeed accelerating rapidly downhill, they returned the boat to the owners at Castle Peak, and drove in Roger's ancient car (he had christened it *Boanerges* for 'sons of Thunder' – it made a fearful row), into the New Territories.

Here the farmers and fishermen lived as they had for hundreds of years. They lived in great poverty among their paddy fields and fish ponds. They were the seafaring Tanka people, and the farming Hakka people whose women with their shabby jackets and wide-brimmed valenced hats; Izolda could never see without being reminded of her strange encounter with Ying Su. Women smoked long-stemmed pipes. Babies were slung on backs while mothers tended the market gardens, herded fat squealing piglets, and threw food to swarms of half-tame ducks swimming crowded together.

Star of the Rising Sun

On their last day Roger and Izolda walked hand in hand through the sixteenth-century walled village of Kam Tin. It was squalid, smelly and poverty-stricken, but Izolda could only see it as romantic.

She gave Roger the spare key to her Kowloon flat when he saw her off on a train at Fanling on the day he had to report back to duty. The man she loved had become so much a part of her that he stayed with her. She carried away the musky scent of his seed in her body, and she blocked her mind to all else.

On a following late afternoon, Izolda caught a bus from the hospital where she worked which took her down Nathan Road. She leapt out at her stop, dashed round the corner and saw *Boanerges* parked outside. She ran up the steps, hair bouncing, up the first flight, round to the second, up the third, round again, bent forwards up the fourth and through the open door into Roger's arms, lips parted, heart thumping.

"It's been a long time!" she panted.

"A mere fifty-eight hours," he said, his eyes crinkling at her in the way that made her weak with loving him. "What a super little place. I've been making myself thoroughly at home."

They sat out on orange boxes in the roof garden and sipped long drinks.

"What about it, dear one?"

"Chippy isn't back yet. I'll ask him when he comes – it'll take ages to get a divorce through."

"I know. That's why I think you should start. Under the circumstances he's bound to give you grounds. What a farce."

"Hugh rang," Izolda changed the subject, "to tell me that

125

Maisie and Tommy have left Manila by boat and are on their way. He's over the moon."

"Crackpot idea," growled Roger.

They went for an evening stroll through the crowded streets of Tsim-Sha-Tsui. They passed nightclubs with their flashing neon signs, and smiled secretly to one another, safe in the knowledge that they had no need for such parlours, and that what went on in their eyrie was far more exciting than anything in the nightclubs below.

They stopped by a fortune teller's booth. A Chinaman with incongruous checked cloth cap on his head opened the cage door of a tiny trained bird. With its beak it picked out one of the cards amongst many. To prove that it was the right card for them, the fortune teller made the bird repeat the act after the pack had been reshuffled. Again it picked out the same card which read: *'To tall dark man you will bear many sons'*. And Izolda hoped indeed it would be so.

At last, and on a Saturday, Chippy turned up at the Macdonnell Road flat. Izolda had been alerted that his MTB was coming in, and she was waiting for him. It was obvious that he was very tired and lacking in sleep, and after the boy had served them a light meal, he went straight to bed. She herself slept in the spare room.

Next day he told her scraps of what he had been doing, including evacuating some VIPs to China. The rest of the time, she gathered, was taken up with patrolling and searching for Japanese infiltrators. They had not got half enough HM ships, he said. They should never have sent those other boats to Indian waters. "It's practically a war situation out here already," he said coughing. He coughed with a hard little cough almost continuously, and he chain-smoked.

"You should see a doctor and you should give up smoking," she said.

"I'm all right," he said. "I have to report back to my ship this evening."

It was Sunday and he was off again. What was the good of that? Not a hope of setting a divorce in motion until he was given some proper leave. She'd tell him then about Roger. He would hate the whole wretched divorce business. There was no point in worrying him with it ahead. In fact she did not think he could take much more.

They went together to the dockyard by *Tamar* and she waved him off. Then she caught the ferry for Kowloon and went back to her little rooftop nest in the city to wait for a call from Roger to say when he could come.

She did not have to fantasise anymore; her childhood *Rose Marie* love story had turned into a reality that far far exceeded the dream: '*You belong to me; I belong to you* . . .'

For a short while longer their lives went on in this idyllic way. Roger's love for Izolda and Izolda's love for Roger in ever-deepening intensity swept all else away in its overriding passion and tenderness, until one morning he kissed her goodbye.

"*Sayonara*, dearest," he said. "Expect me Monday."

With a cheery grin and a wave he was gone.

Part Three

The Roundness of the Sun

1941

Chapter Ten

ON a Monday morning, a chilly but perfect crystalline winter's day, Izolda was drinking her breakfast coffee alone on her roof terrace in Tsim-Sha-Tsui among Peggy's flowering pots. She sipped contentedly. The bright azure of the sea was reflected a deeper blue in the incredible clarity of the sky, and Izolda smiled happily in the knowledge that Roger would be with her again that night.

She lifted her face to the sun. There was a slight pulsing in the still air, and, searching the cloudless vault, she saw . . . what were they? They looked like a hive of buzzing bees. Unperturbed she watched them coming nearer – getting larger. Ah, aircraft; stumpy black shapes with white, red-centred, blobs of roundel markings. Who on earth?

All of a sudden she froze. They were overhead, aiming directly at *her* – only her! Petrified, her eyes were glued on them roaring above, the leading ones diving down towards her. As if turned to stone she continued to watch, face bathed in the warm rays. She shaded her eyes as they came out of the sun, and automatically she began to count.

They were easy to count attacking as they were in formation flights of threes. They were no longer black against the light, but now silver in the full glare of it, and what they were dropping was black: black bombs.

"One-two-three," Izolda counted, mesmerised, watching

them dive close over her head, "four-five-six; seven-eight-nine, twelve, fifteen . . ." It was not possible. No, they were not aiming at her but at the airport, bombing that tiny cluster of Wildebeestes she could just see parked by the runway, and that smaller group of Amphibians and a Clipper riding in the Bay. "Twenty-one, twenty-four, twenty-seven, thirty, thirty-three," on and on they came, roaring overhead, thirty-six of them. White puffs of anti-aircraft fire bursts rose to meet them. Manoeuvres? Couldn't be. There weren't such numbers of war planes here. Those markings? It could only be the Japanese. It had come. WAR. The terror was happening, here, now, and she was in the middle of it.

Even as her brain speculated, Izolda heard and felt the first effects of bursting war with the whine of crashing bombs, the thuds as they hit their targets and blasted the aircraft into flames, leaving craters in the runway. The building under her shuddered; dust from falling masonry rose to her floor as if in slow motion; retaliatory gunfire flashed, and all hell was let loose around her eyrie for a shocking five minutes of what seemed an eternity. Then they were gone leaving a shattering silence filled with the memory of the fearsome sound of war.

Izolda sat on remembering the time her grandmother had told her about the Yokohama earthquake in 1923. Four minutes of all hell let loose, in which her mother had been instantaneously killed. Then a stunned silence like this one, when the mind wondered if it had been dreaming until the eyes took in the gaps in houses, saw the dust rising and settling as she could see from where she sat with the coffee cup still in her hands, a film forming over the milky-brown cooling surface. Immobilised, she watched the plumes of smoke from fires spiralling. In the earthquake they had had half an hour of uncanny silence before the turmoil resumed. How long a gap would there be here? With the RAF destroyed on the ground there would be nothing left with which to defend Hong Kong from the air, and the sole responsibility would lie with the artillery – the Gunners. Roger! Oh God, where was Roger?

Izolda, together with the vast majority of the population on that Monday 8th December, was still in ignorance of the assault on Pearl Harbor with its terrible loss of life, aircraft, and ships only seven hours before the attack on Hong Kong. She did not yet know that America had entered the European conflict, and that morning the United Kingdom and the United States had declared war on Japan.

She did not know that at the same time as the planes arrived out of the sky over her head, the Japanese had attacked on land coming from eight miles over the border where their forces had recently swollen from five thousand to twelve times that amount. They were at that moment crossing the Sham Chun River in swarms at Lo-Wu as well as from Mirs Bay to the east. She did not know that in the organised withdrawal to fortified and dug down positions at Gindrinkers Line, Roger with his Mountain Gunners, mules and guns, and backed up by the Indian infantry, was using brilliant deploying tactics in holding up the enemy. He was in the hills where not long ago he had wandered hand in hand with her through the maze of country lanes round the Hakka farms and villages. She did not know that at Taipo, together with the Punjab regiment he had fought with as infantry on the North-West Frontier, he had instigated and laid a trap which had massacred a whole regiment of enemy. She knew none of this, nor that Hugh – desperately worried about his family who had only just arrived and whom he had left the day before – was blowing up bridges and roads behind the retirement. The Sappers were always last in the face of an encroaching enemy to detonate the charges and run the hell out of it.

Neither did Izolda know that Winn was waiting in the Volunteer's defensive positions in Shing Mun Redoubt, or know where Chippy was, or that Maisie and Tommy were at that very moment fleeing before the enemy in the New Territories. They had been awakened by an urgent call from HQ and with other women and children in Fanling, Maisie had thrown their suitcases into the car and stuffed it with last minute bundles before shoving Tommy in. She had driven off, and was now, with thousands of other fleeing citizens in every form of transport, converging onto the congested roads southwards.

Although Izolda had known that her uncle was in Intelligence and her aunt had hinted that he would not be around if war came, she had been kept in the dark as to his real role which was, as a fluent Chinese speaker, one of the VIPs to fly out with Bungy into China to persuade the Generalissimo in Chunking to order General Yu Han Mau's 7th Army at Kutang to move to their aid. It was literally Hong Kong's only chance of survival.

But all Izolda could think of sitting stunned in Peggy's roof-garden, was that the horror of war was here. It had come to Hong Kong in the same fashion as it had come two years ago to England and France: to London bombed like this, to a France straffed and then overrun and occupied. In France the much vaunted Maginot Line had proved useless. Would the Gindrinkers Line that Winn talked about as impregnable, fare any better?

The telephone rang and Izolda jumped. It must be Roger ringing to see if she were safe!

"Izolda?" an anxious-voiced Toni asked to Izolda's disappointment, "are you all right?"

"Yes. I suppose they were Japanese?"

"Who else? We can't see from here, but we heard. What were they bombing?"

"The airport."

"Dear God. Jimmy's there – at least he was. He said as he was leaving early this morning to tell you to pack your case and come over straight away."

"What on earth's Uncle Jimmy doing at the airport?" There was a silence. "Aunt Toni, are you still there?"

"Mother says to fill up the bath and that you are to come *at once*. She insists."

"I won't come just yet. I've got my work to do and . . ." She could hear them talking in the background.

"Jimmy told me the clerical staff in the hospital would be evacuated to the Island in the event of an attack, and we've just *had* an attack." Toni's voice sounded exasperated.

"I saw it. But I'll go to the hospital first." There was more whispering down the phone.

"Your grandmother says you're as obstinate as your mother was when she took an idea into her head."

"I know," Izolda smiled into the mouthpiece, "and I won't come over yet any more than she would have. Give my love to Grandma," she finally put the receiver down.

She went off to work. There was an air of organised urgency about the military hospital with the red-caped Queen Alexandra's nurses scurrying round and putting up beds in corridors. It was her stint at the switchboard in the main building, and already she felt squeamish. She hoped she would be put back into the typing pool annexe before casualties began to arrive and there was blood about. In the distance she could hear thuds as more bombs fell in a second attack.

There was a third attack from the air on Kowloon in the

afternoon, the flights breaking up to make shallow dives. They seemed to be dropping bombs haphazardly, some near to where she was, some far away, certain of finding targets in the crowded urban peninsular. In the evening she and the other girls in the pool were sent home and told not to come back the next day – Tuesday. They would be in touch with them on the Island when needed. The girls had better get over quickly. The ferries were packed out with fleeing population, the nearly empty ones returning to pick up ever increasing numbers.

Izolda went back to her pad half hoping Roger would have beaten her to it. But *Boanerges* wasn't parked outside the block, and Roger did not come. Late, she went to bed and lay awake listening to the explosions of mortars and gunfire booming. From the sound of answering big guns even she could deduce that the Japanese were pounding Gindrinkers Line.

Still awake at two a.m. Izolda heard a lone plane droning off from the airport. Odd that. What was it doing? It couldn't be the RAF. It had been reported at the hospital that all RAF planes had been destroyed on the ground in the first swoop. Must be a civilian one . . . ?

Chapter Eleven

ON the afternoon of 9th December, Major Roger Stamford
MC had been at it for forty-eight hours with no sleep and
no time to stop and eat. Hassan Khan had kept him going
with mugs of hot sweet tea. Strange how untired he felt
after yesterday's sustained harassment of the enemy in a
continuous fight. It was hard on his men though. Soon he
would get the Subadar-Major to start pulling them out in
dribs and drabs for a rest and a kip.

He was now in position Layback One, crouched down
in the observation post with eyes glued to binoculars.
Professionally he assessed the view northwards before him,
his brain performing with calculating exactness. The scene
of green hills interspaced with flat watered plains was wildly
different from the barren mountains of India, but it helped
to have had that experience. War was war much the same
the world over whether in desert, jungle or acres of paddy
fields. Here he could gauge exactly what was happening,
what action to take, and how to execute it; when and where to
move the guns, when to leave them where they were. No fog
of war here, just a black mass of enemy advancing . . .

He had got back yesterday evening to Brigade Headquarters in 'the Box' in one piece, and, in his battle-grimed
clothes, had made his report on conditions at the front.
The news of the success of his ruse – a trap which the

Japanese had walked straight into – had forestalled him, and the Brigadier greeted him with the words that he had been put up for an immediate DSO. It had made him smile rather wanly and say that would please his father, but they still had the war – which had barely commenced – to win!

Now, from the observation post, he could see the enemy crawling down the scrubby hills into the flatter land like an army of black ants. Wave upon wave upon wave. Never in all his life had he seen such a mass of human beings – if they *were* human. The sight of these fanatical fighters from another race and another world, made the body sweat and the mouth go dry. Thousands and thousands of them converging on the left wing . . . better watch that; something preparing there . . .

Faintly, from over the perimeter two miles away, he could hear the chatter of machine-guns together with the thump of bursting mortar bombs. Overhead the whoosh of shells split the air. Once he had sent Izolda a card with *'please forgive blood and thunder'* written under the war picture. Here it was: blood and thunder. What hurt most was seeing his men killed and wounded. Hassan Khan had been wounded right beside him. He'd held him in his arms, blood and all, until the ambulance train had come and evacuated him to the hospital in Kowloon. A fraction to the left and he would have been hit. Who, if anyone, was in charge of fate? The tea did not taste the same made by the new orderly. He missed Hassan Khan and he vowed he would get every man left back to the Island; and the mules as well, too many of whom had been slaughtered in the crossfire. Mules died with a snort and a sigh of expiration. They couldn't cry out as men did. Nevertheless they suffered and they too would be vitally needed on the Island to carry the precious screw guns to their new position. It was going to be tough fighting every inch of the way – and for those that survived it would end with a last ditch fight with their backs to the vast China Seas. Churchill had decreed: no reinforcements.

Just look at the goddam little yellow bastards! They were swarming towards the left front. They ignored heavy gunfire despite many falling. They were making for the 2nd Royal Scots – the oldest and most senior regiment in the British Army. But why concentrate on the Scots? Did the Japanese know the Jocks were a bit sapped? The enemy over there was taking enormous casualties, but they streamed on; where one fell two more instantly appeared to take his place. Little men, pigmies, masses and masses of them. It was a formidable sight; fantastic; barbaric. If he hadn't seen the numbers with his own eyes he would never have believed it possible.

Good show. The Jocks were emerging to engage the Japs on the left. Now was the time for the guns to come into play to cover their advance. Lieutenant Mike Mitchell, his Forward Observation Officer, was up at the front. Great chap; left with one leg slightly shorter than the other as a result of his calf wound in the Mohmand campaign. It was high time Mike called for defensive fire. *Why wasn't he?* Crap it all, was he going to leave it too late?

The field telephone rang. Thank God the line was still functioning. The signaller beside him was giving the call sign.

"For you, sir, FOO. Urgent."

"Sunray," Roger grasped the khaki receiver.

"Target BZ Gunfire," Mike's voice crackled over. "Immediate."

"Wilco. Out."

Normally Mike would have rung the Gun Position Officer direct for his requests. But this time he wanted the whole battery to come into action and not only the guns of his allotted section. For the whole battery he had to ring either his CO or the second-in-command. Roger knew the situation over there must be critical for Mike to call for the lot, and in seconds he'd rung the GPO and given the order. A moment's lull, and then the satisfying whoosh of a salvo flying high overhead, and the ensuing distant bump, bump, bump; bump, bump, bump – all six of the little darlings, bless 'em.

He looked again in the direction of the Royal Scots. Brown billowing mushrooms interspersed with flashes of red appeared in front of the advancing Jocks. Then out of the smoke and dust facing them, the enemy figures appeared. Relentlessly they encroached into the mêlée as if the gunfire were mere fireworks. They staggered on into the blasts, sometimes seem to falter momentarily, many – very many – falling but never in the avalanching momentum of their drive ceasing to go forwards. And their high-pitched battle cries could be heard above the racket of shells. Would nothing stop them coming? How many of them were there? How many endless more in reserve?

Roger had been well briefed, and in his mind he ran over what they were confronting: Lieutenant-General Sakai Takashi had three Divisions in his 23rd Army, and a Japanese Division consisted of rather more men than was the case with the British. The Task Force of Jap veteran troops of the 38th Division, an élite Brigade which was known to be led by Colonel Fushimi – and didn't that name have some connection with old Mrs Winter? Surely he remembered her using it on the *Chitral* – was certain to be kept as fresh troops to crack the harder nut of the Island. However, this lot weren't exactly indifferent fighting men! As brave as . . . and by the look of it the whole Division was out there attacking the left flank. Bullshit . . . the poor stale Jocks were making a run for it . . . *they were giving way!* Hell, bloody hell . . .

Enemy planes screaming overhead and doing untold damage. Where was the RAF? They badly needed a dog-fight up there to interrupt the enemy flow from the sky, and to drop a few bombs way back where his guns couldn't reach. He searched the sky for a sign of the RAF coming in to retaliate. None sighted yesterday, none today. Not ONE. Could only mean one thing . . . with no airforce there was little hope of the Line holding out, even if they stayed and died to the last man, and that was not the idea. They had to live to defend the Island. Mike would fight on to the last, but he couldn't afford to lose him.

"Get me the FOO," Roger lowered his binoculars to turn to his signaller who cranked away.

"Mike? How're you doing?"

"Fine, sir, fine. That last salvo gave them a kick in the crutch. Give me five more minutes' gunfire. Hope the ammo will stand it!"

"If the Jocks give, and from here it looks as if they've begun to, don't delay; get the hell out of it, and report to Layback Two. Can't afford to lose you."

"Wilco," Mike's voice came back faintly.

Roger crouched low again, and supporting his elbows on the sandbags, steadied his binoculars. He could see the Punjabis dashing in to plug the hole left by the fleeing Scots. Well done once again, the Piffers! He thought back to when he'd first been posted as a young lieutenant to the Frontier. He'd been the FOO with the advance guard up in Tauda Cheena when the picquet was surrounded by Wazirs. Literally hundreds of them had appeared out of thin air from behind rocks and up nullahs. He'd called for gunfire just as Mike had. Within half a minute orange flashes had erupted right on target. It'd been too much for the Wazirs who'd scattered, leaving a toll of dead and wounded.

Different now. How different. Here were numberless hordes; not just a few hundreds, but thousands and thousands and each ready to die for their Emperor, nay exulting in such deaths. No question of cutting and running like the Jocks with *them*. You had to give it to the Japs. One had to kill the whole bleeding lot to stop the rot and how could you do that with only 3.7 inch howitzers and the ammunition already half gone despite the stockpile in the Box – and no help from the sky?

The Box was supposed to hold out until the Chinese Army came in over the hills, practically due north from where he was, to take the enemy from the rear. At the rate things were going . . . hell, the left front *had* collapsed, and the Punjabis and Rajputs, still magnificently at it further over, would have to be pulled back quickly or they'd be surrounded. He hoped to God Mike had obeyed orders and hared back with his men . . .

All Tuesday Izolda stayed on in Tsim-Sha-Tsui waiting for Roger. Half-heartedly she packed. Only once did she leave the flat to get some fresh food, and she rushed back in case the telephone should ring. For a second night she went to bed to sleep in fits and starts through the escalating sounds of ever-nearing battle.

At one point when she dozed off she was awakened by the scream of diving aircraft resulting in shattering blasts which shook her block to its very foundations. Next morning she heard from terrified neighbours that it was the Sham-Shui-Po camp opposite Stonecutter's Island which had been bombed, no distance up the Peninsular from her.

No doubt the Japanese knew that Sham-Shui-Po was the barracks of the 1st Middlesex regiment. What apparently they did not know was that it had been evacuated when the regiment had gone lock stock and barrel up to Gindrinker's Line two days earlier.

The water had been cut off, mains presumably blown up in the previous night's bombing, and Izolda thanked heavens that she'd heeded her grandmother's advice and filled the bath. She tested the telephone and found it still worked, so she stayed on. She was rather surprised at herself. Though nervous and jumpy at every bang, she wasn't as frightened as her hysterical Chinese neighbours.

Later on Wednesday afternoon the telephone *did* ring. Instantly she picked it up.

"For God's sake, Izolda, what do you think you're playing at? I've been trying to get you all day through jammed lines," Toni's voice sounded tense. "*Everyone* is leaving the Peninsular. This house is packed with friends from the New Territories and Kowloon. The Holdens are here with Maisie and her little boy. Maisie is in a state of shock, poor girl. They had a ghastly journey. Miss Maureen has arrived, and Mother has a fit every time she hears your name mentioned. I need you to see to her. I've got quite enough on my hands without—"

"Isn't Uncle Jimmy . . . ?"

"No he's *not* here. You'll be taken prisoner if you stay there much longer. Maisie says it was simply terrible how quickly they came. Fanling was overrun in no time. She adds her persuasions for you to come. I can't think what you're waiting for? It's just sheer stupidity—"

"The Gindrinker's Line will hold out."

"No it *won't*. They say it has already broken in one place."

"I promise you I'll come soon. Tell Grandma not to worry."

"Not to worry!" Toni's voice ended on a high note. Izolda rang off.

Desultorily making herself a sandwich for supper, she heard a car door bang, and the familiar steps coming up. She ran to throw open the door.

He stood there, scowling at her angrily. His face was unshaven and burnt black under his steel helmet. The sleeves of his open-necked shirt were rolled up; great patches of sweat stained his armpits. Across his chest his identity disc swung out on a leather string like a round label. His breeches were spattered with mud and what looked suspiciously like dried blood; his putees, wound round his ankles and legs, were torn, and his marching boots were caked in dust. He was slung around with a clutter of maps, a pair of field glasses, and a water flask dangling to one side. Round his waist he wore a cartridge belt bulging with ammunition in a pouch. A revolver protruded from the holster on his left hip.

Izolda stared at him open-mouthed. She could not believe he was the same officer, immaculately dressed in his mess kit, whom she had danced with at the Government House Ball. Neither was he the clean tanned man she had lived with on the yacht.

"What the *hell* do you think you're doing here?" he glowered, and pushed his way past her into the room.

"And where the hell have you been?" she reacted indignantly.

"Good God, woman, where d'you think?"

"You said you'd be here on Monday evening, and it is now Wednesday. I've been hanging around for you for *days*." They stared furiously at each other.

144

"There's only been a bloody war intervening," Roger began to strip off some of his accoutrements.

"You could at least have rung or sent a message or something."

"I had an inkling you'd still be here." Roger's tired face broke into a grin at Izolda's absurd words. "You stupid, idiotic, darling girl," he said, and put his arms around her. He clasped her to him, her face held tight against his shoulder, a deep breath for a moment shuddering through him. She stood there in his powerful grasp, absorbing him: the feel and the smell of him, the warmth of his body, the sweat, the gun oil – him. Then, "I can only stay a few minutes," he released her, "the General has ordered us to withdraw fighting to the Island, and the sooner *you* get there the better."

"What'll you do?"

"Go back to my men – my bloody marvellous men. God, what superb fighters the Indians make. I've just pulled the Battery out from our latest position – held the Japs up for a good while on Lion Rock." Roger sat down heavily in a chair.

"What happened to Gindrinker's? I thought . . ."

"The Royal Scots fell back last night on the left flank of the Line in complete confusion. 'The First of Foot', my foot! More like 'the Fleet of Foot'. Can't blame them though, with the hordes coming screaming over at 'em looking just like a load of devils. Enough to scare the pants off anyone! So much for holding the fort for three *days*, let alone three weeks. It only took them three hours to capture the Box and forty-eight to destroy the Line. Now, be a good girl and go and pack your things before the Nips catch up. I'll take you down to the ferry. Must have a wash . . . and what about some tea?"

"I filled the bath up on Monday on Grandma's orders.

145

The mains have burst." Izolda went to put on the kettle.

"Well done, Grandma. She's a real campaigner! Hurry up, there's a good girl."

He plunged his head and neck into the bath water, soaping his face, ears and hair. Ducking again he rinsed the soap off, reached for the towel she handed him, put on his khaki jersey over his filthy shirt, and then asked for her razor.

"That feels better." He began the sore process of shaving his stubbly beard.

"Why do you bother?"

"Good for morale, mine and the men I command. Nothing like a spruce officer to keep everyone's pecker up. Mains burst, have they? I'll tell Hugh to pull his father's leg about that. Head of the defunct waterworks, ha-ha. Lord what a feeble joke."

"Is Hugh all right?"

"Fine last time I saw him, merrily blowing up the roads. Having the time of his Sapper life I should think."

"You don't look as if you've had any sleep."

"Haven't since I last saw you, unless you can call an occasional ten minute shut-eye, sleep. It's been one hell of a business. Mules bolting, some slaughtered in the cross-fire. Men killed, others wounded including my orderly. Battery position lost, one of our guns destroyed; running short of ammo though we've managed to keep off quite a load of enemy planes. Even shot down the odd one with a Lewis gun. We've been all over the place all right. I've never seen so many Nips, nor want to ever again. The hillsides were swarming with them in the main attack . . . like those ants, the ones you get in Africa . . . what d'you call them?"

"*Saifu*, soldier ants who devour everything in their path."

"That's it, *saifu* . . . Nothing stops them marching on. We

146

mow them down, pack the guns onto the mules and leapfrog backwards, and still they come . . . crawling . . . hell, I'm nodding off. Why do women always have such bloody blunt razor blades? Damn! Make that tea strong."

"It's ready when you are." She put a cosy over the teapot to keep it hot. "It'll be strong enough by the time you've finished chopping yourself." She watched, his blood trickling.

"A nick," he said mopping at it with the towel. "What was I saying?"

"Something about the Japanese crawling . . ."

"Oh yes; in their green uniforms they're difficult to see by day amongst the hills. At nights they come silently in their rubber boots. They make the best use of these moonlit nights. They know their stuff better than we do. Whoever said they were inadequate, short-sighted fighters needs their heads examined. And their crack troops are yet to come. Now that we've fallen back on Kowloon city, the Nine Dragon peaks are collapsing like dominos! No wonder I'm furious with you for being here. Ah, thanks; nothing like a good old cuppa to give one a second wind – third wind more likely, second one's long gone."

Izolda went to finish her packing in the main room. "How do you know the Japs have rubber boots?"

"Plenty of bodies around."

"What about our wounded?" Izolda put her cup down. She didn't want any tea. The remark had made her feel squeamish.

"Being brought back to your hospital; not enough ambulances though, not enough transport, not enough blank anything . . ."

"Do you want to take something from here?" Izolda threw

her nightdress into the bulging suitcase. She set about putting the last of the stores into a carton.

"Wouldn't mind a blanket; gets cold at nights. We'd better get a move on. Will contact you at Macdonnell Road when I get over."

"I'll most probably be at The Falls."

"OK. I saw Winn briefly with Mike at the Battle Box. Great chaps those box-wallah pen-pushers when you think fighting's only their second string – Sunday soldier hobby. Well, they're in it up to their necks now. Winn was getting ready to move back to the Island."

"I'll tell Aunt Toni you've seen him and that he's all right."

"And go and look after your grandmother—"

"Yes, Roger. I'll look after Grandma."

". . . and yourself. Don't be such a bloody ass as to put yourself in the front line in future – leave that to us." He gulped down the last of the tea, filled his water bottle from the kettle, and they descended the four flights of concrete stairs Izolda had so often run up joyously. He threw the luggage into the back of an open truck parked below.

"Is it yours? Where's *Boanerges*?" she asked as he accelerated along a deserted Salisbury Road past the Kowloon-Canton Railway Station with its clock tower. The trains stood stacked nose to tail, silent and empty in the sidings. Behind, the noise of battle seemed very near: machine-gun fire rattled close by in staccato bursts; a house collapsed like a pack of cards a block away from where they were driving; the boom-boom of the 4.5 howitzers pounded at regular intervals.

"Not my truck. I pinched it, and I've bequeathed *Boanerges*, my dear old rattletrap son of thunder, to the Nips," Roger laughed, hands strong on the wheel, the wind blow-drying his wet hair into waves.

With her hand resting on his knee, Izolda scarcely took her eyes off his face for that short journey. Then he was dumping her things down on the Star Pier by the gates.

"Where are you going?" she asked with a despairing lump in her throat.

"To to other end of Nathan Road to see my orderly in hospital and then off to some heights by the crossing for another hold-up fight. We'll probably end up as infantry fighting hand to hand again soon. Wish I had my grandfather's swordstick with me. That'ud show the Japs," he grinned and jammed on his steel helmet. "Can you manage this load?"

"Yes, I'll manage."

"That's my brave girl," he said. "You'll see, we'll make a soldier's wife of you yet!" He took her in his arms and kissed her hard on the lips. "Till we meet again, dearest."

"Till we meet again . . ."

Chapter Twelve

IT seemed to Izolda her whole world was a bomb that was blowing up and soon there would be nothing left, yet the familiar scene from the Star ferry looked much the same. Hooting craft ploughed their way unconcernedly across as usual; the dance at the Peninsular Hotel was to take place that evening, and the strains from the jazz band were about to mingle with the rattle of machine guns, the bangs of hand grenades, the ripping of rifle shots and the close crack of the officer's pistols.

She struggled with her luggage onto the top deck, pushed her way in with other humanity fleeing from war, and found herself a corner of slatted wooden bench on which to perch. She thought of her mother, who had crossed the English Channel at the outbreak of the Great War to marry her sailor – Izolda's father. But she, Izolda, was being forced to put the sea between herself and her soldier lover. A tear escaped from the corner of her eye. Hurriedly she wiped it away.

"Have you heard," a gossipy English woman was saying to another on the bench beside her, "have you heard the appalling news? No, dear? I listened to it on the broadcast. The *Prince of Wales* and the *Repulse* have been sunk! Yes, this morning, in Malayan waters."

They went on talking, tossing bad news back and forth between them: Kai Tak airport had been bombed again as had the barracks of Sham-Shui-Po. The Gunners had evacuated Stonecutter's Island across the way, but not before a hulk suspected of being used as an observation post by the Fifth Columinsts had been sunk, and not before they'd spiked their own coastal artillery guns. The railway lines further up had been bombed as well as Kowloon military hospital which had been crammed with wounded. The VAD and auxiliary nurses, they said, were staying at their posts. Izolda listened. That was bravery when they could have escaped to the Island. She knew some of them. She looked at her watch as they were nearing the landing stage. The ferry ploughed on regardless, on time: seven minutes exactly.

The houseboy at 12, Macdonnell Road opened the door and smirked familiarly at Izolda. She disliked him more than ever.

"Japs go chop-chop. Japs land soon in Island, Missie, vely bad for Englishmans!" he said cheekily.

"You clean house proper," she ordered and ran her finger along a table that was thick with dust.

"How you pay Chinesemans when Japs come?" he ignored her words. "When Missie, Master, give no money, I leave quicklee."

"What lamp for?" Izolda asked sharply, when she saw one under the kitchen table. "Show mees home." It was well known the Fifth Columnist agents in Hong Kong – the Wang Ching-wei's – indicated enemy targets by using lamps and mirrors.

"You go now," she decided to pay him off then and there.

"*Now* Missie? I dust."

"No dust. Go now. Go!" She took two weeks' wages out of her purse. It was dark and she couldn't get rid of him quickly enough.

She spent half the night cleaning the flat. It gave her some-thing to do. Next morning she rang the naval base again to try and find out about Chippy. Curtly she was told that Lieutenant

151

Paine-Talbot was away 'on active service'. As if she didn't know *that*. "We're all on active service now," she said bitterly. She locked the flat and took a bus up to The Falls.

"So you decided to quit the fightin' line, Izarling?" Louise drawled casually. The only thing that gave her away was the use of the pet name. She was sitting in her room calmly crocheting. "This place is like a refugee camp," she went on grumpily, "stuffed with people I don't know. I've got your Aunt Toni to fix you up with a bed," she pointed with the hook, "it'll be quite like old times. Remember how we shared during our summer holidays in the mountains when you were little?"

Izolda looked at the camp-bed by the dressing table on which her grandfather's Order lay propped up against the mirror with a vase of flowers beside it. Good for Aunt Toni to still arrange flowers. "I didn't know you could crochet," Izolda said.

"Sure thing; before your time. I used to crochet strips like this to go round my hand towels. You always seem to think that because I brought you up you must know *everything* 'bout me." The words came out peevishly. She felt left out. Jimmy had gone. Toni was permanently busy and no one took any notice of her. For sure it was war. She'd warned them it would come long ago.

"Why aren't you wearing your wedding ring?" Izolda's sharp eyes saw the thick gold band was missing. Goodness knows what her grandmother had been up to since she'd been away!

"It's being enlarged – all those sesame cakes of Cookie's," Louise smiled. "I can tell you I had quite a time soaping it off. I hadn't removed it since Grandpa put it on at our double wedding with my cousin—"

"—*in the Union Church*. Isn't it all perfectly awful,

Grandma? The troops have been falling back rapidly." She
lay on the camp-bed to feel what it was like. The mattress
looked pretty thin. Bit hard. Not bad.

"Where's your husband?" asked Louise.

"At sea. They won't tell me more."

"What's going on?" Toni came in looking harassed. "Are
you *ill*?" She peered aghast at Izolda on the bed. "I told
you you should have done as your Uncle bid and come
straight over."

"I'm not ill; I was just trying it out," Izolda sat up and
swung her legs to the floor. "I heard Winn was fine. He's
pulling out with HQ. He'll soon be over."

"Thank God for that," Toni said fervently.

"What's happened to Uncle Jimmy?"

"Flew out on the first day, or rather that night. He and
some others were driving to the civilian plane at the other
end of the landing strip, when the first wave of attack came
over . . ."

"Oh, *no* . . . ?"

"He's all right. They were lucky. No one was hurt, nor
was the plane damaged. The Japanese were attacking the
RAF on the ground as you know, but of course the landing
strip was badly holed. The coolies worked flat out to repair
the runway during the rest of the day and half the night.
Another narrow escape came when the Clipper caught fire
and burnt out in that same first attack. Some more VIPs
were about to board when it happened."

"I heard a lone plane taking off in the night and wondered," Izolda said thoughtfully. "Where's Uncle Jimmy
gone?"

"To China. You needn't mention this to anyone."

"Where's Ying-Su?"

"Gone underground. You needn't mention that *either*."

"I guess I'll miss her," stated Louise.

Underground with the commies, Izolda speculated glaring at her grandmother. Well, she'd expected it, hadn't she? But for Aunt Toni to make a bald statement like that in such a nonchalant fashion . . . and for her grandmother to say she would *miss* the girl when she was a traitor of the worst order . . .

"Wouldn't be in the slightest bit surprised if the Chinese don't come; frightened off by the samurai, that's what," Louise observed.

"I wish you wouldn't always be so pessimistic, Mother," Toni said edgily. She had quite enough worries without adding one about the Chinese *not* coming. Every bedroom in the house was packed. The young Holdens were sleeping in the small dining room. She had found a cot for Tommy in the attic, and brought the dining room table into the drawing room. She herself had turned out of her's and Jimmy's room and had gone up to the top floor in order to give their suite to a family of six. There were other families from the New Territories camping in the large dining room downstairs. Bill and Joan Holden were ensconced in the study, and every room upstairs was crammed full, Winn and Ying Su's rooms occupied. If Winn turned up she would find somewhere for him, though it was unlikely he could stay at night with all the fighting going on. Where was it going to end?

The only exception she'd made in the disruption was not turning her mother-in-law out of her large bedroom: the old lady needed the quiet of her own room. The drawing room next door was where the 'family' lived, ate, worked. The four Holdens and Miss Maureen – upstairs sharing with her – were family; that made eight of them now that Izolda had arrived. To manage the feeding for everyone was too much.

154

Each family had to buy their own food and cook their own meals, but Cookie was doing a great job staying up all hours to bake mounds of bread and cakes for the whole household. Every morning she herself went to the town with Ping-Li to get more stores. The list was endless and none easy to come by: powdered milk, three hundred vitamin pills to hand out, iron pills, haliveroil – as much as she could get in concentrated form for Tommy and the other children – calcium, marmite, aspirin, cold cream, nappies, sanitary towels, more candles and matches. God knows how long the war would go on for . . .

After she'd unpacked, Izolda went downstairs to look for Maisie. She found her playing with Tommy on the lower terraces where there was a paddling pool, a swing and a slide, relics of Winn's and Ying-Su's childhood. Izolda had spoken to Maisie briefly over the phone when she'd arrived in Fanling on the 6th. Her ship had been the last one to dock. Subsequent near arrivals had been turned back on the high seas. Maisie had literally walked into war, and within forty-eight hours she'd found herself and her child, with a flood of refugees, fleeing for their very lives.

Now the girls met again and embraced. Delightedly Izolda picked up her godson. The small baby she'd last seen before the evacuation had grown into a sturdy toddler of eighteen months. Maisie, drawn and anxious-looking, proceeded to pour out the horrors she had encountered in the New Territories. She told of the sickening sight of slaughter and blood of innocent civilians on the roadsides, and how she had lost practically all her possessions.

"The amah and I threw masses of stuff into the car, but she wouldn't come with me and when we got to the ferry I could hardly carry anything besides Tommy," she explained agitatedly.

"What did you do with the car?" Izolda asked from the swing, swaying with Tommy on her knee.

"Parked it down a side street and locked it, but when I went back next day to collect things I found it looted, the car wrecked. There was nothing left." She seemed desolate.

"But you and Tommy are safe, and Hugh is on his way – so I heard."

"I won't believe it, not after what I've seen on the roads and in the paddy fields, not until I see him with my own eyes . . ."

Before the fighting started, Izolda, bursting with her newfound happiness, had thought she would tell her friend the truth about Chippy, and also about Roger. But now, meeting a distraught and obviously still shocked Maisie, so utterly different from the carefree, jolly girl she had known, she changed her mind and decided to keep quiet about her own affairs. Maisie was in such a state she would scarcely take in what she was saying, and in any case there was no point in exposing Chippy when nothing could be done about a divorce. Every single lawyer or barrister, however old, on the Island, had taken up arms with the Volunteers. No, she would keep quiet . . .

On the day after Izolda's arrival at The Falls, the family had an impromptu meal with the Holdens and Miss Maureen in the drawing room. Fung Wan served at table as imperturbably as ever. Izolda related how there was no water anywhere in Kowloon due to persistent Japanese shelling of the water mains.

"Will be same target over here, I expect," forecast burly Bill Holden, tucking into the soup. He had put on even more weight in the last two years and was quite enormous. "If you have to use the water from the falls, Toni, be sure to boil it first."

"Of course," said Toni shortly.

"No water. It sounds mightily like the siege of Paris in 1870," sighed Louise.

"Were you in France at that time?" enquired Joan Holden. She greatly admired Mrs Winter, who seemed to have been everywhere and done everything in her long life.

"Not in *that* war, though I was in Paris in the next. No, I was in Japan then. I read in the newspapers how they were starving and had to eat cats and rats."

"Oh that's nothing to Hong Kong, I'll be thinking," vouchsafed Miss Maureen. She flicked the cuffs of her shirt back and prepared to carve the roast, "Here they have dogs and snakes on the menu any day."

"Ugh," expressed Izolda.

"Did you know the Japanese are very fond of children?" said Louise eyeing Tommy. "I guess I'm quite looking forward to speaking the language again."

"How *can* you say such a thing, Mother," Toni rose to the bait. The telephone shrilled and she flew to the landing.

"Thank God, darling. Thank God! It's Winn," she called to the others, "he's got back with HQ." They all left the table to come and stand round the opium couch, all except Louise who continued to munch away, and Tommy who continued to bang spoons while Fung Wan cut up his meat.

"Yes, yes. We're all right, all of us. How marvellous you're back! What's that? Say again. Hugh? He's wounded?" Maisie went dead white. "Sit down, dear," Toni looked up and patted the couch beside her. Bill Holden took his wife's arm as much to steady himself as support her. "Yes, I'll tell her." They all listened. There was more talking from the other end of the phone. "Where is he?" Toni asked, "Stanley, you say . . . Oh good . . . and how wonderful of Major Stamford. You must get some sleep? . . . But of course. Come up whenever you can. Bless you for ringing, darling. God bless you."

"What's that about Roger Stamford?" hissed Izolda.

"Hugh's quite badly wounded, dear," Toni turned to Maisie, "but they think he's going to be all right. Apparently Major Stamford went to the military hospital in Kowloon to see his orderly and found Hugh there as well. He wasn't going to leave them to be taken prisoner and managed by some miracle to get them both evacuated by stretcher onto a ferry, before making his way to his unit to carry on the fight. We'll go straight down and see Hugh, shall we Maisie? He's in the new hospital which I've been helping Dr Black get organised."

"Can we come too and see how the boy is?" asked Bill Holden.

Toni nodded her head and went off to get her coat. "I must thank Major Stamford for what he has done," Joan said tearfully. "Oh, I do pray he gets back safely too."

Things moved fast. There was a message from Chippy for Izolda. He had been permanently at sea, but he hoped to get into base in a couple of days' time. He was glad to hear she was safe at The Falls.

Either Maisie or his parents visited Hugh daily at the emergency hospital which had been hastily set up in the Stanley College for Boys. Hugh had been wounded in the thigh. He was all the better for seeing them, and asked Maisie to bring Tommy next time. Though effectively and efficiently run under Dr Black and his devoted nursing staff, the building, with its borrowed or scrounged medical equipment, was inevitably rather makeshift and seething with military personnel.

Near the college the neck of the Peninsular was being slashed across with slit trenches, sandbags and Lewis gun emplacements facing inland. The jail warden's quarters and the old prison offices of the Fort were being turned into the East Brigade Headquarters. The whole Peninsular was a beehive of activity.

On the afternoon of Saturday 13th December, Winn appeared at The Falls. Three sergeant's stripes stood out whitely on his fresh uniform. He bore good news which was also bad news. They were all across. Only five days after it had started the soldiers were back on the Island – all except the dead and the wounded. Most of the latter, heartbreakingly, had had to be left behind in the evacuation. Fortunately, considering the extent of the fighting, there were remarkably few casualties. Winn had met Major Roger Stamford and Mike Mitchell – now Acting Captain – at the emergency base set up at Aberdeen where they were resting and catching a few hours' sleep. They were desperately trying to regroup, collect their equipment and count their ammunition before the Japanese gathered for the onslaught on the Island. All the Mountain Gunners were frantically busy.

"How was Roger?" asked Izolda. The family were assembled in the drawing room, and she was hanging on to Winn's every word.

"About as hollow-eyed as the rest of us," Winn laughed, "but a tonic to all. After a couple of hours' sleep he was off searching for spare parts for a gun which had been shot up on the crossing. Trust him to be the last over. Bloody marvellous man!"

"Watch your language, Winn. Your grandmother's listening," Louise said primly.

"Where did they cross?"

"Sorry, Grandma," Winn grinned, not in the least repentant. He perched on the arm of Izolda's chair, hand encircling the back and resting on her shoulder. He felt less cynical about her marriage since her husband had been doing such sterling work in his MTB. Not such a weak-kneed fellow after all. He'd worked himself up into a pique about Izolda marrying because he had wanted his cousin for himself. He genuinely loved her in a devoted way – a possessive sort of family love for a beautiful sibling, a love which, from the beginning, had erotic overtones. He was still in love with her despite her marriage, and strangely enough the erotic overtones during the last few weeks troubled him more than they had done before. During that time she'd changed from the shy ingénue she had been, and blossomed into a sexual woman. He could feel the vibes emanating from her as he sat close to her. Had he the chance to get into bed with her now there would be a passionate plunge and no doubt about it! As it was – good for old Chippy who must have . . . War did strange things to basic urges . . . brought humans to the brink . . . to the point. People said that in the heat of battle sex lay stone cold; but he found it not so, on the contrary . . .

"Go on about Roger," Maisie urged. "I'm so indebted to him for saving Hugh from the Japs."

"Hear, hear," expressed Bill Holden heartily.

"He was in the last ditch defence stand with some Punjabis on Devil's Peak Hill by the Lye-mun Narrows where his screw guns blasted down on the enemy. Remember we walked on the beach across from there, Zol? I gather the Gunners fairly pumped it into the Nips the whole way from one stand to the next – fantastic!

160

"Mike Mitchell told me in Aberdeen that once Major Stamford had extracted his men, guns and what mules were left from Devil's Peak, and got them down to the water's edge, they found total chaos. No transports left. There were other units equally desperate to get across the water, and their second-in-command had just been killed. The Major set-to to bargain with, cajole and bribe any Chinese boatmen he could find to muster enough craft to get them across. Fighting to the last, Mike said it was a sight to behold to see his giant of a CO being paddled across in a sampan blazing away with a Lewis gun from the stern!"

"Why were no naval boats or transports helping the evacuation?" Bill Holden wanted to know.

"What navy is left was fully engaged further west. From all accounts your Chippy, Zol, was in the thick of it off Ocean Terminal doing great work in his torpedo boat. He'd been ferrying troops over non-stop all day and picking up exhausted men out of the water who were making a swim for it. Quite a few of the British troops threw their rifles away and took to the water; most of the Indians couldn't swim. I had a quick word with him at Aberdeen and he told me that Commander Pears on *Thracian* took the Rajputs off the mainland and got them back to the dockyard to fight another day."

"Good for Chippy! How was he?" Izolda was proud of her husband and thrilled to hear Roger was safe.

"Fairly OK. Tired like the rest of us," Winn answered guardedly. They'd all been pretty haggard after the fight and lack of sleep, but Chippy had looked as if he were on the verge of collapse.

"So is the whole of the New Territories now occupied?" Toni asked. She was tired herself. She had been at Stanley hospital working flat out all day and had only come home

161

for a few hours when the call came Winn was on his way to The Falls.

"I used to translate for the doctors," put in Louise. No one other than Izolda knew what she was talking about.

"Do you think the Japanese are sticking to the spirit of the Geneva Convention, over there, dear?" Joan Holden asked her husband.

"We'll soon know," he replied. "The trouble is we have more than one enemy. I heard on the local news that as soon as our troops were withdrawn, out came the Wang Ching-wei's."

"That's right, sir. Kowloon is swarming with them, leading the looters; they openly wear their baggy green uniforms. The swaggering Japs take no notice and don't attempt to stop them. Over here our transport is breaking down all over the Island due to the Wang Chings. The petrol stocks at Aberdeen have been sabotaged with sand and water."

"Oh dear, how can you get over that one?"

"Siphon it, Mum, with a strainer. Takes hours. Slows down everything no end, and they know it."

The company in the drawing room fell silent. "I blame myself for not having put a stopper on you coming into this pickle," Bill said remorsefully to his daughter-in-law.

"Don't say that, Dad," Maisie went over to kiss his forehead, her face drawn. "We're safe enough on the Peak. Just think how I would have felt in Manila hearing Hugh had been wounded?"

"I heard the Japanese have landed in the north of the Philippines," added Joan. "Yes, I think you and Tommy are better off here."

"They say General MacArthur is trying to hold the Japanese off in the Philippines. It was on the wireless. Perhaps they'll invade Australia next? I don't think anywhere in the world is safe anymore," Izolda said despondently. At that moment, in tore a breathless Miss Maureen.

"Did you hear the explosion?" she said, her eyes electrified behind thick lenses.

"We heard a big bang. What was it?"

"Mother o' God," breathed Miss Maureen. She sank into a chair, "as if it wasn't a ferry boat loaded with dynamite. It blew up as it was steaming down the harbour an' every window on Victoria waterfront is shattered. 'Tis sure I'm deaf from it meself."

"Damnation! We can't afford to lose dynamite," Winn burst out.

"I must get back to the hospital," Toni said, looking at the clock. "Keep going everyone here. I'll give you a ring when I can Izolda. Look after everything, won't you, dear? You know how the safe works for wages and cash?"

"Yes, Aunt Toni." They saw her off in the Austen.

"What next Winn?" Bill Holden asked.

"What next?" Winn echoed. "Well, the Nips regroup for the attack, that's what's next. Most likely they'll cross at North Point and attempt to cut the Island in two. We've got to stop them. What with, God knows. We've lost so much stuff we've only got rifles and .38 Smith and Wesson revolvers left in the Volunteers. Keep an eye on the women for me, sir." The men shook hands.

Winn kissed Maisie and Miss Maureen heartily and stood for a moment with his arms around Izolda. She found his compact, familiar figure comforting, and was glad that he no longer avoided her. "Somehow, Zol darling, you've got to survive this bloody war because I intend to and I want to see you again. Remember that when you feel like giving in, won't you?"

"I won't give up, Winn," she kissed him affectionately

163

and watched him climb into the army truck, the same type as Roger had pinched. With a spurt he roared off up the drive, disappearing out of sight under the tiled pagoda archway entrance with its carved dragons in their gaudy greens and reds.

Izolda felt a cold frisson of fear creep up her spine for Winn, Roger, Chippy, Aunt Toni and herself, for all of them – yes, even her indomitable grandmother. The open-mouthed gargoyles and dragons on the pagoda and under the eaves of the mansion seemed to be jeering at her – as if they knew the awfulness of what was going to happen, and were licking their lips in anticipation.

Chapter Thirteen

IT was during the slight lull that followed the withdrawal to the Island that Chippy and Izolda met for lunch. As he was only able to be ashore for an hour, they decided to meet at Mickey's Kitchen which was still a flourishing business. But the sound of battle was never very far away, and those in the restaurant were used to ducking for shelter under the tables. Dive bombing attacks on the naval dockyard at Aberdeen were being stepped up, and the Japanese planes continued to zoom in low over the mountains at will despite sporadic retaliatory fire from hidden guns.

Chippy and Izolda sat side by side on one of the banquette seats as they so often had in the past. She noted Chippy had lost a lot of weight and his face looked thin and pinched and unusually strained under his tan. He chain-smoked throughout the meal, coughed a great deal and to her distress she saw signs of blood on his handkerchief.

"Winn tells me you've been doing great things," she praised brightly. She was genuinely admiring. He had *not* shaken hands with the enemy. He was fighting in the best tradition of the Royal Navy.

"Though I say it, it was not unlike a miniature Dunkirk," Chippy replied modestly. "My MTB was under constant fire but the dear boat didn't receive so much as a glancing blow. Miraculous, really, with all the cross-fire. Picking up the poor blighters trying to swim across was rewarding. They were so grateful to be hauled out, given blankets and a cup of tea. It was wretched, though, to tow *Tamar* into Wanchai Bay and scuttle her with all her treasures on board. What an end to a fine vessel. The harbour is full of sunk and scuttled ships; the order of the day is scorched earth, to mix a metaphor."

"Grandma will be sorry to hear about *Tamar*. She regards herself as a sort of ancient battleship still gamely floating. The news might upset her."

"Don't tell her then. If you don't she'll most probably not hear of it."

"What would you say if I told you I might be having a baby?" Izolda said on the spur of the moment. She badly needed to unburden herself on this thrilling, and at the same time, terrifying, possibility.

"*Might*?" he said, blinking at the implication of what she'd revealed.

"I'm not sure – yet," she said, "I've only missed one . . . It could be strain and nerves with all this awful war and everything," she twisted the table cloth with her hands.

Chippy looked at his wife without speaking for a while, and then he said in cheerful tones, "Good! It's what you've always wanted, isn't it?" And then when she started to speak, "That's enough. You needn't say more."

"We're jumping the gun," she frowned, wishing now she had not let her secret out on impulse. She pulled herself together. "You shouldn't smoke so much, Chippy," she said severely. "You'll give yourself another dose of tuberculosis, and just look at your stained fingers. I think you should go and see a doctor straight away and say you're not fit."

"My nagging wife suggests I quit *now* of all critical times? Bollocks," Chippy laughed hollowly. "So what if I have TB

166

again? I don't give much for my chances of survival, not with these Jap planes raining bombs down on our ships." Both he and Izolda instinctively ducked at a whine overhead followed by a nearby thump. "There are hardly any of us left: *Thracian* is out of action – dive-bombed in dry dock where she was for repairs; and another MTB has been sunk. That leaves the *Cicala* and two of us. It's no use living in cloud cuckoo land, not with the enemy within spitting distance across the water . . . 'Across the water when 'tis dark a million lights shall glow'," he quoted. "Remember, Zol, when I proposed to you?"

"Oh Chippy. And now the lights have all gone out. Will they ever shine again?"

"My God they will, and you make sure, my girl, that there'll be a Paine-Talbot to see them!" He was really rather tickled with the idea. It would make Zol happy. She hadn't mentioned divorce, so obviously did not wish for one. He couldn't care less who the father was. The child would be *theirs* to bring up as he had said once before, and he – because of course it would be a boy – would be born in wedlock and that was how it should be.

They kissed goodbye on the waterfront. "Take good care of both of you, my sweet," Chippy said, pleasure at her news showing in his eyes. And in the tender gesture she had used a hundred times, Izolda smoothed back the hank of hair that had inevitably fallen over his forehead. They turned once more to wave before they each went their separate ways.

On Izolda's return to The Falls she found a letter waiting for her on the hall table. She recognised the handwriting on the envelope instantly. She opened it and found it was penned on a torn-off lined sheet of army memo paper. Headed 'Aberdeen' it was dated the previous day:

> *'Dearest one,*
>
> *I am afraid I cannot get up to see you. There is an enormous amount to be done in preparation for the next, and last, defensive fight, and if you came here you would not see me for dust. So stay where you are, darling girl, and look after wonderful Grandma to whom please give my warmest regards.*
>
> *I have a gut feeling that you and I are basically survivors, and we have everything to survive for do we not? But in this war situation with the dominance of the Japanese in the fight to come, the odds are heavily set against me at any rate.*
>
> *So I want you to know, dearest, that I love you. I'll love you thro' eternity and one day, whether on this earth or in the next, we will be together again.*
>
> *Roger.'*

Tears came to Izolda's eyes as she read the letter. Once in her grandmother's bedroom she read it over again before putting the short note that said so much safely away in her drawer with Roger's first card. Though the letter struck a chill note of doom, it was also heartening and uplifting. Once 'yours-for-ever' had been a fantasy. Now it had come true. Whatever happened in the future nothing could take that away.

Truly, as Louise noted, the British went merrily to war. It was Wednesday 18th December and during the evening's entertainment it sounded to Louise's sensitive ears as if Dante's *Inferno* had been let loose around her.

She sat with Izolda watching Toni acting a minor part in the Amateur Dramatic Society's production of *George and Margaret* at the Jockey Club. She had come not only to see Toni (who was really looking very nice with her hair newly touched up and shining youthfully under the bright lights), but to help take Izolda's mind off impending doom. For four days since the men had got back, they'd been expecting an imminent assault. From the racket outside it would appear to have started.

The play proceeded. The theatre shook. There were gusts of nervous laughter from the audience and clapping from sticky, apprehensive palms. From time to time the voices of the actors were momentarily drowned in a crash of explosions and thunder of barrage mingling with the boom-boom of a large coastal gun. Presumably that particular gun was aimed at one of the light Japanese cruisers said to be lurking barely out of range. Louise hoped they wouldn't sink it. She remembered the beautiful ships of Admiral Togo's at the grand naval review after he'd trounced the Russians at Tsu-Shima. What Emperor Hirohito – remembered as a small shy man – thought he was doing fighting the British and the Americans she could not imagine. Too ridiculous. The Emperor Meiji would have told his grandson and that Tojo Prime Minister a thing or two! They'd lost their heads. If they stopped for a moment to think they would know perfectly well that it was the Russians and Chinese who were their enemies, and just because the Americans had joined with the Chinese Nationalists was *no excuse* for going to war.

Louise sat in the Jockey Club in her long brocade evening gown that had been made for Lady Ho Tung's party a few weeks earlier. She endured the play rather than enjoyed it as it slowly progressed in its amateurish way. Izolda was making a show of clapping heartily at the final curtain. The girl looked peaky. There had been something going on there. All that to-ing and fro-ing to her pad in Kowloon.

When the play ended, Toni came out with her makeup still on. They said goodnight to their friends, and, under a sky lurid red from the bombardment, Louise, Toni and Izolda were driven home by Ping-Li.

That night had been the last social event of free Hong Kong.

In the dark and rain, late the next evening, and when the tide was favourable, the invasion began under cover of a great pall of black smoke from oil storage tanks and a burning paint factory on North Point. Thus well screened, the Japanese troops emerged from a fleet of motor boats, ferries, lighters and sampans. They emerged out of the blackness for the first landings at Lye-mun and Taikoo.

To one side, out of reach of the coastal guns, the Japanese Navy stood silently by, each ship weighed down to the gunwales with reinforcements. And all the while, on their small craft tucked away in innumerable bays and with their escape barred from the seas, thousands upon thousands of Chinese citizens of Hong Kong sat waiting, paralysed with fear.

In streams the invasion boats came across and disgorged their men. Tin hats and bodies were covered with netting and stuffed with leaves and branches. The first parties merged and darted unstoppable and invisible to disappear into the hills.

These were crack troops and no one on the Island had seen anything like it before, for the men who had invaded the New Territories had not worn such camouflage. This lot were Lieutenant-General Sakai Takashi's 38th Division, and they were indomitable, ruthless men led by their veteran commanders, each and every one ready to die for his Emperor. By dawn they had spread right out into the hills and had reached the Wong-Nei-Chong Gap area above the Happy Valley racecourse past where Izolda and Chippy had taken the bus to Repulse Bay in 1940. The British Infantry Brigade's headquarters were situated near the Gap and those left, who had survived the heavy battering from the air, were stoically waiting for the enemy. A multitude of Japanese quickly surrounded them and took up positions to cover the landings of their troops swarming in their wake.

Throughout that night, the harbour smelling vilely of cordite explosions and burning oil, the two remaining MTBs – the remnants of the Royal Navy – fought on valiantly. Repeatedly they made their dashing attacks on the enemy craft. They machine-gunned the hundreds packed into the boats, their tracer fire showing in the dark, the bullets raking. Torn enemy craft split and sank splashing their human cargo into the water.

After each attack the MTBs retreated into the darkness, turned round and ran in again. Each attack was like a naval Charge of the Light Brigade. One MTB was gunned down and then there was only one left – Chippy's.

By now it was dawn, and once again Chippy retreated, turned round and charged into the lone attack. His manoeuvrable torpedo boat bounced through the choppy waves in a turmoil of boiling water. Half dead with tiredness, he clung on to the bridge rail. Ill and exhausted he forced his will and his boat on and into the enemy with every waning ounce of his nerve-drained strength.

"FIRE!" he shouted. "Rake them, rape, rape the bloody little bastards," he screamed into the din in a flood of strained exultation. "Bugger all you banzai-ing sons of peril. Banzai to *you*, banzai, banzai . . . hip, hip hurray; hip, hip hurray; hip, hip hurray to us. Victory, victory . . . I've done it! I've done it!" he yelled into the welter of spray over the bows. That second the bomb hit the deck and he and the boat exploded instantaneously into a ball of fire.

It tore the ship and every living thing in it into a pulp of burning, cascading, hissing fragments.

Thousands were killed, thousands more wounded. Yet still they came, the descendants of the tough seasoned troops that James Winter was so proud of in the wars of the last century when three of them had been of his own blood. They came, well camouflaged, brave, obdurate, shouldering their mortars, their grenades and their machine guns. Silently and stealthily they slipped in by night; vociferous and yelling they assaulted by day.

Yes, they came. But every inch of the ground was stubbornly fought over before the defenders of the Island fell back, destroyed what was left, fought and retreated again, laying waste to everything as they did so. Sappers blew up the ammunition on Magazine Island by the typhoon shelter next to the Royal Yacht Club, and the last man blew himself up with it. All ack-ack guns were spiked before leaving a position. Roger's battery bagged two more low-flying enemy aircraft. In the hills his Mountain Gunners humped their packs, scrounged whatever carts or animals of burden they could lay their hands on, dragged the guns over and set them up on some vantage point. They blazed away holding the enemy up for a considerable time before retreating over the mountains. Behind, in their wake, was left a trail of dead and dying.

True to their proud motto, 'Second to None', the Hong Kong Volunteers played their part alongside the regulars.

A particularly gallant but tragic episode was enacted by a small garrison left isolated at North Point between the typhoon shelter and Quarry Bay. Led by the head of Jardines, a not-so-young man with the rank of Major, they held out for several days. When they were overcome they expected to be taken prisoner – but no. All survivors, whether wounded or not, were bayonetted or shot on the spot.

Winn was more fortunate. He was cornered with a pocket of Volunteers at the China Fleet Club. Long after they were surrounded they fought on with gun or rifle. Winn dashed from window to window to fire out until there was no ammunition left. The white flag went up. There was a lull. The Japanese soldiers knelt at the ready outside, guns pointed, awaiting orders. A senior officer, with a ugly scar down one side of his face, strode in followed by some aides. Steelily his gaze shot round the still defiant ragged Volunteers holding their empty weapons.

"Pile arms," the officer shrilled in tolerable English. He barked out an order in Japanese. They were taken prisoner. It was all in the luck of the draw.

In daylight HMS *Cicala* was shelled and sunk in Lamma Channel by Deep Water Bay, and her brave one-armed captain was drowned. With all ships gone, the Royal Navy personnel remaining armed themselves as best they could and joined the fight on land. The Royal Scots fought furiously, redeeming themselves time and again for the disaster when they had given way in the New Territories. The Middlesex regiment, the Rajputs and Punjabis and all the rest fought like ten men against impossible odds.

On the night of the landings, those at The Falls wrapped themselves in rugs against the cold air. They sat on the verandahs to watch the ferruginous light from fires below reflected in the dark sky. They listened to the pounding of the guns, the screaming of shells, the distant bumps of the mortars, the crack of grenades, and the peculiar bop-bop-bop of the Bofors. They saw the smoke rising over the hills and agonised for those in the thick of it. Up on the Peak it seemed the whole of Victoria was on fire and there must be nothing left of Hong Kong on the cold and overcast day that at last dawned.

Louise had not sat out on the verandah. She'd gone to bed early. What was the point in staying up and getting cold and tired when there was nothing one could do about it? Besides, she had watched one city burning – her home town of Yokohama after the earthquake – on a warmer night than this, and further back in time she had seen the glow in the sky as a child as Atlanta burned. Surely in one lifetime that was enough for anyone to endure?

She propped herself up in bed with pillows and looked across at the dressing table to James's Star. It wasn't there! Then she remembered she'd hidden it. Why, for sure, she had put it in the safest place in the house where no stranger would ever find it. Jimmy had suggested she put the Order in the bank, but she'd told him she didn't trust *his* bank any more than the others, and how right she'd been. The Japanese were in all probability at this very moment breaking open the vaults and stealing the contents.

Louise got out her playing cards and proceeded to deal them on the board before her; her thoughts, as usual, wandered to other things. She was really rather annoyed with the Lord for having subjected her to the situation she found herself in at the end of her life, and she showed her resentment to Him – with respect naturally. She felt He could have done better than this for His faithful servant in her old age. He could have let her die quietly in bed in her sleep *before* yet another war. If He would care for a moment to think about it, she had had enough of violence in all conscience, seen the result of violence whether by man or nature. She had known the stench of death in her nostrils and she did *not* want to see it nor smell it again. Yet the Good Lord had always shown her a path to follow when disaster struck, and it had been made very clear to her that after Izolda's mother's death He had wanted her to take on the care of her granddaughter. Perhaps He had a reason for her to live on in *this* war? Perhaps even in her great old age He had more work for her to do . . .

"Nevertheless not my will, O Lord, but Thy Will be done," Louise mumbled crossly, and slapped down another card.

It was true – though she'd said it to get a rise – she *was* looking forward to speaking Japanese again! She knew the Japanese and their respect for age. Neither would they ill-treat children. Their Bushido 'way of the warrior' code was at its gentlest with children.

She was under no illusions, though, about the uneducated Japanese soldiery. She knew that when they conquered the Island – as they were bound to do – there would be no mercy for any prisoners of war whom they would despise for having given themselves up. 'Better to die with honour than live with shame', was the martial code. They themselves would rather commit *hara kiri* than suffer that disgrace.

The peasant soldier of her day, self-controlled and disciplined in battle, went to pieces in victory in a mad blood-lust stoked by the fiery saké rations that were dealt out in celebration. These peasants could turn into bestial, brutal, hysterical creatures who would murder and behead, bayonet, rape and disembowel.

Louise also knew that in the wake of this uncontrolled behaviour, some of the soldiers, if considered to have behaved to excess, would be taken out and shot. *Usually*, and there was always the exception, the Japanese officers true to their own samurai training did not allow such runaway emotions to surface. They had been trained to show *no* emotion, whether of hatred or of love. James's sons had been so trained, and she was absolutely certain that none of *them* had run amok in victory.

What concerned her at the moment was how to protect Izolda and the other young women in the house from rape, should the soldiers come rampaging in. Her only weapon was her tongue with the capacity to talk to them in their own language and so halt them in their tracks. Up to forty-eight hours after victory was the dangerous period. One could only hope to avoid their paths during that time.

Louise turned out the bedside light and settled for a few hours' uneasy sleep.

Next day Toni turned up at The Falls. She seldom had time to come now, and was never out of uniform. She was uncommunicative about her work and the wounds she dealt with. She proceeded to pay off the servants who had asked to leave, and she gave those staying – Ah Fan, Ping-Li and Fung Wan – wads of notes from the safe which she left empty. She hid the rest of the money away in the pillbox below the house.

"What for, Missie?" the servants looked at the bundles in their hands. They had never seen so much money in all their lives.

"Half for you, half you keep for Missies and young Master when wantchee money, see?" They smiled politely, not understanding, and tucked the money away.

The other families camping at The Falls became restless, found new accommodation on the Peak, and moved off.

The Holdens decided to go to the Repulse Bay Hotel where many families had taken refuge. It had defensive guns in the grounds, and there was a trained nurse in residence. Proper hotel meals were served in the dining room; they made their own electricity (the electric had been cut off at The Falls as had the water, but the telephone still functioned) and the efficient manageress, Miss Matheson, was welcoming guests and preparing for a long siege.

"We'd be better off there than sitting up here living out of the tins dear Toni has accumulated, and denuding her garden of vegetables," Joan Holden stated.

"You're right, dear," Bill agreed, "I suggest we all go, you too, Izolda. Moreover, the hotel has a bar!"

"Yes, do let's," Maisie said, "the nurse would be able to lance Tommy's boil, poor little mite, and it would be so much nearer for us to visit Hugh instead of all the way from here."

"I guess I'm not moving," declared Louise predictably. "You go, Izolda, if you want to."

"Don't be silly, Grandma."

The Holdens sewed bank notes, jewellery and packets of vitamin pills into the linings of their coats. They hugged Izolda goodbye and with waves and smiles they were off.

Next to go was Miss Maureen. But first she went down to do a recce on the town below. Within twenty-four hours she returned via the Peak tram which, amazingly, was running as normal. Visibly shaken she reported on the murder and pillage taking place in Victoria.

She had queued for hours to get a permit to visit the New Territories where she'd found the Irish monks at the Rosary Hill monastery desperate for help. Homeless neutrals were pouring into the hostel the monks had opened. She'd come back to pack her things and go there to work. With her green

Irish passport she was allowed to pass through the Japanese stop-posts. The only white people about were neutrals like herself. (There were plenty of Chinese about, and those who had married Europeans were classed as neutral also. When Izolda heard this she felt a blind rage that Chinese-born Ying Su, who had betrayed the Colony, not to mention her adopted parents, was going to get clean away with it.)

Everybody else was being arrested. The scene below was a terrible one of carnage, debris and bodies left lying in the streets. Maureen had seen a fresh company of smartly turned out Japanese troops, carrying first class equipment, marching prisoners down Des Voeux Road in Central. It was the most degrading sight she had ever seen.

"Winn was there amongst our men," she went on, "they were made to keep their hands over their heads, were spat at, kicked, herded and prodded at bayonet point. I won't tell her about *that*, but I must ring Mrs Jimmy with the news that her Winn is alive and unwounded. 'Tis terrible," she rung her hands, "niver did I think I'd live to see the likes. Winn begged me for water. But there *is* no water, not there nor anywhere in the whole of the town. Mother o' God, I shall niver forget the sight of those poor boys . . ."

Shakily Izolda, numb and white with distress, followed Miss Maureen into her bedroom upstairs and sat down on the bed to watch the her pack. Izolda took a damp handkerchief from out of her pocket and blew her nose.

She had known what Commodore Collinson was going to tell her the moment she heard his voice on the telephone that afternoon saying, "My dear . . ." And her tears for Chippy were also tears of remorse for the way she had openly betrayed him by having an affair which half of Hong Kong must have known about, including the Commodore himself.

She'd known Chippy's chances of survival were slight, and had hoped that perhaps they'd see how ill he was in time, or that he would collapse in front of them and that someone would have to take over. But to go like that so horribly . . . and yet, and yet if he had to die, that was how Chippy would have wished to go: on the bridge of his MTB, giving orders to his Petty Officer at the helm.

Yes, rather that for Chippy than coughing his heart out and spitting blood in some white hospital cot. And then too, when he'd left her on the front he had been pleased, even happy, at the prospect of becoming a family man, and had not grudged her what had happened but rather welcomed it, and indeed, should it come about, the child *would* be christened Christopher Paine-Talbot and bear his name. For truly she *had* loved Chippy, though not in the way she loved Roger, and she felt guilty about this; about marrying him for her own selfish reasons, yet he was so nice, so jolly, so kind . . . they got on so well together . . . they *had* had fun together . . . She felt awful. Her feelings were so mixed . . .

"There, there, dearie," Miss Maureen tried to comfort, embarrassed by the show of emotion.

"Did you hear anything of Roger down there?" Izolda asked, wiping her eyes.

"Major Stamford will be fighting for sure, I'm thinking. That was a brave act of his getting Captain Holden back with the enemy only a few blocks away. And you poor dear, a widow an' all at your age . . . 'tis truly terrible, is war. Thanks be to God I was born Irish. I can be of help to you and Mrs Jimmy coming and going freely as I can. Anything you need I'll get – somehow I will."

"Where were they taking Winn?"

179

"Sham-Shui-Po barracks. They're making it the prisoner-of-war camp, so I hear."

"But they *can't*, not there. I saw it. It's been bombed – twice. It's a ruin!"

Izolda learnt more from Miss Maureen. She learnt that food was already scarce for the Chinese and that there were no vegetables coming in from the New Territories. One of the biggest blows to the people was the sabotage of the huge stocks of rice that had been laid up for just such an emergency as this. On the outbreak of war the godowns were checked by the incoming rice controller, a naval officer, but he discovered that under the first and second layers of sacks of rice, the rest was stuffed with sawdust and straw.

And there was one other story which Miss Maureen told her which moved them both greatly. In the last few days of fighting, incredible scenes took place in the deserted streets of Wanchai, that centre of brothels and red lights. Here the pretty sing-song hostesses of the 'wanton' houses and massage parlours, those graceful girls who wore their gaily coloured *cheongsams* slit provocatively to thigh, had gone out into the street to give water to the men left lying wounded. Those 'Angels of Wanchai', the Lulus, Susies, Kikis and Dollys, when discovered tending the wounded, were beaten by the vanquishing soldiers. When brutally kicked off they came back to tenderly lift men's heads, give them San Miguel beer, to light up cigarettes and place them, stained with lipstick, between the soldiers' lips.

Chapter Fourteen

NOW there were only the two of them at The Falls with three faithful servants. The dining table had been returned to the small dining room, and Izolda had gone back to her room upstairs. Everything was exactly as it had been before she was married except that there was no Jimmy, no Toni, no Winn nor Ying-Su – and there was war, war, war . . .

In place of newspapers, a mimeographed foolscap sheet, delivered to the house, gave the latest information about the fighting. More Volunteers had had to surrender and they were being sent to join the Regulars at the Sham-Shui-Po prisoner of war camp. The Government had not fallen and from the tone of the newssheet did not propose to fall. Sir Mark Young sent greetings to all ranks as the festive season drew near. He encouraged them to hang on. *'In pride and admiration,'* he wrote, *'fight on. Hold fast for King and Empire!'*

Toni rang. "I'm so very sorry about Chippy," she said. "We liked him so much. It is dreadful for you. All my sympathy, Izolda dear."

"Thank you, Aunt Toni," Izolda swallowed. She still couldn't believe that she would never see Chippy again. "You've heard about Winn being taken prisoner?"

"Yes. Miss Maureen is going to try and get in touch with him. I've seen the Holdens. There's quite a crowd of women

181

and children at the Repulse Bay Hotel; sandbags, everything very cramped. The bar's been made into a casualty station with that Scots Nurse Mosey in attendance."

"Is there a hope of the hotel being defended?"

"They're doing their best with guns to the front, and there's an eight-foot drain tunnel leading down to the beach which they can use as a shelter when the bombardment starts. I'm afraid it's only a matter of time – same for all of us. The troops are gradually falling back to Stanley. We're bristling with slit trenches and guns. I'll get to you as best I can when the fighting's over."

"Have . . . have you heard anything of Roger Stamford?"

"No, dear. He's not in hospital here so I expect he's all right, unless . . ." her voice trailed away. "There's a lot of fighting still going on. Fresh batches of wounded all the time coming in. I'd better go. Be brave, dear. Goodbye for now. God bless. Give Mother my love."

"Goodbye, Aunt Toni. Take care." Izolda had gone cold at her aunt's 'unless'.

It was just as well Louise had refused to budge from The Falls. The Repulse Bay Hotel, symbol to the populace of gracious living, and to Izolda the scene of an idyllic time with Roger, soon came under siege. The defensive guns made it the focus of attack. Japanese forces surrounded the hotel and isolated it while their main thrusts passed on towards the Stanley Peninsular and the Chung-Hom-Wan Peninsular to the west.

Meanwhile the hotel was filled with five to fifteen people in every room, and more wounded were constantly being brought in to Nurse Mosey. The place soon became untenable and many people wanted to depart. Maisie, one of them, rued the day she'd ever left The Falls. A message was passed to the forces, and a sortie to break through the cordon successfully held the Japanese off for long enough to allow those who wanted to leave to go. On the coastal road, shortly after, the whole wandering lot were rounded up and taken prisoner. Maisie and Tommy were among them.

Bill Holden was one of the few who refused to leave the hotel, and Joan, torn between husband and daughter-in-law, stayed with him. Elderly, white-haired Nurse Mosey also stayed to tend the badly wounded who could not be moved. They fought on, this small band of elderly men and one or two women. Bill found an old archery set in the basement, and with glee set the arrows alight and fired them flaming into the terraces where the enemy lurked.

It was a defiant bit of bravado which scarcely postponed the hour when the white flag would have to be raised. Astonishingly the telephone was still connected (though by now it had gone dead at The Falls), and the beleaguered group at the hotel felt well rewarded when they received a Christmas greeting over the line from General Maltby at Fortress HQ: '*Let this day be historical in the grand annals of our Empire. The order of the day is HOLD FAST!*'

Now there was no telephone link at The Falls; now there was no mimeographed news-sheet; now all Izolda and Louise had to go on for information was the unceasing background noise of aerial bombardment, the shelling, the mortar fire with the crunches, crumps and bumps. But nothing worse happened at The Falls than pieces of shrapnel dropping into the garden. It set fire to some bushes, which Ping-Li promptly put out with buckets of water from the stream.

Tired dejected Canadian troops carrying Thompson sub-machine guns came down the drive to ask if they could fill their water bottles. Louise and Izolda welcomed them in and gave them food and drink.

"What's happening? How far have the Japanese got?"

"More than half the Island's in their hands, Ma'am," said a gaunt young officer who couldn't have been more than twenty years old. "They've driven a wedge between the East and West Brigades and are mopping up everywhere. We've just passed across Mount Cameron, abandoning it. The Reservoir was captured after one heck of a fight. Yes, there are some families staying on up there. We told them to take their pick of our stores before the Japs catch up."

More days passed to Izolda's growing frustration. Unable to bear the suspense of not knowing what had happened to Roger any longer, Izolda made up her mind to descend to the coast and investigate for herself. She would not get into any trouble; she would take care not to be seen. She would keep to the paths criss-crossing the hillsides of the Peak she knew so well from her Hash Harrier days. She knew every inch of those tracks which no one else used – and certainly not the Japanese. Down nearer the coast she would meet some of their own troops, some gunners perhaps who could tell her about Roger. She'd go soon. But she would first spend Christmas day with her grandmother looking at the presents for the family left by Toni in the drawing room by a decorated Christmas tree.

When Izolda told her grandmother what she proposed to do, Louise said nothing. The old lady just looked at her granddaughter from under her bushy eyebrows and let her go.

Wearing a short-sleeved shirt and a thick cardigan against the morning chill, together with her running slacks and her Hash Harrier ankle-high plimsoll boots, Izolda set forth on what turned out to be the longest day of her life. Slung across her chest was a flask of water, and round her waist was her

Harrier pouch which contained some sandwiches, a banana and a purse with money.

Avoiding the road, Izolda walked up and over the narrow hilltops towards Mount Kellett. Keeping along the ridges she began to scramble down the tracks in the direction of Aberdeen and Wong Chuk Hang. She decided to aim first for the golf course in Deep Water Bay. Surely down there in the Club or near the road, she would come across some of their own men dug in? She would stay in hiding until absolutely certain the land was clear before approaching them.

It was a balmy day, and there was no sign of the ugly black smoke clouds that had menaced the skies for so long. With the sun rising high, Izolda stripped off her cardigan and tied it round her waist, leaving her arms bare to the sun. Every now and then she heard an isolated outburst of machine-gun fire, but the big guns stayed silent. She failed entirely to grasp the significance of the unaccustomed quiet, and naïvely enjoyed the stillness after the continuous noise of the last eighteen days.

After she'd covered nearly three miles of hard going over rough rocky ground where the tracks continually petered out, Izolda sat down to rest. She lay back in a hollow of straggling grass and listened to the twittering of the birds. It struck her how much she'd missed the normal sounds of nature in the days and nights of incessant gunfire, and thought how lovely it was to be out alone on the tracks in the freedom of the beautiful hills after having been incarcerated in the grounds of The Falls for so long. Lazily she watched a flock of blue birds with orange beaks flying into the branches of a flame-of-the-forest tree. As she lay quietly, a cluster of butterflies flew near and landed fluttering and fanning their delicate wings on a myrtle bush inches from her face.

Sitting up she munched a sandwich, took a swig at the

water bottle and thought how much she would miss Chippy and not having him to care for. She wondered what she ought to do about the flat. Though she'd brought most of her own things up to The Falls, all their wedding presents and household belongings were still down there. It had been her first married home and in spite of everything, once she had got over the initial shock of his death, she felt better about having married Chippy. Now there was Roger, and soon, God willing, she would hear that he was well, and soon too it would be time for her next period – and then she would be sure. A flood of happiness filled her at the thought of bearing Roger's child.

For a little while longer Izolda basked in the warmth of the sun, and let her thoughts wander on the joy of what life would be like with Roger. Then she got up and went on and down towards the coast.

Coming out from a thick undergrowth of bushes, she was surprised to find herself just above the coastal road. She had misjudged the distance, but to her left she could see the contours in which the Country Club lay, and she turned back to make her way up to follow the line of the road further above it. At that moment she heard the sound of an approaching lorry, and she made a dive behind the nearest bush – a thin one. She squatted behind its inadequacy and crouched low.

A truck full of soldiers passed; then, a few yards on, braked. The truck came to a scraping halt. It reversed. With a horrified glance, Izolda took in that they were Japanese and that she had been spotted. Taking to her heels she ran uphill.

Not daring to look round, she heard shouts and sounds of the chase behind her. Nimbly she climbed on in her pliable boots and began to outdistance them. She heard the crack of shots and the whistle of a bullet that passed uncomfortably near. Jinking jerkily in an attempt to avoid the fire, she tripped and fell headlong. Scrambling to her knees she saw that one soldier had nearly caught up. Before she could take more than a couple of steps he was upon her. The next thing she knew she was lying on the ground with the man standing over her holding a bayonet to her throat.

Too frightened to scream she lay there on her back looking up at him. He was the first Japanese soldier she had ever seen. He was one of her grandmother's precious Japanese! He was a little man who would barely come up to her shoulder. He wore a peaked cap and was as dirt-splashed and battle-grimed as Roger had been. He had stiff hairbrush black hair and a bull-like neck, and his mouth was wide open screeching furiously and incomprehensively at her. She could feel the point of the glinting blade on her clavicle . . .

It was the same horrifying moment in the taxi with the white slave abductors all over again. The same mental shock of horror with the disbelief that it could really be happening. But it *was* true, and this nightmare was a far, far worse one.

Viciously, the soldier kicked her. He booted her with his hard little boots in the pit of her stomach. She rolled up like a tortured insect into a ball in an endeavour to protect herself from those cruel boots that kicked on, now into the side of her squirming body. With her cheek pressed into the earth she crossed her arms before her, terrified that the kicks and prods from the rifle butt would bruise her breasts.

A great deal of shouting went on. Other soldiers stood by watching, their rifles pointed and held at the ready. One of them came forwards, pulled her roughly to her feet and with his spare hand slapped her face with force: left-right; left-right; left-right. *'No, no, no, please don't,'* her mind screamed as she had in her childhood when the nurse at the Parsonage had beaten her, *'I haven't done anything wrong; not on purpose. Don't, don't . . .'* but no sounds came out, only a heaving sob from a burstingly tight chest that could not breathe for the agony of her ribs. Red rashes on a face . . . weals on a child's body . . .

Jabbing at her with their bayonets, they butted and hustled her down the hill. Other soldiers seated in the truck, dragged her by the arms into the back; the ones who had been with her leapt in. The truck accelerated away. They pulled at her and snatched off her watch, her engagement ring and wedding ring. They confiscated her water bottle, looked into her pouch, emptied it, took her purse and then sat stoney-faced munching her sandwiches. The man who had kicked her ate her banana. They ignored her.

They came upon a crowd of about two hundred European women, children and elderly men who carried suitcases, boxes and bundles. The group straggled along the road guarded by a phalanx of soldiers. Unceremoniously Izolda was tipped out of the truck to join them. Her empty bag and her cardigan were thrown out after her. Automatically she bent to pick them up. A pain stabbed her agonisingly in the side as she stooped. She stayed bent double, unable to move or for the moment breathe for the pain.

"Hold on," a grey-haired man came up to support her figure. "What have they done to you? Are you badly hurt?" Oh, the bliss of hearing that elderly Englishman's concern. Incapable of speaking, Izolda shook her head and managed to straighten herself. She took the jersey and the bag from him and gingerly felt her jaw.

"Good God, if it isn't Izolda!" exclaimed a familiar

voice, and Bill Holden, carrying a heavy suitcase, crossed the road to her. "What on earth are you doing down here?"

"My dear; oh, your face," Joan came over and put an arm round her.

"Devilish monkeys, hitting women," scowled Bill, purple with fury.

"I . . . came down to see. Where's . . . everyone going?"

"We don't know. We were rounded up at the hotel after we showed the white flag. They seem to be bent on taking us somewhere in a hurry."

"Speed-ō, speed-ō," yelled the guards. "Quickli, quickli, march-ō, speed-ō, *Yi-ko!*"

Was it really happening on the dusty road? Had that bestial soldier really stood over her, kicked her, and the other one slapped her with all his force? Was it a nightmare from which she would wake screaming? One heard about things like this happening to other people, those people in the scenes Miss Maureen had described in the town. It was the sort of thing that happened to people one read about, but not to oneself.

"Can you walk, dear? We'd better get on with the others," Joan asked solicitously.

Izolda moved off slowly in the wake of the crowd. The pain in her side, her stinging face, the shouts from the guards with their '*Oi-ni, yi-ko*, speed-os,' told her that this was no nightmare. This was a living terror that had happened – was happening – to her, Izolda Richardson, Zol Paine-Talbot, Roger's girl . . . What did '*Oi-ni*', and '*yi-ko*' mean? "What does it mean?" she asked Bill.

"Something bloody rude, I bet. They're in a goddamned hurry to get us somewhere."

But there was little the Japanese soldiers could do to hurry the mixed company from the very young to the very old shuffling along the road, some of whom had gone through the siege at the Repulse Bay Hotel.

"Have you . . . heard how Hugh is?" Izolda panted shallowly beside the Holdens.

"We went to see him after Dr Black had performed the second operation. He was doing well. Your aunt is the sister in charge of his ward. We feel he could not be in better hands."

"I suppose . . . you haven't heard anything . . . of Roger Stamford?" Izolda asked with hesitation.

"As a matter of fact I have. We were told that he and his Mountain Gunners had taken up positions on the approaches to Stanley."

Izolda gasped. She needed to take a deep breath but found she could not. Her sortie had been worth it. She had found out that Roger was down on the Stanley Peninsular round the next Bay, no distance away from her!

"From the sound of it," Bill Holden was mumbling on, "there's been a general ceasefire. They're rounding up everyone, all over the Peak too."

"Oh God – Grandma." Izolda's relief at the news of Roger turned to one of remorse that she had ever left her grandmother.

They trudged on, going where? Izolda, with her new knowledge that Roger had survived, kept on thinking how furious he would be with her for coming down and getting herself caught so stupidly and needlessly. *'Don't be a bloody ass and put yourself in the front line again,'* he had said in Kowloon. He would also be furious with her for leaving her grandmother.

The batch of civilian prisoners, which included Izolda, who

were being herded along the dusty road, knew next to nothing of what had happened during the last few days. They did not know where they were going, nor why, nor what the insane hurry was about. But they knew only too well that in the few moments of their arrests, their lives had suddenly changed from being free citizens, the white top dogs in the Colony, to being despised prisoners. Now the fierce green-clad soldiers, whose language they could not understand, were in control.

What this latest batch of prisoners also did not know was that, early on Christmas morning, the last stubborn defensive stand on the Stanley Peninsular neck was breached and the Japanese troops had burst through. Trigger-happy and mad with victory they exploded into the promontory Roger and Izolda had once blithely sailed around. They besieged the buildings and proceeded to dash from one building to the other in an orgy of killing.

The Red Cross flag was flying prominently from the Stanley emergency hospital. Dr Black, on seeing from the windows of the Boys College that the game was up, prepared to confront the Japanese. White-coated, he stepped out of the main portal and walked towards them with a hand up as if to bar their way.

"Halt, this is a hospital," he bravely faced them.

They shot him where he stood and stopped for a moment to bayonet his body repeatedly as he lay there on the ground. Then they went berserk. With the tide of killing let loose, they went rampaging on into the hospital. On the ground floor they killed everyone in sight including the wounded men lying in their beds, the red surge of bloodlust carrying them on.

From the screams, the wounded upstairs guessed what was happening. Some crawled under beds or into cupboards.

Some tried to lock themselves into lavatories. Many were too ill to move.

Hugh Holden's bed was by a window. He levered himself up, opened it, and in the moment before his ward was invaded, threw himself out to fall onto his side into the dug flowerbed beneath. He could feel his stitches bursting as he landed. For a while he lay winded and in agony. He crawled towards some cover where he blacked out; then, recovering somewhat, he slithered on painfully.

Like a slow damaged lizard he writhed his way on his stomach inch by inch towards the sea, dragging his useless leg behind him. Only he knew what it cost him in human effort to get to the water, hide among the rocks, fix a makeshift tourniquet from his pyjama cord on his leg and in the dark swim down the bay to the nearest shore, trailing blood and unable to do more than splash feebly with his hands at lurking sharks, sensed rather than seen, and drawn in by his blood. He managed to beach himself before fainting. When he came to he crawled a little further up before passing out again. In the first light he was seen by a passing truck full of Chinamen. They picked him up, put him in a sampan and took him more dead than alive to the Convent of St Teresa's Hospital in Kowloon.

Back in Stanley hospital, where the disembowelled corpses littered the wards, a worse horror was being perpetrated by a section of troops drunk on liquor and led by a saké-inflamed lieutenant. He collected eleven nurses, some British – Toni among them – some Chinese. He shut them in a small room and systematically, during the rest of that night and all through Boxing Day, together with a sergeant and some others, took out one nurse at a time and proceeded to rape each one repeatedly.

One of the British officers waiting by the Fort to be

disarmed, on hearing that his fiancée had been raped in the hospital, went out with a revolver in each hand and shot dead eight Japanese soldiers before he succumbed to a barrage of fire. Another man seized two tommy-guns and went out into the open firing from the hips straight into the victorious enemy and mowing down many men before he too was killed. But neither they nor any of those wounded who were still alive in the hospital, nor the doctors and nurses who had survived, could do anything to stop the atrocity being perpetuated in their midst. Helplessly they listened through the night and the day to the screams of the nurses that ended in mutilation when limp used bodies were discarded like butcher's carcasses into a corner.

Toni, outwardly calm and inwardly resolute, waited all night and well into the next morning locked in with the dwindling other nurses. She had plenty of time to think.

When her turn came and she was paraded before the drunken sergeant, Antonia Winter, Jimmy's dearly loved wife, did as her husband had bidden her. Before his departure to China he had bought her a pistol and made her practise firing it. Now swiftly and deliberately she drew her pistol from under her uniform apron. To the astonishment of his half-focusing eyes, the sergeant saw the small weapon being steadily levelled at him. Before his befuddled brain could barely grasp its meaning, Toni pulled the trigger and shot him stone dead between the eyes. Within seconds the other soldiers lashed out at her. They slashed her to ribbons and threw her body onto the bloody heap of the other nurses in their stained white uniforms. Her peroxided hair stood out shining brightly like a ray of sun in the grizzly pile of bodies.

But the raping stopped.

* * *

None of this was known to the batch of civilian prisoners as they were herded and hurried up the hill by Repulse Bay. They were shouted at and prodded, and perhaps it was just as well that the horrors of what had happened seeped through to them only afterwards, and gradually at that, for to have known it all at once would have been too much to bear. They only knew that the fearsome shock troops in their baggy breeches, puttees and peaked caps, their daggers swaying at their sides and their lethal bayonets fixed, had been all through the Island and were now in a frenzy of elation at their astonishingly quick victory.

As she rounded a corner, Izolda recognised where they were going. They were being led to Eu-Cliffe Castle, an ivy-covered, turretted, grey mansion which she had once visited with her uncle and aunt soon after her arrival in Hong Kong. The vast crenellated castle, situated on a cliff, had been built by a Chinese millionaire. And there the crowd of tired men, women and children were made to stand out in the open and watch fifty British soldiers and officers lined up and executed for no reason other than they were the surrendered enemy. In the sunshine they watched the terrible sight of their bound men being beheaded, some bayonetted, others shot, and their bodies kicked like dogs over the cliff. Women sobbed, some cried hysterically, others fainted. Children screamed and clung terrified to their mothers who tried to hide their faces in their skirts. Old men who had fought in their own war of barbed wire, gas, mud and blood, and had never seen anything like this, stared rheumy-eyed. Bill Holden cursed and damned under his breath; he swore, vilified and raged as he had never raged before.

Izolda, who ran away from the sight of blood in case she should be frightened by it, stood rooted to the ground staring at Roger. He did not look her way nor see her. He stood there hatless, begrimed, ribbons colourful on the breast of his bush jacket, identity disc swinging out. He stood there head and shoulders above the rest, rigid, alert, hands tied behind his back, and right on the edge of the precipice.

In the second before the volley rang out, Izolda saw him turn his head a fraction before his body tumbled over the cliff. Then the world whirled round her and she sank to her knees in the dust, a hot bitter gorge rising in her throat. In physical and mental anguish she knelt on the grass and vomited . . . and vomited.

They were shouted at, prodded and ordered to start marching again. They left the site of the massacre behind with nothing to show for it except the blood-stained grass; and all the fifty bodies were out of sight over the cliff. The road wound up towards the mountain pass, the sun high, the sea blue below. It was still a lovely day, and hot in the afternoon, and it was still the same day that Izolda had started out to find Roger. The scene of green hillsides belied the awfulness of the things that were happening. There were two separate worlds: one could be seen in the beautiful, serene and God-made view; the other was hideous, bestial and man-made. How could these two worlds be one and the same? How could such terrible things happen amid such beauty?

The sun burned on their backs as the civilians struggled on. They had no water. They became parched with thirst. Izolda's tongue felt like a bolster in her mouth. She tried to raise saliva and found nothing to swallow. Her lips cracked when she licked them and she thought longingly of the rill at the Falls.

The mothers begged the guards, whose water bottles were full, for a drink for their children. But they were given none –

the Japanese who loved children? The children cried tiredly and the toddlers were passed in turn by hand among the crowd to give the mothers a rest. And thus in some small way they helped themselves.

Walking in a daze beside puce-faced and still-cursing Bill Holden who looked fit to burst, and flagging Joan whose blue rinse was running down her face with sweat, Izolda found a baby thrust into her arms. She held the child for a while until she was forced to hand him on for the pain in her ribs. But the infant brought a glint of light through the darkness of her despair.

A child was the only hope she had left, now that Roger was dead.

Chapter Fifteen

THE dispirited and shocked column of those who had been made to watch the Eu-Cliffe massacre, slowly progressed in a straggle up to higher ground. Here the land had been bitterly fought over and the sweet-acrid smell of death lay heavy on the air. The crumpled corpses of vanquished soldiers had been left there for days. They lay as they had died on the hillsides.

The Japanese had ordered parties out to remove the bodies of their own soldiers for cremation before sending the ashes back home in little boxes bound in white cloth. But the bodies of the white men and the Indians – they were left to rot. They rotted everywhere: in the gardens of deserted houses and among the crimson flowering poinsettia hedges, each red petal a pointed gout of blood. They rotted on the roadsides, and in the bushes. Flies buzzed busily on contorted faces. Clouds of bluebottles gorged on the bloated carcasses of mules; ants massed over foul-smelling horses; carrion birds sailed overhead and landed to tear at flesh in ghoulish groups; burnt-out trucks littered the road; spiked guns lay overturned. Hilly Victoria Island had become a monstrous midden.

The pathetic procession of men, women and children stupefied with horror by what they had seen and saw, and terrified of what would happen to them next, shambled on. With their burdens they struggled up to the top of Wong-Nei-Chong Gap from where they could see the fires burning in the city below and could smell the fumes of gaseous odour mingling with the unmistakable scent of decomposition.

They began the descent and stumbled on down past the cemetery above the green horseshoe of the Happy Valley racecourse, and Izolda remembered how she and Chippy had laughed light-heartedly at the drunken angles of the old white gravestones. Now she knew what lay under them; what decaying bodies looked like; now she knew about spilled blood and the real hideousness of slaughter as well as the terror of violent death.

Down in the town the Chinese inhabitants lined the pavements before their gutted shops to watch the extraordinary sight of their erstwhile Masters and Missies floundering past like a gang of coolies. Those for whom they had fetched and carried, cooked, cleaned and sometimes slaved, obedient and docile to their every wish, were now lumping heavy suitcases, humping bundles of bedding and clothing, and carrying their own children. They watched the white people limping past with shoes covered in dust, clothes badly soiled, and their faces shiny with sweat.

At first the Chinese spectators were silent, even awed, at the sight. Then one among them shouted abuse in Cantonese, and within seconds the crowd caught on to revile the Europeans. They screamed and spat at them, the hatred and venom in their voices showing the resentment that had long lain deep in their hearts. Someone threw a soft mango at Izolda which split and splodged her shirt; others copied, and the Chinese children, aping their elders, set to with glee to sling anything to hand.

For the first time in her life Izolda experienced and tasted the hopeless conditions of the underprivileged poor. Now she perceived how pent-up passions and subdued human rage could suddenly be let loose like this to catch on as if it were an infectious disease. She knew that her squint-eyed boy would be one of the most vicious. Dog bites dog – white dog.

In that six-hour gruelling and agonisingly slow march under the blistering heat of the sun, some of the old dropped by the wayside to be picked up later in trucks by the Japanese. Those that could, plodded on; Izolda with them.

They were taken to a downtown low-grade block known grandly as the Dragon Hotel and used to house Chinese and Indian travellers. There they were crammed into a main room where the women were relieved of any valuables they still had on them, while fountain pens and pocket-knives were confiscated from the men. Then they were made to stand, and were given a pep talk.

"Our soldiers will plotect you," they were informed by an officer who spoke with an American accent. "Ya, soon you go Plison Camp. OK? Vely happy time there for womens and childrens. No trouble if you good. If you good you healthy and happy. OK. You bow to Japanese now." They all bowed. "Lower, more low to Japanese officer!" They complied again at fifteen degrees, feeling foolish. It would have been funny if it had not been so fraught. One teenager who dared to snigger was immediately slapped.

"Please can we have some water and some food for the children?" Izolda spoke up, angry that they could hit a child.

"Food come soon," the officer turned his pin-small eyes upon Izolda's swollen face and the red bruises which were rapidly turning yellow and blue. "You beaten – ya?" he observed. "You bad womans, ya. I get water childrens now."

The water came in small drinking amounts, but they were given no food. It grew dark and there was no electricity. A few candles were produced to gutter in tin containers.

The sexes were segregated and herded into roughly cubicled rooms with layered cots in tiers, and only enough of them for an eighth of their number. There was a concerted scramble to bag a bed. Izolda and Joan Holden did not bother. Joan was too weary to fight for one, and Izolda was too sore. They settled for the floor. Izolda put on her cardigan to stop the fit of shivering that had set in. She stuffed her canvas bag with newspaper for a pillow, wrapped herself in a blanket Bill Holden had handed to her and lay down on the dirty tick-infected floor.

But there was no sleep for her that night. Her ribs were an agony with every breath she drew. She could find no comfort or rest on the hard boards, and the massacre was always before her, scalding her eyes with the torture of seeing Roger's profile clear against the backdrop before the shots rang out and he fell.

She found she needed to go to the lavatory. Other people were going too. It soon became a sickening business. In the overcrowded 'hotel' in which they were incarcerated, the few European lavatory pans quickly ran over with the floating excrement of frightened people – and there was no water with which to flush the toilets.

"I've got diarrhoea," Izolda said on coming back after a third session to lie down beside Joan. "It must be the water we were given."

In minutes she was up again. She sat, doubled up with stomach pains, on the pan. Other people's faeces splashed her backside, and her plimsolls became soaked in the overflowing filth. With her handkerchief to her nose she sat on purging and scouring and all but fainting. For the best part of an hour she sat there in the worst pain and misery she had ever experienced. She thought she was dying and she wanted to die.

When Izolda did not return, Joan went along to see what was happening. She spoke to her through the shut door.

"No, I'm not all right," Izolda said, the agony in her voice, "I've got the curse – very badly. I haven't got anything. Can you . . . ?"

"I'll see, dear. There's a sheet or towel somewhere."

Izolda cleaned herself as best she could with newspaper and returned to her place on the floor.

"Better, dear?" Joan enquired anxiously.

"No, not better. I'll never be better." She took the towel, and hid her swollen face under the blanket in the depths of her misery.

Next day Izolda could scarcely move for stiffness. Someone gave up their cot and she spent the day there with her face to the wall. Many others developed diarrhoea. The latrines were unusable, yet they had to be used for lack of anywhere else, and the filth flowed out into the passages. The whole building stank from one end to the other. Children cried with hunger and all found themselves covered in huge bites from ticks and bedbugs.

On the third day, exactly forty-four hours after capture, the prisoners were given their first meal of a few spoonfuls of rice and beans. Many, like Izolda who had been picked up on the road, had no plates or implements and had to eat the food with their unwashed hands. Izolda was surprised that she could feel hunger in her physical and mental agony, but she found herself wolfing her meagre ration down.

Later that day the American-speaking officer lined them up again and issued selected persons with passes for the morrow. On each pass was written: *'Please allow to go home'*. Instructions were given, to those who, like Izolda, had been picked up without possessions, that they could collect bedding and clothes and other household goods in suitcases and return before nightfall when their passes would run out. If they did not return, when picked up again they would be shot. *'It was difficult, they must understand, for the Japanese Army to provide for the needs of so many all at once. They must cooperate to be happy, ya!'*

It brought the first smile to the ashen faces of the prisoners in the heavily guared, burstingly full and stinking Dragon Hotel. Good! The conquerors were experiencing difficulties, were they? And in letting some of them go temporarily, did the Japanese soldier have a heart after all?

Next day, clutching her pass and with no intention of ever going back to the loathsome Dragon Hotel, Izolda slipped furtively through the deserted downtown area to Victoria Central. She found it a relief to walk, her stiffness easing a little with the movement. Gingerly she picked her way through telegraph wires draped in the roads and over craters where tramlines ran drunkenly. Buildings on every side were pitted with bomb scars, and there were many bodies lying in the streets.

Whenever she saw a soldier, Izolda slunk into the nearest doorway frightened that her pass would be insufficient to stop her from being rounded up once more, and beaten up again or even butchered on the spot. How many Japanese soldiers could read, *'Please allow to go home'*? Hardly one.

The Japanese flag – known as the *Hi-no-maru* or 'Roundness of the Sun' – was draped from nearly every building. With an air of expectation people in Central were hanging out of windows.

On hearing the blare of a brass band and the clatter of hooves, Izolda hastily tucked herself into an alleyway. She peered out. Along broad Queen's Road emerged a historical sight which even she in her fear and loathing of the enemy could not fail to admire. Down the wide road came a triumphant cavalcade towards the Commander of the Forces. It came towards Lieutenant-General Sakai Takashi at a saluting base. On Izolda's side of the street and to the Divisional Commander leading the cavalcade's right, rode an impressive Colonel on a thoroughbred with a distinguishing white flash on its tossing head. Izolda could not take her eyes off the officer, rivetted as she was by the hideousness of the disfiguring scar down his face. Rows of medals jangled on his chest; holsters bulged on either side of his saddle; his hands were neatly gloved, and his leather boots shone with high polish. He gave the grand salute excessively smartly as he passed the base.

Behind him clanked a phalanx of riders in their peaked caps with star at the centre. They were fine looking, well turned out men on glisteningly groomed horses. No bespectacled pygmies here, no sakédrunk peasants, but cavalrymen of the highest order, all proud and tall in their bearing. What *were* they made of, these enigmatic Japanese her grandmother loved, Izolda wondered. Men who one moment could be brutal and bestial, the next moment indifferent and uncaring, men who lived by their Bushido code, who willingly died for their Emperor and only days after fighting and winning the bloodiest of wars could turn out looking like this? Were they honourable or despicable? She did not want to know *what* they were, not after what they had done . . .

Izolda turned away to walk on slowly up through the Botanical Gardens she had so often run down on her way to join the family at Mickey's Kitchen. She found more suffering in the gardens. The exotic caged birds lay in heaps gasping and dying from lack of water. Water was imperative for survival, and in a kind of mirage dream Izolda convinced herself that she would find water in the Macdonnell flat. There she would wash, discover something to eat; rest before going on her way.

But on climbing the unswept stairs, and seeing the door to hers and Chippy's flat swinging open, she grasped that her conviction was but a delusion and that there would be nothing for her there. The door hung drunkenly on one hinge in creaking desolation that led to rooms ransacked and divested. There were pieces of broken crockery she recognised lying on an uncarpeted floor among the shattered debris of broken panes. The kitchen and bathrooms were stripped bare of fittings – even the lavatory pan and cistern had gone – and there was not a drop of water from the holes where taps had been.

She went out on to the verandah and recalled that her mother had stood there one evening in 1912. In her weakness Izolda felt the presence of her mother flooding round her, for it was when standing there that Camille had had a vision within her of the growth of Hong Kong's tall buildings and of a menace from on high. Her mother had looked up in fear at the dark sky to see only tranquillity and the shining beauty of the evening star leading her on to her own stardom.

Taking comfort at the strange mystic story her grandmother had related, a story which somehow encompassed herself, Izolda went on to Mid-Levels, where she left the road to take to the slopes of the Peak and made her way up the steep, barely defined trails she used to follow when she was young. She panted shallowly as she went, and frequently had to pause. For a while, until her breathing eased, she looked out at the smoke rising in the town and saw beyond it the sea with little islands floating in calm waters, unaffected and unperturbed by barbarous acts of war. And she looked up at the mountain riding above her and despaired that she could ever reach the top.

Once again Izolda dragged herself to her feet and went on up, automatically following the familiar tracks, checking every now and then and taking her bearings from the contours of the ridges. Respiration became a hoarse gasp through her throat and her heart hammered in chest and temples like a drum beating through her body. Utterly exhausted, her clothes filthy and torn, she staggered up the last lap to breast the hill and traverse the slope of the approach to The Falls from below.

On the lower terraces Izolda passed the dug-out which was so well hidden she had to look twice to make sure it was still there. She looked up to find the big house with its turquoise curved imperial roof above her, its red carved dragons leering out from under the eaves, its encircling verandahs high and shaded from the sun; and she could just glimpse the red and green pagoda-arched gateway up behind. No war up here. Nothing had changed. Would she wake up in her little room on the second floor of The Falls and find it had all been a horrible nightmare?

In near delirium, Izolda heard the echo of a jocular voice – Jimmy's. It whispered to her on the wind the words he had uttered on the day of her arrival: *'Yes, my dear, it's a great house, sturdy enough to withstand an invasion – even that of a mother and niece!'*

And there it stood basking in the evening sun, its verandahs garlanded with red and mauve bougainvillaea. It stood firm as it had for forty-two years in its peaceful setting, untouched among the palm trees and shrubberies.

The green grass was cut, the beds tended and bright with flowers. The rill splashed through the property in a soothing, refreshing welcome.

All was very quiet. There was only the fluttering of wings as birds came down to roost in the lengthening shadows, and the gentle splash of blessed running water. Izolda turned the handle and pushed open the heavy front door. She dragged herself up the wide shallow marble stairs by holding on to the wrought-iron bannisters for support. On the landing she glanced at the antique opium couch and at the portrait of the Chinese mandarin in his brocaded robes, glad to see that he was still there; and she entered the serene drawing room with its crimson curtains, blackwood furniture and Tientsin carpets. Everything was in place as she had last seen it. Fresh flowers were arranged in bowls. Had time stood still?

Framed in the open door sat her grandmother in her familiar chair in the large blue bedroom with its tiled bathroom behind. She was crocheting, and the piece was no longer a narrow strip but wider and twice the size Izolda had last seen it. Louise's gold-rimmed spectacles rested low on her nose. She looked up at her granddaughter over them, and her lower lip trembled slightly.

"What are you making?" Izolda asked from the doorway.

"A baby shawl . . ."

"Roger's dead." The words came out huskily, "I saw him shot in a massacre of our men at Eu-Cliffe Castle after I was captured. No Roger; no Chippy; no anything . . . there is nothing left . . ." And she went up to her grandmother, knelt down and put her head in her lap and wept – dry sobs hurtfully shaking her wracked body.

Louise dropped her crochet and gently stroked her granddaughter's tangled hair.

Chapter Sixteen

DAYS later, after Izolda had bathed in the great marble bath with heated water Ping-Li carried up in cans; after Ah Fan had felt her ribs and said they were probably cracked but she would strap them up with wide sticking plaster; after she'd eaten her first meal since that fateful day; after she'd drunk some of her grandmother's brandy and slept deeply for twelve hours, Louise told her of Toni's brave and appalling end.

For a silent while Izolda assimilated this terrible news, the full horror slowly sinking in. It was worse than anything she had conceived. It was not only men who were massacred but women too. The Japanese were utterly bestial.

"I suppose Hugh was killed with the other wounded?" Izolda said at last. She expected to hear that Maisie was going through the same agony as she.

"Praise the Lord, no. Somehow he escaped from the hospital at Stanley." The crochet in Louise's hand trembled at the scene that place envisaged. "Miss Maureen found him at the St Teresa's Convent hospital. Maisie is also in Kowloon. Hearing the Yankees were being put into better quarters than the British, she tagged along with them."

"Who told you about Aunt Toni?"

"The servants first; they make a good grapevine for news; I guess most of it reliable. On this occasion I hoped beyond hope it was unfounded rumour . . . But Miss Maureen later confirmed it was only too true."

"Will someone tell Uncle Jimmy?"

"I expect he'll hear through the usual channels. Poor dear Jimmy, he'll take it mighty badly," Louise shook her white head. "I had a message from Ying-Su . . ."

"You've heard from Ying-Su? She's supposed to have gone to ground with the Japanese. What does she think of her precious allies now that they've murdered her adoptive mother? You're to blame too, Grandma. Teaching her the language like that to betray secrets," Izolda stormed, her jealousy of Ying-Su still rankling. "Well, what did she have to say?"

"None of your business, Izolda. I'm not telling after that outburst," Louise replied sharply. "I guess there's no need for you to stand judgment on something you know nothing about." Louise changed the subject, "There are quite a few families still living in the houses on the higher Peak, so Ah Fan tells me. Several have had Japanese troops callithumping round—"

"What's that mean?" Izolda said suspiciously. What had Ying-Su got in touch with her grandmother for? To send her a word of sympathy over Aunt Toni? If so, the double-crossing . . .

"—it's a term for goin' on the razzle-dazzle. You know I've got an American passport?"

"You've told me that a hundred times."

"No need to be rude." Nevertheless Louise was glad to see life returning to her granddaughter. The child had not spoken at all the first few days after her return to The Falls. She had been in deep shock. "Maybe I'll copy Maisie and use my American passport," Louise went on. "As I was saying, the longer the soldiers *don't* come the better. By now they should have calmed down from their victory muss, though they're bound to arrive sometime. *You* needn't worry," Louise said, seeing Izolda blanche, "I shall talk to them. I told you how I'm looking forward to that. I'll persuade them to allow us to remain here, you'll see."

Louise boasted to cover up the acute sense of isolation she'd felt on the Peak after Izolda had gone off, when, all alone, she heard of Toni's terrible end. With Winn a prisoner she felt it was now her responsibility to keep the house going for Jimmy to come back to – a tall order for a woman of her advanced age especially when it would in all probability take years to restore the status quo. And she had come east to slough off responsibilities . . .

"It's real bad of you, Lord," Izolda heard her grandmother muttering to herself.

Not many days later and true to Louise's prophecy, a whole posse of Japanese soldiers arrived at The Falls. In half a dozen trucks they swept through the temple gates and down the drive, disgorged from their vehicles, and with yells and shouts swarmed round the mansion and the tennis court to take up defensive positions. Each man bristled with weapons. Two non-commissioned officers burst their way into the unlocked house.

"Quick, go and shut yourself in my bathroom." Louise heard the noise from her bedroom. "I'll tell them my granddaughter is living here if they ask. They will think you are a child. Hurry!" Louise ordered.

"But, Grandma . . . they might hurt you. You don't know how brutal they are. I've seen them at it . . . Oh, God, if only I had a pistol!"

"We don't need pistols. There's been too much shootin' already. Passive resistance is best. Do as I tell you at

once. I'll call if I need you. They won't dare touch
ME!"

Izolda did as she was bid and Louise composed herself
on the opium couch on the landing to receive the Japanese
Army. The divan was rather high for her to sit on, and the
tips of her little shoes barely reached the Peking rug on the
floor. She arranged her skirts decently around her, adjusted
her black straw hat on her head, twitched the shawl she
was wearing for extra warmth into place, and thought of
James. She took a deep breath.

"*Ohayō gozaimasu!*" she smiled, bowing her torso politely at a sergeant who had leapt up the stairs ahead of the
others. He pulled up sharply, his jaw dropped open at the
sight of her. Before he had time to think, Louise galloped
on, "What is thy name, *dozo-ka*? Please be so kind as to tell
old lady so that I may address thee in correct manner?"

"Sergeant Kumi is my name," he half saluted, unable to
help himself. He couldn't believe his ears at the pronounciation
of the old-fashioned mode of address which the *ronins* and
court officials still used. She was out of another era;
obviously Japanese, although she wore European dress.
With her complexion, black eyes and beetling brows, she
must be Japanese. Such polite usage from a compatriot
needed a courteous answer and he was only a rough old
sergeant.

By now more soldiers were pressing from behind. They
stromped around the opium bed staring at Louise framed
by the picture of the Mandarin on the wall in his gor-
geously embroidered clothes. There was an explosion from
down below.

"What *dozo* please was that, Sergeant Kumi-*san*?" Louise
demanded imperiously, her eyes flashing.

"They are blowing safe." A corporal answered for him.

"No need to do that, *Gunso-san*," Louise scolded, waving an admonishing finger at the man, "Tch, tch, such bad manners. Sergeant Kumi-*san*, since thou art in charge here please tell thy men to do no more damage in house. If told thy requirements, I shall gladly comply."

Barked orders went out, and the soldiers who were causing havoc downstairs arrived on the landing to join in what was fast becoming a Court audience.

"My duty, Lady-*san*, is to search house for prisoner of wars and womens for internment," the sergeant replied as graciously as he was able.

"Then thou must do thy duty, Sergeant Kumi-*san*. Thou canst take my word for it that there is only myself and my grandchild left here with two Chinese servants and driver for car parked in garage. The great Imperial Japanese Army of chivalrous warriors who have shown this alien land how brave men fight, have no need to intern old women and childrens now has it – *ka*?"

"If Japanese, no. If not, will have to be interned. One day house requisitioned." Sergeant Kumi shifted his large feet uneasily.

"That day has not yet come. Thou wouldst not want to let soldiers under thy command despoil house so that thy superiors are not able to enjoy its comforts, now wouldst thou, *ka*? In meantime I will continue to live here and keep it in perfect order for when officer comes."

"So be it Lady-*san*," the sergeant awkwardly gave his slight bow. After all she *was* Japanese.

"Good! I trust that thou and thy troops will kindly accept my hospitality. Wilt thou honour me by partaking of a meal in my humble home, *desu-ka*?"

Louise purred. She was delighted to find her strategy was working; delighted to find that the Japanese language tripped off her tongue as easily as if she had been speaking it only yesterday instead of eighteen years ago. It was the same flowery manner she'd used when speaking to royalty, though now it was only to a humble sergeant. Briskly she clapped her hands for Fung Wan, who appeared at once from behind the drawing room door where he had prudently kept out of sight.

"Serve soldiers tea and cakes in big dining room downstairs, Fung Wan," Louise switched succinctly to pidgin English.

"Pah! Steal liquor, steal Master and Missie ornaments; blow safe, pah!" scowled Fung Wan.

"Soldiers will be soldiers, Fung Wan. I tell them stop it. Old Missie treat them like naughty childrens and they behave. Now, go get tea re'dy."

"You got *rid* of them? Didn't they touch you? What was that bang?" Izolda came out of hiding after the soldiers clattered downstairs.

"They're being entertained to tea in the big dining room."

"Entertained? How *can* you, Grandma, the loathsome, brutal creatures."

"I expect they'll appreciate the gesture. They're probably hungry and thirsty like you were. Even if they have done mighty terrible things such as – well, we won't go into that – they are brave to the death and I admire that, whatever you say. They are husbands, fathers and sons like any man. War is bestial on whichever side. Look what the Allied troops did in the Boxer Rebellion in Peking. All that destructive looting and worse, tut-tut."

"They didn't bayonet wounded men and rape innocent women; they didn't kill unarmed prisoners out of

212

hand," Izolda clenched her fists at the memories of Eu-Cliffe Castle.

"How do we know *what* they didn't do? It isn't all one-sided you know, Izolda. *I* heard that the Allied troops *did*. They behaved perfectly abominably!"

Sergeant Kumi made his report to Captain Nakamura at Japanese Brigade Headquarters. Captain Nakamura, an up-and-coming young staff officer, arrived and was equally charmed by Louise. He requested to be shown over the building and grounds and reported back to his Colonel that there was an undamaged house up on the Peak in an excellent situation which was eminently suitable for his requirements. Moreover it had a tennis court to the rear which would make a perfect plinth on which to base an anti-aircraft gun against the Chinese should they send bombers over.

In the house, Captain Nakamura went on, was the most curious woman who spoke perfect high-class Japanese. He thought she *was* Japanese married to a Britisher, though he had felt it impolite to ask. She certainly looked Japanese with her smallness and her black eyes hooded with age.

On January 9th 1942, the lights came on again at The Falls – though there was no piped water so Ping-Li had to carry buckets from the stream to flush the lavatories – and Captain Nakamura's Colonel came to investigate.

Alighting from his Packard staff car and leaving the driver and guard outside, this imposing man was ushered by a more respectful Fung Wan up to Louise in the drawing room. The Colonel acknowledged her civilly and she introduced him to Izolda who returned his bare nod by bowing reluctantly low as instructed at the Dragon Hotel. The moment he entered the room she recognised him as the impressive Commander who had led his troops on horseback at the victory parade.

Very formally he sat before them on one of the hard ebony chairs, legs apart, hands held inwards on his thighs. The tip of his long curved and jewelled two-handed samurai sword, its ornate scabbard swathed with black braid, rested on the gold and blue of Jimmy's Tientsin carpet.

He was taller than the average Japanese, a clean-looking neat man with a round head, hair close-shaven. Thick lips could be seen under a military moustache that glinted with a thread of red in an unusually freckled face. The jagged gash of the cheek-to-chin scar which Izolda had noticed before hit the eye grotesquely. He was in dress uniform: gold on his shoulders, full medals.

Unable to follow the conversation, and equally unable to sit still doing nothing, Izolda picked up Louise's crochet and began to work on it. Her hands, though sweating uncomfortably at such close proximity with one of the brutal enemy, at least would be occupied, and when the murmuring of the Colonel's voice came over in a civilised manner without any of the raucous shouting she had come to expect, she began to study him more closely. Well shaped fingernails; well cared for small hands. Nice hands . . . huh! They would certainly have blood on them . . . Izolda listened to the incomprehensible words:

"*Hajimemashite dozo yoroshiku.* I am very pleased to meet thee, Colonel-*san,*" Louise's soft voice opened the conversation. The officer stayed silent and severe in front of her.

"May I enquire if thou be of same nationality?" the Colonel responded in Japanese. He had expected her to speak in English. He rather enjoyed airing his English.

214

"*Ie*, Colonel-*san*, no, I am not of Japanese birth though I lived in thy country for over fifty years and regard it as my own. I sailed to Nippon Koku from the United States when young."

"Ha! That accounts for excellent accent," he acknowledged with a small nod of the head.

"Before trains came to Japan I travelled on horseback to Yedo to teach English in Palaces," Louise expanded.

"That long time ago; that old name for Tokyo."

"*Hai*," Louise sighed, "*hai*, very long time ago in days when young Emperor Meiji reigned on his illustrious ancestor's throne. I am old woman now as you see from my white hairs, one who lives too long into another war, Colonel-*san*."

"Since thou went to Tokyo to teach where did thou travel from, Madam?" The Colonel's interest was slightly roused.

"The great port of Yokohama. Our house on Bluff."

"Ha! My family live in Yokohama. Kitagata district."

"Really?" Louise's heavy eyelids flickered, "Colonel . . . er?"

". . . Fushimi Hojo, Madam."

Her blinking eyes and the tightening of her hands in her lap were the only signs of shock with which Louise heard this name. "Aaah, that is very old *ronin* name," she said carefully, feeling her way, "I knew some Fushimis . . ."

"Perhaps relation," the Colonel replied haughtily. It was all very pleasant sitting in the beautifully furnished room with its treasures – which he had carefully taken in – but he was a busy man with no time to waste on pleasantries, and there was as yet no sign of the tea the old lady had said was coming.

"A fine family of three sons," Louise went on recalling.

215

Her beady eyes digested his face. "One son killed in Korean War, another lost at Great Sea Battle of Tsu-Shuma which defeated Russian Bear. Other son survive."

"Fushimi uncles lost in wars." The Colonel leant forward with sudden interest. "My father, he youngest brother. Cousin have silk firm Yokohama – 'Fushimi and Wakiya'."

"I am glad to hear it. How is business?"

"Good. Prosperous cousin Ozaki son. He live in Kitagata. Curious meet in Hong Kong lady who knew family," Colonel Fushimi beamed with pleasure showing an expanse of gold-capped teeth. The scar on his chin, held rigid, made a parody of the smile.

"Thy honoured father, is he alive, Colonel-*san*? I remember he badly wounded."

"He is well, though old wound received in battle of Liao-yang give much painful trouble to arm. He retired inland country."

"I remember . . . his mother, the beautiful Sumuko."

Izolda looked up from the crochet in her hands. She thought she had heard her grandmother say 'Sumuko' – dear little Sumuko she knew all about from her childhood years of listening to the tales of Old Yokohama. It was her fault that she'd never bothered to learn more than the odd Japanese word. She would have liked to be able to get the gist of what they were talking about. This Colonel seemed affable enough and was apparently treating her grandmother decently, though his one-sided smile was hideous, and the showing of those awful teeth . . . !

"*Hai*," the conversation went on, "that was name. She die before I born. I not know her. My sister killed in her house in earthquake on visit to cousin there."

"Ah, the earthquake . . ."

"You in earthquake, Madam?"

"*Hai,* my daughter die in earthquake."

"My condolences, Madam. Very sad for you. Very sad for both families."

"I lost everything in earthquake. I came to Hong Kong to end my days in peace in my son's house. Then thou camest to make war upon us when our two countries have always been allies. All I have is lost again. Truly, Colonel Fushimi-san, I do not deserve this from thy country that is as if it were my own."

"It was necessary," the Colonel stiffened in his chair, his glittering sword standing out belligerently before him.

"Thy soldiers are great fighters, Colonel Fushimi-*san,* brave men in the spirit of the fabled Samurai warriors of yore; thine was a civilised nation long before the West became so, yet thou dost not always behave as civilised army should. I have heard of treatment of prisoners which is bad, is not in keeping with the Geneva Convention . . ."

"*We not ratify Geneva Convention!*" exploded the Colonel, the sound making Izolda jump. His quiet voice had been too good to be true. "*Prisoner soldiers are peoples beneath contempt, scum of earth!*" he blazed, the scar suffused into a livid line.

"But I know children will be treated kindly," Louise smoothly diverted to less dangerous ground.

"*Hai-ka?*" The Colonel's mood changed as swiftly. "Children – I have four children at my home in Nippon," he said, holding up four fingers for Izolda to see.

Fung Wan brought in tea and little coloured cakes. They sipped in silence, Louise spilling some as usual while Fung Wan stood by with his napkin. Izolda was in danger of doing likewise; her cup rattled in its delicate porcelain saucer. The Colonel's raised voice had unnerved her, and worse, the appraising look he'd given her was extraordinarily

217

sinister. Intended rape? Yet her grandmother did not seem particularly perturbed.

"You British subject now, Madam?" Colonel Fushimi, once tea had been served, got down to business.

"British-American, Colonel-*san*."

"Understand, *domo* please, British *or* American subject both enemy; not permitted stay here." He put down his cup, wiped his lips delicately with the small crossstitch embroidered doily beside his plate, and rose to examine the valuable old scrolls on red parchment paper panelled into the carved draught-screen beside him. "Excellent, excellent!" He felt the surface of the screen appreciatively. "I collect works of art Nippon."

Louise wasn't listening. "Not stay here?" Her heart froze. "I, I understand other families live in houses on Peak do they not?"

"*Hai*, that is so," he said, moving over to examine the contents of the cabinets at close quarters, "soon all taken to Internment Camp; not yet, not in order yet. We get ready Stanley buildings. You and granddaughter go; two weeks, three weeks' time, when prepared."

"We do not wish to go to, to . . . that place. My daughter-in-law nursed there . . ." Louise's voice broke in horror of having to live where . . .

"Ah! Very bad, very bad things happen. All Japanese soldiers have been severely punished, officer in charge shot! Not go near hospital. I arrange with billetting officer to have home ready for you and granddaughter *away* from hospital."

"Colonel Fushimi-*san*, I entreat you, *this* is my home. I am old, old woman. I wish to die here."

"Not possible. Not possible you stay, though it is with deep regret, Madam, that I oblige you to leave home," he said and turned to give her a small bow. "All comforts will be arranged. Captain Nakamura will personally escort by truck when ready."

"But, Colonel, if you knew—"

"Words are final," the Colonel interrupted impatiently. With the eye of a connoisseur he bent from his height to examine the jade in the cabinets more closely.

"*Domo arigato gozaimasu*," Louise deferred to the inevitable. Even in her special circumstances she knew it would not be possible even for a senior officer such as the Colonel to bend the rules. "Shall I be permitted to take luggage – a bed? I shall not live long in camp. I should be grateful for a bed to die on," she sighed heavily.

Izolda recognised the sigh. *Now what is Grandma up to?* she thought.

"You may take reasonable amount. I reserve good suite as you old lady. Guards will be instructed to let furniture in. Cultural treatment according to Samurai martial tradition," Colonel Fushimi declared grandly. "You will be happy in Camp, not die. I take possession of this house," he observed, looking closely at the two valuable jardinières on either side of the mantelpiece. His eyes alighted on the Chinese bowl embossed with yellow dragons on its own table and stand. "Ha!" he exclaimed bouncing with delight, "*Five* claw feet, very valuable, very good; emblem show bowl once belong to Emperors of China. I like! Where your son get from, Madam?"

"In Peking, I believe, Colonel-*san*."

"Ha. Where is son now?"

"He was killed in battle on mainland," Louise lied, without the slightest hesitation.

"Madam," he stood solemnly to attention before her. "Son

219

brave fighting soldier who give up life for country. Die with honour!"

Shoulders braced back, the Colonel walked past the heavy curtains at the french windows and stepped onto the verandah. He looked out at the view and down at the well tended garden. "This good place to spend war. I like! I stay here."

"Thou art welcome to have it for duration of occupation, Colonel Fushimi-*san*," Louise said, presenting it as if he had no power over her, as if it was all hers to give. "I recommend thou keepest Fung Wan, my Number One Boy, and Ah Fan, amah, both excellent servants. Wilt thou be requiring Ping-Li chauffeur and Cadillac car?"

"I shall see," he said, and took out a notebook and fountain pen from his flap pocket. "For official record, *dozo*, names of Europeans living in house."

"My granddaughter's name is Izolda Paine-Talbot." Louise watched him start to write it down and stumble over the spelling. "Here Colonel, let me," she said in English. He frowned at her outstretched hand, and then, looking amused, handed over the pad and pen.

At the tea table, Louise carefully wrote Izolda's name in Western capitals. She looked at it for a moment, then wrote her own name under it in flowing Japanese calligraphy. Expertly the broad nib scratched the serifs down the page. She waved the page in the air to dry.

"My name is," Louise handed back pad and pen, eyes fixed on the Colonel, "Mrs James Winter."

He read the calligraphy at the same moment she spoke the words, but not by so much as a flicker of an eyelid or movement of a muscle did his inscrutable face reveal that the name meant anything to him. Putting pen and pad away, he made the slightest of bows and strode for the stairs.

Louise was left in a whirl, her heart fluttering in her chest. She decided that a teaspoon of brandy was essential to steady her after an interview of such unparalleled coincidence and momentousness, and she made for her bedside table, leaving Izolda no wiser as to what the conversation had been all about. Izolda was also slightly puzzled.

The Colonel was vaguely familiar. He reminded her of someone . . . Ah yes. That was it: his small neat hands reminded her of Uncle Jimmy's!

Part Four

*'When I uproot this seedling
. . . where will they live?'*

1942–1945

Chapter Seventeen

AT the end of January, a truck entered Stanley Internment Camp for British and Allied Civilians with the last of the Europeans to be rounded up. It was a most astonishing sight and one which caused much unfavourable comment.

An old lady sat in front with three hats skewered on her head. Whoever wanted one Sunday hat in Stanley camp, let alone more? She sat between the driver and a Japanese captain, while a slim young girl at the back was perched precariously on luggage piled over a great black ornate couch.

Those passing by stopped in their tracks when they saw the truck bumping over the shallow ditch beyond the neck of the Peninsular, and nearly spilling out its contents. What caused the detrimental comments, and what sparked off hateful suspicions and jealousies that were to beset Louise – and therefore Izolda – was the way guards opened the gates between the barbed wire barricades, and waved the encumbents through without so much as a search.

Actually there had been a cursory examination for arms and liquor ordered by Captain Nakamura at The Falls before Louise and Izolda left, a hunt which gave Izolda the jitters but which revealed nothing. There had been quite a contretemps between grandmother and granddaughter about the divan.

"I guess I'll take the opium couch," Louise had come out with.

"What do you want with that heavy thing?" Izolda remonstrated. "It's sort of square and it hasn't even got a mattress. You told me the Colonel said you could take a bed, so why don't you?"

"I fancy the couch. It'll suit me fine," answered Louise, not to be put off. "Ah Fan can find a mattress upstairs that will fit well enough, and if it doesn't it will be quite useful to have a wooden platform on either side to keep all my things on when I'm bedridden. It'll be my last resting place on earth since they won't let me stay in my own son's home even though . . . Humph. It should be interesting to die on an opium couch – soothin', I guess."

"Oh *Grandma*, I do wish you wouldn't."

"Besides, it has that hidden receptacle. Couldn't be more convenient. I told you I'd put Grandpa's Order in it? I'm sure they'd take *that* off me if they knew. I wonder what our furnished suite'll be like? Fung Wan tells me there are thousands of souls interned in the buildings on the promontory. We'll need to take warm clothing and—"

"The winter is nearly over. You talk as if we're going to be there for years."

"Maybe *you* will, I shan't last . . ."

"Of course we won't," Izolda replied, "not once the Chinese Nationalists get moving."

"Put several pillows in the bedding roll, honey. I must have pillows to die on."

"Oh shut up, Grandma!"

"And don't forget my POTTY, very important. Have you added lavatory paper? I can't see them providing such facilities in a Camp. Oh, my hats – where *am* I going to pack my hats?"

Jimmy's original demonstration of the secret drawer in the back panel of the opium couch had revealed a surprisingly deep recess. Into it now went money, chlorodyne bottles and Louise's half-flasks of brandy which she insisted were purely medicinal but she knew would have been taken off her. She kept on stuffing more things in they had been forbidden to take or which they'd heard from Miss Maureen the guards were partial to. The latter took from inmates any money found on them and such things as pencils and paper, penknives, watches or clocks and, of course, jewellery – none of which were allowed in camp.

Izolda had been in a state of jitters when Captain Nakamura ordered a search of the loaded truck at The Falls. Her grandmother was taking an enormous risk smuggling in liquor which, together with arms of any sort, was absolutely taboo. But Izolda was now in such a cheerful mood that even packing to go into an internment camp didn't upset her because there had been a miracle!

Not long after Colonel Fushimi's visit, Miss Maureen had turned up at The Falls. Attired in her usual shapeless dress with tie and knee-length, drooping cardigan, she'd peered at Izolda through her thick lenses and imparted the marvellous, incredible, intoxicating news that Major Stamford was *alive* and at the Sham-Shui-Po prisoner of war camp with Winn! She had spoken surreptitiously to Winn through the wire, and he told her the Major was in solitary confinement after being caught. Winn and the Gunners in camp had smuggled some food in to him and he'd smuggled his news out.

Roger had a fantastic story to tell, unbeknownst to his guards who had no idea he'd previously been captured or been one of the prisoners at the Eu-Cliffe massacre. A bullet had grazed his neck in the split second he'd anticipated and hurled himself backwards. The crumpled pile of bodies already over the cliff underneath him had cushioned his fall. He believed he was the only one to survive the massacre, and got clean away. He was on the run for nearly two weeks before being picked up by a Japanese patrol boat swimming from an island – where he'd been hiding – to the New Territories and freedom. He said he'd been quite glad to be captured again and given his first solid meal of two tablespoons of rice.

"And how was Winn?" Izolda had asked, her relief and happiness at the amazing news shining in her eyes.

"In good heart, I'm thinking, but bitter and revengeful about his mother. There's nothing he won't stop at now. He sends you and his grandmother all love."

"What are conditions like in there?"

"Bad. The place is bombed to bits an' all. Morale is high, though. Faith, they're busy enough making and mending with scrounged planks of wood and anything they can get their hands on. They need tools – everything. 'Tis true lack of food is the worse problem – oh, I'll be praying night and day to our Blessed Lady to be keeping you all safe. Sure I will."

Miss Maureen had been a mine of information. She told Louise and Izolda that she, with her Irish and Portugese (also neutral) refugee friends in the hospice, were smuggling things in through the wire and taking messages, but they had to be very careful. The rules at Stanley – being a civilian camp – were less severe, and she'd discovered there was some regularisation for the inmates of weekly food parcels not allowed in military camps. She would instruct Ping-Li and Fung Wan to get parcels made up from the food cache in the garden dug-out under the nose of Colonel Fushimi. The rules for parcels were strict: they had to be a certain size and not more than five pounds in weight or they would be confiscated.

In the parcels, disguised notes on labels or wrapping paper would be secreted so the inmates could be kept informed

228

of what was going on in the outside world. Izolda must memorise certain words to be used for specific requirements, and she would show her how to get urgent messages out of the camp. She'd been in touch with the Holden family, now in Stanley, and been able to let them know of Captain Holden's progress in the convent hospital. The three Chinese servants at The Falls would take it in turns to deliver the parcels. She herself was too busy on the mainland to get over except occasionally. It was prudent that the same people were not seen delivering packets or talking through the wire too often or they were beaten up – especially the Chinese. The Korean guards were the worst . . . particularly to be avoided . . . a nationalist Chinese column was rumoured to be on the way to relieve Hong Kong . . . the war, pray Sweet Holy Mary, would soon be over . . .

In Izolda's dramatic resurgence of hope from her dark tunnel of despair, what Miss Maureen related about conditions in the camps, and especially in Stanley, sounded rather like a picnic. Though living there might be difficult, and a bit of a bore due to the restrictions, it wouldn't be for long and could easily be lived through with eyes kept on the brilliant future. Nothing else mattered in the world now except that Roger, whom she'd thought dead, was *alive*. Neither the prospect of internment nor what the Japanese might do to them could frighten her anymore. Her relief from sorrow was so enormous, her mind so ecstatic at the news, that to her nothing could stand in the way of their happiness. Roger, against all odds, had survived the last ditch fight for the Island and he'd survived the massacre at Eu-Cliffe Castle. Now all they had to do was survive the war and they would be together again. It was as simple as that. And with the addition of Miss Maureen's parcels, it would be as easy as pie!

No, although it was maddening having to leave the

comforts of The Falls, the prospect of living in a camp in already established buildings did not sound too bad. Neither did the immediate future seem too impossible to either Louise or Izolda when they could take with them beds and bedding, crockery and cutlery, an electric cooker ring, an oil stove, a carton of tinned food and another of household goods, plus fresh stores to last a week. It didn't seem too bad when they had so much more than the unfortunates who'd been picked up with nothing on them.

Not so bad, that was, until in a rainy drizzle under a dull winter sky, their truck came to a halt on the Peninsular in front of their 'suite': a small, one-storied house already packed to bursting with other families.

Grudging male prisoners from the red-roofed bungalow, which had been part of the college and was but a short step from St Stephen's Bay, were ordered by two armed guards to hump the new prisoners' beds through a communal lobby into a dank seven foot by twelve room with fireplace. The guards looked on indifferently.

The divan fitted neatly across the width leaving enough space for Izolda's camp bed to go down one side. The mattresses, damp from the drizzle, were dumped onto them. The only furniture in the place was a cupboard with mirror and a hard chair. A door led through into a grey windowless scullery, empty except for a sink and a flex with naked bulb hanging overhead. With ill grace, the men piled the rest of the luggage inside.

The truck revved up, and Louise, hiding her horror, went outside with walking stick in hand to stand under a lone pine tree by the porch and bow to Captain Nakamura and politely thank him for his trouble in escorting them.

"Jap lover!" an inmate shouted. Louise took no notice and

was stepping back into the lobby when an untidy-looking English woman barred her way.

"A room each? It's not fair!" she let fly. "Why should you be singled out for luxury, you Jap grovellers, you?"

"Nip sucker!" a man from an inner door spat into Louise's face. "I caught you toadying to that officer; lickspittle swine!"

Again Louise said nothing. Waving her stick at the man she brushed past him and into her room. She banged the door shut on her neighbours.

"I've never been so insulted in all my life," she collapsed onto the divan. "Did you hear what they said? Reviled in adversity – that's what. Disgraceful! Shocking behaviour. There's a deal too many creepin' folk round here and that's a fact. I've always kept myself to myself, Izolda, and I can tell you it looks mightily as if I'll become a *recluse* here. I'll have no truck with such trash, nor you either. Humph," she said mischievously, "they don't know what they're missin'. I was going to hand out those vegetables we brought. Not now!"

"Call this a suite?" Izolda looked round her in dismay at the dingy, dark, shabby room where tins were placed in strategic spots on the bare floor. "What are they for?" she wondered.

It began to pour outside. The rain drummed on the roof and all other sounds were drowned in the noise. One shallow tin overflowed and spilled onto the dirty, rotten floorboards. The puddle it made spread. Izolda collapsed into hysterical giggles. She sat on the bed howling with laughter at her grandmother's disgusted face, tears at the impossible awfulness of the 'suite' wetting her cheeks.

Louise looked at her granddaughter. "Do you *have* to add to the dampness at this particular moment when there's no way of airing our mattresses?" she observed crustily. She peered into the back room and found a switch on the wall. A low wattage bulb lit up. "Well, fancy that now, it works, and so does the faucet," she pronounced sarcastically after trying the one tap over the sink. "*Suite*, my foot. You'd better find out where the water closet is, Izolda. Thank the Lord I brought my potty for night use."

Izolda wiped her eyes and did as she was told. She came back to say there were about twenty people squashed in the building and only one WC.

"No wash-room?" asked Louise.

"No. The bathroom is occupied by a couple with a baby who lives in the tub."

"We'll have to wash in the sink, I guess. Humph. The first thing to do when moving into new quarters is to get the beds made up. Then, when you've had about as much as you can take, your bed is ready for you to tumble into. Once there you can shut your eyes to the outside. Come, honey, get out the bedding . . ."

No sooner was that done than the Holdens arrived. Maisie was the first to rush in with Tommy, soon followed by Bill and Joan. "Oh Maisie, how *good* to see you," Izolda took the child from his mother, "it feels like years since you left The Falls for the hotel."

"That move was a complete disaster. At least you've had an extra month before being taken prisoner," Maisie embraced her friend.

"We would have been here to greet you but we had trouble finding where they'd put you," Joan apologised.

Though they didn't voice their feelings, both Louise and Izolda were surprised by the difference in the Holdens after only a month in captivity. Admittedly Tommy looked much the same, but Maisie had lost the weight she'd put on after having her baby; her dress was stained and she wore flat muddy

232

sandals in place of her smart shoes. Joan Holden's plump figure was already pounds lighter and Bill's purple jowls flapped like the dewlap of an ox.

"You must stay to tea," Louise invited hospitably covering up her unease at the unkempt appearance of the previously smart Holdens. Joan Holden's hair without its blue rinse was *yellow!* "Now where did I pack the cloth? Mrs Holden will you put up the bridge table, please?"

"Where . . . ?" Joan looked round her at the cramped space.

"At the foot of the bed, I guess. We ladies will have to sit on the divan. Mr Holden can have the one chair."

"The rooms are filthy. I thought the Japanese were supposed to be a clean nation. They could have at least swept the place," Izolda said disgustedly. She washed her hands under the cold tap in the sink while Bill knelt down to light the oil stove, staying there until he'd reduced the flame to a steady blue. Izolda put a pan on to boil water and then filled a kettle for the cooker ring. "Blast," she observed, "our plug doesn't fit."

"Will get you another from somewhere tomorrow. You're lucky to have a socket at all," responded Bill.

"I'll help you scrub out if you like?" Maisie offered. "Our room was worse than this, fought over and looted. I can't tell you how awful it was, glass everywhere." She began to lay an array of Fung Wan's freshly baked bread and cakes on the card table, rickety on the uneven floor.

"I know," said Izolda, "our Macdonnell Road flat was vandalised."

"You poor darling . . . I heard about Chippy. Oh, how little did we know what we were in for on the *Chitral*." Maisie caught Tommy snatching a cake off the plate. "Wait," she jumped at him and tried to prize it out of his hand, the cake crumbling. Tommy set up a howl.

"Let him have it, he's hungry the poor mite and there's no need to stand on ceremony in a dump like this," Louise declared. "I reckon we'd better have high tea, Izolda, with boiled eggs to fill up the corners, that is if we can ever get the water to boil." They settled down to wait while Tommy grabbed another cake. "How did you come to Stanley? I hope you brought an umbrella with you?" Louise went on. She looked through the dirty window-panes at the downpour outside.

"Brought over from Kowloon by boat," Maisie started to fill in the gaps. "We landed at the pier on the other side of the isthmus below the old cemetery. I share a room with one other American family – that's good by camp standards. You heard I'd opted to go with the Americans?"

"Yes," Louise nodded, "Miss Maureen told us. I guess I should have done the same rather than get stuck in this hutch."

"You're best off here, Mrs Winter, truly," said Joan. "I promise you you're very fortunate to have these rooms to yourselves."

"That has already been impressed upon us by our neighbours in an extremely rude manner," Louise said dryly.

Bill cleared his throat, "You'll find there are plenty of louts in the camp, Mrs Winter. Better to ignore 'em."

"I have and will."

"The wife and I were put into a dormitory; at our age, if you please. I made one hell of a rumpus."

"Did it make any difference?" asked Izolda.

"The billetting officer, as they call the harassed Japanese in charge, eventually gave us a room in St Stephen's Preparatory School."

234

"Smaller than this. Forty of us share one lavatory. Can you imagine?" Joan sniffed. She couldn't stop herself from looking longingly at the fruit cake.

"At first conditions in the camp were chaotic," Bill continued. "Bodies left lying all over the place . . . the mess of fighting to be cleared . . . no water, no cooking facilities. We've gradually become more organised. Committees set up. We have to do it all ourselves, of course, while the Japs lounge around. We're divided into groups, British – by far the largest contingent – American, Dutch and so on. Each group is responsible for their own cooking. The food provided is foul and quite inadequate. We all get stomach upsets. The daily ration consists of the cheapest kind of mouldy rice sweepings of broken kernels, and there's never enough to go round."

"How do they distribute it?" Izolda wanted to know.

"Queue for hours, and those at the end of the queue don't get. If it wasn't for that bloody marvellous secretary of Jimmy's, we'd have starved by now."

"She told us she'd been in touch with you. How do we collect the parcels?" Louise asked.

"Fetch them from headquarters up the hill, that is *if* they aren't confiscated. We're always being punished and our parcels confiscated for something we're supposed to have done wrong, we usually don't know what. That's what's so disconcerting. One never knows what's going to happen next, and ghastly things do happen. People get beaten, or taken out and shot . . ."

Maisie bit her lip. "I live with the Americans a little way from you; I'll show you where the British kitchens are before I leave, Zol. You'll have to go there to collect your cooked rations. I suggest you start straight away tomorrow morning even though you've brought all these stores in."

235

"We make it sound dreadful, I know," apologised Joan, "and it *is* awful, but I can tell you I was only too glad to come here after the Dragon Hotel. That was the last time I saw you, Izolda, remember? Poor dear; you *were* ill."

"As if I could ever forget it."

"After that stinking hole it was a bit of heaven by contrast to come here and be able to walk out of doors under the blue sky, see the hibiscus, the jacaranda trees, the rocks and the sea. There's even the prison officers' bowling club green for Bill to play on!"

"Just how restricted are we?" asked Izolda. She made the tea and timed the boiled eggs according to taste and dished up. The visitors tucked in with gusto, while she, not hungry herself, helped Tommy with his egg.

"One's allowed to walk about freely on the isthmus out of curfew hours without too much interference from the guards, though you have to watch your step. They're always hanging about to trip you up on any imagined misdemeanour." Maisie scraped every last fibre out of her eggshell and then helped herself to more bread and butter.

"What for goodness' sake do they want with a curfew, stuck out here on a limb?" required Louise petulantly.

"God knows," Bill said, holding out his cup for more tea. "Lights out ridiculously early. If so much as a flicker of a candle shows in the dark, there's trouble. Frightened the Chinese might come to bomb, I suppose."

"Blackout. We should have added curtains to the list, Izolda. We'll have to cut up that bedspread we brought instead. There ain't room for anything. Where *am* I going to keep my hats?" Louise suddenly remembered she had three on her head.

There was a great guffaw from Bill at this – if the old dear would only look at herself in the mirror! "Allow me to put

236

up shelves for you, Mrs Winter," he chuckled. "You'll need some in the kitchen, too. I know where I can scrounge wood and nails. I'll come over tomorrow with the electric plug and set to."

"Very kind of you. In return please feel free to boil water on our stove when you need. I'd say use our conveniences, but I don't reckon we're better off with the scrum in this house than you are. My, what an indelicate subject."

"It is a scandal there's no pooling of parcels for the children in the camp," Maisie complained. "There are hundreds of children here, a great many of them Eurasian who look thoroughly neglected . . ."

Leaving the bungalow, their bellies comfortably filled for once, Mr and Mrs Holden thanked Louise profusely. "My advice to you," Bill said, shaking hands, "is don't be so generous after today. Save up everything you've brought to keep for yourselves. Think of Number One. I mean it. Believe me, dear Mrs Winter, it's the only way to stay alive in the months to come.

It was the third shock of that day of upheaval. There had been the dismay at the smallness and state of their quarters however much others might envy them their privacy; the stinging hate from neighbours and compatriots who should have all been pulling together in their misfortune; and now this warning from Bill Holden.

If he, as big-hearted as his body was large, advised, after only a few weeks in captivity, to keep what little one had for oneself as the only way to survive, conditions in Stanley camp must be dire indeed.

Chapter Eighteen

"WE are just like coolies living in this dump. I shall ask Corporal Seki if he can fetch us a *tatami* mat to cover up these rotten boards. I knew we ought to have brought floor rugs," Louise grumbled.

In February the Japanese gave out the news of their 'great victory' in Singapore which dampened the prisoners' spirits further. It was the month when many of the children went down with measles, several dying. Tommy caught it and became seriously ill. Izolda had not had measles and was advised to keep away, and for weeks she did not see Maisie. She missed her friend, particularly as she had at last felt able to tell Maisie about Chippy – and about her love for Roger.

"There wasn't room in the truck to bring rugs," she said in answer to her grandmother, "Captain Nakamura would have tipped them out. How can Seki get *tatamis* in China, anyway?"

"Even if he can't, he'll appreciate my feelings. Not even the poorest peasant in Japan had to live like this. We used to call the Japanese children 'full moon faced', nice and rounded, not half-starved like the poor little mites here. Talk of parsimony . . ." words failed Louise.

She was sitting on the couch wearing the old mauve kimono Toni had given her – it still smelt of mothballs – over every jumper and cardigan she could lay her hands on. She pulled up the sleeves to scratch the dry skin on her arm with her brittle pointed nails which made her paper-thin skin bleed, and she had these bruises on the backs of her hands. They appeared all of a sudden and disappeared slowly leaving a fading yellow mark only to return overnight in full plum bloom. She must ask that nice missionary, Dr Lawrence, whom Izolda knew, what caused them. She treated them with *Icelma* cream which she also used sparingly on her face. She would eke out the green jar as she would her one bottle of eau-de-Cologne. If she thought about it consciously, she could actually *feel* her skin shrinking from lack of nourishment. Interesting. She would tell Dr Lawrence about that, too.

"What did the Japanese do to keep warm?" Izolda, blue-nosed and with a heavy cold, asked from her camp bed on which she sat cross-legged. She had one of the Chinese quilts (her grandmother insisted on calling them *futons*) clutched round her over her smart black velour coat. The frogged buttons down the front already hung loose.

"*Hibashis*," Louise readily replied, "brazier stoves containing red-hot charcoal. Their houses were hermetically sealed with well-fitting *amado* shutters on every window – no rattling draughty doors like these wretched ones. Sumuko kept her house in Kitagata village beautifully warm all through the winter," Louise went on. She looked contemptuously from her bed at the miserable fire in the grate where a few hissing wooden sticks burned greenly. A gust of wind down the chimney belched a cloud of smoke into the haze of the grimed and patch-walled room.

"If they were hermetically sealed here, we'd suffocate," Izolda coughed.

The door was open to their kitchen-cum-utility room where the stove was turned low to conserve oil. The overhanging light bulb raised the temperature a fraction more in an effort to dry the clothes hanging on a washing line doubled overhead. Garments hung there damply for days on end in the wet season.

As well as being cold, Izolda was tired and depressed. Her joy at knowing Roger was alive had turned to one of worry for him and near-despair as to how she herself could cope. For now she had to face basic present reality, and she found herself totally unprepared, untrained and unsuited both temperamentally and psychologically for the mental and physical struggle for survival.

Though used to taking physical exercise, Izolda had never done any heavy labour, and she found straight away that because of her grandmother's incapacity and the boycotting by the rest of the bungalow, she had to hump and carry, mend their window, doors, floorboards, not to mention parts of the roof as best she could with hammered-out tins, bits of wood, and all worked with inadequate tools. Bill Holden, true to his promise, had put up shelves so that there was a semblance of orderliness about the place; their belongings were now stowed tidily away. She had never done any cooking, never washed up, swept or scrubbed, never even washed her own clothes. Her grandmother, from her scrimping days on Missionary Bluff in Yokohama, and from her plague precautions living in China, was better trained domestically than she.

The reality, belied by the scenic setting in which the Stanley camp was situated, was that not only did the roof over her head leak, but that the rotten floor under her harboured scorpions, centipedes, cockroaches and ants which crawled up into the beds to nip. The first lesson Izolda learnt in self-preservation was to put tins of water under the bed legs in which to drown the ants.

Never in her life had she worked so hard and so long

throughout every day. Each one started before dawn when she rose to take the full chamber-pot to empty it down the one lavatory in the bungalow in the hopes of getting in before the antagonistic neighbours were up, but usually finding she had to wait in the passage with barbed asides and derogatory remarks. After the curfew bell sounded she went out with the rest to queue for their cooked morning meal of *congee* rice gruel. Often she came back drenched, shoes covered in mud, the rain having turned the paths into quagmires, and she had to stay in her wet outdoor clothes for the rest of the day. Queuing for their midday rice ration, cooked in the communal kitchen and doled out into their receptacles, could take three hours, and then there was queuing again for their evening 'stew' which consisted of a cabbage stalk or a fish head floating in coloured water.

Everyone, except the very old and the very ill, was given work to do by the leaders of each nationality, a Mr Ian Gimson for the British section. In view of having to look after her grandmother, Izolda was allotted a morning shift only. Her task was a nauseating one of picking out the weevils and bits of glass and grit by hand from the rice to be cooked next day. To begin with Izolda, squeamish by nature, thought she could not do it, and on her first day retched continuously and all but threw up. But there was no alternative, and surprisingly soon the writhing rice meant no more to her than a dull job that had to be done.

In the afternoons she went down as near to the wired-off beach as they were allowed, to collect bits of driftwood, or cut down (when no guard was in sight) branches on the rocky hillsides for their fire. Back she came in her once smart coat, bundle under her arm, and got down to scrubbing and repairing. She learned to throw nothing away, to keep everything for re-use. She fetched, carried, cleaned, washed, worked at her job – and queued; endless queuing for herself and her grandmother, first standing on one foot and then dropping on the other before shuffling an inch or two forwards.

There was never enough food to go round, and sometimes, if she was late starting she returned empty-handed and had queued for nothing. The stores they'd brought into camp were eked out by Louise. Even so, in a few months these were used up. They found that the parcels sent in (the supply was irregular, many going missing) only made them slightly less undernourished than if they'd had to exist solely on the rations provided. Nevertheless the parcels were tremendously welcome and much savoured for their change of diet as well as heartening messages which Izolda searched for and repeated to Louise: '*Winn and Roger were well. They sent their love*'!

There were a great many police in Stanley camp, and, being mostly younger men, they shouldered the heavy sanitary squad work of digging outside latrines for emergency use: 'if water cut off', so the guards foretold. The police were accompanied by their families and inevitably scandals abounded, though how anyone could take a lover in the congested conditions together with the strict night curfew, stumped many. There were births, both legitimate and illegitimate, though less and less of either occurred as time went on. There were outbreaks of enteritis, dysentery and tick fever, and people died – so very many deaths.

It was a mixed camp of diverse races, colours, castes and classes; there was envy, jealousy, discontent, bribery, bickering, stealing and open hatred. Glowing through these unpalatable truths were pockets of affection, of love and devotion, of unselfishness and hidden bravery, the latter often unknown and unrecognised, as was to be in the case of Louise.

There was particular public spiritedness and leadership shown among the doctors, and in this, Dr Lawrence, who had treated Chippy and who had become Izolda's friend and only confidante after her marriage, was very much to the fore. The doctors messed together by choice in the old Leprosarium on the Peninsular, a place which everyone else had shunned. But the medicos knew that a building could not hold infection of that sort, and they spread themselves luxuriously inside. Out of practically nothing they turned a smallish house nearby above Tweed Bay into a hospital. Rooms were reconstructed to hold seventy-two patients. And they were always full of ill and dying.

The supply of drugs and medicines brought or smuggled in was completely inadequate. The most frustrating aspect for the doctors was that so many lives could have been saved had they the drugs, even such mundane ones as quinine. Growing despair crept round as the first months passed and there came no sighting from land, sea or air of the promised Chinese forces.

With her wise old eyes and her intuitiveness, Louise had sniffed the canker in the fetid air when she'd been driven in between the wire. The barbed gate had clanged behind her, shutting away her ordered life where she was loved and respected. She met the hatred face to face on her doorstep; had to shoulder the added burden of being classed as a collaborator, the vilest accusation in war. And though Louise was born an American citizen and still thought of herself as American, she was a British patriot at heart, devoted to the memory of her husband. No, Louise was no collaborator, but she had been accused of being one because she'd come into camp with a truckload of goods, and had spoken a few polite words to a Japanese captain.

Louise had hoped that she might be of some use in internment despite her age. There was a great deal she could tell the leaders in camp about the psychology of the Japanese with their mixed mentality which came from their ancient roots. Truly she had looked forward to helping by translating as she had in another war. But she found that in a camp full of businessmen, bankers, professors, doctors, police, diplomats, taipans and tycoons among them, there were more than enough fluent speakers to act as interpreters. Louise saw only too clearly that an old woman who happened to speak Japanese was of no use in the community, nor was she of interest other than to cause resentment as the dead weight of another mouth to feed, and a 'Jap-lover' mouth at that – too true.

So she kept to herself. She played her part in the squalid rooms by always being there. And she retained her standards. She dampened her white hair and curled the top and side pieces in pipe cleaners every single night; and by day she always rang the changes with one of her three hats.

Louise may have kept up her standards, but she looked like an ancient witch, and she felt like an ancient witch when she sat on her camp stool by the oil stove and stirred their cooked rations of rice with the stalky stew or the undercooked soya beans to a pulp so that she could digest it. The way it was cooked in the main kitchens gave her and Izolda (and a good many other people) diarrhoea. The 'trots' had attacked them the moment they went on to the unsavoury diet. The salt fish in the mixture added its bad smell; the musty rice sat heavy in stomachs. She dished out doses of chlorodyne until they were better, and she took to re-cooking every ounce of the rations.

Often Izolda was near to tears with fatigue, and often Louise was cross and grumbled too much. Surprisingly often they laughed when they stopped to look and saw the bizarre picture of two unkempt peasant women about their chores, one in a shawl and a hat, the other with scarf tied under chin and a spotted black velour coat that drooped around her figure.

Always, though, whatever their moods or their feelings, whether they felt like crying or whether they laughed or just got on with it – they were companionable together.

Louise seldom left their quarters during that winter, but once a week she did. She went to Church! Louise had never missed a Sunday worship the whole of her life unless illness precluded it, and an internment camp certainly wasn't going to prevent her from attending. Led by the Dean – who had married Chippy and Izolda and was now interned with the rest – the service was held by priests of various denominations in the hall of the college. The devotions reminded Louise of her uncle's Union Church in Yokohama, the first church to be built there to which, in the early days before others built their own, all denominations came.

With an air of pleasurable expectation, Louise, dressed in her 'best' for the outing, put on one of her hats at the right angle for the prevailing fashion, and with her stick to steady her footsteps, set off in good time up the hill to St Stephen's. She carried her camp stool on which she sat for the duration while the other worshippers crowded round and squatted on the floor or on grass mats they had brought with them.

Normally that outing lasted Louise for the week, but one day she was forced to go out when the whole camp was made to assemble by the high white prison walls. There they waited for hours in the rain while their rooms were searched for arms, liquor and any army equipment. They were forbidden to talk.

"Oh God," mouthed Izolda. "What if they find your brandy . . ."

"Do some proper praying instead," Louise hissed in return. For once she was as worried as Izolda that on return they would find some of their precious possessions gone, but the hidden drawer served them well again. When they at last were allowed back, with Izolda supporting Louise who was in a near state of collapse, though all was in disorder in the rooms, only Izolda's water-bottle was found to be missing.

"That's the second one they've pinched off me. What do they want them for?" she asked Bill Holden on his next visit.

"Army equipment, my dear."

"But it wasn't! It was Hash Harrier stuff."

"That the colour is khaki is good enough for them. They don't know the difference, the ignorant bastards."

Through all the cold shouldering, the sordidness, and the growing irritability brought on through malnutrition, Louise and Izolda were often touched by small presents, many of them anonymous, that were left inside their entrance lobby: a flower, a chocolate, an apple, a piece of soap cut off from a bar. They were given to the one because she was the oldest person in camp, and to the other because she was young and beautiful and took good care of her grandmother. Occasionally, and very surreptitiously, the piggy-eyed, short-necked Corporal Seki who guarded their area and to whom Louise talked quietly in Japanese, brought small gifts – even once a *tatami* mat for their main room.

When the warmer weather came and Louise could sit outside on her camp stool, she took to holding conversations with him despite the rule that guard and prisoner were forbidden to talk to one another. To the suspicious neighbours, this flaunting of regulations was proof indeed that the old woman was hand in glove with the enemy.

"You lived in Nippon Koku, *desu-ka?*" Corporal Seki leaned on his rifle by the door of the *Seyo no Fujin*, the European Lady.

"*Hai*, and I taught Japanese princes to speak English," Louise had her boast.

"What Japanese princes?" the small guard asked disbelievingly.

"Prince Yashimoto for one."

"*Ie*, Great Emperor uncle?" his little eyes opened wide with awe.

"*Hai, hai*," Louise nodded her hatted head grandly, "also the Countess Sannomiya and Princess Terashima."

These conversations and the church services gave great pleasure to Louise, but best of all she enjoyed the long evenings in bed after the seven o'clock curfew bell and lights out. No one dared disobey this rule to save electricity after a mother in the bungalow had been beaten up for being wasteful of light when she'd got up in the night and turned on the light to tend her sick child. Through the walls Izolda and Louise had heard the screechings of the guards followed by thumps and the cries of the mother.

Thus, after Louise had brewed their nightcap of weak tea with an infusion of pine needles she had gathered from the tree overshadowing the porch, the light was turned out punctually at seven, a candle lit to gutter weakly between them, and they settled for the long night. Louise liked the candlelight. It reminded her of the old days in Japan before electricity or even gas had come, and they had clusters of candles on the missionary walls. Besides, it was warm and friendly and disguised the worst of the discolouration marks in their room.

"Your mother used to make patterns on the wall like this,"

247

Louise put down her cup on the exposed wooden part of her bed to demonstrate a church and a steeple, a butterfly. "See, Jup's ears!"

"Who's Jup?"

"Your Uncle Edouard's dog."

Izolda smiled. One of Roger's names! Her great-uncle had died before she was born. It was all so long ago. She was tired and it was cozy in bed with mosquito nets up to keep the buzzing insects at bay. One had to be careful about mosquitoes. Bites in camp turned septic. Izolda began to read her book fetched from the library where the inmates had centralised their volumes.

"Don't read too long, honey, you'll strain your eyes in this light." Louise adjusted her pillows piled against the mother-of-pearl floral pattern of her couch. She took up her board and deck of cards and began to play her Thirteen Demon game.

Izolda's thoughts, however, were not on her book. "Mrs Holden told me today that Hugh had left hospital and is with Winn and Roger in Sham-Shui-Po. I wonder how they're faring. Isn't it strange – all three of them together. Chippy ought to be there too . . ." But she knew Chippy would not have lasted long in the camp.

"Far worse for them than for us," Louise replied with truth, "the Japanese soldier has no respect for PoWs as you heard Colonel Fushimi say."

"No, I didn't hear your Colonel say that; I couldn't understand *what* you were talking about."

"Perhaps it's just as well you couldn't," muttered Louise darkly, "we can only pray the men will come through."

"I've given up praying – given up believing in God."

"Very foolish to give up your beliefs just when you need God more than you've ever needed Him in your life," Louise dealt her cards with a reproving flip. "Major Stamford's escape was a miracle straight from heaven."

"Roger came through miraculously through his own ingenuity, but all the others were . . . Every time I hear the shouts and screams from the Jail I see it all again, the executions, the blood, the horror . . ."

"When I was a good bit younger than you I rode on my black pony past scenes of execution in Tokyo – it was called Yedo then—"

"I *know* it was called Yedo. You must have told me a million times."

"I guess there's no need to be rude, Izolda. There's enough bad manners in this dump without having to add more. The Japanese have always executed people by beheading and you can't expect them to suddenly change anymore than you can expect them to stop committing *seppuku*."

"What's that?"

"*Hara-kiri*, belly-cut; ritual suicide."

"I suppose you've seen that too?"

"Not actually *seen* it done, of course not, but it happened to two courtiers I knew, a husband and wife, after the Dowager Empress's death; the same period when Mrs Carew was saved from the hangman's noose by the clemency of the Emperor."

"The Mrs Carew who gave her husband strychnine because she had a lover? Do you believe she killed him?"

"Search me."

"You haven't explained how you can go on praying."

"Well, if you stop being flippant and want a serious answer," Louise gathered up her cards triumphantly after the game had actually come out, "I have a kind of relationship with the Lord." She pressed a petal behind her and took out James's Star from the recess and studied the it in the candlelight.

"What do you mean 'a relationship' with God?"

249

"Just what I say – one establishes a relationship. Akin to a human one, I guess. Talking, listening, asking . . . don't you want to ask God to keep Major Stamford safe?" Louise demanded pertinently. Although Izolda had told her nothing she'd guessed most of it.

"Yes."

"Or pray for me at my end?"

"Oh, Grandma, I wish you—"

"You see!" Louise said with a crow, "you *do* pray. All religions have something in common, that's why I like the services here. Buddhism and Shintoism went hand in hand in Japan. Sumuko used to worship in the Myokoji Temple by Kitagata village, near where their boys went to school when they were small . . ." Louise went on about the old days. She was always mentioning Sumuko and her children these days. Izolda fell asleep while she was still talking.

"God help them," Izolda awoke to hear her grandmother praying in the middle of the night when the piteous cries from the Jail came over to the bungalow.

Why did the dreaded Kempei-tai torturers have midnight interrogations? Why always at night when by day the sounds would have been smothered by the busy noise of the camp? Was the torture inflicted by the Japanese Secret Police considered to be more efficacious at night, the prisoners more vulnerable then?

The prisoners all knew about the gurgling chokes of the water torture when heads were held under till the victims fell unconscious. Ducking five times was said to be the limit reckoned to extract the maximum information. There was the unbelievable horrendousness of drowning by forceable drinking when a prisoner was tied up, hands to feet, a pipe put down his gullet, water forced through nose and mouth . . .

unconscious . . . brought round by stamping on the stomach
. . . process repeated. Other well-known punishments were
bamboo slivers forced under fingernails, toenails wrenched
out, burns to genitals, joints torn out of sockets – the list was
sick-making and endless.

"Dear Lord, help them. O God forgive them," came fervently from the opium couch.

Izolda clapped her pillow over her head and stuffed her
fingers in her ears. But the sounds of strangled groans and
terrible shrieks continued to come over to her in the otherwise
quiet nights.

And she hated the Japanese with all her being as she had
never hated before. Her grandmother prayed for them, but
she hated them – the bestial, barbarous, creatures. She
loathed them for their crucifying of the prisoners. One of
them in there was Sir Vandaleur Grayburn, head of the Hong
Kong Bank, who had once said he did not believe war would
come to Hong Kong. When it had he had bravely, but in the
event tragically, refused to leave for China on the last boat
with other VIPs.

No, Izolda did not believe in God anymore. Not in a deity
who could allow such things to happen, who let the world
become one huge sore of suffering. Izolda wanted no truck,
no 'relationship' with a God who sat up there on His clouds
in His comfortable heaven doing absolutely bloody nothing
about the hideousness of the world He had created below.

Chapter Nineteen

STANLEY CAMP felt forgotten. What were the Allies doing, or rather *not* doing? All they had to go by was the Japanese controlled *Hong Kong News* which could be illuminating: '*The victorious Army advancing in reverse*' brought wan smiles to the inmates.

Rumours abounded that they were all to be taken out and shot. No one felt safe in the ominous quiet of the jail after a van was seen driving out. The van did not leave the Peninsular. It stopped by the jetty below the old cemetery on the hill. Hulks of tortured and still-bound men tumbled out. The loved and much respected Sir Vandaleur Grayburn was one of them. They were kicked and hustled into place to be mercilessly executed in full view of those prisoners standing above who forced themselves to watch in order to identify both executed and executors for future records.

But though the horror never left them, with the warmer weather conditions in the camp did improve. The food distribution had been reorganised, queuing reduced to a minimum, and the inmates were each given a card to prevent dishonest ones coming back twice. Moreoever Michael of Mickey's Kitchen was allotted the task of British quartermaster. He did marvels with the rations (supposed to be half a pound of rice per person per day, but more like four ounces) by varying the cooking. Sometimes he steamed the rice to make it less soggy, or fried it into rice-balls. Each day he kept a portion of raw rice to be ground on a stone mill, which was fashioned by an engineer in the camp, and made into a kind of bread. A brilliant professor, interned from the Hong Kong University, produced yeast from a hop 'starter'.

The Swiss Red Cross representative, Eric Zindel, succeeded in introducing evaporated milk into the camp for the smaller children and invalids, but the International Red Cross parcels, which were known to have arrived on the Island, were not handed out.

Tickets were issued by the Japanese for the canteen set up in the old prison officers' club where they, by encouraging the black market, made an enormous profit for themselves. Sometimes Izolda went along there with a bank note from their cache, and after a long wait returned with a pot of jam and, occasionally, some fresh eggs. Even with the food they managed to get from outside – a tin of sardines made to last for several days, some bully beef, a piece of cheese, biscuits, raisins – Louise rapidly lost the plumpness she had put on since coming to Hong Kong. She looked at her bare third finger, the indentation left of her wedding ring clearly visible, and thought how she need never have taken it off to be enlarged. Naked fingers. Naked into the world . . . naked out of it . . .

As for Izolda, her face lost its youthful roundness and became fine drawn, the effect to make her more beautiful than ever. Her slender body turned ribby, and her long legs were too thin. At Easter they pasted up the mirror in their room.

Izolda finished her stint at de-weeviling and volunteered to teach French at the children's classes. She met Peggy there, also teaching, her friend from the Kowloon pad. Peggy was pregnant and desperately worried about her husband in the

1st Middlesex, of whom she'd heard nothing since hostilities began. Izolda offered to get a message to Miss Maureen in the hopes she could find out something.

Crèches were arranged for babies, where Joan Holden helped. Afterwards she rushed back to be with Bill who was ill with fever. Many of the toddlers seen running around were still being breast fed, and mothers were encouraged by the doctors to continue for as long as they could. Kindergartens were formed; lectures arranged for adults, and the professors organised various courses. Paper and pencils were like gold, and handwriting was kept minute to preserve space. Sports for the adults and games for the children took place on the tennis courts. There were theatricals and musicals in the Hall. It all gave the illusion of a holiday camp.

But underlying these normal activities was the hunger, the dread of being punished, and perhaps worst of all, of becoming ill. And there was always the presence of the guards, mostly unobtrusive, but liable at any moment to turn nasty. As Miss Maureen had warned, the Koreans were most feared. Suddenly, with a snapping of orders, one of these would turn, screech, jab and prod with bayonet if anyone so much as stepped out of line, particularly at the assemblies for the bowing, counting sessions.

At Easter the weather was perfect, with day after day of sunshine. People lolled on the grass. Like happy picnickers they lazed among the green hills from where they could look across to the verdant mountains over the neck of the isthmus and their prison boundary.

The setting of Stanley camp was lovely with white surf breaking gently against red rocks, and emerald islands seen basking in the deep blue of a tranquil sea. Looking down on them, who could have guessed the anguish of those in that false Arcadia relaxing there, chattering, discussing, wondering, quarrelling and bickering? They were beautiful, those finely slim figures in their ragged shorts and bikini scarf tops; the men tanned and stripped to the waist, all surplus fat vanished, muscles toned with manual labour. But after Easter their beauty began to fade.

"Have you heard the rumour of an impending escape? I hope to God Roger doesn't try something like that," Izolda said in an undertone to Maisie. They were paddling in the sea, Izolda was holding Tommy under the arms encouraging him to splash and kick in the cool clear water. He'd been lethargic since his bad attack of measles.

"Roger is Roger and you can't expect him not to try and escape," Maisie replied low-voiced, an eye fixed on one of the guards. "Regulations say it's the duty of officers to do so. I imagine Hugh and Winn are of the same mind, though I don't think Hugh is fit enough. Miss Maureen reported he has a bad limp. I hope to God he doesn't try when you think of what happens if they're caught," she shivered. "Winn, not being so tall and with his knowledge of the language, would have a better chance, I would think."

"How they must detest being imprisoned." Izolda gazed out across to the little island offshore, and over to Cap D'Anguilar round which she and Roger had sailed in another time, in another free world. "Miss Maureen told us before we came in here that Winn had been put in solitary confinement for a month. Apparently after he heard how Aunt Toni was killed he hit out at the first guard he saw. She said he was lucky to have got away with a beating and being left in the guard room. Grandma worries about him. She's in a funny mood. She talks more than ever about the past."

"Did Winn know about Chippy?"

"He guessed there was something wrong. I have a hunch

Grandma wanted me to marry Winn. That was before Roger
. . . Come on, Tommy," she encouraged, "kick out and splash
your hands in the water. There, that's better."

They went to sit further up the beach and Maisie began to
towel Tommy down. The change of venue was a boon to the
women, especially the mothers. After much wrangling and
persuasion from Ian Gimson, the commandant allowed that
for a few hours daily the women and children could bathe
in Tweed Bay below the hospital. Men were not permitted
to go there or to swim, but they were given access under
guard to another beach where they could collect water for
cooking. From the sea water the prisoners produced salt by
evaporation, a very necessary adjunct to the quite insufficient
salt ration.

When the families approached to bathe at the allotted
times, the guards removed the barbed wire and counted
them as they went down the steep steps to the beach, and
counted them up again when they returned. They always got
it wrong, and there was invariably a rumpus. Apparently the
Japanese found it hard to count correctly.

"In the early days before you arrived," Maisie informed
while pulling on Tommy's shorts and setting him to play with
a battered bucket in the sand, "and before they got the count
right – well, as right as they ever can – there were several
escapes."

"How?" Izolda lowered her voice to a whisper. She kept
her eyes on the soldiers watching them from the cliff above.

"By swimming across to the mainland. In the mix-up at
that time none were recaptured. More difficult now . . .
guards, I gather, swarm in the New Territories. They say
the doctors are up to their eyes at the Leprosarium in a highly
secret escape route that was formed before the Japs invaded.
The doctors have found a way down here where they can

fish at night from the rocks, and local fishermen have been coming in the dark to sell their catch. You can imagine what the next step is."

"Some Chinese spit at us, some, like our servants, risk their lives for us. None of it makes sense. How do you know about all this?"

"I only know that something is in the offing which won't affect me as an American."

"Why?"

"My contingent may be repatriated."

"How fantastic! Why didn't you tell me before? When? Where to?"

"Shush . . . it's only a rumour. Anyway I don't want to go."

"*Maisie.* Don't be a damned fool."

"It would feel like deserting Hugh."

"Of course you must go if you get the chance. Think of Tommy. Look at him. He's never fully recovered from measles, and you said it had affected his eyes. He should have cod-liver oil – oh, all sorts of things will get him right in the States. Hugh would be the first to *insist* on your going."

"I suppose he would. Would you go and leave Roger?"

"Yes! He once told me not to be a bloody fool and put my neck in a noose, or words to that effect. Think what a fool you'd feel if you turned down the option and then *he* escaped. I also think you owe it to Hugh's father. He's never forgiven himself for pulling strings in getting you back here only to be put in the bag."

"Poor Pa-in-law. He's rottenly ill with malaria. But he shouldn't blame himself. I'd be in a worse bag in Manila. They say the women there are chained up in dungeons. What a ghastly mess it all is." Her hand pushed at her hair

257

which curled damply about her pinched face. "You know your grandmother could be repatriated?"

"I hadn't thought of that."

"Tell her from me that I'll look after her on the journey if I decide to go. She could live with my parents in Boston. They'd love to have her. You must try and make her go, Zol. It's an absolute disgrace to intern her at her age."

"You don't know Grandma once she's dug her toes in." Izolda said uneasily. She blocked her mind to the thought of being left there alone . . .

Izolda had cause to visit Dr Lawrence at the Tweed Bay Hospital. She had never been quite well since that terrible night of pain, misery and despair at the Dragon Hotel after her beating. The doctor had been such a good friend to both her and Chippy, and she was so grateful to him for his understanding. When she'd first come into camp he had condoled with her in her bereavement, and observed that her husband never lost his dignity and humour through all his difficulties. He said that he had been a courageous man if ever there was one.

Now he examined her and, with his blue eyes screwed up in his kind rubbery face, said, "Sad that Mrs Paine-Talbot had a miscarriage. You need a D and C. Don't worry, only a scrape, it's nothing; a couple of days in hospital. At the moment we haven't a bed, but I'll be in touch with you when we do. What? Worried about constipation?" the doctor's voice rose to a squeak. "Well, that's a change for the better! No need to evacuate. Stomach consumes everything in an effort to keep the body going. I have a perfectly healthy patient who hasn't been for three weeks."

"Bang goes my grandmother's 'regular habits' upbringing," Izolda smiled.

"How is my oldest patient?"

"Marvellous really, though she has lost a lot of weight. She keeps her spirits up by talking endlessly about the past."

"Better than talking about the present, and haven't we all lost weight?" he said, putting his hand comically into the loose band of his khaki shorts. "Tell her I'll be popping in to see her soon."

Dr Lawrence, with those 'in the know', walked delicately during the next few days. There was bound to be a terrible blow-up, and there was when two policemen were found to be missing. There were shouts and rushings around, whistles and curfew bells rung in the middle of the day. The inmates peered fearfully out of their windows and speculated about reprisals. The fear grew when they were made to parade and line up. But it was only for roll-call, and soon fear left and fatigue set in when no sooner were they dismissed than they were called out again for another roll-call.

Under the hot sun, and several times during that exhausting day, the whole camp of some three thousand three hundred, including the elderly like Louise and the ill like Bill Holden who were normally exempt from roll-calls, were made to go out in the heat to line up and be counted.

"*Ichi, ni, san, yo, gō, roku, nana, hachi, ku, jū,*" they began all over again.

"Just like Paris, August 1914, I guess. Your mother and I queued all day in the heat to get into the British Consulate for our exit permits," Louise recalled. She looked down at Izolda sitting on the ground beside her camp stool.

"*San-jū, san-jū-ichi, san-jū-ni,*" the voices droned on. They came nearer. Louise stood up. Izolda did not. "STAND UP," screamed the Korean guard, jabbing at Izolda's feet with his rifle butt. She quickly did so.

"Bow!" a Japanese yelled, "show respect for guard!" She bowed – glaring.

"*Go-jū, go-jū-ichi, go-jū-ni,*" it went on.

"*Hyaku.* What's that? Where've we got to?" Izolda asked in the burning heat.

"A hundred," said Louise. She put up her umbrella and sat down firmly on her camp stool.

"Oh God. Only got to a hundred."

"I wish you wouldn't go on saying 'Oh God' all the time, Izolda," Louise reproved, "I've never liked to hear it, least of all on a lady's lips."

"*Lady?* Look at us all – ladies, huh!"

"*Put down umbrella!*" A Japanese officer confronted them what seemed like hours later.

"Sun is too hot for old grandmother like me," Louise said in Japanese, bowing politely from her sitting position, "most gracious for chivalrous Japanese officer allow an old woman sit under shade of umbrella."

He looked at her, a grin spreading over his high-cheekboned face. "Allow to sit!" he barked.

"Where have we got to now?"

"Getting on. *Ni-sen*: two thousand."

There were shouted lectures and dire threats of reprisals if anyone else tried to escape, and eventually they were allowed to go.

"Nip-lovers; Jap-servers!" The words were spat out at Louise and Izolda when they neared their bungalow. By then Louise was tottering with fatigue. "Oh, fiddle-di-dee to you," she expressed crossly in a voice loud enough for them to hear.

"How can they be so stupid, Grandma?" Izolda said once they were in their room. "No one can hate the Japs more than I. I loathe having to bow to them."

"I can't think why you object to bowing, honey. I've done it all my life. There is nothing subservient about it. Is it humiliating to doff the hat? It is polite to bow and it's the Japanese custom. They do it before each other constantly and that's all there is to it."

"Oh, *Grandma*. You and your Japanese!"

Louise was gardening again for the first time since she had left France. She dug the soil by grasping a table fork in her sorely cracked fingers.

It had all started with Peggy. Both Izolda and Louise had taken her under their wing in her distress after she'd heard her husband of a few weeks had been killed on the Island in one of the last battles, and that her child would be a posthumous baby. In gratitude, Peggy had brought over a straggly pot of geraniums. Louise proceeded to kneel down and hoe up the bed full of weeds under the window. She prepared the soil by adding sand from the paths – now bone dry – and mixing in pieces of stool collected in a flower pot after she had been to the closet.

"How revolting," Izolda had been disgusted.

"Not revolting, natural. The Japanese grew rice that yielded two and sometimes three crops a year from a good coating of human manure. Nothing wrong with that, though the fields did smell rather like the *fu-fu* barges do here. We used to wear bandanas over our noses riding past the paddy."

She took cuttings from Peggy's plant and stuck them into her new bed. They flourished. She sent a message to Miss Maureen for seeds and was soon growing lettuces, tomatoes and nasturtiums beside her geraniums. No longer did Izolda have to get up at dawn to empty the chamber-pot when all she had to do was splash water

261

onto it from the tap and tip it onto the beds with such favourable results.

Dr Lawrence, when he called to see Louise, was so impressed with her special tea boiled for fifteen minutes with an infusion of young pine needles from their tree outside the window, that he formed the habit of coming in to see her once a week, and always at afternoon tea time. He was making a study of malnutrition and why it affected the young more than the old. Their conversations were as enlightening as were, in a different way, Louise's with Corporal Seki.

"Pine needles contain Vitamin C," Dr Lawrence nodded approvingly as he sipped the hot brew.

"In Japan pine was known to be nutritious long before vitamins were heard of," Louise answered with a snort. "Did you know that nasturtium seeds are good to eat, Dr Lawrence?" she enquired on another day when he was looking at her plants. "With Michael's bread, the leaves are quite delicious in a sandwich. And diluted urine is good for tomatoes. Just look how mine have come on," she pointed proudly.

"Excellent," he admired. "What else can you enlighten me about, Mrs Winter?"

"Seaweed," Louise sparkled. "Is there any round the Peninsular? Full of health-giving properties. The Japanese eat a great deal of pressed seaweed in their own country."

"Good idea. I'll get the men to have a search when they collect the sea water."

"And tell anyone starting a garden to use the sludge in the drains for manure. Also make them deposit their wood ash on the soil. You know, doctor, it came to me in the middle of the night that it is the *low* diet which makes the mind so clear. I guess we're becoming aesthetics. Put that down in your book on malnutrition!"

"Pellagra," said Dr Lawrence, "beri-beri, oedema, burning electric feet, bones hurting, the itch (he had examined Louise's forearms), all deficiency diseases and all multiplying in the camp. We need every available vitamin we can scrounge. As for medical supplies, if only I could lay my hands on some." The doctor's face twisted with frustration. "We are desperately short; running out of everything. No quinine left. I have a dozen cases including that of Mr Holden whom I could cure in a matter of days had I got quinine. I wish you could think of some way, Mrs Winter," he teased, "to grow drugs!"

Dr Lawrence did not know it at the time, and neither did his oldest patient, but on that day his jocular remark sowed a tiny seed in Louise's receptive mind.

Louise was not the only one to start a garden that first year. Once Stanley camp had shaken down to dull routine, inventiveness increased through dire need. Gardens sprang up all over the hillsides. Bare patches of land vanished under a plethora of vegetable plots interspersed with the old mimosa bushes and hibiscus hedges flowering beside scented deep orange lilies that grew everywhere and gave an exotic touch to the shabby, half-derelict houses.

Humane little Corporal Seki was particularly appreciative of the gardens and could be seen wandering through them with approving eye, rifle and bayonet slung over his shoulder. He had developed a great respect for the *Seyo no Fujin* who had known royalty, and he liked to stop by the bungalow and watch her kneeling on some sacking tending her tomatoes.

"You have family in Nippon, Seki-*san*?" Louise looked up at him.

"*Hai*, Lady-*san*, I have childrens Nippon," he took out a

snapshot from his pocket and showed it to her. Louise nodded approvingly. "Have you been up Matchless Hill of Mount Fujiyama?" she sat down on her camp stool for a chat.

"Sacred mountain where the gods live? No Lady-*san*, not ever."

"I have! On a rainy day . . . with my husband-to-be before we were married. We looked across the rim at the top and saw ourselves reflected in a rainbow!"

"That good omen for long and happy marriage, Lady-*san*."

"Yes," expressed Louise softly.

"They grow straight and tall like granddaughter," he observed the geraniums, his head held critically to one side.

"I was first to grow them from cuttings in Yokohama. Many moons before you were born, Seki-*san*."

"*Aie*, it is good to have long venerable life."

"This patch is nothing. You should have seen my garden on Bluff. So many beautiful flowers and an orchard of *kakis* and *bewas*."

"*Ai*. What would I not give to eat juicy *kaki* here."

"I too," sighed Louise.

"*Domo arigatō*, Lady-*san*," Corporal Seki bowed slightly taking his leave. It was unheard-of for a guard to bow, and he would have been beaten for doing so had his superiors seen him.

Next day in the lobby, although there were no persimmons nor medlars, Louise found a small offering of fruit.

Chapter Twenty

JUNE came. The American repatriation scheme was put into operation. Maisie and Tommy were going. Would Mrs Winter come with them? Izolda added her persuasions to Maisie's for she could see how her grandmother had deteriorated in body, though not in spirit, during the five months they'd been in captivity; and she held her breath at the thought of her going.

But she did not have to hold it for long. Louise made a string of excuses as to why she would not go: she was too old to move to a new country even though it was the land of her birth. The ship – a Japanese one – would be uncomfortable and crowded. The food would probably be worse than here where at least she could recook it. The boat might even be sunk by the American navy. *That* would be an ironic end if ever there was one!

It was obvious to the handful in camp who knew Louise, that she had no intention of leaving her granddaughter. But what not even Izolda perceived, was that in an extraordinary way her grandmother liked being where she was. She liked seeing the Japanese round about the place even if they were rough and sometimes brutal soldiery. She liked hearing them talk even if it was mostly barked orders, and she loved her conversations with Seki. Besides, when very old, needs were few.

Louise was comfortable on her couch with her precious possessions in the secret drawer behind her pillows. She had the Order to look at and dream over; the chlorodyne drops to take when she needed them and the sips of brandy if she felt cold or trembly. She was not in any pain, and though the itch was aggravating, she could put up with a little thing like that. The diet was unpalatable to say the least, but she was not hungry, let alone ravenous as Izolda was all the time. She only hankered for dainty food like Cookie's sesame cakes. Moreover, and perhaps best of all, she liked the long candlelit nights when she played her Patience and listened to her granddaughter sleeping close beside her so that sometimes she forgot Izolda was grown-up and thought of her as the child she had taken to live with her in the sun. Here she was never lonely as she had been at The Falls where the family were out a great deal and always busy. To sum up, Louise, in her great old age with the biggest adventure of all ever drawing nearer – that of death into another life of reunion with her loved ones – was content to be where she was.

There was a great deal of envy in the camp for the lucky three hundred Americans who were leaving, though the envy was ameliorated somewhat by the knowledge that a few of those remaining would benefit from vacated rooms. Much excited speculation went on as to who would be the next nationality selected to leave. All bets were on the Canadians, and if so was it not conceivable that certain British age groups might follow? Hope rose.

The great day arrived, and leaving Peggy in charge of their rooms, as pilfering was rife, Louise and Izolda, together with the Holdens and a crowd of onlookers, made their slow way up and over to the narrow cemetery athwart the hillside from where they could best watch the unique occasion. Bill Holden's walk had turned into a painful shuffle. Unrecognisable from the man first met at The Falls, Bill puffed and swayed like a drunkard on swollen legs. Flaps of empty skin fell over the trouser band under his open shirt. He managed to breast the hill, and sat down panting on the cemetery wall to roll his tobacco (made of dried hibiscus leaves) into the semblance of a cigarette. All the while his mottled hands shook with ague.

The *Asama Mara* lay anchored well out in Stanley Bay. She was a shabby Japanese steamer with newly painted white crosses standing out on her sides for all to see. Boats ferried the American repatriates out from the jutting pier on the Peninsular near to where the executions had taken place. The watching crowd raised a cheer and the Americans waved back.

The distance was too great to pick out Maisie and Tommy, and the throats of the small party waving them off were too constricted to give much of a cheer. Izolda's feelings were mixed. She was glad for Maisie and Tommy and at the same time sad for herself that they were leaving. But what brought a lump to her throat and tears to her eyes was the view from up there which reminded her so much of her time with Roger and brought back in desperate measure her longing to be with him again. The scene before her showed the dramatic old Fort they had sailed around, the new white Jail of more recent horrors, the old brigade quarters by the playing fields, and the science block with the prison officers' quarters behind. Beyond the promontory lay the picturesque little fishing village of Stanley where she and Roger had left the junk overnight. Long low Repulse Hotel in the next bay where they had dined, she could not see for the fold of hills, but she could remember every detail of that blissful time. Now the

Peninsular, sailed round so blithely, had become her prison. She knew every yard and corner of it horribly intimately.

With a last look at the ship, the four turned away and began to wander back down the tree-shaded old cemetery with its graves of those ravaged by malaria in the last century, and its many sad new graves. Most of these latter ones were unnecessary deaths due to weakness and lack of resistance to disease through starvation. The funerals here were particularly affecting with the same coffin having to be used again and again. Each body, shrouded in sacking, was removed from the box and limply, awkwardly lowered six feet into the earth – that was, six feet at first. Now the graves were getting more and more shallow as the living prisoners' strength for digging diminished.

Louise did not like the thought of such an undignified burial for herself anymore than anyone else did. Other younger ones hoped beyond hope that they would survive the camp. But Louise was too old for such delusions. Her end in the gradual deterioration she felt within herself was too inevitable to shrug off with equanimity, and by virtue of being Louise she did not let it rest there. Instead, in the face of impossible odds, she determined to do something about it, and that night, lying awake as usual, she worked out a plan.

She had all her life prayed and planned. With her the two went hand in hand particularly after an emergency or when faced with a dilemma. Even if it never came to anything it was a good idea to plan. It kept the mind busy and made one think of something positive. Besides, quite often her plans *did* come off!

On the morrow she would write a letter and have it delivered through Corporal Seki.

Soon after the American contingent left, news came through

268

of an epidemic of diptheria sweeping through the Sham-Shui-Po prisoner of war camp. The only treatment the doctors were able to give their patients was to keep them lying flat for three weeks in an attempt to ease the strain on their hearts. It was not enough, and the death toll rose alarmingly. Louise, already worried that her grandson might catch the disease in Sham-Shui-Po, now worried for her other grandchild, Izolda, who had gone into the Tweed Bay hospital, and had had her minor operation successfully, only to develop a fever twenty-four hours later.

At first Dr Lawrence feared that diptheria had come to Stanley and Izolda was the first case, but after two days he diagnosed an infection, for which he needed M & B sulphanilamide as treatment. On investigation he was told that they had run out of supply. The fever took hold and rose, swinging Izolda into delirious incoherence. When Louise next visited the hospital, her granddaughter scarcely recognised her.

To Joan Holden's deep grief and the sadness of their many Hong Kong friends in the camp, Bill passed away in his room from the results of malaria. On the same day two children died of dysentery and another was at death's door. Several adults were dangerously ill with scrub typhus and tick fever. Peggy's baby was born prematurely and did not survive more than a few hours, and Izolda's condition was slowly deteriorating. The war had not ended, nor looked like ending, nor did anyone any longer expect the Chinese 7th Army to come to the rescue. The whole of Stanley Camp was plunged into its worst depression so far.

Lying on her couch alone and awake in the dark of her room, Louise desperately searched in her mind for what she could do. She'd had a satisfactory reply to her letter via Seki in answer to her 'plan'. With the reply had come a present of sweets and fruit. Why not try another petition to the same source?

Louise felt for the matchbox on the side of her couch and lit the candle. She sat up in bed, tore a page out of the exercise book in the hidden panel and wrote a second letter in her flowing Japanese calligraphy.

In the morning she gave the missive marked 'For Immediate Delivery' to Corporal Seki to hand in to Headquarters. Then she called urgently for Dr Lawrence to come and see her. He arrived with sombre face. Izolda was weaker. Her heart could not stand many more days of high fever. Louise confided her plans to him. It was absolutely essential to get certain facts right before she could proceed.

To Louise's great relief, Jimmy's black Cadillac arrived pronto outside the bungalow with a Japanese Army driver at the wheel. She climbed into the back; an armed guard sat in front with the driver, and to the fury of some inmates of the camp, old Mrs Winter was seen to be driven through the guard post and away over the neck of the isthmus.

On entering Jimmy's ground floor study at The Falls, Louise's eyes were immediately drawn to the Fushimi family 9th-century Emaki scroll hanging on the wall facing her. The picture was exactly as she remembered it in the old Fushimi home. Of finely drawn bamboo grass and a rising moon painted on silk, the *tanku* hieroglyphics read:

> *The*
> *gods*
> *will*
> *guard*
> > *the*
> > *pure*
> > *in*
> > *heart*

270

"Very old, very valuable, very beautiful . . ." Louise murmured, her eyes translating the Japanese writing as she composed herself on a chair before the desk. She sat there looking at the scroll and remembering. Her shiny straw hat rested at its slight angle on her white hair nicely crinkled at the sides from the pipe cleaners. On her lap a black leather bag was clasped tightly in her gloved hands.

With his samurai sword clanking, Colonel Fushimi sat down behind the desk with his back to, and his figure framed by, the Emaki scroll. He said nothing but he noticed how very much older Mrs Winter had grown in the months since their last meeting. Although she sat upright in her chair without touching the back, to him she appeared a shrunken little wizened old woman, extraordinarily Japanese-looking. Pity she was not Japanese. Had she not been an enemy alien he could have allowed her to stay on at The Falls.

On her part, as they took one another in, Louise noticed the streaks of grey in the Colonel's blue-black hair, and the new medals. Also, was he never parted from his sword?

"Congratulate on good health and long life," Colonel Fushimi pronounced into the silence. "Camp good place for internees. Plenty fresh air and exercise. Everyone happy there!" His scarred face puckered into the twisted smile Louise found not unattractive.

"*Domo arigatō gazaimasu*, Colonel Fushimi-*san*," and Louise thanked him for the present of fruit and sweets. For a good five minutes the two in the study exchanged, in measured Japanese tones, the polite preliminaries of the day, during which time the Colonel mentioned the contents of Louise's first letter.

271

"May I be allowed to enquire reason for urgent request for interview, Madam?" he then asked with an amused and courteous air.

"Men in camps are dying unnecessarily of diptheria," Louise plunged in. She spoke in English, for some of the medical words she had to use were unknown to her in Japanese – and anyway she knew the Colonel liked to air his English and she hoped to keep him in the benign mood of his introduction. "You know, I am sure, Colonel Fushimi, that my grandson is prisoner of war in Sham-Shui-Po camp. It is he who should inherit this house and all its treasures from his father, my . . . er . . . late son. They die there of diptheria due to no serum for the required injections to save life. In Stanley camp for civilians, children and grown-ups are dangerously ill in hospital with dysentery, others with tick fever or with malaria for which there is no quinine nor atebrin left. The state of those with ulcers is terrible to see when gangrene sets in, and there are many cases of beri-beri due to hydropic deficiency. More and more of these cases appear all the time because of lack of Vitaman B."

The Colonel's mild expression changed to one of annoyance as Louise's tirade continued, and she, seeing this, hurried on for fear he might cut her off short before she had time to get out all she had to say.

"My granddaughter is ill in the hospital," she went on quickly. "She has an infection and high fever which may kill her since the doctors have run out of sulphanilamide, the wonder drug recently discovered. The rations you give us are of starvation level, and in our weakness we succumb easily to disease when we have no medicines nor drugs with which to combat them. Hospitals in the camps are known as 'Death Houses', because so many in them die. It is not the Bushido chivalry I once knew of a great

272

nation to treat hapless prisoners thus. It is butchery!" There.
She'd said it.

Colonel Fushimi stiffened alarmingly in his seat. His face
flushed and reddened his scar in a way Louise recognised as
a warning. Had she been too blunt too soon? Careful – she
must go carefully or she would not get anywhere.

"You come here on personal call, Madam," Colonel
Fushimi said in a clipped and irritated tone. He laid his
neat hands to hold the desk before him and leaned towards
her with a glower, "How camps run no concern of mine. I
not guard," (he spat out the word contemptuously) "I am
fighting officer serving in Headquarters House, Hong Kong.
You are under occupation. If have complaint you send in
correct manner to camp commandant. He will listen. He will
do everything he can to make prisoners well."

"Commander Yamashita has been approached repeatedly
by the chairman of our camp committee, to no effect. He
seems indifferent to the suffering; indeed he is unconcerned
to such an extent it makes us believe he welcomes the fact
that the more of us die the fewer mouths there are for him
to feed."

"Do not worry, please," Colonel Fushimi said in bored
tones, "you must be happy under Japanese protection."

"Happy?" flashed Louise, glaring at him with her hooded
eyes. "How can people be happy when they are starving?
How can I not worry when my granddaughter is seriously
ill? The camp commandant tells us drugs are not to be had
on the Island, but we know that is *not true*. Neither have
we received *any* Red Cross parcels to which we are entitled
under international law. I know, I know," Louise would
not be interrupted when the Colonel opened his mouth to
speak, ". . . your government has never ratified the Geneva
convention. You told me that last time we met. That does

273

not exonerate you from following international law of all civilised nations. It is a disgrace. Japan was a civilised nation long before the West. We know that the Swiss consul Mr Zindel has delivered parcels to the commandant, yet we do not receive them. What happens to them? It is obvious that your well-fed soldiers enjoy their contents."

"You go too far, Madam!" the Colonel hissed out the words furiously at Louise. He had not brought her here to insult him. His trimmed and reddish moustache twitched with anger, "My soldiers *not* better fed; you served same rations as soldiers. There is shortage of food for everyone, shortage of drugs for my men also. Many Japanese soldiers die of diphtheria – all same war shortages. Life very difficult after war. We deal with prisoners kindly; we leave you alone; you only have to be good in order to be healthy and happy. *No* confiscate parcels if you good!"

"We are not children, Colonel Fushimi. For the slightest thing such as leaving the lights on a few minutes after curfew, for untidiness, or lack of bowing sufficiently which custom I find gracious though my compatriots find it alien to their culture, for all these small things our rations are cut as punishment. Why do you treat us like this?" Louise went on relentlessly in her absolute determination to hammer him and get rid of the usual senseless patter of being happy. Well into her stride now, sometimes she drummed it home in English, sometimes when she saw he was about to burst, she reverted to the softer tones of her flowery Japanese.

"This disobeying orders *not* small matter; this bowing very important for discipline. I repeat, Madam, how this camp run *no* affair of mine. About Red Cross parcels I will look into. Law of civilised country! If soldiers interfering they will be severely punished."

"*Domo arigatō*, Colonel Fushimi-*san*. I thank thee most kindly for this generous statement."

She had scored one point – the Red Cross parcels – but that was not enough, nothing like enough. She must go on and she was tiring. She felt the nervous energy she'd built up draining out of her. She must not allow herself to faint however much her heart fluttered with the strain. She wished she could have a sip of brandy to steady her and warm her limbs which felt frozen even though the temperature in the study was high and the fan on the ceiling whirled warm air. She had not had her usual nip that morning. She had more sense than to arrive at Hojo's breathing brandy fumes!

Once more Louise took a deep breath. "The question of the Red Cross food parcels unfortunately does not help over drugs for those dying of diphtheria, dysentery and malaria, nor provide anaesthetics for those waiting for operations, nor give the sulphanilamide for septicaemia that my granddaughter desperately needs to stay alive. Colonel Fushimi, you know that this granddaughter is . . . she is more dear to me than anything in the world." The words came slowly, wrung out of her.

"I repeat, Madam, I cannot help in this matter, *not* interfere in internal affair of Stanley civilian camp. I do best for you, give you suite, give you fruit, to help granddaughter. I am Nippon fighting soldier of the shock troops of the Imperial Japanese Army *not* concerned with menial task of guarding prisoners. I bring you here in answer to 'most personal matter'," the Colonel tapped her letter on the desk with a well-shaped fingernail, "your request, Madam, NOT personal matter!"

"That it would save my grandchildren's lives in the two camps should be very personal to you, Colonel Fushimi-*san*. After all, we both know—"

275

"WISH NOT TO HEAR!" the Colonel interrupted with a bellow, "I have given answer. Interview closed!" He rose as he spoke, sinewy figure looming, ornate jewelled scabbard glittering.

Louise clasped her handbag more tightly, her eyes on the scabbard. She was sure it was the same valuable one his father had worn at James's funeral on the Bluff. It clanked against the desk that separated them, a desk which seemed to emphasise the impossible divide she was vainly trying to bridge. The flimsy connecting silken thread she had woven between them was at breaking point. All was nearly lost with his anger and curt dismissal of her, and her main reason for coming – the essential drugs – were as far out of reach as ever.

Louise did not move when the Colonel rose. She sat stolidly on, a little old lady with bright black button eyes fixed unwaveringly upon him. She still had her trump card to play. She had kept it to the very last in the hopes that she would not have to use it. But now, since all other appeals and persuasions had failed, play it she would have to in the same manner as in her 'One Man' patience game she turned over a card to give herself one more chance to win.

She noticed again, as the Colonel stood behind his desk glowering at her, and waiting impatiently for her to rise and take her leave, the two new medals on his chest – for the taking of Hong Kong she presumed. A fine and brave fighting man . . . James would have been proud of him . . .

"There is one more subject, *dozo* please. I request thy patience, Colonel Fushimi-*san*, before I finally cease to be of trouble to thee," Louise expressed in Japanese, "if, as it were, thou receivest message from The Tenno, Holy of Holiest, Heavenly King descended from the Sun Goddess

Amaterasu, 'She who shines in sky', Great Emperor of Japan himself . . ."

Still standing, the Colonel stared at Louise, his eyes like slits. Was she mad this old old woman whose house he enjoyed living in, whose late son's treasures he guarded as if they were his own – the old woman whose presence in Hong Kong so disturbed him? She must be insane to take the name of the sacred Emperor himself in vain. He would have no more dealings with her. He had been foolish to allow her to come here out of a certain sense of . . . kinship, out of a feeling she did have something important of a personal nature to impart; out of curiosity perhaps. Instead she had bombarded him with a lot of irrelevant requests.

". . . if thou wert to receive insignia of honour from Emperor, wouldst thou obey and wouldst thou keep thy word to the bearer of such a gift, Colonel Fushimi-*san*?"

"Foolish question," the Colonel jeered with a flash of gold teeth, "thou knowest well tradition of Japanese. Very well thou knowest samurai officer obey the Tenno willingly with his life. Thou knowest I AM THE SWORD OF MY EMPEROR!" The proud words rang out loud and clear in Jimmy's study.

"I know that thy holy Emperor's forebear, the great Emperor Meiji, presented to my husband most prized possession . . ."

"*Hai?*" The Colonel breathed when Louise hesitated, his temper receding as quickly as it had flared, his imagination caught like a child's at her mysterious words.

"If thou couldst see this possession, touch it, hold it, keep it and hand on to thy sons and their sons and heirs, wouldst thou give me thy word as honourable-in-war-and-peace Samurai warrior, feared and admired for centuries by thy peoples, to

277

do thy utmost to bring drugs and medicines urgently needed in Stanley, Sham-Shui-Po and the other prison camps in the quickest possible time?"

"The . . . uh . . . possession, given by person of Emperor himself?"

"*Hai*, Colonel Fushimi-*san*, by his very hands. I watched him do so at the Imperial Palace in Tokyo. With these same eyes I saw His Majesty in the audience throne room, and afterwards spoke myself with Her Gracious Majesty. *Hai*, verily, that was great day in our lives."

"And thou wouldst give this precious relic in return for drugs?"

"*Hai*, I would. Right it is that thou shouldst have it with the blood that flows in thy veins."

"Where does this relic lie? In Falls maybe? I not see it?" he looked about the study in some puzzlement.

"I keep in safe place."

"Where is that?"

"First thy word, Colonel-*san*."

Imperceptibly Colonel Fushimi, standing behind his desk, hesitated. If the old lady was not mad and could in fact produce something of considerable value to him – some antique perhaps or porcelain vase that had once belonged to Emperor Meiji, he indeed knew exactly where he could lay his hands on a considerable amount of drugs. His own soldiers were not so badly off as he had indicated. He could, with impunity, give his word. It was tempting to, yet still he did not quite trust her.

"Thy word, Colonel," Louise insisted. She held her breath and prayed that the lure was too great for him to resist.

Then, "With my honour as samurai for bond I give my pledge," and Colonel Fushimi, tall behind the desk, excessively smartly touched the hilt of his sword with his right hand, brought it up to his left shoulder, then raised it to his cap in the grand salute.

"I have it on me," Louise said rising to her feet. She took two unsteady steps towards him and dumped her black leather handbag onto the desk. She opened the clasp, drew out and gently laid on the table the *Order of the Star of the Rising Sun*, half caressing it as she did so.

They stood there on either side of the desk gazing at the Star, and Louise looked long and for the last time upon its beautiful smooth surface. The central round ruby stone shone gloriously as if alive. Surrounding the ruby, silver-tipped rays sparkled and reflected like brilliant stars circling the sun.

Louise had treasured the Order since that never-to-be-forgotten day in the last century at the Imperial Palace. It had rested for years in the place of honour on the grand piano in their drawing room on the Bluff with the Emperor's signed photograph in a silver frame next to it. It had lain with its ribbon on James's coffin surrounded by mountains of flowers, one of them a wreath from the Emperor. The Star, found by her in the still warm ashes which was all that was left of her home after the earthquake, had given her the courage to go on in life, and it had travelled with her from that day wherever she went. It was the Star which she treasured above all else, her husband's precious Order, her last and most prized possession – a very part of her.

And now it was Colonel Fushimi's. Louise watched him taking it in and taking it over. His eyes were wide open, dark globes of wonder and delight. He lifted the jewel from off the desk and with reverence held it up to the light to see its lustrous colour the better, and to read the inscription delicately engraved on a green and purple flowered hasp. He turned it in his small square-fingered hands as lovingly as Louise had held it to her hot cheek after the earthquake. And she knew that what she had done was good.

"It is fitting that the Order given to thy grandfather should go back with thee to our beautiful Land of the Rising Sun," Louise said softly. "*Sayonara*, Colonel *Hojo Fushimi-san.*" He did not answer, but before he called the guard to show her out, he bowed very low in front of her.

It was the bow that Japanese men only use before ladies of high birth.

Chapter Twenty-One

COLONEL FUSHIMI was true to his honourable word. Most unexpectedly – to everyone except Louise and Dr Lawrence – the various doctors in the camps were summoned to headquarters where they were handed out a considerable quantity of drugs. The immediate effect of the application of these medical supplies, could only be described as miraculous, not the least the rapid normalising of Izolda's temperature once sulphanilamide had been administered.

Amoebic dysentery was cured with emertine injections. Men with strangled breathing at Sham-Shui-Po recovered after being given the anti-diphtheria serum. Quinine restored the malarial victims, and operations which had been debilitating waiting patients could now take place under the new batch of anaesthetics.

And not only that. Red Cross parcels arrived. They were the size of shoe boxes, with no less than fifteen items in each, soap as well as other forgotten goodies. In Stanley camp the internees were given *two* parcels as if to make up for the backlog. It was incredible! Some gorged themselves all at once, others – as did Louise and Izolda – eked out their portions, with every day one delicious mouthful to look forward to. And the more pessimistic inmates saved some in case they were still incarcerated at Christmas, which God forbid. A whole year in camp was unthinkable.

For a while speculation was rife as to what had precipitated the influx and what had caused the Japanese to have this sudden change of heart. Was the war not going so well as the Japanese *Hong Kong News* made out? Were they starting to curry favour in a turn of the tide towards the Allies? The doctors were suspected of knowing the truth, but if so they were not saying anything – and nor was Louise. Not even to Izolda. Louise was pleased with the success of her plan and enormously relieved to have her granddaughter back with her and restored, albeit needing a great deal of rest to gather her strength again. But Louise missed the Star more than she had thought possible. She kept forgetting that she'd given it away and, finding it no longer in the secret drawer, was reminded and hurt all over again.

To help her convalescence, Izolda went down at every opportunity to the charming little cove just round from the Tweed Bay hospital to swim. By now it was the autumn of 1942 and the weather, after the long hot summer of her illness, was still very warm. She bathed with the other women and children, and then took herself off with her bowl of rice to picnic on the rocks. She always settled down in the same spot away from the others and beyond the quarry to where the boulders hid her from the guard's outlook on the cliff. It was from this secluded spot that the doctors fished at night and fishing boats came in surreptitiously to sell their catch to the British prisoners.

Browner than she had ever been, as bronze-tanned as a native, her hair chopped short and bleached, Izolda was bone-thin and oddly dressed in scantily patched shorts and sun top, her brown midriff showing. As slowly as she could she ate her rice ration, grain by careful grain, at the same time studiously memorising every rock and contour of the beach. All the while her thoughts were on Roger, and every night she dreamed of meeting him again . . .

The conditions in Sham-Shui-Po camp had been appalling right from the start – far worse than at Stanley. But the morale therein was far better. After its repeated bombing, Sham-Shui-Po had been looted and gutted, and when the first batch of prisoners arrived they found only blasted windows and no doors, let alone bathroom or kitchen fitments, furniture, beds or bedding. In the marvellously ingenious ways of organised groups of capable, disciplined regulars and volunteers, the men had, with makeshift tools, scrounged bits and pieces and with vital parts smuggled in through the wire, pitched in and patched up the camp into some sort of habitation.

On being picked up, Roger had been taken to Sham-Shui-Po in January 1942 and thrown into solitary confinement in what was little more than a hole in the ground behind the guard room. It had been a bad time. He had no idea who was in the prisoner of war camp, or where his officers and men were, or even whether others had escaped the massacre at Eu-Cliffe castle before which, at the surrender, he'd been stripped of everything except his bare clothing and identity disc.

Now, left incarcerated and inactive in the confined blacked-out dungeon space too small to stand up in or lie down; starved, thirsty, dirty and with only a stinking latrine bucket for companionship, he thought longingly of the North-West Frontier and his clean dug-out where he'd lain fully stretched out with face to the stars in the velvet heavens.

He strained his ears for the sound of English voices but could only hear the barked orders and hisses of Japanese guards. In those first days of void, blackness and isolation

283

before a guard shoved two tablespoons of rice and some water through the grill, strong-willed professional soldier Roger Stamford hit as near to rock bottom as it was possible to get.

Then on the third day he heard the unmistakable voice of his Forward Observation Officer, Mike Mitchell, singing in Urdu. At the top of his voice the young man sang a bawdy version of the Pathan song learned on the Frontier, and it was the sweetest sound Roger had ever heard:

'There's a boy across the river, with an arse like a peach, but alas I cannot swim . . .'

The words came to an abrupt end, and Roger could imagine how Mike was being butted with a rifle and shoved unceremoniously away from the vicinity of the guard room. But the words had done what they'd intended. He was not alone. His friends were in the camp. The snatch of song brought a smile to Roger's grey lips and gave him an incalculable uplift of hope. He began to exercise in his cramped position.

When after a month Roger was released from solitary confinement, Mike was there waiting to take him to their quarters. He was put in the picture and told where his men and his orderly Hassan Khan – released from hospital – were in another part of the camp. He went over to see them and re-met Winn, who, being uncommissioned, had the extra hardship of having to work as a coolie outside the camp. Winn, looking much the same – it was the big men who seemed to suffer worst – took Roger to the wire to speak with Miss Maureen and hear news of Izolda in the civilian camp.

The next and last prisoner of war to arrive in Sham-Shui-Po camp was Hugh Holden from the convent hospital. His appearance was a shock to his Sapper contemporaries. He was limping badly, still a sick man who should never have been discharged so soon. Friends rallied round him and did what they could to collect his rations and see he was exempted from parades.

A great many friendships arose in the brutal conditions of the Sham-Shui-Po and there was none greater than the one formed between Roger, Hugh and Winn. Regular soldiers Roger and Hugh already had much in common – and now Winn, the gritty Volunteer, joined them in collaboration for the most audacious venture of their lives that was to take nine months to formulate and devise with help from outside.

It was Winn who was the lynchpin to their escape plan. He was the one who got in touch with the epic British Army Aid Group known to its members as 'Bag' for short, and his own particular link, the anonymous 'Why'. The Chinese agents – except for one or two British executives the agents were mostly loyal Chinese – met regularly in a café in Queen's Road on the Island right under the noses of the Japanese. The great advantage and essentiality of having Winn as a potential escapee was his ability to meet his contact in Kowloon while out at work.

Together with all the other 'desk men' who had fought in the Hong Kong Volunteer Defence Force as other ranks, Winn was unused to manual labour, let alone navvying with the fit (to begin with) British and Canadian regular troops. But Winn was an athlete and made of tough Winter stock.

The routine for the other ranks was ruthless and relentless. They rose at four a.m., swallowed some rice, trudged off under heavy guard the four miles to Kai Tak airfield where for the rest of the punishing day they worked collecting stone from the walls of the city to build a new cross-runway on the landing strip. They were given a small amount of rice during the one short break in the day. At dusk they tramped back to the camp, were searched, and given an evening meal of watery soup.

In filthy conditions, the other ranks fell spent onto their bedboards where they attempted to sleep whilst being tortured by bedbugs hidden by day in the cracks of wood on their tiered bunks. It was unmitigated hell, and many of the older executives died within a few weeks under these penal conditions. With those who lived on, the deprivations began to tell in bones aching, legs swelling down to agonisingly hot feet which nothing would cool. On average, five burials took place daily in Sham-Shui-Po.

"My men are worn out," Roger, ever a tower of unbending strength, fought every inch of the way for better conditions for his *jawans* and especially for Hassan Khan whom he'd saved from the hospital in Kowloon only to see him now dying before his eyes of deprivation and overwork. "The Indians are starving," he said on another occasion. "Their mortality rate is higher than any other. They cannot be expected to work the long hours unless you give them more food and better living conditions. I demand they be given a day off in the week to rest, clean up and mend."

More often than not when Roger put up his petitions, he was knocked down and beaten for his pains and thrown once more into solitary confinement, which imprisonment, though bad enough, had lost the trauma of his first experience owing to his friends having discovered a way to smuggle in food and notes. No sooner was Roger released than he was at it again standing up to the guards, demanding rights by the Geneva convention, insisting on better treatment for his men and generally being such a nuisance with his outstanding presence towering over them, that he earned the grudging admiration of the Japanese guards who eventually gave way and relaxed some of the more farcical rules imposed on the Indians.

But though in the summer the health of the prisoners improved, and indeed many lives were saved through the mysterious batch of drugs which were supposed to have arrived through some benefactor on Victoria Island, the rations in Sham-Shui-Po camp deteriorated to famine proportions. It was said that there *was* no food left in Hong Kong and that the Chinese peasants were starving.

A draught of prisoners was sent off to Japan where it was spread around that there was plenty of food, living conditions were better, and the work in shipbuilding or mines was less arduous than the work in Hong Kong. Then other reports came through of death ships on the way and death camps when they got there. In the ships the prisoners of war were battened down like cattle and left without water in the heat of the holds. One report told of a ship torpedoed by the Americans off the coast of China and sunk with thousands of prisoners left trapped below to drown, while the crew took to the boats. Conditions in the Japanese homeland camps were reportedly even more brutal than in Hong Kong.

"If we're sent on the next draught as looks rather likely, I don't give much for our chances of survival," Roger said to Hugh in the bunk next to his after mulling over the latest rumours. "I'm all for getting the hell out of here where at least there's a chance of escaping to China. What d'you think, old chap?"

"They only send the fitter men to Japan, so that counts me out," replied Hugh resignedly. He was putting a wireless set together, his capable fingers manipulating cleverly in the dark under the blanket. His leg was playing him up and he looked dreadfully gaunt. "It counts me out for the escape also. I can't walk yards, let alone miles, with this damned leg. The gup is that those not draughted are to be sent to the

Argyle Street camp to join the senior officers. Commodore Collison is there."

"And separate us from our men – the swine."

"That's the idea. Anything to break down the troops' morale," groused Hugh. "So whether you get sent to Japan, Roger, or stay in Hong Kong, you won't be with your men much longer, nor will we be with Winn for that matter. No, rather than starve to death in this hole, you and Winn 'ud better have a bash at it and quickly before you're further debilitated. Why not get Mike Mitchell to take my place?"

And so it was arranged by the escape committee in the camp. They chose only those who were most likely to succeed, and Winn was of top priority because of his expertise at the language and his knowledge of the New Territories. So far only six escapees had got away to China. A seventh was believed to have gone underground with a prostitute in the old walled city of Kowloon. The rest had been caught, tortured and shot. Failure was not a pretty picture and only the strongest, bravest and most determined were helped in their attempts through 'Bag'.

Time moved on. Roger walked like a caged lion up and down the six-foot-six sea boundary, which his height nearly equalled. Winn, out at work, was alerted to time and date, and a daring plan for the escape of five prisoners was put into action.

With balaclava-type homemade caps on heads, their faces and hands blackened, Roger first and then Mike squirmed their way into a previously dug shallow hole under the wire fence. After they'd disappeared, a member of the escape committee approached and made good the damage behind them so well that it was impossible to detect where the ground had been disturbed. The two Mountain Gunners crept their way to the harbour wall a few yards from the wire, climbed over it and, undetected, dropped into the sea.

In pitch black, slowly, without making any but the faintest of ripples, yard by yard they swam breast-stroke out into the harbour. Their dark heads bobbed one behind the other on the water. In this way they traversed the mile to deserted Stonecutter's Island which the British had evacuated during the retreat. The Japanese had swarmed over the island but had not bothered to occupy it, and it remained deserted except for a few visiting fishermen.

At a specified spot the escapees located a small hidden sampan containing paddles, provisions, and change of clothing. They lay hidden in the bushes well up from the lapping shore. Roger handed out their packs of rations.

"It's a piece of cake! Worth it if only for this," they grinned to one another in the dark while devouring the best meal they'd had since captivity.

All day the two hid in the undergrowth. They rested, slept and listened to the hue and cry on the foreshore of the mainland. There were yells and shouts from the infuriated guards when it was found at roll-call that two were missing. The escape committee had hoped to cover up their disappearance for a few days, but had been unsuccessful. A squad of guards proceeded to trot out of the camp gates, run up and down the nearby roads, bayonets at the ready, and search houses and shops. They were convinced the escapees must be somewhere nearby in the town. None considered Stonecutter's Island. To the Japanese, such a swim was an impossibility.

While it was still dark, and early on the same morning Roger and Mike made their escape, an extra man of similar build to Winn set out with the other ranks' working party. Near the airport Winn vanished into thin air. The numbers of the exhausted navvies taken that night during roll-call showed all present and correct, and it was not until two days later than Winn was found to be missing, by which time Roger and Mike had long left Stonecutter's Island.

As soon as it was dark after their day of hiding, these two embarked in the sampan and paddled off south-west navigating by compass. They came to rest on Lamma Island where they laid up near a deserted beach for a second day. Unless they had the misfortune to run into a patrol Roger and Mike knew the first part of the escape was the least hazardous. It was after they'd rounded Victoria Island and landed at Clear Water Bay Peninsular that the worst of the dangers would begin.

On schedule, and at dusk again, a fisherman in a larger sampan appeared on the deserted Lamma Island beach. Before showing themselves, Roger and Mike identified the man by a certain distinctive blue smock. Then the Gunners, leaving their small sampan well hidden, climbed in and were paddled off, this time due east.

With nerves tensed, Roger's expectations rose with every paddle stroke.

Chapter Twenty-Two

IZOLDA waited in the Tweed Bay hospital surgery. She'd arrived well before the seven o'clock curfew and had told her grandmother she was spending the night with Peggy. As time slowly passed and the hours lengthened towards the allotted moment, her excitement built up to fever point. She held a book in her hand but though she turned the pages, she hadn't taken in one word. Instead, unanswerable questions rose and fell in her brain: *Were they going to be late? Had they been caught in the first lap? Had they even started?* Time ticked by interminably slowly.

At last Dr Lawrence came in and with a dry smile Izolda rose, put her book on the chair, and followed him out into the dark night.

Well away from the path that the women and children took by day, she followed stealthily to scramble down the rocky way she'd rehearsed over and over again sitting with her bowl of rice nearby. Feeling in the dark for outcrops as handholds, and carefully testing each foothold before placing her feet, she followed closely behind Dr Lawrence's dim outline. Once on the beach she crouched down beside two escapees already waiting. Her heart thumped wildly with expectation and anxiety.

There were no guards posted on this beach where the women and children bathed, where the doctors fished and

291

the fishermen surreptitiously sailed in. The nearest outlook was on the other side of the beach above the quarry where there was a cliff path patrolled by two armed guards who were relieved at regular intervals during the night curfew. Their every move had been monitored for weeks. They always met half-way by the quarry where they stopped, usually lit cigarettes, and chatted for a few minutes before each strolled on in opposite directions. With any deviation from this routine, those on the beach would hear the warning screech of an owl given by one of the Leprosarium doctors keeping watch above. When all was clear, the 'tip-tip' signal of the nightjar would sound.

From her crouched position on the beach, Izolda heard the slap of a splash followed by the faintest scrape of a boat crunching gently on sand. Dr Lawrence moved over to hold the bow, and Izolda saw the tall outline of Roger's figure stepping out. His shadow loomed up . . . and she was in his arms.

He held her to him and bent to kiss her face. They stood by the sea in the dark and he passed his hands all over her, feeling her like a blind man feels. They sat down on the beach near the boat where the other men were busy. Their arms were about one another. In their ears there was the bare sound of lapping water, and Izolda was sure she could smell the sweet fragrant scent of frangipani all around them. She was glad she couldn't see the details of Roger's face all that well in the dark for his bare arms and powerful shoulders felt very thin at her touch. By the way his eyes glowed in sunken sockets she had no doubt his face was lean looking to gauntness and almost unrecognisable.

She was glad too that he couldn't see her clearly with her thinness, delicate and wand-like in her slenderness. No longer was she Roger's golden girl, but a dead tired one, her straight lank hair scissor-chopped, and she dressed in patched and faded trousers cut with ragged ends to the knee.

"How are you, dearest?"

"Fine. How are you?"

"All the better for seeing you!" She could feel how the words were said with eyes wrinkling at the corners. "How's your grandmother?"

"Very frail. And Winn?"

"All right when I last saw him in camp. We'll be meeting soon . . . God willing. He sent you love."

"Give him mine. Oh, Roger, you will be careful . . . ?"

"You bet!" He kissed her again, his face rough and unshaven.

"Is Hugh better?"

"So-so. Leg plays him up. Doing sterling undercover work in camp."

They heard Japanese voices in the near distance and sniffed the flair of a newly lighted match on the air. Roger stiffened.

"The guards meeting on patrol." Izolda breathed into his ear, her voice strained with tension. She waited, hardly daring to breathe . . . no screech of an owl? "Thank God, they've moved on."

"I heard about Chippy's end. I'm sorry, darling. Great bloke."

"Yes. He was such fun . . ."

"Will you marry me?"

"Of course! When?"

"As soon as this bloody war is over."

There was an indication from Dr Lawrence that it was time to go. They stood up.

"I love you, my dearest one," he said.

293

"I love you, Roger," she said, "Oh God, how I love you. I wish I could come . . ."

"Look after Grandma. Wonderful Grandma." She saw his eyes glistening.

"Yes," she whispered despairingly. She could barely see his outline for her own tears.

"You are the sweetest and bravest woman I have ever met. Know yourself, darling." They kissed farewell and tasted the salt of their tears mingling. There was no passion in their embrace, no strength left for passion in their starved bodies, their love perhaps all the greater for that. Any strength they had left now was the strength of mind with the determination and will to live.

Izolda stood in the water and stretched out her hand to Roger after he'd stepped into the boat and joined the dark shapes of the others in the stern. Their hands clung together, his hand large, warm, comforting, firm round hers, the strong hand that Chippy had responded to on their first meeting, the hand that she loved so much she thought her heart would break when she had to let it go.

"Till we meet again, dearest."

"Till we meet again . . ."

"Bless you, doctor!" Roger whispered his thanks.

"God be with you all," the reply came from the beach beside Izolda.

There was a faint splash and the boat drew away.

When Winn vanished into thin air, and the extra man covered up for him at work on the early morning of that fateful escape, Winn disappeared into the maze of crowded Kowloon's city back alleyways. Anyone who did not live in those dark and rat-infested squalid slums, and especially a white man, would have been hopelessly lost within minutes; but Winn did not get lost. Before the outbreak of war, Ying-Su had taken him there and shown him the 'Bag' upstairs room above the same herbal magician's shop that Chippy and Izolda had once visited. Now, when Winn arrived, the old man with his yellowy-grey wispy beard, stumps of teeth and long Chinese robe, was opening up his shutters in preparation for the day. The Chinaman grinned his near-toothless grin and ushered Winn upstairs.

"Ying-Ying!"

"Winn!" She fell into his arms. "Thank God you've come. My hair has gone grey waiting for you. You haven't been followed?"

"No – too dark. With any luck the guards won't know I'm missing for the first thirty-six hours. As easy as pie getting here!"

Ying-Su, in her relief at seeing him, the strain of being the link 'Why' on the escape route committee telling after all she'd been through since the outbreak of war, allowed herself a silent weep in Winn's arms. Constantly, she had crossed and re-crossed the Chinese border and on down the New Territories to call in at the herbalist. Then over to Victoria Island and the café in Queen's Road where she made contact with other links. All the time she was arranging, organising, collecting the PoWs and others from hideouts and conducting them over the border; and all through this she was keeping tabs on her scattered family and making sure parcels and messages were sent through Miss Maureen, Ping-Li and the amah. Now, this incredibly plucky Chinese girl who had already saved many Allied lives and was to save many more, served Winn a nourishing meal and sat down beside him to watch him wolfing it down.

"Not so fast," she smiled. "You'll give yourself tummy-ache."

"What does it feel like to be Mrs Brigadier-General Sha-Kwo?" he asked, mouth full.

"Nice," she said, "*when* I'm able to see him."

"He's in Chungking?"

"Yes, with the Generalissimo. He and Madame have been marvellous to Dad."

"How did he take . . . ?"

"Very badly. Oh Winn, it was too awful, wasn't it – darling Mum. This bloody war. Dad's thoroughly disillusioned. No luck with the 7th Army. They won't change now. We've just got to slog on and hope the tide turns soon in the Pacific."

"Do you know if Roger and Mike have got away?"

"Must have. A great hue and cry was reported by one of our links. They should be lying up on Stonecutter's Island now." She looked out of the grimy window at the new day. "Tonight we'll start off for the meeting point. We'll divide up before we get to the border. That'll be the danger time. Teeming with soldiers, sniffer dogs, the lot."

"I'm worried about Roger. He's so tall."

"You're good friends with him?"

"Rather. He's a tower of strength and booster of morale in there, the one who takes any amount of punishment in petitioning for us other ranks. I have the greatest admiration for him."

"I just wondered because . . . you're in love with Zol, aren't you?"

"I am, the wretched girl. First she goes and marries poor old Chippy, and then . . ." Winn paused.

"And then she has a passionate affair with the man you have the greatest admiration for! I'm surprised at your friendship with him. More in keeping I'd have thought to hate his guts. Anyways, our prim little Victorian maiden cousin has at last burst away from prudery."

"Before we set forth on this caper, Roger and I made a pact that whoever survives shall marry Zol."

"Would she marry you if . . . ?"

"I'm pretty sure she would," Winn replied confidently. "I know, and she knows, we'd fuse in bed," he grinned.

"Still, you have to face it, Winn. You would be second best."

"Pshaw. Not so sure about that. We'll see. The best man wins! You know that Zol thinks you're a communist spy?"

"Yes. Rather useful bit of deception. Safer she got it that way. Dad showed me the snap she took by the stall. What a coincidence. That's my life all over: my fate hangs upon a thread."

Winn bathed luxuriously in a tub of hot water with Ying-Su scrubbing his back and putting ointment on his bedbug sores. He then slept the day through on a pile of quilts. That evening, after donning Chinese Hakka garb, brother and sister slipped through the herbalist's shop and began the journey up the New Territories towards the rendezvous with the others. They walked only at night, avoiding roads and paths as much as possible. Ying-Su seemed to be able to see in the dark and her ears were attuned to hear Japanese patrols from a long way off. Her worst fear was of meeting dogs. She wasn't afraid of them for herself, but for Winn. The animals were trained to sniff out Europeans.

They walked over the battle-strewn ground of Gindrinker's Line, eerie and deserted with its broken fortifications and tunnels. They climbed up and over Yellow Hill where AA guns and the Mountain Gunner's 3.7 Howitzers lay spiked and overturned. Many were the shallow unmarked humped graves that they stumbled over in the dark. And there were plenty of picked-dry bones of horses and mules around.

When the faint glimmers of dawn could be seen in the

East, Ying-Su headed for a selected farmhouse. She tapped on the door which was opened a crack, big enough for her to give the code in Hakka dialect. She was allowed in, money was handed over, and she and Winn were given food and shelter to sustain them for the next night's even more dangerous march.

Roger, Mike, the two civilian escapees from Stanley camp together with the smock-clad boatman, cleared Victoria Island in the dark and made for Clear Water Bay with its temples and memories of Izolda, now so near and dear in their recent encounter. They paid the boatman a goodly sum they'd been given for that purpose, and, leaving the sampan, made their way overland to Shatin near where the Gunners had fought so stubbornly on the retreat through the Territories. One of the men from Stanley, who spoke Cantonese, gave the code words at cetain houses on the escape route and they were admitted. Every day feeling stronger with a regular evening meal, the party walked on round Taipu to short of Fanling where, in the arranged rendezvous, they met up with Ying-Su and Winn. Everything had gone marvellously according to plan, but there was no rejoicing. All were very aware of the crucially dangerous next part.

Ying Su briefed them. She told them they would have to go it alone for a while. They could divide up into groups but each group must have a Chinese-speaking member with them. It was decided that Roger and Mike would go with Winn, while the two from Stanley would stay together. The next night Ying-Su embraced Winn and Roger, shook hands with the others, wished them all the best of luck and said that she would be waiting for them over the other side of the boundary river. She slipped away into the dark.

The five men set forth dressed as coolies, Roger looking ridiculously conspicuous with his height despite a brown stain on face, arms and legs. The two men from Stanley peeled off on a north-westerly course, while Roger, Mike and Winn made their way due north, navigating by compasses and the stars.

All went well until they failed to locate a farmhouse short of Lo-Wu from where they planned to cross the river the next night. From several near-misses, it was evident this area was stiff with Japanese patrols. They went on searching for the farmhouse until, with dawn soon to break, they decided to hide as best they could in a Chinese graveyard. Here they settled down for a long wait.

Not many hours later, and quite accidentally, they were almost stepped on by some wandering locals, who, frightened by the men's strange looks, ran off. It was obvious to the escapees that the Chinese were about to raise the alarm, and the three took to their heels in the opposite direction. Soon they could hear the chase in full cry behind. The sound of screaming soldiers came over ominously to their ears, all the time closing in on them. Roger made a sign and the three halted.

"Our best chance is every man for himself. Quick, off you go," he panted and in the same breath doubled away to the left. Mike leapt to obey by turning off to the right. He ran straight into two soldiers. Winn saw what was happening to Mike at the same time as he heard Roger crashing on to the left with the main hue and cry in that direction. Winn's best chance of survival was to double back between the soldiers chasing Roger and those attacking Mike. For a split second he wavered, the instinct to save his skin strong. Then he turned to divert those chasing Roger.

A clear vision of what was happening had flashed through

his brain. Mike had downed one guard and seemed to be getting the better of the other, but Roger hadn't a hope with the posse after him. He or Roger – and Izolda. She was part of him, his beautiful cousin of his own blood and he wanted her as he had never wanted another girl. But Zol was in love with Roger as Roger was with her and it was no good pretending that they were not. And Ying-Ying had truly said that if Roger died and he survived to marry Zol it would be second best for her. But not only did he love Zol. In camp he had come to love Roger as all men loved him for his straightness, his toughness, his bravery – his care of his men. He had seen him nurse his orderly, Hassan Khan, when he was dying, as tenderly as any woman, and he loved him for his unfailing giving of himself, his strength of purpose, his born leadership, the very presence of the man. What a waste for a man of his quality to be caught, tortured, shot by one of these bloody little Japanese guards chasing them. Rather than that should happen he would go straight in there and kill the whole bleeding lot with his own bare hands . . .

Out of the corner of his eye, Winn caught sight of Mike several yards away. He was bloodied, hands tied behind his back and was being prodded along by a soldier. The man lifted his rifle and took aim at Winn. "I killed the other bastard; bashed the man's head open with a rock," Mike shouted. Then, "Winn . . . what the hell are you doing? Don't go that way, man . . . go *back*, you idiot." The shot rang out.

But Winn had fled. Unarmed and single-handed he jumped across the path to intercept the three guards in the van catching up on Roger. A shot narrowly missed him at the same instant that he knocked one man with a punch on the jaw like a prizefighter's and sent the man sprawling. Grabbing the Jap's rifle, Winn was just in time to shoot the second soldier dead as the man was aiming for him. He knew then that if he did not get away now, his fate was sealed every bit as much as Mike's was. One to go . . .

The third guard leapt on Winn from behind and they fell, rifles scattering. They wrestled on hard earth. Even as he was getting the better of this small soldier by rolling with him on the ground and half-throttling him over a mound, the first guard recovered sufficiently to crawl up, and, bleeding profusely at the mouth where his teeth had been knocked in, grabbed Winn's legs and held onto them. The third guard, now released from Winn's full stranglehold and gasping for breath, sat on Winn's head while the first soldier doggedly continued to hang onto his legs.

The fight continued. Winn, struggling manfully, kicked off the man at his feet, and managed to disentangle himself from the other Japanese by battering him repeatedly. Winn staggered upright, breathing heavily, and as he did so saw captive Mike and his guard approaching. The guard shoved Mike to his knees in the dust, took two steps forward and shot Winn as the white man stood there, chest bared. The guard came nearer and shot Winn again and then bayonetted the sprawled body through the heart.

More soldiers arrived carrying between them the body of the Japanese Mike had killed. They dumped this man beside the soldier Winn had shot. They stood around looking impassively at the dead foreigner on the ground, blood oozing through his coolie clothes. They took the compass, food and money they found on him, tore off his identity disc and kicked his body out of the way. They trussed Mike up more firmly and marched him to the local guard post. Next day they took him by truck and boat to Stanley jail. There he was fearfully beaten up, manacled, chained and left in solitary confinement without food or water. Then he was tortured.

Peggy, who had met Mike with her late husband before hostilities started, saw him being brought in by truck. She went straight to the doctors to tell them the name of the latest British officer to be imprisoned in the jail. Soon the whole camp knew it was Captain Mike Mitchell, second-in-command of the Mountain Gunner battery, who was being interrogated and tortured behind the high white walls.

When Izolda heard, she went and sat with her back against the wall to be as near as she could get to Mike, Roger's friend from the North-West Frontier. Desperately she tried to get through to him by telepathy to tell him she was there suffering his agony with him every inch of the way, and asking him to forgive her for being so preoccupied with Roger on the beach she hadn't given him a thought. She went on in her mind to ask him what had happened to the others. Had they been with him when he, Mike, was taken prisoner? What, what, what had happened to Winn? Oh God, what had happened to Roger? Why, why, had they attempted to escape only for it to end like this? Oh God, kill the Japs in the jail. Bring the building down with an earthquake or a tidal wave and kill them all stone dead! Oh, God, if you won't kill them, DO something . . .

A month later, Mike Mitchell who had been mentioned in despatches on the North-West Frontier where he was wounded, and had been recommended for the Military Cross for his part with Roger in the destruction of a whole regiment of Japanese on the first day of the invasion into the New Territories, was brought back to Sham-Shui-Po camp in shackles. He was tied to a stake in the middle of the parade ground as an example to all of what happened if they dared to try and escape, let alone kill guards.

It took two days for him to die, left in the broiling sun

trussed up like a martyr. The PoW camp watched, stunned and more shocked than they had ever been. The men walked about on tiptoe, their voices kept low as if at the bedside of the dying, as indeed it was. The senior naval and military officers again and again demanded to see Colonel Tokunang, the Commandant of the PoW camps – to no avail.

One of the Gunner officers could bear it no longer and crept towards the bound figure with a mug of water. He was skewered with a bayonet and carried away wounded by his friends. After that the British gave the order that no one was to go near. But on the last day Hugh limped by closer than most, and Mike through blurred, swollen eyes and waves of unconsciousness, saw him, recognised him, and winked. It was a horribly grotesque tortured wink in the drained, parched, twisted, dying man's face: grotesque, yes, but at the same time valiant and unbowed.

The Japanese took down his body and said he was a courageous man, and a very brave soldier. They said they would give him a great military funeral. 'Death is lighter than a feather, duty is higher than a mountain', they said. The officer had done his duty by enemy standards in endeavouring to escape. He had done his duty by Japanese standards in the ultimate act of dying. All was exonerated with his death. Now they had 'great respect' for him.

A padre in white robes took the service at which the entire camp of PoWs paraded smartly in their washed, ironed and even starched best uniforms, produced from heaven knows where. The Japanese attended in full dress uniform with swords. The Union Jack was draped over the coffin, which the Japanese officers bowed before, and the band of one of the incarcerated regiments was ordered to play suitable music. Afterwards the guards left some food gifts for the Mountain Gunners.

The prisoners of war found the whole episode quite incomprehensible after leaving the Gunner Captain to die by slow inches. They could not begin to understand the Japanese mentality.

But Louise understood.

Chapter Twenty-Three

LOUISE may have understood the Japanese mentality, but when news of Winn's death seeped through it could not help her sorrow for her other grandchild. She grieved at his loss, as Izolda did, and was immeasurably saddened for Jimmy and for Ying-Su who were both once again bereaved. The next 'void and infinite' year of 1943 was hard for Louise, but for Izolda, living without any news of Roger, it was well nigh unbearable. And time went by slowly, slowly.

"Try taking salt for your hunger cramps," Dr Lawrence advised after examining her ankles which were swollen and puffy and left indentations when prodded. Izolda took to wearing a wide cloth tightly tied round her wasp waist to stop the gnawing pangs of hunger which beset her all the time.

Dr Lawrence himself was suffering from abdominal distension to such an extent that he looked pregnant. In the camp they were desperately short of stores. There was no sugar left, hardly any tea; candles ran out and they used oil with rags for wicks in saucers after lights out. Louise's face became so thin that her dentures would not stay in and she had difficulty in masticating at all. She lay on her bed mumbling to herself and sewing bits of soap into cotton bags to preserve every scrap for use.

With the coal shortage on the Island, electricity had to be cut. Water from the tap came on for only one day in four.

305

Men staggered weakly up from the beaches with sea water to flush the toilets, and the dug latrines came into use. What everyone had dreaded most happened: they ran out of oil for cooking and heating. The trees on the headland had long been stripped, and now furniture, floorboards and doors were broken up and used as fuel. Izolda chopped up the cupboard in their room and then in desperation took down and did the same with their inner door. A blanket was draped over the gap into the lobby.

The influx of drugs had long since been used up, and there had been only more issue of Red Cross parcels. Vitamin pills were kept for the very ill in a last attempt to save lives. Menstruation in the younger women stopped altogether. Clothing and shoes began to fall to pieces. Those who had contacts outside could have asked for clothes, but who was going to ask for a pair of shoes when they would lose the equivalent in weight of food? Worst of all was the terrible lassitude and inertia which came after a year of malnutrition. The inmates of Stanley camp had to force themselves to get up in the mornings, *make* themselves do anything.

Most of the inmates looked dreadful by now. Long gone were the gods and goddesses of the first spring. Now they were gaunt, ribby and stark cheek-boned. Sores that would not heal were left roughly bandaged; stick-like arms, gross legs and teeth loose in soft gums were the norm. A few people's bodies seemed to have come to terms with the diet, their weight loss stabilised. One of these was Joan Holden who came over by day to look after Louise when Izolda was away at her French teaching classes. She liked to talk to old Mrs Winter about her son Hugh who had been transferred to the Argyle Street camp where Miss Maureen kept in touch with him. Conditions there were said to be better than Sham-Shui-Po with the result that his wound was at last healing.

Reserves of money ran out in Stanley; people were up to their necks in debt from promissory notes; black market dealers with fat faces turned up in new clothes, and the vindictiveness and quarrelling in camp became more bitter. The Hong Kong dollar was abolished; military Yen was established in its stead, hundreds of which were paid for a bar of soap or a pot of jam in the canteen to line the pockets of the Japanese. And people continued to die, many of them the older members. The old cemetery filled relentlessly; the graves were shallow . . .

"Oh Roger, Roger, where are you . . . ?" Louise heard Izolda crying out in the night in her half-sleep. "I can't bear it. I can't bear it . . ."

"I know, I know, honey. I couldn't bear it many times . . ." What could she say to bring comfort to the child? To say 'no news is good news' was too trite and pat for such a situation and would not bring relief from anxiety. Louise searched in the hidden drawer for James's Order and was once again hurt when she found it was not there and that she had given it to Hojo Fushimi. It had been her last earthly link with James once her wedding ring had gone, and now that the Star had gone it was time she went too.

"When couldn't you bear it, Grandma?" Izolda lay awake on her back in the night, her legs hurting, a cardboard box placed under her sheet to protect them from the weight.

"They buried your mother on the day of the earthquake in the grounds of the Royal Naval hospital. I saw her grave with its rough cross – that was one time when I couldn't bear it. Later I was told that her body was moved to the great foreign cemetery near to where your grandfather lies. One day you will go and see the graves."

"*Me* to Japan? Never!"

"When all this is forgotten and forgiven . . . you will want to go."

Izolda, unable to bear the physical and mental pain any longer, got up and, drawing the blanket in place of a door aside, went out into the hot midsummer night and sat screened by the bungalow wall where the guards couldn't see her. She looked at the Mount around the silent, silent jail where they had done their worst to Mike, and thought of Roger and prayed for Roger.

The tropical night was unutterably beautiful. The light from the moon, as bright as a white-muted sun, made a swathe of silver across the shimmering surface of the silky sea. The Southern Cross blazed in a sky shining with constellations over Stanley Fort.

"May I have a word?" Dr Lawrence waylaid Izolda when she came out from her class, French textbooks in hand. He took her by the elbow and led her over to the cliff above Tweed Bay where the guards patrolled at night. "Let's sit here and rest our funny figures!" He drew her down to sit beside him.

"Is it about my grandmother?"

"Mrs Winter is coming peacefully to the end of her long life. No, it's not about her, it's about what happened to your cousin . . ."

"I don't want to know about the details," Izolda made to get up. She had suffered enough, grieved enough for Winn, for the awfulness of Mike Mitchell's end. She did not want the wounds reopened, wounds which with the passing of months had become numb with the beginnings of healing.

"You should know about your Winter cousin," Dr Lawrence put out his hand to stop her going.

"Why? What is the point of digging that up when nothing can help him now?"

"I'll tell you why. When the late Captain Mitchell was returned to the PoW camp from here," Dr Lawrence went on, taking no notice of Izolda's protests, "he was, before his execution, able to convey the story of what happened to his friends. I'll tell you about that in a minute, but first you should know that the two escapees from here got clean away across the border where they met up with our link."

"And Roger never turned up," Izolda said dully.

"I'm afraid not, my dear. Nothing has been heard of him since. Had he survived, 'Bag' would have got to know about it. The link waited for a whole week further in extreme danger in Japanese-occupied Kwang-tun Province in the hopes the others would come. The absolute limit for waiting is three days. She risked—"

"She? Did you say *she*?" Izolda flashed the question. Suddenly, as if coming out of darkness into a bright room, she saw it all: why Ying-Su had kept on disappearing before the war; why Winn and her uncle and aunt were guarded when talking about her whereabouts; why her grandmother was so fascinated by Ying-Su. *She* would have guessed. Trust Grandma!

Of *course* it was Ying-Su who had organised the escape of the five – and how many others? "And I believed she was a communist traitor," Izolda now confessed. "I was jealous of my grandmother's affection for her. I had no idea . . . too blinded by my own invented suspicions. Oh, how stupid I've been and how I maligned and belittled her. Please tell me more, Dr Lawrence. Please tell me everything . . ."

They sat side by side on the clifftop looking out to sea, and Dr Lawrence in his quiet voice, arms folded over his stomach, thin knobbly-kneed limbs protruding from

309

drooping wide-legged khaki shorts, told Izolda, without mentioning any specifics, a little about the British Army Aid Group and Ying-Su's part in 'Bag'. He told her how Captain Mitchell, after running into the two armed guards, one of whom he killed, came hands-bound upon the scene and perceived how Winn had deliberately taken on three other soldiers to divert them from following in Roger's tracks. And once again Izolda saw it all, saw the great friendship that had developed in Sham-Shui-Po between these two men who loved her. She saw how Roger, whom all men admired and would follow gladly into battle, was about to be cut down by the three pursuing Japanese when Winn had crashed into their midst with his diversionary tactics. Winn had deliberately given up his life for Roger – and for her.

Dr Lawrence talked on. He reminded Izolda of the wonderful influences in her life, first and foremost her grandmother who had given away her most prized possession to save hers and others' lives . . .

"The Star?" Izolda gasped. Dr Lawrence nodded. "I wondered why Grandma kept on . . . she never told me. To whom did she give . . . ?" But once again she knew the answer: 'Sumuko', the name spoken between the Colonel and her grandmother at that first meeting at The Falls. The Colonel's tallness and colouring, his well-kept neat hands so like her Uncle Jimmy's. The fog of resentment and misunderstanding she had been living in for so long, now, as if at the end of a long dark tunnel, had all of a sudden dispersed. It left her with a clear mind, and at last she was able to see the light ahead and with it, the truth.

"I have known you since your marriage," Dr Lawrence turned to face Izolda, "and I have been watching you in this camp. I know what you have been through, and I have seen you *come* through, my dear. In the responsibility you have had to shoulder in caring for your grandmother, in the dire time of your illness, through your loyalty to your husband and for your love for another, I have seen you gain new purpose, gain confidence in yourself. Through all the trials endured in here," he concluded, "you have developed from unsureness to strength tempered with compassion that will serve you well all your days." The doctor squeezed Izolda's hand and put it down in her lap. Stiffly he got up to go.

Izolda sat on, her hands cupping her chin, eyes bright with comprehension and unshed tears. Her grandmother had, in the first year of their imprisonment, said something along the same lines as the doctor about the camp being a hard school, but one that in the end would not be regretted, impossible to believe at the time. But now she found it was true. After Stanley camp she could face life and death as valiantly as Roger, Winn, Toni and Ying-Su faced them.

And with this self-knowledge Izolda found that her loathing of the enemy had dissolved, leaving an acceptance that such things happened, with a willingness to try and understand. Now only gratitude was left that she had known brave men and women. Whatever happened in the future she would not be found wanting. The blood that ran in her veins was, on the Richardson side, seafaring blood, on the Winter side pioneering blood, and on her grandmother's side American missionary blood that time and again had risen above affliction.

The clouds gathered overhead unnoticed as Izolda sat on the cliff above the beach where she had last seen Roger. A clap of thunder startled her back to the present, and the heavens opened as she rose to walk to her quarters.

She lifted her face to let the soft pure water trickle down and drench her. The rain finally purified her from her burden of insecurity and fear. She had learned strength behind barbed wire.

Izolda found herself free in captivity.

In the evenings Izolda boiled water and gently washed her grandmother's emaciated figure. She turned over the frail frame, as light as a child's, to treat her bedsores, and looked into the dark old eyes alight with ancient memory; she now treasured every moment that remained.

During the autumn Louise never left her opium couch. She spent her days sitting propped up on it in Toni's old mauve kimono, her toothless mouth quavering as she swatted at flies with the broken swat, or flitted with the flit gun that was long since empty of flit. She scratched away at her flaking skin and made it bleed, and she mumbled about how she missed the Star. She took her sips of brandy when her feet were cold, which was all the time. And her only worry was that she would outlive that last bottle of Dr J Collis Browne's Chlorodyne, and that last half-flask of medicinal brandy.

And when she reiterated that she really could not live much longer, Izolda no more said, "Oh, Grandma, I wish you wouldn't," but just smiled at her, stroked her bruised transparent hand, and tenderly kissed the soft wrinkled cheek.

When Louise began to call her 'Camille', Izolda knew the time was near. She heard her grandmother rambling on in the night about her days in the Land of the Rising Sun, and how she had ridden in her red habit along the Great Tokaidō Highway to Yedo, her long black hair blowing out behind her, the pony's mane in her face, and with growing insight Izolda began to comprehend the power and inspiration which had animated her grandmother, so dear to her, so very frail – now somehow eternal. Was it all part of the same thing, this life and death? All sprung from the same source of love, ecstasy, hereafter . . . ?

At Christmas the last words Louise said on the opium couch while her granddaughter held her hand were, 'James', 'Edouard' and 'Camille' and her seeing of them was so real that Izolda could not but believe that they would meet again in another world as beautiful and as peaceful as the wonderful tropical nights.

Next morning Izolda awoke in the small room to hear and feel the stillness of a spirit gone.

It was Japanese custom to post a guard in honour of the dead while a body remained, and Corporal Seki was ordered to stand outside Louise's room. He stood there in his baggy trousers, large tears unashamedly rollingly down his face for his one alien friend in the camp, the *Seyo no Fujin* European lady who had 'gone to the better land'.

The funeral service was taken in the College Hall by the Dean, and even those inmates of Stanley camp who had boycotted Louise for being a 'Jap lover', were surprised to see the arrival of a tall Japanese colonel with a scar down his face. He came with a consignment of smart shock troops – no lowly guards these – and he himself was dressed in impeccable uniform with gold braid and rows of shining medals. A ceremonial sword of ancient beauty and studded with jewels dangled and clanked at his side as he marched up.

Leaving his troops outside, this imposing figure attended the ceremony. The congregation was so astounded by his presence on the one chair rustled up from somewhere for his use, that in their lowly positions on the floor all round, they were unable to concentrate on the Dean's sermon on Mrs Winter's missionary upbringing and her staunch Christian faith.

After the service, and with everyone gawping at them, Izolda was driven away with the colonel in the back of his polished Packard staff car. They followed the hearse to attend the cremation outside the camp, after which the ashes were placed in one of the small white-covered boxes reserved for Japanese officers.

In death Louise had neatly completed her 'One Man' patience in a tidy box-like pack that was taken to Japan to rest on James Winter's grave in the great foreign cemetery on the Bluff in Yokohama. And it is said that in the whole of the far east during the war no other enemy alien was given so great an honour by the Japanese.

As for Izolda, she was driven back in the staff car to Stanley for what was to be the last gruelling year and eight months of internment. But when the Packard bumped over the shallow ditch beyond the neck of the Peninsular and the guards opened the gates between the barbed wire barricades and waved her through, anyone seeing her would have noticed a broad smile on her thin face. For she could hear her grandmother's voice:

'*VERY satisfactory,*' Izolda could distinctly hear Louise drawling, '*that, I guess, was much more dignified than being put in a sack to rot in THIS dump!*'

314

Chapter Twenty-Four

"ARE you sure you want to be dropped here, Miss?" the smartly uniformed Royal Marine driver of the jeep asked Izolda.

She was sitting on the front seat squashed in between him and another brawny marine. Three others sat in the back talking grim-faced amongst themselves about the appalling conditions of the inmates they had just seen in the Stanley camp.

The driver who had spoken first looked dubiously at an overgrown and ill-defined track taking off into the hills from the road and then at the English girl beside him. In the internment camp she had asked if he could give her a lift to near Aberdeen, and he had readily agreed thinking she would want to be left in some habitable spot among friends, not out in the wilds like this. This pretty girl, who was so thin she looked to him as if a puff of wind would blow her away, had brought no suitcase with her, only a school satchel carried over one shoulder. After asking for the lift, she had climbed into the jeep just as she was in her worn and ragged clothes.

"Yes, I'm quite sure this is the right spot," Izolda replied, "the track will take me over the hills to where I want to go. Thank you so much for the ride. Goodbye, all!"

The driver obligingly slid out and held the door open for

her. "By gum," he expressed, watching her walk off, "that slip of a thing has some guts. Crikey, after years behind the wire she walks out on her own without so much as a word to anyone and sets off to climb a mountain!" He shook his head in amused admiration, revved up the jeep and shot off down the Aberdeen coastal road.

It was high summer, and Izolda had been anticipating this moment of liberation ever since a very cold early January day at the beginning of 1945 when three hundred Allied bombers appeared over Hong Kong. She had watched the sight of massed droning formations breaking up to dive-bomb and sink tanker shipping in the bay. The sound of bombs exploding, with retaliatory Japanese anti-aircraft gunfire, had taken her right back to when the battle had raged for Victoria Island and there had been not one British aircraft left to take to the skies. This raid, then, must at last be the beginning of the end.

But smiles were wiped off faces when on January 16th, American bombs were dropped on Stanley Peninsular itself and ten inmates were killed: 'friendly' fire. It seemed the final irony. There was a long wait ahead during which time hopes rose and fell and rose again until in August came the rumour of a bomb as big as the sun which, after being dropped on Hiroshima in Japan, brought about the enemy's capitulation.

Yet still the internees could scarcely believe it. They were told by their representatives to stay put, and the conditions remained much the same with the Japanese ordered to go on running the camp and provide meagre rations. Stories circulated that the Chinese Nationalist Army – the army which had *not* come to their aid – was now preparing to jump in and take Hong Kong for themselves before the Royal Navy could arrive! Though the attitude of the guards changed – many currying favour – and there was no bullying nor shouted orders or roll-calls, nor any curfews or restrictions to the beaches, the food situation was as bad as it had ever been. And tragically the daily death toll went on rising. By August 30th there could be no doubt left in anyone's mind that the war was truly over. Izolda, Peggy and Joan Holden went up to the old cemetery vantage point to watch the British Pacific Fleet sailing in from twenty miles off-shore. HMS *Swiftsure* and *Euryabus* anchored in Kowloon Bay. Rear-Admiral Cecil Harcourt, Commander of the 11th Aircraft Carrier Squadron, received the Japanese surrender of Hong Kong. Almost immediately on Sir Mark Young's release from captivity, the latter took up the Governorship of Hong Kong again, and in no time after that Admiral Harcourt arrived in person in Stanley camp with a convoy of Royal Marines, five to a jeep. The ex-prisoners went mad with excitement. There were cheers and weeping, joy and relief on every face, while the officers and men tried to hide their shock at the sunken-eyed and skeletal appearances of the inmates. They had seen deprivation in the PoW camps, but they had not expected it to be so bad in a civilian camp. There were three rousing cheers for King George VI followed by the singing of 'Oh God, our help in ages past'. And a great deal of food and cigarettes were distributed.

Izolda did not enter into the excitement. Instead she stood on the edge of the crowd staring at the marines. Their faces were so *plump*! They looked like men from another planet. She herself was deeply suntanned and very thin, her face pinched looking. For the last year and a half, she had been dependent on one source from outside to supply her with food parcels, and, almost more importantly, money with which to buy stores from the black market canteen. As a result her body was less emaciated than some.

In 1943 Miss Maureen had been repatriated to Ireland with

many of the other Irish refugees in Kowloon who had had to abandon their hostel work because of the general shortage of food. Ping-Li, finding the Japanese colonel had no use for his services as a chauffeur, had made his way back to his people in Wei-chu in China. Fung Wan had been discovered smuggling messages through the Sham-Shui-Po camp wire and had been so badly beaten up he had died from his injuries. That left the amah, Ah Fan, who stayed on at The Falls. Due to her age no one took much notice of her pottering about the house and lower terraces of the mansion from where she collected money and goods from the dwindling cache, and made up the parcels into the required size for the only one of the family left. The hidden cache was never discovered, and Ah Fan's part, in the latter half of the war, was the essential ingredient in Izolda's survival, though any personal contact with the amah through the wire had long been given up for fear of reprisals.

Izolda had no idea if The Falls was habitable – it could have been bombed by the Americans, its anti-aircraft guns behind the tennis court an obvious target – nor whether the Colonel was still there. Nor indeed did she know if she had any family left. Since Miss Maureen's departure, all messages had ceased which indicated Ying Su wasn't around either. And it was Ying-Su who, since she had learned the truth from the doctor, Izolda wanted to claim wholeheartedly as 'family'. She badly wanted to laugh with her over her own ridiculous suspicions and to show her true feelings of affection and admiration.

So, after years of incarceration, Izolda had no intention of staying one more hour than she needed to in Stanley camp, and at the first opportunity that came her way she told her friends she was off, cadged the lift, and left. Now, waving goodbye on the deserted hillside to the stalwart British marines, she began to make her way up the overgrown, yet still familiar steep track.

Her progress was slow, her breath coming shortly, and she was constantly reminded of her painful climb on the other side of the mountain after the beating and imprisonment in the filthy Dragon Hotel. As she had done then, she now sat down on a hummock of grass to rest, and in the hot sunshine she looked again at the view below of innumerable small green islands floating in the sparkling blue of the China Sea. It was the view that always brought back to her the idyllic days with Roger before the horror of war engulfed them – and she doubted she would ever see him again. Remembering Dr Lawrence's words that they surely would have heard through one of the 'Bag' links had Major Stamford got away to China, and that even if he had been successful unbeknown to anyone, without a guide to lead him through the Japanese-occupied Chinese province, an escapee's chances were reduced to practically nil.

The most likely outcome – Izolda had to face it – was that Roger had been discovered still on this side of the border and had died in a fight, for Roger would have fought as Winn had fought, to the death. No one would have known of Winn's end if Mike Mitchell hadn't witnessed it and passed the information on before his own death. Yet there *must* have been witnesses, both Chinese and Japanese, of what had happened to Roger up there so near the border.

That Roger's tall body could disappear forever without trace Izolda simply could not believe. Now the war was at last over, her driving aim was to go into the New Territories, recover Winn's body and see that it was brought back and properly laid to rest near his mother. At the same time she would make other enquiries along the border. She would not stop until she had unearthed something about Roger one way or another. She could not rest until she had evidence that Roger was no longer on this earth. Then she would close for ever the most beautiful chapter of her life.

In the quietness of the peaceful scene, and as Izolda looked down on the lovely panorama below her, the trilling of an insistent bird overhead seemed to urge her to continue. On rising she felt momentarily giddy from weakness. Brushing her hand across her eyes she looked up the hill the way she had to go and saw, in her imagination, a distant figure descending the track. Who these days would know this path? Ah Fan, perhaps? But, no, it was not a woman. Neither was it a Chinese . . .

Izolda shut her eyes and shook her head. Malnutrition had caused her to see a mirage. During the last year in camp she had often had these dizzy spells when she bent down or stood up too quickly. With the blurred vision, hallucinations took place – more often than not visions of banquets! But this time, opening her eyes again, she saw the distant figure had not dissolved.

How could it be when a few moments ago she had once again forced herself to conclude . . . ? Yet the walk . . . The similarity was striking . . . and . . . and . . . it could only be . . . it *must* be; who else with that unmistakable loose-figured step and that magnificent bearing of a dark-haired man hatless in the sun? It *was* Roger, and he was coming down in great strides to meet her!!

With amazed hope spreading over her thin face, Izolda found the strength to run up the track towards the figure, still believing herself to be in a dream – a glorious dream! But there, before her, he was. He, only he.

Laughing and crying Izolda ran on, her heart bursting with love, her lungs strained to their utmost. She stretched out her hands and he took them as they met, and she found herself in his embrace, his beloved face against hers, the warmth and strength of his arms about her. And he was not the emaciated Roger she had glimpsed on the beach, but one restored to superb fitness and strength.

"Roger, oh Roger!" Her eyes, huge upon him, shone with happiness and joy. This was no ethereal dream; this was substantial reality. How she loved him!

"My dearest." His eyes took in with stark horror her thinness.

For a long while they did not speak. Roger just held Izolda to him and stroked her blanched chopped hair. Then the words burst forth:

"When . . . when . . . did you get here?" she gasped.

"This morning." His eyes caressed her face.

"But, but from where? I'd given up . . ."

"Hope? Never. You and I only had to survive and we have!" he said joyously.

"How did you . . . ?"

"We flew in."

"*We?*"

"With your uncle. When I found you weren't at The Falls I came straight down the shortcut. Ah Fan showed me. I had a sort of feeling you'd be in your pad in Kowloon when the Japs were at the door, and I had the same sort of feeling you'd decide to walk up here at the first opportunity. You see how well I know you, my dearest, and what faith I have in your ability to climb mountains!" He kissed her face all over and held her tremulous body to his and once again felt terror at her thinness and all that that implied; all that she had been through.

"China. You came with Uncle Jimmy from Chungking. But . . . however did you *get* all that way?" She gazed at him, breathless. He looked wonderful. The man on the *Chitral*; the man at the Government House Ball; the man with the magnificent body on the junk . . . She leant against him, her legs feeling as if they would give way.

"Are you all right?" He tightened his arms about her, "I'll carry you up if you like. You look pretty light . . ."

"No, thank you," she laughed. "There's nothing wrong with me a few good meals won't cure!"

"That's the spirit," he said. Still, he noticed she was trembling. He made her sit down beside him on the hillside. And he began to tell her what had happened.

After breaking away from his three companions in the graveyard, each taking a different route in his *sauve qui peut* strategy, Roger had deliberately made his way eastwards as quickly and as far from Lo-Wu as he could get. There was bound to be a doubling and trebling of guards near Lo-Wu now they had been spotted.

After some days he reached the border area right up in the north-east corner of the New Territories. There he had had the most scare-raising moments of the whole escape.

"In the dark," Roger related, his arm warm and supportive round Izolda's slight figure, "I was creeping along a *chong* over the border river, when I heard guards approaching from the opposite side of the bridge. There was only one way to avoid them and that was to slip over the side. This I did. I clung onto the planks from under the bridge, my legs swinging in mid-air above the drop to the water below. Had I let go and splashed into the river, they would have been after me as quick as you could say Jack knife, so, with muscles aching and fit to burst, I clung on by my fingernails for dear life. The worst part came when the guards walked over and the patrol's hounds sniffed and snuffled at my knuckles. I have never been so terrified in all my life!"

"What happened?" Izolda held her breath at the image of it.

"By some miracle, for which one can only thank God, the dogs didn't give me away, and the patrol passed on over. I was so filthy by then I expect I smelt like a coolie. Anyway I crossed the border at last and made my way into hilly country near Har-chang, by which time I was pretty well starving having long finished the rations I had on me. I was getting more and more desperate wandering around lost and alone in the isolated countryside, when I was challenged by some wild-looking armed men. They took me to a military camp. They turned out to be Chinese guerrillas and once they verified I was an escaped British officer they befriended me and seeing I was starving, fed me on pork, chicken and fish; the most delicious food I'm ever likely to taste."

"Yummy," Izolda murmured with longing.

"When did you last feed?" Roger asked, looking concerned.

"You make me sound like one of your mules," she laughed. "At the moment I feel bloated. The Royal Marines brought in masses of goodies this morning and I've been stuffing myself with chocolate."

"Well then, you know what it feels like to have a good tuck-in," Roger grinned, and went on to tell Izolda how he had stayed with the irregulars who knew the country intimately, and how he had fought with them. "One of them spoke a few words of English and I picked up their dialect quite quickly – had to. They were keen to learn any strategy I could teach them. I was made into a sort of fighting consultant general. I, at the same time, learnt a great deal from them about guerrilla warfare of quick strikes and withdrawals and brilliant tactical use of territory."

For hundreds of miles Roger marched with the guerrillas. The foreigner became revered among them and the other pockets of fighters with whom they joined up. He in his turn saw great chunks of interior China with its huge rivers, mountainous crags, and extraordinary precipitous landscapes. Then in 1944, hearing on the camp wireless the Allies were attacking from the Indian border to retake Burma, he decided it was time he joined his own army. He took leave of his guerrilla friends with promises to come and visit when they were the government in power, which every man of them was convinced they would be one day.

"They are an amazingly tough, resilient lot of visionaries," Roger said, "their eyes are set on a new era for China and one can only wish them luck. They arranged for me to join some custom officials who led me over the roof of the world on the famous 'Rice Route', a journey of a lifetime which I wouldn't have missed for anything! We stopped at nights at remote Chinese inns, marched by day and ate well. We climbed through the Kwei-yang mountains to Kwongsi Luen and then Wa Shan – I'll show you on the map one day, darling – and on through Ch'ien-Ch'ien-Chiang to Chungking. As you see I've become as hardened as a mountaineer and blackened by the sun in high altitudes."

"Certainly no sign of prisoner-of-war pallor," Izolda laughed. "How wonderful it all sounds, and here I was steeling myself to think you were dead. Yes? Go on . . ."

"I told you we were survivors, remember? Well, in Chungking I got in touch with your uncle. We sent a message through 'Bag' to say I was safe, but I suppose it never got through. I made contact with the American forces of the USAAF and was given the post of British liaison officer. They were bringing in supplies to Chiang Kai-shek via the dangerous 'over the hump' mountainous route from India."

"It must have been spectacular. Did you do the journey?"

"Rather, to Assam and back. Fantastic. No landing place the whole way. Then suddenly it was all over after the atomic bombs were dropped and the Japanese capitulated. A VIP plane was made available for your uncle who was urgently called for by the Governor here, and I cadged a lift. Managed to wangle myself on board as your uncle's military aide."

"You heard Winn was killed?"

". . . and Mike." Roger's face saddened. "Ying-Su told me. Had we stayed together there would have been even less chance of survival. It was the right tactic to scatter. After that it was just the luck of the draw."

Izolda did not tell him then how Winn had attacked the guards so that Roger should have a better chance of getting away. That could wait for later. Instead she asked, "Did Ying-Su come with you and Uncle Jimmy? I'm longing to see her again."

"No. We left her behind with her husband whom I met at General Chiang Kai-shek's HQ. They say she's been put up for a George Medal for her undercover work."

"Oh, tremendous! Every bit of it deserved. Did you tell her general about the guerrillas?"

"Most certainly not; not even your uncle," Roger said. "There is honour among thieves! By the way, Ying-Su sends you her love."

"Thank you," Izolda said slowly.

"And Grandma?" Roger rose. He took Izolda's hands and pulled her to her feet.

"She died peacefully at Christmas in 1943." Izolda told Roger how her grandmother had made arrangements with the Japanese colonel to be cremated and have her ashes returned to lie on her husband's grave in Japan.

"Brilliant! Wonderful Grandma," Roger exclaimed. He

kissed Izolda until her face glowed. "Come, Izarling," he said, shouldering her satchel.

And they turned and began to walk together up the mountain.

Afterword

1995

I

IZOLDA arrived at Kai Tak airport in good time to meet Roger's plane. He had been in Europe on a two-week business trip. After parking the car she made her way inside from where she could view the arrivals. She took a seat and sat quietly, hiding the inner frisson of fear that always assailed her at times like this. Accidents *could* happen! Watching the other planes coming in, the approach seemed to her to be one of the most hazardous in the world, and by now she was acquainted with a good many landing strips after years of 'following the drum'.

Roger's Jumbo jet was on time. There it came, dipping low over the skyscrapers of Hong Kong, silent, throttles back, gliding towards the dramatic 11,130-feet-long main runway that jutted far out towards the Lye-mun Gap on what used to be sea. She remembered the short affair the runway had been when she'd arrived in Hong Kong, and how the Japanese had blasted it that fateful morning when war had come unannounced. Now, a slight bump far out near the sea, another . . . and safely down, brakes applied. Beautiful! Thank God. Izolda relaxed. Smiling in anticipation she watched the great plane trundling over to its allotted bay. She made her way to the gate.

Fifty years on from the end of the war, Izolda was remarkably unchanged. She had the kind of serene beauty

which the years seem not to touch. The main difference was
that her erstwhile golden locks had turned white. This had
happened when she was still quite young; her children had
never known her otherwise. In a dramatic way the white
enhanced her looks. She wore her hair as before: softly
waved in a pageboy style. Roger had made her grow it
from its chopped look when they had met again on the old
track leading up to The Falls and he'd been so shocked by
her appearance after years of internment.

Three weeks later, to exactly allow for the banns to be
read, the two had been married by the Dean in the cathedral,
the latter as gaunt-looking as Izolda. Only Jimmy, Ying-Su
and Dr Lawrence had attended; the doctor was there in case
Izolda should faint, a weakness to which she was prone for
some months after her release. After his war leave, Roger
had been posted to the staff college in Quetta, a healthy spot
where a quarter had been made ready for them. Altogether it
was a wonderful start to married life, a year of togetherness
and recovery with the soothsayer's predictions coming true
in the following years of 'many sons' to follow.

The eldest boy was born in Quetta where Izolda had been
left 'an abandoned wife' on the posting of her husband on
active service to the Near East where she was not allowed to
follow. (In the future, when her sons were invariably at the
accouchements of her daughters-in-law, she was likely to tell
them that Roger had not attended ONE of their births. 'He
was never THERE,' she would groan to their amusement.)
The first child was christened Christopher Paine-Talbot
Stamford as Izolda had promised Chippy.

Much to Roger's delight, Chris, when grown up, had
expressed a wish to join the Army and go to Sandhurst. At
one time he'd even served with the Gurkhas out in the New
Territories. He had married Maisie Holden's daughter born

in Boston, USA. Tommy, who had been as a small boy in the internment camp with his mother until the Americans were repatriated, married Izolda and Roger's only daughter. Thus Tommy and his family, though his business inherited from the Lauders kept him in Boston, were regular visitors to The Falls. Sadly Hugh Holden had died in 1960. He never fully recovered from his severe wounding and medical neglect in the PoW camp. Chris, on early retirement with the run-down of the Army, had taken a job in Jimmy's bank. He was the only one of the sons to settle permanently in Hong Kong.

When Roger appeared through the barrier at Kai-Tak airport, Izolda experienced the now familiar jolt of admiration for his physique. She had fallen in love with him when she was eighteen and she was still in love with him. They embraced warmly. Now in his seventies, with his iron-grey hair, his great height and upstanding figure, he was more distinguished looking than ever. Knighted on his last appointment at the War Office, he was now General Sir Roger Stamford with a string of decorations after his name. His rapid rise to become the youngest Major-General in the British Army had come about in the Korean War. After some lengthy battles in appalling weather and impossible terrain in the stickiest fighting he had yet encountered, he had been awarded the VC for personally rescuing a number of wounded soldiers under a barrage of relentless fire. He had carried one after the other to safety at the time his brigade had been forced to retreat from the Maryang-San and Knoll Ridge positions.

From that period it had been further promotion until his retirement to Hong Kong where he and Izolda had gone to be with Jimmy. From their time together in China, Jimmy had come to consider Roger as a son in place of Winn, and before his death he had made a new Will leaving The Falls to Izolda and Roger. It had been Ying-Su who had proposed the idea to her father. Married to the well-known property developer, the Chinese General Sha-Kwo, a relative of the Generalissimo Chiang Kai Shek, 'Bungy' was a fervent supporter of the nationalists in Taiwan. The Sha-Kwos were *personae non gratae* in 'Red' communist China. They had come back from Chunking after the war to secure their property where they lived in some style.

Bungy's loyalties never changed, and he had become the leader of some eight thousand refugee nationalist soldiers in Kowloon to put himself in an even worse light with the Chinese government; nothing the British Hong Kong government could say in the way of reassurance could alter the fact that his and Ying-Su's lives would be in danger after the handover in July 1997. Any property that belonged to Mrs Sha-Kwo, GM and her husband, would most likely be confiscated.

Jimmy, looking ahead in his old age, had agreed. Now the brave Chinese girl, to whom Izolda and so many other escapees owed their lives, in her seventies packed up her home and stoutly declared that she would be back to visit the family. Knowing all the ways of infiltrating in and out of the Crown territory as she did, Izolda was sure she would turn up secretly in her peasant guise.

As for Roger, he had much preferred the idea of retiring to Hong Kong than living in England and having to commute to London to a desk job. Moreover, in Hong Kong he was offered any number of honorary posts, one of which was head of the auxiliary police in which served quite a few Sikh Indians. Another was colonel of the famous Volunteers with whom Winn had fought so valiantly, now being disbanded. Izolda herself, in the footsteps of her late aunt, took up much philanthropic work for the Red Cross, for hospital visitings, and served on various housing committees for Vietnamese refugees.

They altered the house so that the whole of the ground floor and the second floor were self-contained flats for friends and family to visit. Chinese servants were a thing of the past. Izolda now had two Filipino maids to cook and clean. As she said, everyone in Hong Kong, well off and poor alike, rose early, worked late and played hard! Above all, now that their brood were grown up and Roger had retired, they had time to simply be together.

Outside the airport Izolda led Roger to where she had parked the car. He took the wheel and, exchanging news, they drove off through the congested tunnel under Victoria Harbour. Once on Victoria Island, Izolda pondered on the many changes which had taken place since she had first known the Colony. Though the ferries were still plying to and fro as packed as ever, and with the journey taking much the same time as before and for much the same price, whole clutches of new sky-scrapers crowded and dominated the Star ferry terminus. Everywhere she looked she could pick out new tall hotels, offices, banks and great blocks of flats rising further up the hillsides. Much land had been reclaimed in front of Wanchai. The China Fleet Yacht Club, where Chippy had proposed to her, lay in a different location and had been renamed the Royal Hong Kong Yacht Club. She supposed the prefix 'Royal' would be the next thing to go. Roger had already wound up the Volunteers, though they hoped to establish a small museum to house their memorabilia and accounts of their deeds. As for her work, there would soon be no more Vietnamese refugees to care for. The plan was to repatriate all, willy-nilly. The Chinese had said they had no wish to take *them* over!

"How will it all end?" she said aloud.

"What end?"

"This place, this life. Only two years to go."

"It won't end. The Chinese know which side their bread is buttered. We're staying, and so is Chris. Being under the Chinese can't be as bad as it was under the Japanese," Roger expressed in his usual ebullient manner.

The car passed a new block on the site of the Hong Kong Club where Izolda and Chippy had had their wedding reception, with not even a plaque to say the old Club had once stood there. The lawn of the Cricket Club which had once reverberated to the click of bat on ball – Izolda had often watched Chippy and the naval team playing there – had long since vanished under new buildings. However, the old façade of the colonial courthouse still stood across the way as did the dark premises of Mickey's Kitchen in Ice House Lane with memories of Michael, who had managed to concoct edible dishes from the parsimonious and weevil-infected rice rations doled out by the Stanley camp guards.

Those times would never leave Izolda entirely. The nightmare dreams still came and she would wake sweating to find the comfort of Roger sleeping peacefully beside her. He amazed her. He was as interested in the psyche of the Japanese as her grandmother had been! He had put the massacre at Eu-Cliffe castle, the tortures of himself and his fellow men, the bestiality of the Kempetai interrogators, the slaughter in the Korean War, all behind him.

Leaving the shopping area behind, the car passed the white outline of St John's cathedral where Izolda had twice been married and her mother Camille had, in another age, given a singing recital. Above the cathedral the Botanical Gardens were ablaze with colourful flowers and exotic tropical birds in their cages where once they had lain panting and dying for lack of water. Across the way still lay the Helena May hostel where Izolda had first met Peggy, and where the Hash Harrier ladies still gathered for their runs. Above the Peak tram station there was such a network of under- and overpasses that unless one knew where to look it was difficult to locate the Kennedy and Macdonnell Roads, though Government House, where another Chris, Governor Chris Patten, was now installed – and he doing his best in an almost impossible task – remained serene in its lovely garden of frangapani trees. Would the new Chinese incumbent appreciate the scent of the frangipani flowers? The building always reminded Izolda of Sir Mark Young's fabulous Ball which had brought her and Roger together again.

"Remember," she murmured to Roger as they passed the gates, "Sir Mark's wartime call of: 'The Colony stays a British bastion *for ever*'? That was on the day he was inspecting the Middlesex – Peggy's first husband's regiment. It was on the Colony's one hundredth year under British sovereignty."

"Sir Mark was mistaken, though you cannot deny we had a jolly good innings," Roger replied, changing gear for the climb up to the Peak where, as before, the buildings mostly petered out. The subject of the handover was a burning issue in Hong Kong just then, everyone having their say on what had happened historically, what should happen now, and what might happen in the future.

Izolda clung to a point of view which she had inherited from her uncle. "I still cannot think why the politicians decided to hand the *whole* of the Colony back to China on a plate," she expressed to Roger who had many times heard her out on this. "Ying-Su always said it should never have been taken away from China in the first place, but look at

335

her now . . . having to up sticks and live in Taiwan. The New Territories leased in 1898 for ninety-nine years, yes, but wouldn't you think an attempt might have been made to negotiate the freehold Crown colony of Victoria Island, the Kowloon Peninsular and Stonecutter's Island ceded in perpetuity in 1842 and—"

"—1860 respectively!" Roger, with a smile, finished for her. "You and your hobby-horse! It won't do, darling. We live in a different world from when Jimmy settled here. No one is going to take a blind bit of notice of those old-fashioned views."

"No, of course not. It's far too late anyway, but at least I can still *say* it without fear of being imprisoned."

"Well, I've had a soft spot for the Red Army ever since they, as a bunch of guerrillas with high ideals, took me into their camp when I was on the run and starving. Tremendous chaps. The first thing I'm going to do when they arrive at the barracks here is to call on their commanding officer."

"Oh, Roger – you're impossible . . ."

"Why not? Soldiers are soldiers the world over. Anyway, if we'd tried to keep the Crown Colony bit it wouldn't have worked, and Ma Thatcher knew it. The water comes from China . . ."

"That old argument does not make sense to *me*. There's the sea; we used it when in camp; and look at Gibraltar. They're dependant on Spain for water . . ."

"There are springs in Gibraltar."

"So there are at The Falls . . ." She gave up. It wasn't worth wasting breath on. Water under the bridge! The Chinese held all the cards. They had *not* come to the aid of the British in 1941 even though they were fighting the Japanese in pockets. They had watched from a safe distance over the border and done nothing. Her grandmother had always said that despite the 'hiccough' of war – some hiccough! – the real threat to the western world was not Japan but China.

Governor Patten would sail away in the Royal Yacht . . . the Chinese would take over . . . and Roger would call on them! To her and Roger at their age it didn't matter all that much, and as Roger always said it couldn't be as bad under the Chinese as it had been under the Japanese. It was their son and his family that she worried about: Chris Paine-Talbot Stamford would somehow have to cope with the changes that were bound to come . . .

Roger turned off the main Peak road to pass under the familiar red and green pagoda gate and down the gravelled drive to The Falls. It stood there before them with its deep shady verandahs, serene, peaceful, solid in the sunlight, all sounds of traffic blocked off by the mountain behind them.

"Nothing will ever make me leave it," said Izolda as once her grandmother had said. She walked up the marble stairs and glanced at the opium couch resting in its old place with the portrait of the mandarin above. Yet they had been *forced* to leave. Would history repeat iself once again?

II

PEGGY was the first visitor to arrive for the golden wedding celebrations at The Falls. She had long meant to do the pilgrimage to see her first husband's and baby's graves, and had seized the opportunity when Izolda's invitation to stay had come. The women chatted away as if it had been yesterday they had gone their separate ways, and not fifty years ago. On the coastal road, the long low lines of the Repulse Bay restaurant façade, now rebuilt, was all that was left to remind them of the famous old hotel. Behind it great tall blocks of flats lined the horizon, but the sandy expanse of the bay to the fore with its gaudy modern temple figures and its shark look-out had not changed.

Round the corner on the Stanley Peninsular they came across the old colonial graveyard of the previous century with its many newer plots from the last war, including Bill Holden's. There they found the infant's grave. The very smallness of the plot was acutely moving. Peggy knelt down to put flowers on it, and Izolda put her arm round her old friend. After losing her baby at birth in the cruel conditions of the camp, Peggy, though married subsequently to another Middlesex man, could never have children. During all the years of their incarceration together, the two friends hadn't shown the level of emotion they did now.

Moving on they found most of the old buildings and

bungalows had been demolished with new ones built in their places. The site meant nothing to them anymore, not even the grim-stoned old Fort, nor even the pretty beach where they had bathed with Maisie Holden and Tommy under guard, and where Izolda had briefly met Roger in the most poignant and heart-rending encounter of their lives.

Izolda drove Peggy on to Chaiwan where the bay was mostly reclaimed and where there were many large Chinese cemeteries. They came to the war memorial cemetery and found the Middlesex section. Peggy's second husband had been with them in the thick of the Korean War. Now she left more flowers and thanked God for this husband's survival.

They moved on to the well tended grave of Antonia Winter, Jimmy's wife and Izolda's aunt, killed while nursing. On her stone was also inscribed a memorial to her son, Winn Sutherland Winter of the Hong Kong Volunteer Force, killed attempting to escape over the Chinese border. His body had never been recovered though Jimmy and Izolda had left no stone unturned in their attempts to find it. At the end of the inscription was quoted: *'Greater love hath no man than that he lay down his life for his friend'*.

Finally the pair moved on to a monument where, among those of other naval men with no known graves, was inscribed the name of Lieutenant Christopher Paine-Talbot DSC, RN. "Dear Chippy, how he adored you, Izolda," Peggy said. "So much tragedy, so much bravery. How fortunate you and I were to have come through."

On their way back to The Falls, Izolda told Peggy that the Japanese colonel who had requisitioned their house was her grandmother's step-grandson, and how Louise had bartered her late husband's Japanese Order for a quantity of drugs, and how in this way the old lady, too, had saved many lives.

"I was one of them," mused Peggy who had previously

not known of the relationship. "I had puerperal fever after my baby was born. We all wondered at the sudden influx of drugs. Dear old Mrs Winter . . . she was heroic too . . ."

The golden wedding celebrations passed off splendidly. The guests, in long evening dresses and dinner jackets, walked through the house and down the steps into a huge marquee for the reception and dinner dance. Dancing went on through the night, and breakfast was served at dawn for the young. The whole of The Falls was opened for the older generation so that they could sit in comfort on the verandahs looking down on the scene lit with fairy lights and culminating at midnight in a grand firework display. The newspapers reported next day that the Stamford party equalled in size and style the diamond jubilee celebration of Sir Robert and Lady Ho Tung's just before war broke out.

Looking at her clan gathered round, Izolda found it hard to believe she had once been that little girl living with her grandmother and dreaming of having a large family. They were all there, her sons and their families and her daughter over from Boston with her son-in-law Tommy and her old friend, Maisie. There were her grandchildren and there was even a great-grandchild. Chris, in his middle age a tower of strength, was the one who had organised everything so that she and Roger had nothing to do but greet everyone and enjoy it all. Chris was a jolly man as her Uncle Jimmy had been, a banker now too who looked after their affairs. A big man with a huge laugh, dependable . . . Chippy would have been proud of him.

III

THE Stamford celebration was not the only momentous event of 1995. The next occasion was entirely Roger's idea, and it was he who put it into action.

When the buzz and excitement of the fiftieth anniversary had died down and all the relations and guests had left, Roger wrote to Colonel Fushimi in Yokohama to say that as an old soldier himself he would very much like to meet him to discuss the tactics of the battle for Hong Kong they had both fought. His wife, née Izolda Richardson, Mrs James Winter's granddaughter, would like to see her grandparents' grave in the foreign cemetery on the Bluff. For their visit he proposed to book into the old section of the Grand Hotel facing the harbour where James Winter, his ancestor and Izolda's grandfather, had attended many functions right from the early settler days of the last century.

Colonel Fushimi wrote back in tolerable English to say he would be delighted to see the General to discuss tactics, and to meet again the late Mrs James Winter's granddaughter. He wrote that he would draw up an itinerary for their visit and ensure the local press was informed. He said there had been several occasions in recent years when war veterans had been invited to Japan with reciprocal visits to England, all enjoyable occasions of 'old soldiers'. But this one as family would be of special appeal and interest. He would arrange for them to come to his home in Kitagata village to see the late James Winter's Order which he treasured and which his eldest son would inherit.

Thus Roger, with Izolda in high excitement and some trepidation as to what her reaction would be at seeing the Colonel again and her grandmother's 'beloved' Japan for the first time, set forth to fly to Tokyo. On arrival they boarded a coach for Yokohama and the Grand Hotel, which was everything she had ever imagined with its marvellous view of the harbour.

Colonel Fushimi, now in his nineties with thick spectacles, slightly deaf, and with sparse white hair short and bristle stiff, could not have been more courteous and welcoming. Everything – as Roger had expected it would be for a distinguished Japanese colonel – was organised up to the hilt. Izolda, looking for the scar which had so perturbed her at The Falls, now found it sunk deep in the wrinkles of his cheek and no longer alarming. Moreover the gold teeth had gone, in their place handsome new ones!

They met the eldest son and other members of the Fushimi family and learnt that one of James Winter's daughters, Kura, had married 'Tomi' Glover, the son of the Scot Thomas Blake Glover, founder of the Mitsubishi dock and coal empire. Their home had been Glover House in Nagasaki. Though Thomas Glover had been some ten years older than James Winter, they had met in the old pioneering days, become friends, and had both married Japanese ladies. It was eminently suitable, therefore, that Tomi and Kura had fallen in love.

It later came out that Kura had been killed in the Nagasaki atomic bomb of 1945; Tomi, by then old and ill, took the honourable way out of his time and committed *hara-kiri*.

Even that tragedy seemed not to upset the amicable atmosphere of old enemies now meeting, and later Roger and the Colonel discussed how in Hong Kong the Japanese had surprised the British by their overland attack in such numbers while the main attack had been expected from out to sea where the Colony's coastal defence guns were at their thickest. Both veterans agreed that casualties on all sides would have been far greater had not the atomic bomb been dropped by the Americans which enabled – as the Colonel said – the Emperor to 'with honour' sue for peace.

Colonel Fushimi gave Roger and Izolda tea at his house filled with the antiques he had collected during his long life, including an especially valuable collection of Samurai swords. Izolda was shown the *Order of the Star of the Rising Sun* in its place of honour set on a plinth between little wicker lights which were never extinguished. And to Izolda's delight she was permitted once again to handle the Order as she had as a child and as innumerable times she had seen her grandmother do.

But the highlight of the visit came when Izolda met her Japanese half-cousins of the second and third generations in the great foreign cemetery on the Bluff where the dead of forty-one nations rest, and where there are over four thousand known graves. There, near the old Bluff Road, and opposite Christ Church – twice destroyed and twice rebuilt – where James Winter's funeral had taken place in 1909, Roger and Izolda found a big gathering waiting, including the press. Cameras flashed as they neared. Immensely moved to see her mother's grave of 1923 nearby and then that of her grandparents for the first time, Izolda read the added inscription she had asked for at the cremation in Hong Kong:

Evelyn Hart

Louise Winter, née Winn of Georgia USA
and of Yokohama
1854–1943
A Beloved Grandmother

Late that night, back in their Grand Hotel suite, tired but exhilarated, Izolda, already in bed, watched her husband undress and put his pyjamas on. "Grandma," she remembered, "once said to me in camp when I was in despair and full of hatred, that one day all the horrors of war would leave me and that I would visit Japan. At the time I denied vehemently that my attitude could change. It has taken me fifty years to understand her point of view and forgive as she forgave."

"Wonderful, wonderful Grandma," Roger said and added, "Nice chap, Fushimi – great fighter."

He got into bed beside his wife.